Georges Simenon

A MAIGRET TRIO

Maigret's Failure

Maigret in Society

Maigret and the Lazy Burglar

A Helen and Kurt Wolff Book

Harcourt Brace Jovanovich, Inc.

New York

CONTENTS

Maigret's Failure

3

Maigret in Society

111

Maigret and the Lazy Burglar

217

MAIGRET'S FAILURE

THE OLD LADY OF KILBURN LANE AND THE BUTCHER NEAR THE PARC MONCEAU

JOSEPH, the office messenger, tapped on the door as lightly as a scurrying mouse. The door did not creak as he pushed it open, and he slid into Maigret's office so quietly that—with his bald head surrounded by its almost ethereal halo of white hair—he might have been playing at ghosts.

The Superintendent sat bending over his files, his teeth clenched on the stem of his pipe; he did not look up, and Joseph stood there, motionless.

For a week now Maigret had been extremely touchy, and his assistants walked on tiptoe when they entered his room. In this he was not alone in Paris, or in France as a whole, for never had there been such a damp, cold and gloomy month of March.

At eleven o'clock in the morning, the murky light of a hangman's dawn still lay over the offices; the lamps were still burning at noon, and dusk came down at three o'clock. One could no longer say it was raining; one was actually living in a cloud, with water everywhere, trails of it on the floors, and no one able to utter three words without blowing his nose.

The papers carried photos of suburban dwellers going home by boat along streets that had turned into watercourses.

Arriving that morning, the Superintendent inquired:

'Is Janvier here?'

'He's ill.'

'Lucas?'

'His wife rang up to say that . . .'

The inspectors were going down one after another, sometimes in whole batches, so that never more than a third of the team was on hand.

Madame Maigret hadn't got 'flu. Her trouble was toothache. Every night, in spite of the dentist's efforts, it came on towards two or three o'clock, and she didn't get another wink of sleep till dawn.

She was brave and never complained, never let out a moan.

It was worse than that. Suddenly, in the midst of his own sleep, Maigret would realize she was awake. He could feel she was restraining her complaints so hard that she hardly dared to breathe. For a time he would say nothing, lie keeping watch, as it were, over her suffering; then he would be unable to resist muttering:

'Why don't you take an aspirin?'

'Weren't you asleep?'

'No. Take an aspirin.'

'But you know they have no effect any more.'

'Take one all the same.'

He would get up and go barefoot to fetch the box and bring her a glass of water, trying in vain to hide a weariness that verged on ill humour.

'I'm so sorry,' she would sigh.

'It's not your fault.'

'I could go and sleep in the servant's room.'

They had one on the sixth floor, which was hardly ever used.

'Let me go and sleep up there.'

'No.'

'Tomorrow you'll be tired, and you have so much to do.'

He had more worries than actual work. For this was the moment when Mrs. Muriel Britt, the old Englishwoman all the papers were talking about, had chosen to disappear.

Women disappear every day, and it usually happens quietly; they may be found or they may not, but it's not worth more than three lines in the papers, at most.

Muriel Britt's disappearance had made a great stir, for she had come to Paris with fifty-two other people, a whole coachful, one of those herds that travel agencies assemble in England, America, Canada or elsewhere and take the rounds of Paris for a mere song.

It was the very evening the group had 'done' Paris by Night. The mixed company—nearly all middle-aged men and women—had been taken by motor-coach to the Central Market, the Place Pigalle, the Rue de Lappe and the Champs-Elysées, their tickets covering the cost of a drink at each establishment they visited.

Towards the end, they had all been very gay, many of them with flushed cheeks and bright eyes. A little man with a waxed moustache, a clerk in the City, had been lost before the final stop; but he was found the following afternoon in his own bed, to which he had discreetly withdrawn.

Mrs. Britt was a different matter. The English papers pointed out that she had no reason to vanish. She was fifty-eight years old, thin and stringy, with the tired face and body of a woman who had worked all her life; she ran a boarding-house in Kilburn Lane, somewhere in West London.

Maigret had no idea what Kilburn Lane might be like. Judging by the press photographs he imagined a melancholy house where typists and junior clerks lodged and assembled at a round table at mealtimes.

Mrs. Britt was a widow. She had a son in South Africa and a married daughter living somewhere along the Suez Canal. Stress was laid on the fact that this was the first real holiday the poor woman had taken in her life.

A visit to Paris, of course. With a party. At an all-in price. She was staying with the others at a hotel near the Gare Saint-Lazare which specialized in tours of this kind.

She had got out of the bus with the rest of the party, and gone up to her room. Three witnesses had heard her shut the door.

The next morning she was not there, and no trace of her had since been found.

A sergeant from the Yard had arrived, looking embarrassed, and after contacting Maigret had begun to make tactful inquiries on his own.

The English papers, less tactful, were proclaiming that the French police were inefficient.

The fact was that there were a few details Maigret felt reluctant to let out to the Press. For one thing, bottles of spirits had been found hidden all over Mrs. Britt's room—under the mattress, under the clothes in a drawer, and even on top of the wardrobe.

For another thing, no sooner had her photograph appeared in an evening paper, than the grocer who had sold her the bottles had come to the Quai des Orfèvres.

'Did you notice anything special about her?'

'Well . . . She was half-seas over . . . Though water wasn't in her line . . . To judge by what she bought from me, it was gin she usually drank . . .'

Had Mrs. Britt already been a copious secret drinker at the Kilburn Lane boarding-house? The English papers carefully avoided any mention of that.

The night porter at the hotel had also made a statement.

'I saw her come creeping downstairs again. She was a bit tight and she tried to flirt with me.'

'Then she went out?'

'Yes.'

'Which way did she go?'

'I don't know.'

A policeman had seen her hesitating to go into a bar in the Rue d'Amsterdam.

That was all. Nobody had been fished out of the Seine. No dismembered woman had been found on a plot of waste ground.

Superintendent Pike, of the Yard, whom Maigret knew quite well, telephoned from London every morning.

'Sorry, Maigret; still no clue?'

What with this, the rain, wet clothes, umbrellas dripping in every corner and Madame Maigret's teeth into the bargain, things were pretty unpleasant and one could feel that the Superintendent would jump at any excuse for an outburst.

'What is it, Joseph?'

'The Chief would like a word with you, Superintendent.'

'I'll go along at once.'

This was not the time for the report. When the head of the Judicial Police sent for Maigret during the day, something important was generally afoot.

All the same he finished looking through a file and filled a fresh pipe before going to the Chief's office.

'Still nothing, Maigret?'

He merely shrugged his shoulders.

'I've just received a letter from the Minister, sent by messenger.'

When anyone said 'the Minister' with no further indication, it meant the Minister of the Interior, to whom the Judicial Police are responsible.

'Saying what?'

'There's a fellow coming here at half past eleven . . .'

It was now a quarter past.

'. . . Chap called Fumal, who seems to be a big shot in his own circle. At the last election he subscribed I don't know how many million francs to the party funds. . . .'

'What's his daughter done?'

'He hasn't got a daughter.'

'His son, then?'

'No son, either. The Minister doesn't tell me what it's all about. It just appears that this gentleman wants to speak to you personally and that everything must be done to meet his wishes.'

Maigret's lips moved, and it was easy to guess that the word he did not utter began with the letters *sh*.

'I apologize, old man. And I realize it's bound to be a bore. But do try your damnedest. We've had enough bothers just lately.'

Maigret paused beside Joseph in the anteroom.

'When this Fumal arrives, show him straight in to my office.'

'This what?'

'Fumal! That's his name.'

A name, incidentally, that reminded him of something. Curiously enough he could have sworn it was something unpleasant, but he had enough annoyances already, without racking his memory for more.

'Is Aillevard here?' he asked, at the door of the inspectors' office.

'He hasn't come in this morning.'

'Is he ill?'

'He hasn't telephoned.'

Janvier was back at work, still with a red nose and a pasty complexion.

'How are the kids?'

'All got 'flu, of course!'

Five minutes later came another light tap on the office door, and Joseph, with the air of uttering a rather rude word, announced:

'Monsieur Fumal.'

'Sit down,' growled Maigret, without looking at his visitor.

Then he glanced up, to discover a huge, flabby individual who could hardly squeeze into the armchair. Fumal was staring quizzically at the Superintendent, as though expecting a certain definite reaction.

'What have you come about? I was told you wanted to speak to me personally.'

There were only a few drops of rain on the visitor's overcoat; he must have arrived by car.

'Don't you recognize me?'

'No.'

'Think.'

'I haven't time.'

'Ferdinand.'

'Ferdinand who?'

'Fattie Ferdinand. . . . Boum-Boum!'

At that, Maigret remembered, and he had been right in thinking, shortly before, that it was an unpleasant memory. It went back a long way, to the village school at Saint-Fiacre, in the Allier Department, where Mademoiselle Chaigné had been schoolmistress.

In those days Maigret's father was bailiff at the Château de Saint-Fiacre. Ferdinand was the son of the butcher at Les Quatre-Vents, a hamlet a mile or so away.

In every class there is always a boy like him, taller than the others and fatter, with a kind of unhealthy corpulence.

'Got there, now?'

'I have.'

'What does it feel like, seeing me again? Personally I knew you'd become a cop, because I saw your photo in the papers. We used to be on Christian name terms, by the way.'

'We aren't any longer,' said the Superintendent laconically as he knocked out his pipe.

'Just as you like. You've read the Minister's letter?'

'No.'

'Weren't you told about it?'

'Yes.'

'Come to think of it we've done pretty well, both of us. In different ways, of course. My father wasn't a bailiff, only a village butcher. I was thrown out of high school at Moulins when I was fourteen . . .'

His attitude was definitely aggressive, and this was not only for Maigret's benefit. He was the type of man who would be hard and churlish with everybody, with life in general, with heaven.

'All the same, Oscar said to me today . . .'

Oscar was the Minister of the Interior.

'. . . Go and see Maigret, since he's the fellow you want to see, and he'll put himself entirely at your disposal. . . . *I'll take care he does.* . . .'

The Superintendent did not move an eyelash, he just continued to gaze stolidly into his visitor's face.

'I remember your father well,' Fumal went on. 'He had a sandy moustache, didn't he? He was thin . . . narrow-chested. They must have brought off some good schemes, my dad and he . . .'

This time Maigret had difficulty in remaining expressionless, for Fumal had touched on a sore point, one of his most painful childhood memories.

Like many country butchers, Fumal's father, Louis, had been a bit of a cattle-dealer as well. He had even rented some low-lying meadows where he used to fatten his beasts, and little by little he had widened the range of his local activities.

His wife, Ferdinand's mother, was the local beauty; it was said that she never wore drawers, and that she had even declared cynically:

'In the time it takes to pull them off, one might miss a chance.'

Are there shadowy patches like this in everyone's childhood memories?

As bailiff for the local landowner, Evariste Maigret was responsible for selling the estate cattle. For a long time he had refused to do business with Louis Fumal. But one day he changed his mind. Fumal had come to the office, his worn pocket-book stuffed with banknotes, as usual.

Maigret must have been seven or eight years old then, and he hadn't gone to school. It wasn't 'flu, like Janvier's children, it was mumps. His mother was still alive. It was very hot in the kitchen, all grey, with pale water running down the window-panes.

His father had come rushing in, hatless—unusual for him—with tiny raindrops on his moustache, and very excited.

'That dirty dog Fumal . . .' he had muttered.

'What has he done?'

'I didn't notice right away . . . when he'd gone I put the money in the safe, then I made a phone call, and it wasn't till after that, that I noticed he'd slipped two banknotes under my tobacco jar . . .'

What had been the sum involved? After all these years Maigret hadn't the faintest idea, but he remembered his father's anger and humiliation . . .

'I'm going to chase after him . . .'

'He drove away in his trap?'

'Yes. I'll catch him up on my bike, and . . .'

The rest was vague. But after that, Fumal's name had not been mentioned in his home, except in a peculiar tone. The two men never spoke to each other again. There had been another incident, about which Maigret knew even less. Fumal had apparently tried to make the Comte de Saint-Fiacre (it was still the old Comte) suspicious of his bailiff, and the latter had been obliged to defend himself.

'Well?'

'Have you heard anything about me, since we were at school?'

There was an implied threat in Ferdinand Fumal's tone now.

'No.'

'Do you know the "United Butchers"?'

'By name.'

This was an extensive chain of butcher's shops—there was one in the Boulevard Voltaire, not far from where Maigret lived—against which the smaller butchers had protested, but in vain.

'That's me. Hear of "Economic Butchers"?'

Vaguely. Another chain, in the poorer districts and the suburbs.

'That's me again,' declared Fumal with a defiant glance. 'Do you know how many million francs those two are worth?'

'It doesn't interest me.'

'I'm also behind "Northern Butchers", whose head office is at Lille, and "Associated Butchers", whose head office is in the Rue Rambuteau, here in Paris.'

Eyeing the bulk of the man in his armchair, Maigret almost muttered:

'That makes a lot of meat!'

But he didn't. He had a hunch that this business was going to be even more bothersome than the disappearance of Mrs. Britt. He loathed Fumal already, and not only because of his father's memory. The man was too cocksure, with an insolent self-confidence that was insulting to ordinary people.

And yet one could sense, below the surface, a kind of uneasiness that might even be panic.

'Aren't you wondering why I've come here?'

'No.'

That was the way to exasperate types like this—to confront them with utter calm, with the force of inertia. There was no curiosity, no interest in the Superintendent's face, and the other man began to lose his temper.

'Do you realize I've enough influence to get a senior official thrown out?'

'Really?'

'Even one who thinks he's important.'

'I'm still listening, Monsieur Fumal.'

'Please note that I came here as a friend.'

'And so . . . ?'

'You at once adopted an attitude that was . . .'

'Polite, Monsieur Fumal.'

'Very well! As you choose. It was you I asked to see, because I thought that in view of our old friendship . . .'

They had never been friends, never played together. In fact, Ferdinand Fumal had never played with anyone, he had always spent the recreation break alone in a corner.

'Allow me to remind you that I, too, have a lot of work waiting for me.'

'I'm a busier man than you, and I came to see you all the same. I might have got you to come to one of my offices . . .'

What was the good of arguing? It was true that he knew the Minister, had been useful to him—and doubtless to other politicians as well—and that the thing might get awkward.

'You need the police?'

'Unofficially.'

'Please explain.'

'It is understood that what I'm about to tell you will go no further.'

'Unless you've committed a crime . . .'

'I don't care for jokes.'

Maigret's patience was exhausted. He got up and went to lean on the chimney-piece, resisting the urge to throw his visitor out.

'Someone wants to kill me.'

Maigret nearly retorted 'I can understand that.'

But he forced himself to remain impassive.

'For the last week or so I've been receiving anonymous letters, to which I paid no particular attention at first. People in my position can expect to arouse jealousy and sometimes hatred.'

'Have you the letters with you?'

Fumal pulled out of his pocket a wallet as fat as his father's had been in the old days.

'Here is the first of them. I threw away the envelope, not realizing what was in it.'

Maigret took it, and read the pencilled words:

You're going to pop off.

Without a smile, he laid the paper on his desk.

'What do the others say?'

'This is the second, it came next day. I kept the envelope—as you see from the postmark, it was sent from a Post Office near the Opéra.'

This note, too, was in pencil, in a copybook hand; it said:

I'll have your skin.

There were others; Fumal passed them over one by one, taking them out of the envelope himself.

'I can't read the postmark on this one.'

'Your days are numbered, dirty dog.'

'I suppose you've no idea who sent them?'

'Wait. There are seven of them altogether, the last arrived this morning. One was posted in the Boulevard Beaumarchais, another at the Central Post Office in the Rue du Louvre, and the last in the Avenue des Ternes.'

The wording varied.

'You've not got long to live.'

'Make your will.'

'Swine.'

The last message was a repetition of the first:

'You're going to pop off.'

'You'll leave this correspondence with me?'

Maigret had chosen the word correspondence on purpose, not without ironic intention.

'If it will help you to find out who sent it.'

'You don't think it's a joke?'

'The people I have to do with are seldom given to joking. Whatever you may think, Maigret, I'm not a man who's easily scared. After all, one can't rise to my position without making a number of enemies, and I've always despised them.'

'Why have you come here?'

'Because it's my right as a citizen to be given protection. I don't want to be shot down without even knowing where the shot came from. I spoke to the Minister about it and he told me . . .'

'I know. In short, you'd like to have a discreet watch kept over you.'

'That seems to be indicated.'

'And probably you'd like us to find out who wrote the anonymous letters, too?'

'If possible.'

'Can you think of anyone in particular?'

'In particular, no. Except . . .'

'Go ahead.'

'Please realize I'm not accusing him. He's a weak man, and though he might be capable of threats he would never dare to carry them out.'

'Who is it?'

'A chap called Gaillardin, Roger Gaillardin, of the "Economic Agencies".'

'He has reasons for hating you?'

'I ruined him.'

'On purpose?'

'Yes. After warning him that I was going to.'

'Why?'

'Because he got in my way. Now his business is in liquidation and I hope to get him sent to prison, because there's a matter of some cheques as well as the bankruptcy.'

'Have you his address?'

'26 Rue François Premier.'

'Is he a butcher?'

'Not a professional. He's a financial adventurer. He finances his adventures with other people's money. I finance mine with my own. There's a great difference.'

'Is he married?'

'Yes. But it's not his wife who counts. It's his mistress; he lives with her.'

'You know her?'

'The three of us often went out together.'

'Are you married, Monsieur Fumal?'

'Have been for twenty-five years.'

'Did your wife come with you on these outings?'

'My wife stopped going out long ago.'

'She's an invalid?'

'If you like. Anyhow, she thinks so.'

'I'll make a few notes.'

Maigret sat down and drew a folder and some paper towards him.

'Your address?'

'I live in a house of which I am the owner, 58 bis Boulevard de Courcelles, opposite the Parc Monceau.'

'A good district.'

'Yes. I have offices in the Rue Rambuteau, near the Central Markets, and others at La Villette, near the slaughter-houses.'

'I understand.'

'Not to mention those at Lille and in other towns.'

'I suppose you employ a large staff?'

'In the Boulevard de Courcelles I have five servants.'

'A chauffeur?'

'I've never managed to learn to drive.'

'A secretary?'

'I have a private secretary.'

'In the Boulevard de Courcelles?'

'She has her own room and an office there, but she goes with me when I visit our different branches.'

'Young?'

'I don't know. Early thirties, I suppose.'

'Do you sleep with her?'

'No.'

'With whom?'

Fumal smiled contemptuously.

'I was expecting that question. Yes, I have a mistress. I've had several. At the moment it's a girl called Martine Gilloux; I've fixed her up in a flat in the Rue de l'Etoile.'

'Just round the corner from you.'

'Of course.'

'Where did you meet her?'

'In a night-club, a year ago. She's even-tempered and hardly ever goes out.'

'I suppose she has no reason to hate you?'

'I suppose the same.'

'Has she a lover?'

'If she has I don't know about it,' he growled, furious. 'Is that all you want?'

'No. Is your wife jealous?'

'To judge by the tact you're displaying, I suppose you'll ask her that.'

'What kind of family does she come from?'

'Butcher's daughter.'

'Fine.'

'What's fine?'

'Nothing. I'd like to know more about your immediate surroundings. Do you open your letters yourself?'

'Those that come to the Boulevard de Courcelles.'

'That's your private mail?'

'More or less. The rest is sent to the Rue Rambuteau or La Villette, where the staff deals with it.'

'It isn't your secretary who . . .'

'She opens the envelopes and hands them to me.'

'Have you shown her these notes?'

'No.'

'Why not?'

'I don't know.'

'Nor to your wife, either?'

'No.'

'To your mistress?'

'No again. Is that all you want to know?'

'I suppose you'll authorize me to go to the Boulevard de Courcelles? Under what pretext?'

'That I've lodged a complaint because some papers have disappeared.'

'May I go to your various offices as well?'

'In the same way.'

'And to the Rue de l'Etoile?'

'If you must.'

'Thank you.'

'Is that all?'

'I shall have your house watched, as from this afternoon, but it seems to me it will be more difficult to have you followed as you go about Paris. You use a sedan, I suppose?'

'Yes.'

'Are you armed?'

'I don't carry a gun, but I keep a revolver in my bedside-table.'

'You and your wife have separate rooms?'

'For the last ten years.'

Maigret had risen and was looking towards the door, then he glanced at his watch. Fumal stood up, trying in his turn, with some difficulty, to find something to say, and only came out with:

'I wasn't expecting you to take this attitude.'

'Have I been discourteous?'

'I don't say that, but . . .'

'I have your matter in hand, Monsieur Fumal. I hope nothing unpleasant will happen to you.'

The big butcher, now out in the corridor, snapped back furiously:
'I hope not, too. For your sake!'
Whereupon Maigret closed the door, rather violently.

II

THE DISTRUSTFUL SECRETARY AND THE WIFE WHO DOESN'T TRY TO UNDERSTAND

Lucas came in, carrying some documents and smelling like a chemist's shop, and Maigret, who had not yet sat down again at his desk, asked gruffly:
'Seen him?'
'Who, Chief?'
'Fellow who just went out.'
'I almost collided with him, but I didn't look at him.'
'You should have. Unless I'm very much mistaken he's going to cause us more trouble than the Englishwoman.'

Maigret had used a stronger word than 'trouble'. He was not merely glum, but worried, with a weight on his shoulders. It upset him, this emergence from the distant past of a fellow who had always repelled him and whose father had done his own a bad turn.

'Who is he?' asked Lucas as he spread his papers out on the desk.
'Fumal.'
'The meat man?'
'You know about him?'
'My brother-in-law was assistant book-keeper in one of his offices for a couple of years.'
'What does your brother-in-law think of him?'
'He gave up the job.'
'Would you like to deal with the thing?'
Maigret pushed the threatening letters across to Lucas.
'Show 'em to Moers first of all, on the off-chance.'

The laboratory people nearly always get something out of a document. Moers knew every type of paper, every kind of ink, probably every make of pencil too. Besides, there might be some known fingerprints on the letters.

'How are we going to protect him?' Lucas inquired after reading them.

'I've no idea. Begin by sending someone to the Boulevard de Cour-celles—Vacher, for instance.'

'Into the house, or outside?'

Maigret did not reply immediately.

The rain had just stopped, but things were no better for that. A cold, wet wind had sprung up, forcing the passers-by to cling to their hats, and blowing their clothes hard against them. People on the Pont Saint-Michel were leaning backwards as they walked, as though some-one were pushing them.

'Outside. He'd better take someone with him to make inquiries in the neighbourhood. You yourself might go and take a look into the offices in the Rue Rambuteau and at La Villette.'

'You think it's a genuine threat?'

'On Fumal's part, at any rate. If we don't do what he wants he'll stir up all his political friends.'

'What does he want?'

'I've no idea.'

This was true. What exactly did this wholesale butcher want? What lay behind his visit?

'Are you going home for lunch?'

It was past noon. For the last week Maigret had been lunching in the Place Dauphine every other day, not because of his work, but because his wife had a dentist's appointment for half past eleven. And he didn't like eating alone.

Lucas went with him. As usual there were several inspectors stand-ing at the bar, and the two men went into the little back room, where there was an old-fashioned coal stove, something the Superintendent always liked.

'What would you say to a *blanquette de veau?*' suggested the *patron.*

'The very thing for me.'

On the steps of the Palais de Justice a woman was struggling des-perately to pull down her skirt, which a sudden squall had turned inside-out like an umbrella.

A little later, as the hors d'oeuvres were being served, Maigret said again, as though to himself:

'I don't understand . . .'

It is not unusual for lunatics, or semi-lunatics, to write letters of the type Fumal had received. Sometimes they even carry out their threats. They are humble people, and in almost every case they have been brooding over their grievances for a long time, not daring to bring them into the open.

A man like Fumal must have wronged hundreds of people. His arrogance would have wounded others.

What Maigret didn't understand was the nature of his visit, his aggressive way of behaving.

Had Maigret himself begun it? Had he been wrong to show faint signs of a long-standing resentment that went back to the village days at Saint-Fiacre?

'The Yard hasn't telephoned to you today, Chief?'

'Not yet. That'll come.'

They were served with a *blanquette de veau*—Madame Maigret herself could not have made a creamier sauce—and a moment later the proprietor came to announce that Maigret was wanted on the telephone. Only the people at the Quai knew where to find him.

'Yes. Hello? . . . Janin? . . . What does she want? . . . Ask her to wait for a bit . . . Oh, say a quarter of an hour . . . Yes . . . In the waiting-room, that's best . . .'

As he sat down again he told Lucas:

'His secretary wants to speak to me. She's at the Quai.'

'Did she know her boss was calling on you?'

Maigret shrugged his shoulders and began to eat. He took no cheese or dessert, only a cup of coffee, which he gulped down, boiling hot, as he filled a pipe.

'Don't you hurry. Do what I told you, and keep me informed.'

He felt certain he had a cold coming on, too. As he went under the archway of the Judicial Police building the wind whipped away his hat; the constable on duty caught it in the nick of time.

'Thanks, my boy.'

Reaching the first floor, he looked with curiosity through the glass portion into the waiting-room and saw a young woman, about thirty, fair-haired and with regular features; she sat with hands folded over her bag, waiting with no sign of impatience.

'Is it you who want to talk to me?'

'Superintendent Maigret?'

'Come this way . . . Please sit down . . .'

He took off his coat and hat, sat down at his desk, and gave her another searching glance. Without waiting for him to question her, she began, in a voice which soon gained confidence, finding its natural tone almost at once:

'My name is Louise Bourges and I'm the private secretary of Monsieur Fumal.'

'Since when?'

'Three years.'

'I understand you live in the Boulevard de Courcelles, in your employer's house?'

'In the ordinary way, yes. But I've kept my little flat on the Quai Voltaire.'

'Yes . . .'

'Monsieur Fumal must have been to see you this morning.'

'Did he mention it to you?'

'No. I heard him telephoning to the Minister of the Interior.'

'In front of you?'

'I shouldn't have known about it otherwise; I don't listen at doors.'

'It's that visit you want to see me about?'

She nodded, took her time, choosing her words.

'Monsieur Fumal doesn't know I'm here.'

'Where is he at the moment?'

'In a big Left Bank restaurant where he has several guests for lunch. He has a business luncheon nearly every day.'

Maigret was neither helping her nor doing anything to put her off. As a matter of fact he was wondering, as he looked at her more closely, why in spite of a good figure and regular, rather pretty features, she lacked charm.

'I don't want to waste your time, Superintendent. I don't know exactly what Monsieur Fumal told you. I imagine he brought you some letters.'

'You've read them?'

'The first, and at least one other. The first because it was I who opened it, and the other because he left it lying on his desk.'

'How do you know there have been more than two?'

'Because I handle all the letters and I recognized that copybook writing and the yellowish envelopes.'

'Has Monsieur Fumal talked to you about them?'

'No.'

She hesitated again, though she was not embarrassed in spite of the Superintendent's fixed stare.

'I think you ought to know that he wrote them himself.'

Her cheeks were a little pinker now and she seemed relieved to have got past the difficult point.

'What makes you think so?'

'To begin with, because I once caught him writing. I never knock before going into his office. It's he who wanted it that way. He thought I'd gone out. I'd forgotten something. I went back to the office and saw him writing copybook letters on a sheet of paper.'

'When was this?'

'The day before yesterday.'

'Did he seem upset?'

'He covered the sheet of paper with a blotter at once. Yesterday I was wondering where he'd got the paper and envelopes. We have none of that kind in the house, nor in the Rue Rambuteau or any of the other offices. As you will have noticed it's a cheap kind of paper which is sold in small packets at general stores and in tobacconists' shops. While he was out I had a look.'

'Did you find any?'

Opening her bag, she produced a sheet of lined paper and a yellowish envelope, and held them out to him.

'Where did you find these?'

'In a cupboard full of old files that aren't used any longer.'

'May I ask, Mademoiselle, why you decided to come and see me?'

She looked faintly abashed for a second, but recovered herself at once and replied in a firm, slightly defiant tone:

'To protect myself.'

'From whom?'

'From him.'

'I don't understand.'

'Because you don't know him as well as I do.'

She didn't suspect that Maigret had known him long before she did!

'Please explain.'

'There's nothing to explain. He does nothing without a reason, you understand? If he's taking the trouble to write threatening letters to himself, it's for some purpose. Especially if, afterwards, he gets in touch with the Minister of the Interior and comes to see you.'

Her argument was perfectly convincing.

'Do you think, Superintendent, that there can be such a thing as a person who's basically cruel, I mean someone who's cruel just for the pleasure of it?'

Maigret thought it better not to reply.

'Well, he's like that! He employs hundreds of people, directly or indirectly, and he does his utmost to make their lives a misery. He's shrewd, too. It's almost impossible to hide anything from him. His managers, who are under-paid, all make some attempt to cheat him, and he delights in surprising them just when they least expect it.

'In the Rue Rambuteau office there was an old book-keeper he detested, for no reason, but he kept him on for nearly thirty years because he was useful. The man was a kind of slave, he trembled when the boss came near him. His health was bad and he had six or seven children.

'When his health got worse, Monsieur Fumal decided to get rid of him without paying him any compensation or showing him any gratitude. Do you know what he did?

'He went one night to the Rue Rambuteau, where there was a safe to which only he and this book-keeper had keys, and he took some banknotes out of it.

'Next morning he went to the office and put several of the notes into the pocket of the jacket the book-keeper used to take off and hang up when he arrived—he had an old one for work.

'Monsieur Fumal had the safe opened, on some excuse. You can guess what happened. The old man cried like a child, fell on his knees. It seems there was a terrible scene, and up to the last moment Monsieur Fumal was threatening to call the police, so when the poor man left he was thanking him.

'Now do you understand why I wanted to protect myself?'

'I understand,' he murmured pensively.

'I've given you only one example. There are others. He does nothing without a motive, and his motives are always unpredictable.'

'Do you think he's afraid for his life?'

'I'm sure he is. He's always been afraid. It's because of that—strange as it may seem—that he's forbidden me to knock on the door. The sound of a sudden knock makes him jump.'

'From what you say, there must be a number of people with good cause for resentment against him?'

'A great many, yes.'

'Pretty well all those who work for him?'

'And the people he does business with, too. He's ruined dozens of small butchers who refused to sell their businesses. More recently he ruined Monsieur Gaillardin.'

'Do you know him?'

'Yes.'

'What sort of a man is he?'

'A very good kind of man. He lives in a beautiful flat in the Rue François Premier with a mistress twenty years younger than himself. He had a flourishing business and lived in a big way until Monsieur Fumal decided to launch "United Butchers". It's a long story. They fought for two years and in the end Monsieur Gaillardin had to throw up the sponge.'

'You do not like your employer?'

'No, Superintendent.'

'Why do you go on working for him?'

She blushed for the second time, but was not put off her stride.

'Because of Felix.'

'Who is Felix?'

'The chauffeur.'

'You are the chauffeur's mistress?'

'If you wish to put it crudely, yes. We're engaged, too, and we shall get married as soon as we've saved enough to buy an inn somewhere near Giens.'

'Why Giens?'

'Because we both come from there.'

'Did you know each other before coming to Paris?'

'No. We met in the Boulevard de Courcelles.'

'Does Monsieur Fumal know of your plans?'

'I hope not.'

'And about the relationship between you?'

'Knowing him, I should say he probably does. He's not a man from whom one can hide anything, and I'm certain he has spied on us sometimes. He takes care to say nothing about it. He never does until the moment when it can be useful to him.'

'I suppose Felix feels about him as you do?'

'He certainly does.'

The young lady could not be accused of lacking frankness.

'There is a Madame Fumal, isn't there?'

'Yes. They've been married a very long time.'

'What is she like?'

'What could she be like, with such a husband? He terrorizes her.'

'What do you mean?'

'She lives in the house like a shadow. He goes and comes as he pleases, brings friends or business acquaintances home with him. He takes no more notice of her than if she were a servant, he never takes her to a restaurant or to the theatre, and in the summer he just sends her off to spend her holidays in some lost village in the mountains.'

'Used she to be pretty?'

'No. Her father was one of the biggest butchers in Paris, in the Rue du Faubourg Saint-Honoré, and in those days Monsieur Fumal wasn't yet rich.'

'Do you think she's unhappy?'

'Not even that. She's stopped caring about anything. She sleeps, drinks, reads novels and sometimes goes all alone to the nearest cinema.'

'Is she younger than he?'

'Probably, but she doesn't look it.'

'Is that all you have to tell me?'

'I'd better go now, so as to be at the house when he gets back.'

'Do you have your meals there?'

'Almost always.'

'With the servants?'

Her cheeks flushed for the third time and she nodded silently.

'Thank you, Mademoiselle. I expect I shall go over there this afternoon.'

'You won't tell him that . . .'

'Don't worry.'

'He's so cunning . . .'

'So am I!'

He watched her as she walked down the long corridor, until she reached the stairs and vanished from sight.

Why the devil was Ferdinand Fumal sending himself threatening letters and then coming to ask for police protection? One explanation sprang to the mind straight away, but Maigret didn't like explanations that were too simple.

Fumal had a host of enemies. Some of them hated him enough to make an attempt on his life. Perhaps he had recently given someone even greater cause to hate him?

He hadn't the nerve to come to the police and tell them:

'I'm a swine. One of my victims may be meaning to kill me. Protect me.'

He'd chosen the devious method of writing anonymous letters to himself and waving them in the Superintendent's face.

Was that it? Or was one to suppose that Mademoiselle Bourges had been lying?

Feeling slightly uncertain, Maigret went upstairs to the laboratory. Moers was working, and he handed him the sheet of paper and the envelope the secretary had just given him.

'Have you found anything?'

'Finger-prints.'

'Whose?'

'Three people's. First those of a man I don't know, who has broad, square-tipped fingers, and then yours and Lucas's.'

'That's all?'

'Yes.'

'This sheet of paper and this envelope are exactly like the others.'

After a brief examination Moers confirmed this.

'I didn't look for prints on the envelopes, of course. There are always a mass of them there, including the postman's.'

When Maigret got back to his office he was tempted to wash his hands of the whole Fumal business. How could he protect a man who went all over Paris, unless he put at least a dozen inspectors on the job?

'The stinker!' he muttered between his teeth now and then.

A call came through about Mrs. Britt. Yet another clue, picked up yesterday, had led nowhere.

'If anyone asks for me,' he announced in the inspectors' office, 'say I'll be back in an hour or two.'

Down in the courtyard, he chose one of the black cars.

'Boulevard de Courcelles. Number 58 *bis*.'

The rain had begun again. One could see from the faces of the passers-by that they were fed up with splashing about in cold rain and mud.

The house, a detached one built at the end of the last century, was spacious, with a carriage entrance, bars across the downstairs windows, and very tall windows on the first floor. Maigret pressed a brass button and after some delay a manservant in a striped waistcoat opened the door.

'Monsieur Fumal, please.'

'He's not at home.'

'In that case I will see Madame Fumal.'

'I don't know whether Madame can see you.'

'Tell her Superintendent Maigret is here.'

The former stables, on the far side of the courtyard, were now used as garages, and two cars could be seen there, which proved that the ex-butcher owned at least three.

'Will you come this way . . .'

A broad staircase with carved banisters led up to the first floor, where two marble statues stood like sentinels. Maigret was requested to wait here, and sat down on an uncomfortable Renaissance chair.

The manservant went up higher and was away for a long time. Whispering could be heard from the floor above. From some other direction came the click of a typewriter—that must be Mademoiselle Bourges at work.

'Madame will see you directly. She says will you please wait . . .'

The man went downstairs again and nearly a quarter of an hour elapsed before a lady's maid came down from the second floor.

'Superintendent Maigret? . . . This way, please . . .'

The atmosphere was as gloomy as that of the law-courts in a provincial town. There was too much space and not enough life, voices echoed between the walls which were painted to imitate marble.

Maigret was shown into an old-fashioned drawing-room where a grand piano was surrounded by at least fifteen arm-chairs upholstered in faded tapestry. Again he waited for a short time, and at last the door opened to admit a woman in a housecoat: with her expressionless eyes, puffy, colourless face and jet-black hair she gave the effect of an apparition.

'I'm sorry to have kept you waiting . . .'

She spoke in a colourless voice, like a sleepwalker.

'Please sit down. Are you sure it's I you want to see?'

Louise Bourges had hinted at the truth by mentioning drink, but the truth went beyond the Superintendent's expectations. This woman's face, as she sat opposite him, was weary but resigned, without sadness, and she seemed to be utterly remote from real life.

'Your husband came to see me this morning, and he has reason to believe that someone has designs on his life.'

She did not start, but merely stared at him in mild surprise.

'Has he told you about it?'

'He never tells me about anything.'

'Do you know if he has enemies?'

The words seemed to take a long time to penetrate to her brain, and more time was needed for her reply to take shape there.

'I suppose he has, don't you think?' she murmured at last.

'Was yours a love marriage?'

This was beyond her understanding and all she said was:

'I don't know.'

'You have no children, Madame Fumal?'

She shook her head.

'Would your husband have liked to have some?'

Again she replied:

'I don't know.'

Then she added indifferently:

'I suppose so.'

What else could he ask her? It seemed almost impossible to communicate with her, as though she lived in a different world, or as though they were separated by the sound-proof walls of a glass cage.

'I'm afraid I interrupted your afternoon rest?'

'No. I don't have a rest.'

'Then all that remains is for me . . .'

All that remained, in fact, was for him to take his leave, and he was on the point of doing so when the door opened abruptly.

'What are you doing here?' Fumal demanded, his eyes harder than ever.

'As you see, I am making the acquaintance of your wife.'

'They tell me one of your policemen is downstairs questioning my servants. And I find you up here, pestering my wife, who . . .'

'Just a moment, Monsieur Fumal. It was you who applied to me, was it not?'

'I didn't give you the right to interfere in my private life.'

Maigret bowed to the woman, who was watching them without understanding.

'I beg your pardon, Madame. I hope I have not disturbed you too much.'

The master of the house followed him to the head of the stairs.

'What did you talk to her about?'

'I asked her whether she knew if you had enemies.'

'What did she say?'

'That you probably had, but that she didn't know who they were.'

'Does that get you any further?'

'No.'

'Well?'

'Well, nothing.'

Maigret almost asked him why he had sent anonymous letters to himself, but he felt the moment for that had not yet come.

'Is there anyone else here to whom you want to put questions?'

'One of my inspectors is attending to that. You have just told me he's downstairs. In point of fact, if you really want to be protected, it might be best to let one of our men come with you wherever you go. It's all very well to watch this house, but when you go to the Rue Rambuteau, or somewhere else . . .'

They were going downstairs now. Fumal seemed to reflect, staring at Maigret as though wondering if this were not a trap.

'When would it begin?'

'When you like.'

'Tomorrow morning?'

'Very well. I'll send you someone tomorrow morning. What time do you usually go out?'

'It depends on the day. Tomorrow I'm going up to La Villette at eight o'clock.'

'There will be an inspector here at half past seven.'

They had heard the front door open and close again. Reaching the first floor, they saw a man coming towards them; he was short and bald, dressed all in black, and carried his hat in his hand. He seemed to be quite at home in the place, and glanced inquiringly at Maigret and then at Fumal.

'This is Superintendent Maigret, Joseph. I had a little matter to settle with him.'

To the Superintendent, he said:

'This is Joseph Goldman, my lawyer—my right hand, you might say. Everyone calls him Monsieur Joseph.'

Monsieur Joseph had a black leather briefcase under his arm; he gave a peculiar smile, baring a row of bad teeth.

'I won't go down with you, Superintendent. Victor will let you out.'

Victor, the manservant in the striped waistcoat, was waiting at the foot of the stairs.

'Then it's agreed for tomorrow morning.'

'Agreed,' Maigret echoed.

He could not remember ever having such an impression of helplessness or rather of unreality. Even the house looked unreal! And it seemed to him that the servant, closing the door behind him, wore a mocking smile.

Back at the Quai, he wondered who to send next day to watch over Fumal, and finally chose Lapointe, to whom he gave his instructions.

'Be there by seven-thirty. Follow him wherever he goes. He'll take you in his car. He'll probably try to annoy you.'

'Why?'

'Doesn't matter. Don't you turn a hair.'

He had to attend to the old Englishwoman, who was now reported to have been seen at Maubeuge. In all probability it wasn't she. He had lost count of the false alarms, the old Englishwomen who'd been seen all over France.

Vachet rang up to ask for orders.

'What am I to do? Watch inside the house, or out of doors?'

'Whichever you like.'

'It's pouring, but I'd rather be outside.'

Somebody else who didn't relish the atmosphere of the house in the Boulevard de Courcelles.

'I'll send someone to relieve you towards midnight.'

'That's fine, Chief. Thank you.'

Maigret dined at home. That night his wife was not in pain and he slept right through till half past seven. His usual cup of coffee was brought to him in bed, and his eyes turned straight towards the window; the sky outside was leaden, as it had been for days.

He had just gone into the bathroom when the telephone rang. He heard his wife say:

'Yes . . . yes . . . One moment, Monsieur Lapointe . . .'

This meant disaster. It was at half past seven that Lapointe was to go on duty in the Boulevard de Courcelles. If he was ringing up . . .

'Hello . . . Maigret here . . .'

'Listen, Chief . . . Something's happened . . .'

'Dead?'

'Yes.'

'How?'

'We don't know. Perhaps poisoned. I don't see any wound. I scarcely took time to look. The doctor's not here yet.'

'I'll be right along!'

Had he been mistaken in thinking that Fumal could bring him nothing but . . . bothers?

III

THE MANSERVANT'S PAST AND THE THIRD-FLOOR TENANT

WHILE he was shaving, Maigret's conscience was ill at ease. Perhaps because he had a personal grudge against Fumal? Automatically this made him wonder if he had done his full duty. The man had come to ask for his protection. True, he had been aggressive about it, had himself pushed by the Minister, and his manner towards the Superintendent had been almost openly menacing.

But that did not absolve Maigret from doing his duty. Had he really done it to the very utmost? He had gone to the Boulevard de Courcelles himself, but he had not taken the trouble to inspect all the doors and other ways of access; he had postponed that task till next day, together with the job of interviewing the servants one after another.

He had sent an inspector to mount guard outside the house. From half past seven this morning, if Fumal had not been killed, Lapointe would have been at his side while Lucas pursued his investigations in the Rue Rambuteau and elsewhere.

Would he have acted differently if he hadn't found the man unlikeable, if he had not had an old score to settle with him, if—Fumal had been just any big Paris business man?

Before breakfast, Maigret telephoned to the Public Prosecutor's office and then to the Quai des Orfèvres.

'Aren't you having a car sent round?' inquired Madame Maigret, who made herself as small as possible on such occasions.

'I'll take a taxi.'

The Boulevards were almost empty, with only a few dark figures emerging from the *Métro* entrances and hurrying into doorways. A car—a doctor's—was standing outside no. 58 *bis* Boulevard de Courcelles, and when the Superintendent rang the bell the door opened at once.

The manservant, the same as yesterday, had not had time to shave, but he was already wearing his yellow-and-black striped waistcoat. He had very bushy eyebrows, and Maigret stared at him for a second as though trying to remember something.

'Where is it?' he asked.

'On the first floor, in the study.'

On his way upstairs he made a mental note to look into this Victor later on; the man roused his curiosity. Lapointe came to meet him on the landing, which was doing duty as a waiting-room.

'I made a mistake, Chief; I'm sorry. The way he was lying when I first saw him, the wound couldn't be seen.'

'He wasn't poisoned?'

'No. When the doctor turned him over he found a gaping wound in the back, level with the heart. The shot was fired point-blank.'

'Where's his wife?'

'I don't know. She hasn't come down.'

'The secretary?'

'She must be over there. Come with me. I'm only just beginning to find my way about.'

On the side overlooking the railings of the Parc Monceau was an enormous drawing-room which gave the impression of never being used, and was damp in spite of the central heating.

Along a red-carpeted corridor, on the right, was the outer office, a not very large room looking on to the courtyard. Louise Bourges was there, standing by the window; a maidservant was with her. Neither of them said anything, and Louise Bourges looked anxiously at Maigret, probably wondering what attitude he would adopt towards her after her visit to the Quai des Orfèvres the day before.

'Where is he?' was all Maigret asked.

She pointed to a door: 'There.'

This second office was larger, also red-carpeted, and furnished in the Empire style. A human form was lying near an arm-chair, and a doctor Maigret did not know was kneeling beside it.

'I'm told it was a shot fired at point-blank range?'

The doctor nodded. The Superintendent had already noted that the dead man was not in pyjamas, but wore the same clothes as the day before.

'When did it happen?'

'So far as I can judge at first glance, late in the evening, between eleven and midnight, or thereabouts.'

Involuntarily, Maigret found himself thinking of the village of Saint-Fiacre, the school playground, the fat boy whom nobody liked and who was known as Boum-Boum, or sometimes Jujube.

In turning him over the doctor had laid him in a curious attitude, with one arm outstretched as though pointing to a corner of the room where there was nothing to be seen except a yellowing marble Nymph on a pedestal.

'I suppose death was instantaneous?'

This was a foolish question, for the wound was so large that a fist could almost have been thrust into it. But the Superintendent was ill at ease. This was no ordinary case.

'His wife has been told?'

'I think so.'

Maigret went into the next room and put the same question to the secretary:

'His wife has been told?'

'Yes. Noémi went up and told her.'

'She hasn't come down?'

He was beginning to realize that nothing happened here in the way it would in a normal household.

'When did you last see him?'

'Yesterday evening, about nine o'clock.'

'He sent for you?'

'Yes.'

'Why?'

'To dictate some letters. The shorthand notes are on my pad. I haven't typed them yet.'

'Important letters?'

'No more and no less than any others. He often used to dictate in the evening.'

Without her needing to add anything further, Maigret realized what the girl was thinking; it was to annoy her that her employer used to send for her in that way, after the day's work. Ferdinand Fumal seemed to have spent his life trying to annoy people.

'Did he have any visitors?'

'Not while I was here.'

'Was he expecting anyone?'

'I think so. He had a telephone call and told me to go to bed.'

'What time was that?'

'Half past nine.'

'Did you go to bed?'

'Yes.'

'Alone?'

'No.'

'Where is your room?'

'With the other servants' rooms, above the old stables that are used as garages nowadays.'

'Monsieur Fumal and his wife slept alone in the house?'

'No. Victor sleeps on the ground floor.'

'That's the manservant?'

'He acts as porter too, looks after the house, runs errands.'

'He's not married?'

'No. At least, not so far as I know. He has a little room with a round window looking out under the archway.'

'Thank you.'

'What am I to do now?'

'Wait. When the post comes, bring me the letters. I wonder if there'll be another anonymous one.'

He had the impression she blushed, but was not certain. Steps were heard on the stairs. The Public Prosecutor's deputy arrived, with a young magistrate called Planche, with whom Maigret had not worked before. The clerk who followed them had a cold. Almost as soon as they had come in, the front door opened again, to admit the people from the Criminal Records Office.

Louise Bourges remained in her own office, standing by the window, waiting for instructions, and it was to her that Maigret turned once more, a little later.

'Who told Madame Fumal?'

'Noémi.'

'Is that her personal maid?'

'It's the one who attends to the second floor. Monsieur Fumal's bed-room is on this floor, beyond his office.'

'Go and see what's happening up there.'

And as she hesitated:

'What are you afraid of?'

'Nothing.'

It was strange, to say the least of it, that the dead man's wife had not come downstairs and that there was no sound from above.

Since Maigret's arrival Lapointe had been silently ferreting about, looking for a weapon. He had opened the door of the bedroom, which was enormous, and furnished, like the office, in Empire style; the bed was turned down and pyjamas and dressing-gown laid out on it.

Despite the tall windows the atmosphere of the house was grey, and only a few lights had been turned on; the photographers were setting up their cameras here and there, the Public Prosecutor's men were whispering in a corner while they waited for the official pathologist.

'Have you any ideas, Maigret?'

'None at all.'

'Did you know him?'

'I knew him in my village schooldays and he came to see me yester-day. He'd been to the Minister of the Interior to get our protection.'

'Against what?'

'For some time he'd been receiving anonymous threats.'

'Didn't you do anything?'

'An inspector spent the night outside the house and another was going to watch him all day.'

'In any case it looks as though the murderer had taken his gun away with him.'

Lapointe had found nothing. Neither had the others. Maigret, hands in pockets, made for the stairs and went down to the ground floor, where he pressed his nose against the round window he had been told of.

The room inside resembled a porter's lodge, with a tumbled bed, a wardrobe, a gas heater, a table and some book-shelves. The manservant was sitting astride a chair, with his elbows propped on the back of it, staring blankly into space.

The Superintendent tapped softly on the window-pane and the man started, looked at him with a frown, then got up and came to the door.

'You recognized me?' he asked at once, his face a mixture of fright and suspicion.

The day before, already, Maigret had felt he'd seen the man before somewhere, but he still could not think where.

'I recognized you at once.'

'Who are you?'

'You didn't know me in the old days, because I'm a good bit younger. When I was born you'd already left.'

'Left where?'

'Saint-Fiacre, of course! Don't you remember Nicolas?'

Maigret remembered Nicolas very well. He was an old drunkard who put in a few days' work here and there on the farms, ran the threshing-machine in summer and rang the church bells on Sundays. He lived in a hut on the edge of the woods and had the peculiarity of eating crows and polecats.

'He was my father.'

'He's dead?'

'Long ago.'

'And how long have you been in Paris?'

'Didn't you see about it in the papers? After all, they printed photos of me. I got into trouble at home. In the end they realized I hadn't done it on purpose.'

He had bristly hair and a low forehead.

'Tell me about it.'

'I used to go poaching, that's a fact, and I never denied it.'

'And you killed a gamekeeper?'

'You did read about it?'

'Which gamekeeper?'

'A young one, you didn't know him. He was always after me. I swear I didn't do it on purpose, though. I was watching for a deer, and when I heard a noise in the bushes . . .'

'What made you think of coming here, afterwards?'

'I didn't think of it.'

'Fumal came to fetch you?'

'Yes. He needed a man he could trust. You've never gone back to the district yourself, though they've not forgotten you down there and I can tell you they're proud of you. But as soon as Fumal had some money he bought the Château de Saint-Fiacre . . .'

Maigret felt a slight pang in his heart. He'd been born there—only on the estate, of course, but still he had been born there, and for a long time the Comtesse de Saint-Fiacre had been his ideal of womanhood.

'I see,' he growled.

Fumal had always surrounded himself with people he had some hold over, hadn't he? What he needed was not so much a manservant as a kind of bodyguard, a watch-dog, so he had brought back to Paris a young fellow who'd had a narrow escape from the hulks.

'It was he who paid your lawyer?'

'How did you know?'

'Tell me what happened yesterday evening.'

'Nothing happened. Monsieur didn't go out.'

'What time did he get home?'

'A little before eight o'clock, for dinner.'

'Alone?'

'With Mademoiselle Louise.'

'The car was put into the garage?'

'Yes. It's still there. All three of them are there.'

'The secretary has her meals with the servants?'

'She likes to, because of Felix.'

'Everyone knows about her affair with Felix?'

'It's not difficult to see.'

'Your boss knew, too?'

Victor said nothing, and Maigret challenged him:

'You told him, didn't you?'

'He asked me . . .'

'You told him?'

'Yes.'

'If I understand correctly, you told him about everything that went on in the servants' quarters?'

'He paid me to.'

'Let's get back to yesterday evening. You left your lodge?'

'No. Germaine brought me my dinner here.'

'It was the same every evening?'

'Yes.'

'Who's Germaine?'

'The oldest of the women.'

'Did anyone come to the house?'

'Monsieur Joseph got home about half past nine.'

'You mean he lives here?'

'Didn't you know?'

Maigret had had no suspicion of it.

'Give me the full details. Where's his room?'

'It isn't a room, it's a whole flat, on the third floor. They're attics, with sloping ceilings, but they're bigger than those above the garage. In the old days they were the servants' rooms.'

'How long has he been living in the house?'

'I don't know. It began before I came.'

'And how long have you been here?'

'Five years.'

'Where does Monsieur Joseph have his meals?'

'Nearly always in a café in the Boulevard des Batignolles.'

'He's a bachelor?'

'A widower, or so I'm told.'

'Doesn't he ever sleep out?'

'Only when he's away from Paris, of course.'

'Does he travel a lot?'

'It's he who goes to the country branches to inspect the books.'

'What time did you say he came home?'

'About half past nine.'

'He didn't go out again?'

'No.'

'No one else came?'

'Monsieur Gaillardin.'

'How do you come to know him?'

'Because I've often let him in. At one time he and the boss were great friends. Then there was trouble between them, and yesterday was the first time for months that . . .'

'You allowed him to go upstairs?'

'Monsieur phoned me to let him in. There's an inside telephone from the office to my lodge.'

'What time was this?'

'About ten o'clock. I've been used to telling the time by the sun, you know, and I don't often think to look at the clock. Particularly as this one is always at least ten minutes fast.'

'How long did he stay up there?'

'A quarter of an hour, perhaps.'

'How did you open the door for him when he left?'

'By pushing the button, here, same as in any concierge's lodge.'

'You saw him go past?'

'Of course I did.'

'You looked at him?'

'Well . . .'

He hesitated, growing uneasy again.

'It depends what you mean by look. There's not much light under the archway. I didn't clamp my face against the window. But I saw him, I mean recognized him. I'm sure it was him.'

'But you don't know what mood he was in?'

'I certainly don't.'

'Did your employer telephone you after that?'

'Why?'

'Answer my question.'

'No . . . I don't think so . . . Wait . . . No . . . I got into bed. I read part of the newspaper in bed and then I put the light out.'

'Which means that after Gaillardin left, nobody came into the house?'

Victor opened his mouth, then shut it again.

'Isn't that so?' Maigret persisted.

'That is so, of course . . . But yet it may not be so . . . It's difficult to describe people's lives in a few minutes, like this . . . I don't even know how much you know . . .'

'What do you mean?'

'What have they told you, upstairs?'

'Who?'

'Well, Mademoiselle Louise, or Noémi, or Germaine . . .'

'Somebody may have come in last night without your knowing about it?'

'Of course!'

'Who?'

'The boss, for one—he may have gone out and come in again. Haven't you noticed the back door, in the Rue de Prony? That used to be the tradesman's entrance, and he has a key to it.'

'Does he ever use it?'

'I don't think so. I don't know.'

'Who else has a key?'

'Monsieur Joseph, I'm sure of that, because I've sometimes seen him going out in the morning when I hadn't seen him come in the night before.'

'Who else?'

'Probably the tart.'

'Whom do you mean by that?'

'The boss's tart, the latest one, a little brunette; I don't know her name, she lives somewhere near the Etoile.'

'Did she come last night?'

'I tell you I don't know. Once before, you understand, when there was that business about the gamekeeper, they asked me so many questions that they made me say things that weren't true. They even made me sign them, and later on they brought them up against me.'

'Did you like your boss?'

'What difference does that make?'

'You refuse to answer?'

'I only say that has nothing to do with it, it's my own business.'

'Just as you like.'

'If I speak to you like this . . .'

'I understand.'

It was better not to push things further, and Maigret went slowly back to the first floor.

'Madame Fumal still hasn't come down?' he asked the secretary.

'She doesn't want to see him till he's been tidied up.'

'How is she?'

'The same as usual.'

'She didn't seem surprised?'

Louise Bourges shrugged her shoulders. She was more tense than she had been the day before, and several times Maigret noticed her biting her nails.

'I can't find any gun, Chief. They're asking whether they can take the body away to the Medico-Legal Institute.'

'What does the examining magistrate say?'

'He agrees.'

'Then so do I.'

Just at that moment Victor came up with the letters and paused, hesitant, when about to give them to Louise Bourges.

'Hand them over!' said Maigret.

There were fewer than he would have expected. Presumably most of Fumal's correspondence went to his various offices. These were mostly bills, two or three invitations to charity entertainments, a letter from a solicitor at Nevers, and finally an envelope the Superintendent recognized at once. Louise Bourges was peering at it from a distance.

The address was written in pencil. The sheet of cheap paper bore only two words:

'Final warning.'

Wasn't this becoming almost ironical?

At that moment Ferdinand Fumal, lying on a stretcher, was leaving his house in the Boulevard de Courcelles, just opposite the main entrance of the Parc Monceau, with its dripping trees.

'Find me the telephone number of a man called Gaillardin, in the Rue François Premier.'

It was the secretary who passed the telephone directory to Lapointe.

'Roger?' asked the latter.

'Yes. Get him for me.'

It was not a man who answered the Inspector's call.

'Excuse me, Madame, but may I speak to Monsieur Gaillardin? . . . Yes . . . I beg your pardon? . . . He's not at home?'

Lapointe looked questioningly at Maigret.

'It's very urgent . . . Do you know if he's at his office? . . . You don't know? You think he may be away from Paris? . . . Just a moment . . . Hold on, please . . .'

'Ask her whether he slept in the house last night.'

'Hello. Can you tell me whether Monsieur Gaillardin slept at home last night? . . . No . . . When did you last see him? . . . You had dinner together? . . . At Fouquet's? . . . And he left you at . . . I can't hear . . . A little after half past nine . . . Without telling you where he was going . . . I understand . . . Yes . . . Thank you . . . No, there's no message . . .'

He explained to Maigret:

'As far as I can make out it was his mistress, not his wife, and he doesn't seem to be in the habit of confiding in her.'

Two inspectors, who had arrived a long time earlier, were lending a hand to the Criminal Records men.

'You, Neveu, cut along to the Rue François Premier . . . The address is in the telephone directory . . . Gaillardin . . . Try to find out whether the fellow took any luggage away with him, whether he was expecting to go, and that kind of thing . . . Manage to get hold of a photo . . . And to be on the safe side, let the stations and airports have a description of him . . .'

It all sounded too simple, and Maigret was afraid to rely on it.

'Did you know Gaillardin was coming to see your employer yesterday evening?' he asked Louise Bourges.

'As I told you, I knew someone had telephoned and that he had replied with something like: "All right".'

'What sort of humour was he in?'

'The usual.'

'Did Monsieur Joseph often come down to see him in the evening?'

'I believe so.'

'Where is Monsieur Joseph at the moment?'

'Upstairs, I expect.'

He might have been, a moment earlier, but he wasn't any longer, for they saw him coming across the landing, gazing round him in amazement.

It was rather unexpected, after all the comings and goings that had upset the household, to see the little greyish man come downstairs as though everything were as usual and hear him ask in a quite natural tone:

'What is going on?'

'Haven't you heard anything?' inquired Maigret gruffly.

'Heard what? Where is Monsieur Fumal?'

'He's dead.'

'What did you say?'

'I said he was dead, and he's already out of the house. You are a sound sleeper, Monsieur Joseph?'

'I sleep like anyone else.'

'You have heard nothing since half past seven this morning?'

'I heard someone go into Madame Fumal's room, on the floor below mine.'

'What time did you go to bed last night?'

'About half past ten.'

'When did you leave your employer?'

The little man still did not seem to grasp what was happening.

'Why are you asking me these questions?'

'Because Fumal was murdered. You came down to see him after dinner yesterday?'

'I didn't come down, but I looked in on him when I got home.'

'At what time?'

'About half past nine. A little later, perhaps.'

'And after that?'

'After that, nothing. I went up to my own rooms, worked for an hour, and went to bed.'

'You didn't hear a shot?'

'Up there one can't hear a sound from this floor.'

'You have a revolver?'

'Me? I have never touched a weapon in my life. I never even did my national service, owing to bad health.'

'You knew Fumal had one?'

'He had shown it to me.'

They had at last discovered, under some papers in the drawer of the bedside-table, a Belgian revolver which had not been fired for years, and so could have nothing to do with the crime.

'And you knew Fumal was expecting a visitor?'

In this house nobody gave a straight answer to a question; there was always a blank pause, as though the person questioned had to repeat the words to himself several times in order to understand them.

'What visitor?'

'Don't pretend to be a fool, Monsieur Joseph. Incidentally, what is your real name?'

'Joseph Goldman. You heard it yesterday when we were introduced.'

'What was your profession before Fumal employed you?'

'I was a bailiff for twenty-two years. As for being employed by him, that is not quite correct. You speak as though I were a servant or a clerk. Whereas in point of fact I was a friend, an adviser.'

'You mean your job was to keep his dirty tricks on the right side of the law, more or less?'

'Take care, Superintendent. There are witnesses present.'

'And so what?'

'I might call you to account for your incautious words.'

'What do you know about Gaillardin's visit?'

The old man compressed his lips, which were by nature remarkably thin.

'Nothing.'

'And I suppose you know nothing about a certain Martine who lives in the Rue de l'Etoile and probably, like yourself, has a key to the back door?'

'I never concern myself with women.'

It was scarcely an hour and a half since Maigret had arrived in this house, and already he felt as though he were choking, he longed to get outside and breathe free air, however damp.

'I must ask you to remain here.'

'May I not go to the Rue Rambuteau? I'm expected there about some important decisions. You seem to be losing sight of the fact that we supply Paris with at least one-eighth of its meat, and that . . .'

'One of my inspectors will go with you.'

'Which means?'

'Nothing, Monsieur Joseph. Absolutely nothing!'

Maigret was ready to explode. In the big drawing-room the Public Prosecutor's men were putting the finishing touches to their report. Planche, the examining magistrate, asked the Superintendent:

'Have you been up to see her?'

He meant Madame Fumal, of course.

'Not yet.'

He would have to go. He would also have to question Felix and the other servants. He would have to get hold of Roger Gaillardin and interrogate Martine Gilloux, who perhaps had a key to the back door.

Finally, he must search, in the Rue Rambuteau offices and in those at La Villette, for any evidence that might . . .

Maigret was disheartened from the start. He felt he had made a bad beginning. Fumal had come to ask for his protection. The Superintendent hadn't believed the man, and he'd been killed by a shot in the back. Soon, no doubt, the Minister of the Interior would be ringing up the head of the Judicial Police.

As if the vanishing Englishwoman hadn't been enough!

Louise Bourges was watching him from a distance, as though trying to guess his thoughts; and it so happened that he was thinking of her, wondering whether she had really seen her employer writing one of the anonymous letters.

If not, that would alter everything.

THE DRUNKEN WOMAN AND THE STEALTHY-FOOTED
PHOTOGRAPHER

NEARLY thirty years ago, when Maigret, newly married, was still the secretary of the Police Station in the Rue Rochechouart, his wife sometimes used to call for him at the office, at noon. They would make a quick lunch so as to have time for a walk along the streets and boulevards, and Maigret remembered that one such walk had brought them, on a spring day, to this same Parc Monceau that he could now see, all black and white, outside the window.

There had been more nannies than there were now, most of them in trim uniforms. The babies' prams made an impression of luxurious comfort, and the iron chairs along the paths were bright with yellow paint; an old lady with violets on her hat was throwing bread to the birds.

'When I'm a Superintendent. . .' he had said jokingly.

And the two of them had looked through the railings, whose gilded lance-points glittered in the sun, at the wealthy houses bordering the park, imagining the calm elegant life that must go on behind those windows.

If there was anyone in Paris who had gained experience of brutal realities, anyone who, day after day, had been shown the truth that lay under the surface of things, it was Maigret himself; and yet he had never quite resigned himself to shedding his belief in certain of the pictures that belonged to his childhood or early youth.

Hadn't he once declared that he would have liked to be 'a mender of destinies', because he had such a desire to restore people to their real places, the places that would have been theirs if the world had been like a simple folk-tale?

There was probably more tragedy than harmony in eight out of the ten sumptuous houses that surrounded the Park. But he had seldom breathed an atmosphere so oppressive as in this one. Everything seemed false and discordant, from the moment one passed by the lodge of the porter-valet who was neither porter nor valet but, for all his striped waistcoat, an ex-poacher, a murderer turned watchdog.

And what was Monsieur Joseph, the shady bailiff, doing in the attics of the house?

Even Louise Bourges was not reassuring, with her dream of marrying the chauffeur and opening an inn at Giens.

The former butcher from Saint-Fiacre had seemed even more out of place than the others, and the high, panelled walls, the furniture—presumably bought together with the house—looked as out of their element as the statues on either side of the stairhead.

What upset the Superintendent most of all, perhaps, was the malice he could sense behind Fumal's every word and deed, for he had always refused to believe in the existence of pure malice.

It was after ten o'clock when he left the first floor, where his colleagues were still working, and went slowly upstairs. On the second floor there was no maid to prevent him from opening the door of the drawing-room, with its fifteen or sixteen empty arm-chairs, and he coughed to announce his presence.

Nobody came. Nothing stirred. He went across to a half-open door leading into a smaller drawing-room, where a breakfast tray stood forgotten on a small table.

He knocked on a third door, listened hard, thought he heard a stifled cough, and finally turned the handle.

This was Madame Fumal's room, and she lay in bed, watching his advance, an expression of dull astonishment in her eyes.

'I beg your pardon. I found no servant to announce me. I suppose they're all downstairs, with my inspectors.'

Her hair was tousled and she had not washed. Her nightdress was wide open, revealing one shoulder and a curve of pallid breast. The day before, he might have felt some doubt. But now he was certain the woman facing him had been drinking, not merely before she went to bed, but that morning already, and a strong smell of alcohol still hung about the room.

The butcher's wife was still watching him with an indefinable expression, as if, though not yet entirely reassured, she was feeling a kind of relief, even a secret mirth.

'I suppose you have been told?'

She nodded, and it was not grief that glittered her eyes.

'Your husband is dead. Someone killed him.'

At this she brought out, in a rather halting voice:

'I always thought it would end like that.'

And she tittered faintly—even more drunk than he had thought when he came in.

'You were expecting a murder?'

'With him, I was expecting anything.'

She pointed to the tumbled bed, to the untidy room, and faltered:

'I beg your pardon . . .'

'You didn't have the curiosity to go downstairs?'

'Why should I?'

Suddenly her gaze became keener:

'He really is dead, isn't he?'

When Maigret nodded she slipped her hand under the bedclothes, pulled out a bottle and put it to her lips:

'Here's to his health!' she said jestingly.

But even in death Fumal still frightened her, for she looked timidly at the door and asked Maigret:

'Is he still in the house?'

'They've just taken him away to the Medico-Legal Institute.'

'What are they going to do to him?'

'—Hold a post-mortem.'

Was it the news that her husband's body was to be chopped up that brought that spiteful smile to her face? Did she look on it as a kind of revenge, a sort of amends for all she had suffered through him?

As a girl and a young woman she must have been like anyone else. What sort of a life had Fumal led her, to reduce her to this lamentable condition?

Maigret had come across other such wrecks, but nearly always in sordid surroundings, in shabby districts, and poverty had invariably been the cause of their degradation.

'Did he come to see you yesterday evening?'

'Who?'

'Your husband.'

She shook her head.

'He used to come sometimes?'

'Sometimes, yes, but I would have preferred not to see him.'

'You didn't go down to his office?'

'I never went down there. It was in his office that he saw my father for the last time, and three hours afterwards they found my father hanging.'

That seemed to have been Fumal's vice—to ruin people, not only those who got in his way or offended him, but just anybody, in order to assert his power, to convince himself of it.

'You don't know what visitors he received last night?'

Later, Maigret would have to tell an inspector to search these rooms.

The idea of doing it himself was repugnant. But it had to be done. There was nothing to prove that this woman might not at last have screwed up the courage to go and kill her husband, and it was not impossible that the gun might be found in her room.

'I don't know . . . I don't want to know anything any more . . . Do you know what I want? . . . To be left all alone and . . .'

Maigret hadn't heard. Still standing up, not far from the bed, he saw Madame Fumal's eyes focus on a point behind him. There was the flash of a light-bulb, and at the same instant the woman flung off the bedclothes and hurled herself, with unsuspected energy, at the photographer who had appeared, without a sound, in the doorway.

He tried to beat a retreat, but she had already grabbed his camera, threw it furiously on the ground, then picked it up, only to throw it down again with greater violence.

Maigret frowned, recognizing a reporter from one of the evening papers. Someone, he didn't know who, had told the news to the Press, and he would find the whole pack of them downstairs.

'Just a moment,' he said firmly.

It was his turn to pick up the camera, from which he removed the film.

'Out you go, my boy . . .' he said to the young man.

To Madame Fumal he added:

'Go back to bed. I apologize for what happened. I will see you are left in peace from now on. But one of my men will have to search your suite.'

He was in a hurry to get out of the room, and would have liked to leave the house for ever. The photographer was waiting for him on the landing.

'I thought I might . . .'

'You went a bit too far. Are the other reporters here?'

'Some of them.'

'Who gave them the alarm?'

'I don't know. About half an hour ago my editor sent for me and . . .'

It must have been the man from the Medico-Legal Institute. All over the place there are people who are hand-in-glove with the newspapers.

There were seven or eight Press representatives downstairs already, and more would be arriving.

'What happened exactly, Superintendent?'

'If I knew that, my lads, I shouldn't be here any longer. I want you

to leave us to work in peace, and I promise you that if we discover anything . . .'

'Can we photograph the rooms?'

'Well, be quick about it.'

There were too many people to interrogate for them all to be taken
to the Quai des Orfèvres. There were big empty rooms available here.
Lapointe was already at work, so was Bonfils, and Torrence had just
arrived with Lesueur.

He told Torrence to go and search the second-floor rooms, and sent
Bonfils to Monsieur Joseph's flat. The latter was not yet back from the
Rue Rambuteau.

'When he comes in, ask him some questions on the off-chance, but
I don't think he'll say much.'

The Public Prosecutor's men had left by now, and so had most of
the experts from the Criminal Records Department.

'Send up one of the servants, by herself—Noémi, it's her job—to see
to Madame Fumal, and tell the rest to wait in the drawing-room.'

When the telephone rang in the dead man's office, Louise Bourges
took the call, as a matter of course.

'This is Monsieur Fumal's secretary . . . Yes . . . Oh yes, he's here
. . . I'll put you through . . .'

She turned to Maigret:

'It's for you . . . From the Quai des Orfèvres . . .'

'Hello—yes?'

It was the Director of the Judicial Police.

'The Minister of the Interior has just rung me up . . .'

'He knows already?'

'Yes. Everybody knows.'

Had one of the journalists spread the news to the wireless? Quite
possibly.

'Furious?'

'That's not the word. Bothered, rather. He wants to be kept informed of the inquiry, step by step. Have you any idea?'

'None.'

'They're expecting it to make a stir presently. The fellow was even
more important than he made out.'

'Do they miss him?'

'Why do you ask?'

'No special reason. Up to now, people have seemed rather relieved.'

'You're doing all you possibly can, aren't you?'

He certainly was! And yet he'd never felt so little eagerness to find a murderer. True, he was curious to know who had at last decided to get rid of Fumal, which of these men or women had had enough of it and risked everything at one throw. But would he blame the criminal? Wouldn't he feel a pang at heart when the handcuffs were put on?

He had seldom been faced with so many hypotheses, all equally plausible.

There was Madame Fumal, of course; she had only to go down one flight of stairs in order to avenge herself for twenty years of humiliation; and as well as regaining her freedom she would doubtless inherit Fumal's fortune, or most of it.

Had she a lover? To look at her it appeared unlikely, but that was a subject about which he had grown sceptical.

Monsieur Joseph?

He seemed entirely devoted to the big butcher, in whose shadow his life was led. God knew what dirty business they were in together. Hadn't Fumal had some hold over the creature, as he seemed to have over all who worked for him?

Even worms like Monsieur Joseph sometimes turned!

Louise Bourges, the secretary who had come to see him at the Quai des Orfèvres?

So far she was the only person who alleged that her employer had written the anonymous letters himself.

Felix, the chauffeur, was her lover. They were in a hurry to get married and settle at Giens.

Suppose she or Felix had robbed Fumal, or tried to swindle him, even to blackmail him? . . .

Everyone in this business seemed to have a reason for killing Fumal —even Victor, the ex-poacher, for his employer kept him on a tight rein.

The lives of the other servants must be looked into thoroughly. Then there was Gaillardin, who hadn't gone back to the Rue François Premier after visiting Fumal.

'Are you leaving, Chief?'

'I'll be back in a few minutes.'

He was thirsty, and felt the need to get out for a change of air.

'If anyone asks for me, Lapointe can take a message.'

On the landing he had to shake off the journalists, and downstairs he found several Press cars and one radio car drawn up at the curb. Because of this, a few passers-by had stopped to watch, and a uniformed policeman was standing at the door.

Hands in his pockets, Maigret strode rapidly towards the Boulevard des Batignolles and went into the first café he came to.

'A beer, please,' he ordered, 'and a counter for the telephone.'

He wanted to ring up his wife.

'I certainly shan't be home for lunch . . . Dinner? . . . I hope so . . . Perhaps . . . No, there are no special bothers . . .'

Indeed, perhaps the Minister too was not sorry to be rid of a compromising friend. There must be others who were delighted. The people in the Rue Rambuteau office, for instance, those at La Villette, and the managers of all the butchers' shops, who'd had a hard life with Fumal.

He didn't yet know that the afternoon papers would be announcing:

'King of the Meat Trade Murdered'

Newspapers love the word 'king', as they do the word 'millionaire'. One paper quoted the experts as saying that Fumal controlled one-tenth of the meat trade in Paris and more than a quarter in Northern France.

Who would inherit that empire? Madame Fumal?

As he left the *bistro*, Maigret caught sight of a prowling taxi, and this gave him the idea of taking a look at the Rue François Premier. He had already sent Neveu there, and had had no news from him, but he wanted to see for himself, and above all he was glad of an excuse to escape for a time from the sickening atmosphere of the Boulevard de Courcelles.

The building was a modern one, the concierge's lodge almost luxurious.

'Monsieur Gaillardin? Third floor left, but I don't think he's at home.'

Maigret went up in the lift and rang the doorbell. A young woman in a housecoat opened the door—or rather, until he told her who he was, just peeped through a narrow crack.

'You still have no news of Roger?' she asked then, showing him into a drawing-room as bright as any room in Paris could look in such weather.

'And haven't you?'

'No. Since your inspector came I've been worried. Just now I listened to the wireless . . .'

'They talked about Fumal?'

'Yes.'

'You know your husband went to see him yesterday evening?

She was pretty, with a luscious figure, and could hardly be over thirty.

'He's not my husband,' she corrected, 'Roger and I are not married.'

'I know. I used the word by mistake.'

'He has a wife and two children, but he doesn't live with them. Not for some years . . . wait a minute . . . five years, exactly . . .'

'You know he's in trouble?'

'I know he's practically ruined, and that it's that man . . .'

'Tell me, does Gaillardin own a revolver?'

Because she had visibly turned pale, she could not lie.

'There's always been one in his drawer.'

'Will you make sure it's still there? May I come with you?'

He followed her into the bedroom, where she had clearly slept alone in a huge, very low bed. She opened two or three drawers, seemed surprised, opened others, more and more feverishly.

'I can't find it.'

'I suppose he never carried it on him?'

'Not that I know of. You don't know him? He's a peaceable man, very cheerful, what they call a *bon vivant*.'

'Weren't you uneasy when he didn't come home?'

She did not know what to reply.

'Yes . . . Of course . . . I told your inspector so . . . But you see, he felt quite confident . . . He was sure he'd find the money at the last moment . . . I thought he'd gone to visit friends, perhaps out of town.'

'Where does his wife live?'

'At Neuilly. I'll give you her address.'

She wrote it for him on a scrap of paper. At that moment the telephone rang, and with a word of apology she lifted the receiver. The voice at the other end boomed so loudly that Maigret could hear what it said.

'Hello! Madame Gaillardin?'

'Yes . . . That is . . .'

'You are speaking from 26 Rue François Premier?'

'Yes.'

'From the residence of a certain Roger Gaillardin?'

Maigret could have sworn that the invisible questioner was a sergeant at some local police station.

'Yes; I live with him, but I'm not his wife.'

'Will you come to the Puteaux police station as quickly as possible?'

'Has something happened?'

'Yes, something has happened.'

'Roger's dead?'

'Yes.'

'Can't you tell me what happened?'

'The first thing is for you to identify the body. Some papers were found on it, but . . .'

Maigret signed to the young woman to hand him the receiver.

'Hallo! This is Superintendent Maigret, of the Judicial Police. Tell me anything you know.'

'At nine thirty-two a.m. a man's body was found on the bank of the Seine, three hundred yards below the Puteaux bridge. Owing to a pile of bricks unloaded there some days ago, the passers-by didn't notice it before. It was a bargeman who . . .'

'Murdered?'

'No. At least I don't think so, because he was still clutching an automatic with only one bullet missing from it. It looks as though he shot himself in the right temple.'

'Thank you. When the body has been identified, send it to the Medico-Legal Institute, and have the contents of the pockets sent to the Quai des Orfèvres. The lady who answered you just now will be along soon.'

Maigret hung up.

'He shot himself in the head,' he said.

'I heard.'

'Has his wife got a telephone?'

'Yes.'

She gave him the number and he dialled it at once.

'Hallo! Madame Gaillardin?'

'This is the maid.'

'Is Madame Gaillardin out?'

'She left for the Riviera two days ago, with the children. Who is that? Monsieur Gaillardin?'

'No. The police. There's something I want to know. Were you in the flat yesterday evening?'

'Certainly I was.'

'Did Monsieur Gaillardin call there?'

'Why?'

'Answer me, please.'

'Well, yes.'

'At what time?'

'I'd gone to bed. It was after half past ten.'

'What did he want?'

'To speak to Madame.'

'Did he often come to see her in the evening?'

'Not in the evening, no.'

'In the daytime?'

'He used to come to see the children.'

'But yesterday he wanted to speak to his wife?'

'Yes. He seemed surprised that she'd gone away.'

'Did he stay long?'

'No.'

'Did he seem upset?'

'He was certainly tired. In fact I offered him a glass of brandy.'

'Did he drink it?'

'At one gulp.'

Maigret rang off and turned to the young woman.

'You can go to Puteaux now.'

'Aren't you coming with me?'

'Not now. I expect I shall be seeing you again, though.'

To sum up the position: Gaillardin had taken his revolver with him the previous evening when he left the Rue François Premier. He had gone first of all to the Boulevard de Courcelles. Was he hoping that Fumal would give him more time? Relying on some argument to make the man change his mind?

He must have been unsuccessful. A little later he had gone to his wife's flat at Neuilly and found that only the maid was there. The flat was not far from the Seine. Three hundred yards away was the Puteaux bridge; he had crossed that.

Had he roamed along the river bank for long, before shooting himself in the head?

Maigret went into a rather smart bar and growled:

'A pint of beer and a telephone counter.'

He wanted to ring the Medico-Legal Institute.

'Maigret here. Is Doctor Paul there yet? What's that? Yes, Maigret . . . He's still busy? Ask him if he's found the bullet . . . Half a second . . . If he has, ask him whether it was fired from a revolver or from an automatic . . .'

He heard the sound of footsteps, and voices at the other end of the line.

'Hallo . . . Superintendent? . . . It seems the shot was from an automatic . . . The bullet was lodged in . . .'

Never mind where the bullet that killed Fumal had lodged.

Unless one could assume that Roger Gaillardin had been carrying two weapons that evening, it was not he who had killed the big butcher.

*   *   *

As Maigret crossed the first-floor landing of the house in the Boulevard de Courcelles, the journalists assailed him again, and to get rid of them he told them of the discovery made on the river bank at Puteaux.

The inspectors were still busy in the different rooms, questioning the secretary and the servants. Only Torrence was unoccupied. He seemed to be waiting impatiently for the Superintendent, and at once led him away into a corner.

'I've found something up there, Chief,' he said in an undertone.

'The gun?'

'No. Will you come with me?'

They went up to the second floor and into the drawing-room with the many arm-chairs and the doubtless never-opened piano.

'In Madame Fumal's room?'

Torrence looked mysterious and shook his head.

'It's a huge apartment,' he said. 'You'll see.'

He seemed to be quite at home, and pointed out the various rooms to Maigret, paying no attention to Madame Fumal, who was still in bed.

'I haven't said anything about it to her. I think it'll be better if it comes from you. This way . . .'

They went through one empty bedroom and then another; these had obviously not been used for a long time. There was also an unused bathroom, where buckets and brooms were kept.

On the left of a corridor was a fair-sized room, full of stacked-up furniture, trunks and dusty suitcases.

At the far end of this corridor, Torrence opened the door of a room smaller than the others, and narrow; it had only one window, looking out on to the courtyard. The room was furnished as though for a servant—it had a divan bed with a red cotton cover, a table, two chairs and a cheap cupboard.

The inspector, with quiet triumph gleaming in his eyes, pointed to an ash-tray, of the type given away as advertisements; two cigarette-butts lay on it.

'Sniff that, Chief. I don't know what Moers will say about it, but I'd swear those cigarettes were smoked not long ago. Probably yesterday. Perhaps even this morning. When I came in the room still smelt of tobacco.'

'You've looked in the cupboard?'

'Nothing in there except a couple of blankets. Now get up on that chair. Look out, it's not strong.'

Maigret knew by experience that people who want to hide something usually put it on top of a cupboard or wardrobe.

Up there now, under a thick layer of dust, were a razor, a packet of blades and a tube of shaving-cream.

'What do you say to that?'

'You've said nothing about them to the servants?'

'I preferred to wait for you.'

'Go back to the drawing-room.'

As for himself, he knocked on the bedroom door.

There was no answer, but when he opened it he found Madame Fumal staring in his direction.

'What do you want now? Can't I be allowed to sleep?'

She was neither better nor worse than before, and if she had been drinking again it was hardly noticeable.

'I am terribly sorry to bother you, but I have my job to do and I must ask you a few questions.'

She was still gazing at him with a frown, as though trying to guess what would come next.

'I believe I'm right in thinking that the servants all sleep in the rooms above the garage?'

'Yes. Why?'

'Do you smoke?'

She hesitated, but there was no time for a lie.

'No.'

'It's always in this room that you sleep?'

'What do you mean?'

'And I suppose your husband never came to sleep in your apartment?'

This time it was clear she had understood; and abandoning her defensive attitude she shrank down further under the bedclothes.

'Is he still there?' she asked in a low voice.

'No. But I have every reason to believe he spent at least part of the night there.'

'That's possible. I don't know when he left. He comes and goes . . .'

'Who is he?'

She seemed surprised. She must have thought he knew more, and now she was sorry to have said so much.

'Haven't they told you?'

'Who could have told me?'

'Noémi . . . Or Germaine . . . They both know . . . In fact Noémi . . .'

She smiled strangely.

'Is he your lover?'

At this she burst out laughing—harsh laughter that must have been painful.

'Can you see me with a lover? Do you really suppose any man would still want me? Have you looked at me, Superintendent? Would you like to see what . . .'

She clutched the sheet as though to throw it back, and for a horrified second Maigret thought she meant to show him her nakedness.

'My lover!' she said again. 'No, Superintendent. I have no lover. It's a long time since I . . .'

She realized she was giving herself away.

'I have had lovers, that's true. And Ferdinand knew it. And he's made me pay for it, all my life. With him, one has to pay for everything—everything. You understand? But my brother never did him any harm, except for being my father's son, and my brother.'

'It was your brother who slept in the end room?'

'Yes. He often does, several nights a week. When he's capable of getting this far.'

'What does he do?'

She looked at him straight in the eyes, fiercely, with a sort of restrained fury.

'He drinks!' she announced. 'Like me! There's nothing else left for him to do. He had money, a wife, children . . .'

'Your husband ruined him?'

'He took his last penny. But if you imagine it was my brother who killed him, you're wrong. He's not even capable of that any longer. Any more than I am.'

'Where is he at the moment?'

She shrugged her shoulders.

'Somewhere where there's a drink-shop. He's not a young man now. He's sixty-two and looks at least sixty-five. His children are married and refuse to see him. His wife works in a factory, at Limoges.'

She groped for her bottle.

'Was it Victor who brought him to the house?'

'If Victor had known about it he'd have gone and told my husband.'

'Your brother had a key?'

'Noémi had one made for him.'

'What is your brother's name?'

'Emile . . . Emile Lentin . . . I can't tell you where to find him. When he sees in the papers that Fumal is dead, I expect he'll be afraid to come here. In that case you'll pick him up sooner or later by the river or in the Salvation Army doss-house.'

She threw him another defiant glance, and with a bitter twist to her lips, began to drink from the bottle.

V

THE HOME-LOVING LADY AND THE
FOOD-LOVING GIRL

THERE was no need to say who he was, or to show his badge. A small glass lens was set into the front door at eye-level, in such a way that whoever rang the bell could be seen from inside. And now the door opened at once and a delighted voice exclaimed:

'Monsieur Maigret!'

He, for his part, recognized the woman who opened the door and ushered him into a room which was over-heated by a gas stove. She must have been at least sixty by this time, but she had scarcely changed at all since the days when she kept a discreet brothel in the Rue Notre-Dame-de-Lorette and Maigret had rescued her from an awkward situation.

He had not expected to find her running this hotel in the Rue de l'Etoile, where the notice beside the door offered 'Luxurious bachelor flats to let by the month or the week'.

It was not exactly a hotel. The office was not a proper office either, but a private room with comfortable arm-chairs on whose silken cushions two or three Persian cats lay purring.

Rose's hair had thinned a bit but it was still peroxide blonde; her face and body were plumper and her complexion rather pallid.

'Who have you come about?' she asked Maigret as she cleared one of the arm-chairs. She was quite thrilled, for she had always had a bit of a crush on the Superintendent; whenever she got into trouble in the old days she would go to see him at the Quai des Orfèvres.

'Have you got a girl here called Martine Gilloux?'

It was midday. The newspapers had not yet announced Fumal's death. Feeling a bit of a coward, Maigret had left his staff at work in the depressing atmosphere of the Boulevard de Courcelles and made his escape, for the second time that morning.

'She's done nothing wrong, has she?' asked Rose, adding quickly:

'She's a good girl, absolutely harmless.'

'Is she upstairs now?'

'She went out, perhaps a quarter of an hour ago. She's one who doesn't like late nights. At this time of day she'll probably be making her little tour of the district before going to lunch at Gino's or some other restaurant in the Avenue des Ternes.'

The little sitting-room was like the one in the Rue Notre-Dame-de-Lorette, except that the walls were not adorned with the pornographic prints that had been part of the professional stock-in-trade at the old place. It was just as hot. Rose had always been a chilly creature, or rather she'd always loved warmth for its own sake, overheating her rooms, swathing herself in quilted housecoats, and in winter sometimes spending weeks on end without putting her nose out of doors.

'Has she been living here long?'

'More than a year.'

'What sort of a girl is she?'

They spoke the same language, the pair of them, and understood each other.

'A nice child who had no luck for years. She comes from a very poor family. She was born somewhere in the suburbs, I've forgotten where, but she told me she'd gone hungry for a long time and I realized she wasn't putting it on.'

Again she asked him:

'Anything bad?'

'I don't think so.'

'I'm sure not. She's not really very bright, and she tries to be nice to everybody. Men have taken advantage of her. She's had her ups and downs, more downs than ups. For a long time she was in the hands of a brute who led her a dog's life; but luckily for her he went to prison in the end. She told me all this herself, for she didn't live here in those days, she was somewhere in Montmartre, off the Boulevard Barbès. By chance, she found someone who took a flatlet here for her, and since then she's had a quiet life.'

'Fumal?'

'That's his name. A big wholesale butcher, with several cars and a chauffeur.'

'Does he come often?'

'Sometimes not for two or three days, and then he'll turn up every afternoon or every evening.'

'Anything else?'

'I can't think of anything. You know how it goes on. He gives her enough to live comfortably, but not in luxury. She has some nice dresses, a fur coat, two or three bits of jewellery.'

'Does he take her out?'

'Now and then, especially when he's dining in a restaurant with men friends who bring their own girls.'

'Has Martine another man friend?'

'I used to wonder, at first. Girls like that generally do feel the need to have somebody. I put some cunning questions to her. I always find out in the end what's going on in the district. I can tell you definitely she has no one. She finds it more restful. In fact, she doesn't really care for men.'

'Does she drug?'

'She's not the type.'

'What does she do with her time?'

'She stays at home, reading or listening to the wireless. She sleeps. She goes out for her meals, takes a little stroll, and comes in again.'

'Do you know Fumal?'

'I've seen him go down the corridor. Often the chauffeur waits outside in the car while he's upstairs.'

'You say I shall find her at Gino's?'

'You know it? The little Italian restaurant . . .'

Maigret knew it. The restaurant was not large or impressive-looking, but it was celebrated for its spaghetti and particularly for its ravioli, and the clientele was select.

When he went in he paused at the bar to ask:

'Is Martine Gilloux here?'

There were already about a dozen people at lunch, men and women.

He followed the direction of the barman's glance and saw a young woman eating alone in a corner.

After depositing his coat and hat in the cloakroom, Maigret went over to her and stopped, his hand on the empty chair at the opposite side of the table.

'May I sit down?'

She looked at him blankly, so he added:

'I have to talk to you. I'm from the police.'

He had noticed that ten or a dozen small dishes of hors d'oeuvres were ranged in front of her.

'Don't be frightened. I only need a few particulars.'

'About whom?'

'About Fumal. And yourself.'

He turned to the head waiter, who had approached the table.

'I'll have some hors d'oeuvres too, and then a *spaghetti milanese*.'

At last he said to the young woman, who was still looking uneasy, and even more bewildered:

'I've just come from the Rue de l'Etoile. Rose told me I should find you here. Fumal is dead.'

She must have been between twenty-five and twenty-eight years old, but there was something older in her face—weariness, apathy, perhaps a lack of curiosity about life. She was fairly tall, rather fat, with a gentle, timid expression, reminding one of a child that has been beaten.

'You didn't know?'

She shook her head, still eyeing him, not knowing what to think.

'You saw him yesterday?'

'Wait a minute . . . Yesterday . . . Yes . . . He came to see me about five o'clock . . .'

'How was he?'

'Just as usual.'

One point had just struck Maigret. Up to now, everyone to whom he had broken the news of Fumal's death had greeted it with delighted astonishment, more or less controlled. At the very least, one could sense their relief.

Martine Gilloux, on the contrary, had received the news gravely, perhaps with distress, certainly with anxiety.

Was she reflecting that her future hung in the balance yet again, that her tranquillity and comfort had come to an end, perhaps for ever?

Was she afraid of the streets, where she had roamed for so long?

'Go on eating,' he said, as his own order was brought.

She did so, mechanically, and one could see that, for her, eating was the greatest thing in life, the thing that reassured her. For the past year she had probably been eating in order to wipe out the memory of her long years of hunger, or to avenge herself for them.

'What do you know about him?' he asked her gently.

'You're sure you're from the police?'

She was almost ready to ask advice from the barman or the head waiter, who were watching them. He showed her his badge.

'Superintendent Maigret,' he said.

'I've read about you in the papers. Is it really you? I thought you were fatter.'

'Tell me about Fumal. Let's begin at the beginning. Where did you meet him, when and how?'

'Just over a year ago.'

'Where?'

'In a little night-club in Montmartre, *Le Désir*. I was at the bar. He came in with some friends who had drunk more than he had.'

'He didn't drink?'

'I've never seen him drunk.'

'And then?'

'There were other girls. One of his friends called one of them over. Then another—a butcher, I think, from Lille or somewhere in the North—came and fetched my girl-friend, Nina. So Fumal was the only one at their table who hadn't got a girl. Then he beckoned to me to come over. You know how it happens. I could see he wasn't really keen, he only wanted to do like the others. I remember he looked at me and remarked:

'*"You're thin. You must be hungry."*

'It's true I was thin in those days. Without consulting me, he called the head waiter and ordered a complete supper for me.

'*"Eat and drink all you can,"* he said, *"you won't have the luck to meet Fumal every evening!"*

'That's more or less how it began. His friends left before him, with the two other girls. He asked me about my parents, about my child-hood, what I was doing. There are a lot like that. He didn't even paw me.

'In the end, he decided:

'*"Come along! I'm going to take you to a decent hotel".*'

'He spent the night there?' asked Maigret.

'No. It was near the Place Clichy, I remember. He paid a week in advance, and that night he didn't even come upstairs. He came back next day.'

'And that time he did come upstairs?'

'Yes. He stayed for a bit. But not so much for the reason you suppose. He wasn't very strong in that direction. Most of the time he talked to me about himself, and what he was doing, and his wife.'

'In what way did he talk?'

'I think he was unhappy.'

Maigret could scarcely believe his ears.

'Go on,' he murmured.

'It's difficult, you understand? He talked to me so often about those things . . .'

'In short, he came to see you so as to talk about himself.' Maigret had lapsed automatically into the familiar '*tu*'.

'Not only that . . .'

'But chiefly?'

'Perhaps. It seems he'd worked hard, harder than anybody in the world, and had become a very powerful man. Is that true?'

'It *was* true—yes.'

'He used to say things like:

'"*What good does it do me? People don't realize it and they take me for a brute. My wife's mad. My servants and employees think only of robbing me. When I go into a smart restaurant I can guess that people are muttering:*

'"*Hallo—here comes the butcher!*"'

The waiter brought spaghetti for Maigret and raviolo for Martine Gilloux, who had a flask of Chianti in front of her.

'Do you mind . . . ?'

Her worries had not spoilt her appetite.

'He said his wife was mad?'

'Yes, and that she hated him. He'd bought the château in the village where he was born. Is that true, too?'

'Quite true.'

'I didn't take much notice, you know. I thought he was probably boasting a good deal. The peasants in that village still call him the Butcher. He'd bought a big house in the Boulevard de Courcelles and he used to say it was more like a station waiting-room than a proper house.'

'Ever been there?'

'Yes.'

'Have you a key?'

'No. I only went there twice. The first time was because he wanted to show me where he lived. It was at night. We went up to the first floor. I saw the big drawing-room, his office, his bedroom, the dining-room, then some other rooms with hardly any furniture, and it really didn't seem like a proper house.

'"*The madwoman lives up above,*" he told me. "*I expect she's on the landing, spying on us.*"

'I asked him if she was jealous and he said no, she just spied on him for the sake of spying, it was a mania with her. Does she really drink?'

'Yes.'

'Well then, you see, almost everything he said to me was true. And that he could walk in to see Cabinet Ministers without sending up his name?'

'Only a slight exaggeration.'

There was surely something ironical about the relationship between Fumal and Martine. For over a year she'd been his mistress. And really he'd taken her, and kept her, solely in order to have someone he could swank in front of and complain to at the same time.

Some men, when their troubles get too much for them, pick up a tart on the street, just so as to confide in her.

Fumal had taken on a personal confidante for his exclusive use, settling her comfortably in the Rue de l'Etoile so that she had nothing to do but wait on his pleasure.

Yet in point of fact she had never believed him. Not only that, but she had never so much as wondered whether what he told her was true or false.

It was all the same to her.

Now he was dead she was awestruck to learn that he really had been as important as he made out.

'He wasn't worried, just lately?'

'How do you mean?'

'He didn't think his life was in danger? He didn't talk about his enemies?'

'He often told me a man couldn't become powerful without making hordes of enemies. He used to say:

'"*They fawn on me like dogs, but in actual fact they hate me, all of them, and they'll never be so happy as the day I kick the bucket.*"

'And he would add:

'"*You too, for that matter. Or rather, you would be pleased, if I left you something. But I shan't. If I die or if I drop you, you'll go back to the gutter".'*

She was not shocked by this. She had seen too much before he came along. He had brought her months of security, and that had been enough for her.

'What happened to him?' she asked in her turn. 'A heart attack?'

'Had he a weak heart?'

'I don't know. When people die suddenly one usually hears . . .'

'He was murdered.'

She stopped eating, so startled that she sat open-mouthed. It was quite a time before she asked:

'Where? When?'

'Last night. At home.'

'Who did it?'

'That's what I'm trying to find out.'

'How was it done?'

'A revolver shot.'

For the first time in her life, most likely, she had lost her appetite, and pushing her plate away she reached out for her glass and emptied it at a gulp.

'Just my luck,' he heard her whisper.

'Did he ever mention a Monsieur Joseph to you?'

'An old, rather small man?'

'Yes.'

'He called him the Thief. It seems he really had been a thief. Ferdinand might have had him put in prison. He preferred to keep him in his service, because he said scoundrels were more useful than honest men. He even fixed him up in the attics, so as to have him always at hand.'

'And his secretary?'

'Mademoiselle Louise?'

So Fumal really had made detailed confidences to his mistress.

'What did he think about her?'

'That she was frigid, ambitious and grasping and that she only worked for him so as to put money aside.'

'Is that all?'

'No. Something happened with her. Did she tell you?'

'Go on.'

'Oh well—now he's dead . . .'

She glanced round and lowered her voice, for fear of being over-heard by the head waiter.

'One day in the office he pretended to be making a pass at her, he be-gan to paw her and then he told her:

'"*Get your clothes off.*"'

'And she did?' asked Maigret in surprise.

'So he said. He didn't even take her into his bedroom. He stood there, by the window, while she undressed, watching her ironically. When she'd taken off every stitch, he asked her:

'"*You're a virgin?*"'

'What did she say?'

'Nothing. She blushed. And after a bit he grunted:

'"*You're not a virgin. That'll do! Put your clothes on again!*"'

'At the time I didn't believe that story. I've had insults to put up with too. But I'm not well brought up or educated. Men know they can be-have however they want with me. But a girl like that . . .

'If he wasn't lying, he watched her while she dressed, and then pointed to her chair and her shorthand pad and began to dictate let-ters to her . . .'

'You haven't a lover?' asked Maigret point-blank.

She said no, promptly, but at the same time she glanced at the bar-man.

'He's the chap?'

'No.'

'You're in love with him?'

'Not in love.'

'But you easily could have been—no?'

'I don't know. He takes no notice of me.'

He ordered coffee and asked Martine:

'No dessert?'

'Not today. I'm so whacked I shall go to bed. You don't need me any more?'

'No. Never mind the bill, I'll attend to that. You're not to leave the Rue de l'Etoile until further notice.'

'Not even for meals?'

'Only for meals.'

The inspectors had lunched in a little Normandy restaurant they had discovered just off the Boulevard de Courcelles, and were already back at work when Maigret arrived.

There were a few bits of news, of no great importance. It had been confirmed that Roger Gaillardin had committed suicide—the revolver had not been put into his hand when he was dead. And it was definitely the one he had had in his flat in the Rue François Premier.

The ballistics expert also said that the automatic found in Fumal's room had not been fired for months, probably not for years.

Lucas had come back with Monsieur Joseph from the Rue Rambuteau, where everything was in wild confusion.

'There's no one to give orders and nobody knows what turn things will take. Fumal couldn't bear to delegate authority to anyone, he managed everything himself, turning up at the most unexpected moments, and his staff lived in perpetual terror. Only Monsieur Joseph knew the ins and outs of the business, it appears, and he has no legal powers and is as much hated as his boss used to be.'

The evening papers, which were just out, corroborated this state of affairs. Nearly all of them had the same headline:

'KING OF MEAT-MARKET MURDERED'

'*A man who was never much in the public eye,*' they explained, '*but who nevertheless played a considerable part . . .*'

They gave the list of the companies he had formed, with their branches and sub-branches, making a positive empire.

They recalled the fact—unknown to Maigret—that five years previously the said empire had almost collapsed when the tax authorities had pushed their noses into Fumal's affairs. Scandal had been averted, though according to well-informed circles the Treasury had been defrauded of over a billion francs.

How had the business been hushed up? This the newspapers did not explain; only giving it to be understood that the former village butcher had protectors in high places.

One of the newspapers asked:

'*Will his death bring the matter forward again?*'

In any case some people must be feeling uncomfortable this afternoon, including the Minister who had telephoned the Judicial Police.

What the Press did not know yet, and might perhaps find out, was that, only the day before, this same Fumal had asked for police protection.

Had Maigret done all that was in his power?

He had sent an inspector to watch the house in the Boulevard de Courcelles, which is the routine procedure on such occasions. He had gone himself to have a look at the place, and he had instructed Lapointe to follow Fumal wherever he went, as from the next morning. They had been about to continue the inquiry when . . .

He had not been at fault professionally. All the same he was not pleased with himself. In the first place, hadn't he allowed his judgment to be influenced by childhood memories, especially by the way Fumal's father had behaved to his own father?

He had not felt the least sympathy for the man who had come to see him with a recommendation from the Minister of the Interior.

Whereas when Louise Bourges, the secretary, had come along, he had taken her entirely at her word.

He felt sure the story Martine had told him just now, at the restaurant, was true. Ferdinand Fumal was exactly the kind of man to humiliate a woman in some disgusting way. It was true, too, that the secretary felt nothing but contempt for him, or hatred, and that if she remained in his employment it was solely with the idea of marrying Felix and having enough, between the two of them, to buy an inn at Giens.

Was she satisfied with the salary she was earning? Being so close to Fumal, knowing all his business secrets, might she not have other ways of making money?

The man used to tell his mistress:

'Their one idea is to rob me, the lot of them . . .'

Had he been so far wrong? Up to now, Maigret had met nobody who cared a jot for him. To remain in his employment went against the grain with them all.

Fumal, for his part, did nothing to make himself popular. On the contrary, he seemed to find a malignant pleasure, a secret thrill, in calling forth hatred.

It was not merely for the last few days, or weeks, or even years, that he had felt this hatred around him.

Why had it taken him until yesterday to become uneasy enough to ask for police protection?

Why—if his secretary was telling the truth—had he taken the trouble to send himself anonymous threats?

Had he suddenly discovered that he had one enemy more dangerous than the rest? Or had he given somebody a reason for doing away with him at short notice?

That was a possibility. Moers was not only examining the anonymous notes, but specimens of the handwriting of Fumal and Louise

Bourges as well. He had called in one of the leading Paris graphologists to help him.

From the office in the Boulevard de Courcelles, Maigret—his glum, heavy manner unchanged—rang through to the laboratory.

'Moers? . . . Getting any results? . . .'

He could imagine them, up in the attics of the Palais de Justice, working by electric light, throwing the documents on a screen, one by one.

Moers made his report in his even tones; he had verified that all but one of the threatening letters bore only Fumal's finger-prints. With those of Maigret and Lucas. On the first of them the prints of Louise Bourges had been found.

This seemed to bear out what Louise had said, for she claimed to have opened the first letter, but not the following ones.

On the other hand that proved nothing, because if she had written the notes she was quite intelligent enough to have worn gloves while doing it.

'What about the writing?'

'We're still working at that. It's awkward, because of the copybook style. So far there's nothing to show that Fumal didn't write the letters himself.'

The staff was still being questioned in the next-door room, people being confronted in pairs and then interviewed again separately. There were already pages and pages of statements; Maigret had them brought to him and ran through them.

Felix, the chauffeur, confirmed what Louise Bourges had said. He was a short, thick-set, swarthy man with a somewhat arrogant expression.

Question: You are the lover of Mademoiselle Bourges?

Answer: We are engaged to be married.

Question: You sleep with her?

Answer: She'll tell you about that, if she chooses.

Question: You have been spending most nights in her room?

Answer: If she told you so, it must be true.

Question: When were you intending to get married?

Answer: As soon as possible.

Question: What were you waiting for?

Answer: Till we had enough money to set ourselves up with.

Question: What were you doing before you entered Monsieur Fumal's employment?

Answer: I was a butcher's assistant.

Question: How did he come to take you on?

Answer: He bought the shop where I was working—he was always buying up butchers. He noticed me and asked if I knew how to drive a car. I told him I was the one who drove the delivery van.

Question: Was Louise Bourges already working for him then?

Answer: No.

Question: You didn't know her?

Answer: No.

Question: Your boss didn't often go about on foot in Paris?

Answer: He had three cars.

Question: He didn't drive himself?

Answer: No. I took him everywhere.

Question: Including the Rue de l'Etoile?

Answer: Yes.

Question: You knew whom he went to see there?

Answer: His tart.

Question: Did you know her?

Answer: I've driven her with him in the car. They sometimes went to a restaurant together, or up to Montmartre.

Question: Fumal never tried to give you the slip, just lately?

Answer: I don't understand.

Question: He never had himself driven somewhere and then took a taxi, for instance, to go on elsewhere?

Answer: I never noticed it.

Question: He never stopped the car at a stationer's shop or a news-agent's? He never asked you to buy him some writing-paper?

Answer: No.

There were pages and pages of this. At one point it ran:

Question: You found him a good boss?

Answer: There are no good bosses.

Question: You hated him?

No answer.

Question: Did intimacy ever occur between Louise Bourges and him?

Answer: Fumal or no Fumal, I'd have smashed his teeth in, and if you're insinuating . . .

Question: He never tried?

Answer: Luckily for him.

Question: Were you robbing him?

Answer: Pardon?

Question: I am asking you whether you used to take a rake-off on petrol for instance, or on repair bills and so forth . . .

Answer: It's obvious you didn't know him.

Question: He kept a close eye on things?

Answer: He didn't want to be taken for a sucker.

Question: So you had nothing but your wages?

In another file was a statement by Louise Bourges. Maigret read:

Question: Did your boss never try to go to bed with you?

Answer: He kept a girl specially for that.

Question: He no longer had any relations with his wife?

Answer: That is not my business.

Question: Did no one ever offer you money to get you to influence him, for instance, or to give away some of his plans?

Answer: He was not open to influence and he told nobody about his plans.

Question: How many more years did you expect to remain in his employment?

Answer: As few as possible.

Germaine, the woman who did the heavy cleaning work, had been born at Saint-Fiacre, where her brother was still a small farmer. Fumal had bought the farm. He had bought nearly all the farms that used to belong to the Comte de Saint-Fiacre.

Question: How did you come into his employment?

Answer: I was a widow. I was working on my brother's farm. Monsieur Fumal suggested I should come to Paris.

Question: Were you happy here?

Answer: When have I ever been happy?

Question: Were you fond of your master?

Answer: He wasn't fond of anybody.

Question: And you?

Answer: I've no time to ask myself such things.

Question: You knew Madame Fumal's brother often spent the night on the second floor?

Answer: It's no business of mine.

Question: It never occurred to you to tell your master about it?

Answer: The master's affairs are none of our business.

Question: Do you intend to remain in Madame Fumal's service?

Answer: I shall do what I've done all my life—I shall go wherever I'm wanted.

The desk telephone rang. Maigret picked up the receiver. It was the police station in the Rue de Maistre, in Montmartre.

'The chap you're looking for is here.'

'What chap?'

'Emile Lentin. He was found in a *bistro* near the Place Clichy.'

'Drunk?'

'Fairly.'

'What does he say?'

'Nothing.'

'Take him to the Quai des Orfèvres. I'll see him presently.'

No gun had been found in the house or in the outbuildings.

Monsieur Joseph, seated in one of the uncomfortable Renaissance arm-chairs in the anteroom, was biting his nails as he waited for one of the inspectors to question him for the third time.

VI

THE MAN IN THE LUMBER-ROOM AND THE SUMS BORROWED FROM THE PETTY CASH

I T W A S five o'clock when Maigret got back to the Quai des Orfèvres; the lights were on already, and that made one more day without a glimpse of sun—one wouldn't even have suspected it was still there, behind the thick layer of angry-looking clouds.

There were a few papers waiting on his desk, as usual, most of them about Mrs. Britt. The public never gets worked up right away. It's as though it were distrustful of any case the papers are only just beginning to talk about. After two or three days the first reaction begins to be felt in Paris, and then in the provinces. The story of the vanished Englishwoman had already penetrated to the most remote villages, and even to foreign countries.

One of the messages reported she had been seen at Monte Carlo by two people, one of them a croupier at one of the tables; and as this was not at all unlikely, the Superintendent went into the inspectors' office to give instructions about the matter.

The office was practically empty.

'Someone was brought along for you, Chief. Considering the state he was in, I thought I'd better lock him up in the lumber-room.'

This was the name given to a narrow room at the end of the corridor, which had the advantage of being lit only by a skylight that was out of reach. After the day when a suspect, shut up in an office to await interrogation, had thrown himself out of the window, a grey-painted bench had been put into the unused room and a stout lock on the door.

'How is he?'

'Dead drunk. He lay down at once and he's asleep. I hope he's not been sick.'

All the way along in the taxi that had brought him from the Boulevard de Courcelles, Maigret had been thinking about Fumal and the strange way he had met his death.

He was a very suspicious man, all the evidence pointed to that. He was no simpleton. And it must be admitted he had a kind of skill in summing people up.

He had not been killed in his bed, nor taken by surprise when off his guard for some reason or other.

He had been found fully dressed, in his office. He had been standing in front of a cupboard containing files, when he'd been shot from behind, at point-blank range.

Could the murderer have come in without a sound, and crept up unnoticed? Most unlikely, especially as a big stretch of the parquet floor was uncarpeted.

So Fumal must have known him, known he was behind him, and not been expecting the attack.

Maigret had glanced at the papers in the mahogany cupboard, most of which were business documents, contracts, deeds of sale or transfer about which he understood nothing, and he had asked the Finance Department to send him an expert, who was now on the spot, inspecting the papers one by one.

In another piece of furniture they had found two packets of writing-paper similar to that of the anonymous letters, and that, too, would mean work for the police. Moers would first try to trace the manufacturer. After that, inspectors would go out to question all retailers who sold that type of paper.

'The Director hasn't asked for me?'

'No, Chief.'

What would be the use of going to see him now? To tell him one had found nothing? Maigret had been instructed to guard Fumal's life, and Fumal had died a few hours later. Was the Minister furious? Or on the contrary, was he secretly relieved?

'Have you the key?'

The key of the lumber-room. He went down the corridor, listened at the door for a moment, heard nothing, opened it, and saw a man stretched out on the bench at what seemed great length, his head resting on his folded arms.

He was not exactly a tramp, but his suit was old, crumpled and stained like that of a man who sometimes sleeps fully dressed in all kinds of places. His brown hair was too long, especially at the back.

Maigret touched him on the shoulder, then shook him, and after a time the drunkard stirred, grunted, and finally rolled over almost completely.

'Whadyou wan'?' he growled thickly.

'Would you like a glass of water?'

Emile Lentin sat up, still not realizing where he was, opened his eyes and gave the Superintendent a long stare, wondering why this man was standing in front of him.

'Don't you remember? You're at Judicial Police Headquarters. I am Superintendent Maigret.'

Little by little the man was coming to, and his expression changed, became timid and crafty.

'Why was I brought here?'

'Are you in a condition to understand what is said to you?'

He passed his tongue over his dry lips.

'I'm thirsty.'

'Come to my office.'

He made Lentin walk in front of him, and the man's legs were so shaky there was no danger of his running away.

'Drink this, anyhow.'

Maigret offered him a large glass of water and two aspirins, and he swallowed them obediently.

Madame Fumal's brother had a worn face with red eyelids and his eyeballs seemed as though floating in some fluid.

'I haven't done anything,' he began without being asked, 'and Jeanne's not done anything either.'

'Sit down.'

He sat down hesitantly on the edge of an arm-chair.

'Since when have you known your brother-in-law was dead?'

The man only gazed silently at Maigret, who went on:

'When you were found in Montmartre the afternoon papers hadn't yet appeared. Did the police talk to you?'

He made an effort to remember, repeating:

'The police . . . ?'

'The police who picked you up in the bar.'

He tried to smile politely.

'Perhaps . . . Yes . . . There was something like that . . . I beg your pardon . . .'

'Since what time today have you been drunk?'

'I don't know . . . For a long time . . .'

'But you knew Fumal was dead?'

'I knew it would turn out like this.'

'That what would turn out like this?'

'That all the blame would be laid on me.'

'You spent the night in the Boulevard de Courcelles?'

One could feel he had to make an effort to follow Maigret's meaning and his own train of thought. He must have a terrible hangover, and the sweat stood out on his forehead.

'I suppose you wouldn't give me a drink? . . . Not much . . . You know, just enough to pep me up . . .'

It was true that at the stage he had reached a little glass of spirits would steady him a bit, at least for the time being. In his drunkenness he had arrived at the same point as a drug-addict, who suffers tortures when the time comes for his usual dose.

Maigret opened his cupboard and poured a little brandy into a glass, while Lentin watched him with a mixture of gratitude and stupefaction. It must have been the first time in his life that the police had given him a drink.

'Now try to answer my questions exactly.'

'I promise!' he said, already sitting straighter in his chair.

'You spent the night, or part of the night, at your sister's flat, as you often do?'

'Whenever I'm in the district.'

'What time did you leave the Boulevard de Courcelles?'

Again he looked closely at Maigret, like a man who hesitates, trying to weigh the pros and cons.

'I suppose I'd better tell the truth?'

'Undoubtedly.'

'It was a little after one o'clock at night, perhaps two o'clock. I'd gone there in the late afternoon. I'd lain down on the divan, because I was very tired.'

'Were you drunk?'

'Perhaps. I'd certainly been drinking.'

'What happened after that?'

'After a time Jeanne, my sister, brought me something to eat—some cold chicken. She hardly ever has her meals with her husband. Her lunch and dinner are brought up to her on a tray. When I'm there she nearly always asks for something cold—ham or chicken—and shares it with me.'

'You don't know what time it was.'

'No. It's long enough since I've had a watch.'

'You chatted, your sister and you?'

'What would we say to each other?'

And that was one of the most tragic remarks Maigret had ever heard. True enough, what could they have said to each other? They were both practically at the same point. They had got beyond the stage at which people still rehash memories or vent their bitterness.

'I asked her for a drink.'

'How did your sister get hold of drink? Did her husband supply her?'

'Not enough. I used to go and buy it for her.'

'She had money?'

He sighed, with a glance at the cupboard; but the Superintendent did not offer him a second tot.

'It's so complicated . . .'

'What's complicated?'

'Everything . . . The whole of that life . . . I know people won't understand and that's why I cleared out . . .'

'Just a moment, Lentin. Let's go on taking things in their order. Your sister brought you something to eat. You asked her for a drink. You don't know what the time was, but it was already dark, isn't that so?'

'Certainly.'

'You drank together?'

'Just a glass or two. She wasn't feeling well. There are times now when she can't breathe properly. She went off to bed.'

'And then?'

'I went on lying there and smoking cigarettes. I'd have liked to know what time it was. I listened to the sounds from the Boulevard, where only an occasional car was going past. Without putting on my shoes I went out on the landing and found the house was in darkness.'

'What did you intend to do?'

'I hadn't a cent. Not even a ten-franc piece. Jeanne had no money either. Fumal didn't give her any, and often she had to borrow from the maids.'

'You meant to ask your brother-in-law for money?'

The man almost laughed.

'Of course not! Oh well, if I've got to tell you everything . . . Here we go! Have you been told how suspicious he was? He didn't trust a soul. Every piece of furniture in the house was kept locked. But I had discovered a trick. His secretary, Mademoiselle Louise, always had money in her drawer. Not much. Never more than five or six thousand francs, chiefly in change and small notes, to buy stamps, pay for registered letters at the Post Office, and give tips. It was what they called the petty cash.

'So from time to time, when I was cleaned out, I'd go down to the office and take a few hundred-franc pieces . . .'

'Fumal never caught you at it?'

'No. I went on evenings when he was out, for choice. Once or twice it so happened he was in bed, but he didn't hear anything. I'm cat-footed.'

'He wasn't in bed yesterday?'

'No, he was not!'

'What did he say to you?'

'He said nothing to me, for the very good reason that he was dead, stretched out at full length on the carpet.'

'You took some money all the same?'

'I was even on the point of taking his wallet. You see I'm being frank. I told myself it was I who'd be accused sooner or later, and that it would be a good long time before I could come to the house again.'

'Was there a light on in the office?'

'If there had been I should have seen it under the door and I wouldn't have gone in.'

'Did you switch it on?'

'No. I had a pocket lamp.'

'What did you touch?'

'First of all I touched his hand, which was cold. That meant he was dead. Then I opened the drawer of the secretary's desk.'

'Were you wearing gloves?'

'No.'

It would be easy to make a check. The experts had taken impressions of the finger-prints in both offices. They were upstairs now, filing them. If Lentin was telling the truth, his prints would have been found on Mademoiselle Bourges's desk.

'You didn't see the revolver?'

'No. My first idea was to leave without saying anything to my sister. Then I thought she'd better know about it. I went upstairs again and woke her. I told her:

'"*Your husband's dead.*"

'She wouldn't believe it. She came down with me in her nightdress, and I shone the light on the body while she watched from the door.'

'She didn't touch anything?'

'She didn't even come into the room. She said:

'"*He really does look dead. At last!* . . ."'

This explained the woman's lack of response when Maigret had spoken to her, that morning, about Fumal's death.

'And then?'

'We went back upstairs and began to drink.'

'To celebrate the event?'

'More or less. After a bit we both got very merry, and I believe we started to laugh. I don't remember whether it was she or I who remarked:

'"*Father hung himself too soon* . . ."'

'It didn't occur to you to send for the police?'

Lentin stared at him, dumbfounded. Why should they have sent for the police? Fumal was dead. For them, that was all that mattered.

'In the end I thought I'd better leave . . . If I were found in the house . . .'

'What time was that?'

'I don't know. I walked as far as the Place Clichy and nearly all the bars were closed. In fact I believe only one was open. I had a glass or two there. Then I went on along the Boulevard as far as Pigalle, where I went into another bar, and finally I must have gone to sleep on a *banquette* in some café, but I don't know where. They turned me out at crack of dawn. I walked on again. I even went to look at the house in the Boulevard de Courcelles.'

'Why?'

'To find out what was happening. There were some cars outside and a policeman at the door. I didn't go close. I walked on . . .'

Those words kept recurring like a *leitmotiv*; and indeed, walking and propping his elbows on bars were Lentin's principal occupations.

'You never do any work?'

'Sometimes I lend a hand at the Central Markets, or on road repairs.'

In all probability he sometimes opened car doors outside hotels, too,

and perhaps did a bit of shoplifting. Maigret would get the clerks upstairs to find out whether he'd ever been in prison.

'Have you a revolver?'

'If I'd ever possessed one I'd have sold it long ago. Or the police would
have taken it off me long ago, for I've spent I don't know how many
nights in the cells.'

'Your sister?'

'What about my sister?'

'She had no gun?'

'You don't know her. I'm tired, Superintendent. You must admit I've
behaved well, I've told you everything I know. If only you'd give me
one tiny drop more . . .'

His expression was humble, pleading.

'Just a tiny drop!' he repeated.

There was probably nothing more to be got out of him, and Maigret
walked over to the cupboard, while Lentin's face brightened.

Maigret suddenly began to address him as '*tu*', just as he had done
with Martine Gilloux.

'Don't you miss your wife and kids?'

Glass in hand, the man hesitated, swallowed the spirits at one gulp
and murmured reproachfully:

'Why bring that up? To begin with, the kids are grown up now. Two
of them are married and they wouldn't recognize me if they saw me in
the street.'

'You don't know who killed Fumal?'

'If I knew I'd go and thank him. And if I'd had the courage I'd have
done it myself. I'd sworn to myself I would, after my father's death. I
told my sister I was going to. It was she who pointed out that
all it would do would be to land me in prison for the rest of my days.
But if I'd found a way of not being caught . . .'

Had the man or woman who had really killed Fumal argued in the
same way, waited for a chance to do it without risk?

'Do you want to ask me anything else?'

No. Maigret could think of no other question to put to him.

All he said was:

'What will you do, if I let you go?'

Lentin made a vague gesture, indicating the city into which he would
vanish once again.

'I'll keep you for a day or two.'

'With nothing to drink?'

'You shall have a glass of wine tomorrow morning. You need to rest.'

The bench in the lumber-room was hard. Maigret rang for an inspector.

'Take him to the cells. Tell them to feed him and let him sleep.'

As he got to his feet the man threw a last glance towards the cupboard, opened his mouth to beg for yet another drink, but didn't dare, and walked out, faltering:

'Thank you.'

Maigret called the inspector back.

'Have his prints taken and give them to Moers.'

He explained briefly why. Meanwhile, Madame Fumal's brother waited half-way down the empty corridor, making no attempt to escape.

Maigret spent ten long minutes sitting at his desk, staring straight ahead of him and smoking his pipe as though in a dream. At last he heaved himself out of his chair and walked across to the inspectors' office. This was still nearly empty. Low voices could be heard from the neighbouring room, and he went in, to find that all those who had spent the day working in the house in the Boulevard de Courcelles were gathered there.

They had left only one man at the house—Inspector Neveu, whom one of them would relieve presently.

Acting on the orders of the Superintendent, the inspectors were comparing the answers made to them during the various interrogations.

Nearly everyone had been questioned two or three times. As for Monsieur Joseph, he had been called in five times, going back each time to wait on the landing, with its Renaissance chairs and its marble statues.

'I suppose I have the right to go out and see to my business?' he had asked in the end.

'No.'

'Not even for a meal?'

'There's a cook in the house.'

The kitchen was on the ground floor, behind Victor's lodge. The cook was a fat, elderly woman, a widow, who seemed to know nothing about what went on in the house. Some of her replies were true to type:

Question: What do you think of Monsieur Fumel?

Answer: What do you expect me to think? How should I know the man?

She pointed to the service-hatch with its lift for dishes, and to the ceiling of her kitchen.

Answer: I work down here and he eats up there.

Question: Did he never come down to see you?

Answer: He sent for me to come up every now and then, to give me orders, and once a month for me to show him the accounts.

Question: He kept a close eye on those?

Answer: What do you call a close eye?

Asked about Louise Bourges, she declared:

Answer: If she sleeps with someone it's natural at her age. That won't happen to me any more, worse luck!

About Madame Fumal:

Answer: It takes all sorts to make a world.

How long had she been in the house?

Answer: Three months.

Question: You didn't find the atmosphere peculiar?

Answer: If you'd seen all I've seen in houses like this!

It was true she had changed jobs dozens of times in her life.

Question: Were you never comfortable anywhere?

Answer: I'm fond of change.

Every few months she would turn up again in the employment agency, where she was a regular customer. She specialized in replacement work and in jobs with foreigners visiting Paris.

Question: You saw nothing and heard nothing?

Answer: When I'm asleep I'm asleep.

Maigret's reason for burdening his men with the meticulous work they were now doing was that he still hoped that some revealing contradiction between two witnesses might come to light, even if only on a point of detail.

If Roger Gaillardin was not the murderer—and it was practically certain he was not—then Fumal had not been killed by anyone from outside.

Inspector Vacher, who had been watching the house throughout the evening, corroborated Victor's statements to within a few minutes.

Shortly before eight o'clock, Fumal's car had driven into the courtyard. Felix, the chauffeur, was at the wheel. Fumal and his secretary were sitting in the back of the car.

After admitting the car Victor had closed the gate again and it had not been reopened that night.

Always according to Victor, Louise Bourges had gone up to the first floor with her employer, but had stayed only a few minutes, after which she had come down to the servants' dining-room, near the kitchen.

She had dined there. Germaine, the housemaid, had gone up to wait on Fumal, while Noémi carried a tray up to the second floor for Madame Fumal.

All that seemed to be definite. No conflicting evidence had been discovered.

After dinner, Louise Bourges had gone up to the office again and stayed there for approximately half an hour. At about half past nine she had crossed the courtyard and gone into the servants' quarters.

Felix, when questioned, had stated:

Answer: I went to join her in her room, as I did almost every evening.

Question: Why do the two of you sleep in her room and not in yours?

Answer: Because hers is bigger.

Louise Bourges, without a blush, had said exactly the same thing. Germaine, the housemaid:

Answer: I heard them at their little affairs for at least an hour. She seems frigid, just to look at. But if you had to sleep in the next room, with only a thin partition between your bed and hers . . .

Question: What time was it when you got to sleep?

Answer: I wound the alarm-clock at half past ten.

Question: You didn't hear anything during the night?

Answer: No.

Question: You knew about Emile Lentin's visits to his sister?

Answer: Like everyone else.

Question: What do you mean by everyone else?

Answer: Noémi, the cook . . .

Question: How did the cook know, considering she never goes up to the second floor?

Answer: Because I told her.

Question: Why?

Answer: So that when he was there she should send up double portions, naturally!

Question: Victor knew, too?

Answer: I didn't tell him anything. I've always distrusted him, but he's not a man from whom you can hide things.

Question: And the secretary?

Answer: Felix must have told her.

Question: And how did Felix know?

Answer: Through Noémi.

So everybody in the house was aware that Lentin often came to sleep in the little room on the second floor—everybody except perhaps Ferdinand Fumal.

And Monsieur Joseph, who slept right overhead?

Question: You are acquainted with Emile Lentin?

Answer: I was acquainted with him, until he took to drink.

Question: It was his brother-in-law who ruined him?

Answer: People who ruin themselves always blame others for it.

Question: You mean he behaved rashly?

Answer: He took himself to be smarter than he really was.

Question: And he found himself up against someone who was really smart?

Answer: If you like. That's business.

Question: Afterwards he tried to borrow from his brother-in-law?

Answer: Probably.

Question: With no result?

Answer: Even a man who's very rich can't come to the help of all failures.

Question: Did you ever see him in the house?

Answer: Years ago.

Question: Where?

Answer: In Monsieur Fumal's office.

Question: What happened between them?

Answer: Monsieur Fumal threw him out.

Question: You've never seen him since then?

Answer: Once, on the pavement near the Châtelet. He was drunk.

Question: Did he speak to you?

Answer: He asked me to tell his brother-in-law that he was a swine.

Question: Did you know he sometimes slept in the house?

Answer: No.

Question: If you had known, would you have told your employer?

Answer: Probably.

Question: You're not sure?

Answer: I haven't thought it over.

Question: Did nobody speak to you about it?

Answer: People weren't keen on speaking to me.

That was true. It tallied with what the servants said. Noémi had expressed the general feeling about Monsieur Joseph in her own words:

Answer: He was in the house like a mouse in a wall. Nobody knew exactly what he did.

For the rest of the evening, too, the different notes tallied. It had been a little after half past nine when Monsieur Joseph had rung the bell. The little door in the big gate had opened and closed behind him.

Question: Why didn't you come in by the back door, since you had a key to it?

Answer: I only used that door when it was late or when I was going straight up to my own rooms.

Question: You stopped on the first floor?

Answer: Yes, I've already said so three times.

Question: Monsieur Fumal was alive then?

Answer: As much as you or me.

Question: What did you talk about?

Answer: Business.

Question: There was nobody else in the office?

Answer: Nobody.

Question: Fumal didn't tell you he was expecting a visitor?

Answer: He did.

Question: Why didn't you mention this before?

Answer: Because you didn't ask me. He was expecting Gaillardin and knew why he was coming. He was still hoping to be given more time. We decided not to give it to him.

Question: You didn't stay to be present at the conversation?

Answer: No.

Question: Why not?

Answer: Because I don't enjoy executions.

The strangest thing was that it seemed to be true. Looking at the fellow, one could sense that he was capable of every kind of dirty trick and every kind of meanness, but incapable of looking someone in the face and telling him of a fatal decision.

Question: From upstairs you must have heard Gaillardin arrive?

Answer: From upstairs one can hear nothing that goes on in the house. You try!

Question: You didn't have the curiosity to come down afterwards and find out what had happened?

Answer: I knew beforehand.

Realizing at once that two constructions could be placed on his reply, he corrected himself:

Answer: I mean I knew Monsieur Fumal would say no, that Gaillardin would implore him, talking about his wife and children, as they all do, even when they're living with a mistress, but that he would get no results.

Question: You believe he killed Fumal?

Answer: I have already said what I think.

Question: Have you quarrelled with your employer recently?

Answer: We never quarrelled.

Question: How much were you paid, Monsieur Goldman?

Answer: You have only to look at my income tax return.

Question: That is no answer.

Answer: It is the best possible.

In any case no one had seen him come downstairs again. But then, no one had seen or heard Emile Lentin come down—the first time by himself, the second time with his sister—or leave, in the end, by the back door into the Rue de Prony.

At a few minutes to ten, a taxi had stopped in the Boulevard. Gaillardin had emerged from it, paid, and rung the doorbell.

Exactly seventeen minutes later, Inspector Vacher had seen him come out again and walk off towards the Etoile, looking back now and again in the hope of finding a taxi.

Vacher had not been able to watch the back door, because he did not know of its existence.

Did not the responsibility for that rest with Maigret who had not believed in the anonymous letters and had been half-hearted in arranging for a watch to be kept?

The atmosphere in the office was thick with pipe and cigarette smoke. From time to time the inspectors exchanged sheets of paper annotated in red or blue pencil.

'What would you say to a glass of beer, boys?'

It would take hours longer to scrutinize every sentence of the interrogations, and later on they'd have sandwiches sent up.

Telephone. Someone lifted the receiver.

'It's for you, Chief.'

It was Moers, who had been dealing with the finger-prints. He confirmed the fact that Lentin's prints had been found only on the door-handle and on the secretary's drawer.

'But somebody must be lying!' exclaimed Maigret angrily.

Unless there had been no murderer, and that was impossible.

VII

A SIMPLE SUM IN ARITHMETIC AND A
LESS INNOCENT WAR SOUVENIR

MAIGRET was feeling a relief as pervasive and sensual as that given, for instance, by a hot bath after three days and three nights in a train.

He knew he was asleep, that he was in bed, and if he put out a hand he would touch his wife's thigh. He even knew it was the middle of the night, about two o'clock or not much later.

And yet he was dreaming. But doesn't it sometimes happen that in dreaming one has a sudden intuition that wouldn't have come in a waking state? Isn't it possible, at times, for the mind to be whetted instead of lulled?

That had undoubtedly happened to him once, in his student days. He had spent the entire evening poring over a difficult problem, and suddenly, in the middle of the night, he had hit on the solution in a dream. When he woke up he couldn't remember it at first, but in the end he had succeeded.

The same thing was happening now. If his wife had turned on the light she would doubtless have seen a mocking smile on his face.

He was laughing at himself. He'd taken the Fumal case too tragically. He had charged at it with lowered head, and that was why he hadn't seen where it was leading him. Didn't he know better, at his age, than to be scared of a Minister, who would perhaps have sunk back into the crowd in a week or a month from now?

He had set out on the wrong foot. He'd been aware of that from the start, from the moment when Boum-Boum had called on him in his office. And afterwards, instead of pulling himself together, smoking a quiet pipe and drinking a glass of beer to soothe his nerves, he hadn't given himself a second's respite.

Now he'd found the solution, like that of his long-ago problem. It had come into his mind rather in the way a bubble rises to the surface of a pool, and at last he could relax.

Finished! Tomorrow morning he would do the necessary, and there would be no more Fumal case. After that he'd only have to deal with that pestilential Mrs. Britt and find her, dead or alive.

The important thing was not to lose track of his discovery. In the first place he must get it into his head clearly, not just as a fuzzy gleam. He knew what he meant by that. In one or two sentences. The only truths are short ones. Who said that? No matter. One sentence. Then wake up and . . .

He opened his eyes, suddenly, in the dark room, and at once he frowned. His dream was not quite finished. He had the impression that the truth was still within his grasp.

His wife was sleeping, warm and snug, and he turned over on his back to think more easily.

There was something perfectly simple to which, during the day, he had failed to attribute its proper importance. He'd laughed when he hit on it in his dream. Why?

He struggled to recover the thread of his thoughts. He felt sure there was someone involved with whom he had been in contact several times.

And some insignificant fact. Was it actually a fact? Or some material clue?

The relaxed mood induced by his dream was now followed by a state of tension almost physically painful. He persisted, forcing himself to envisage the house in the Boulevard de Courcelles from top to bottom, with everyone who lived in it or had come there.

He and his inspectors had stayed at the Quai des Orfèvres until ten o'clock that night, working on the statements till in the end they had known by heart even the most trivial remarks, which ran through their heads like the chorus of some song.

Was it in the documents? Was it something to do with Louise Bourges and Felix?

He was inclined to believe so, and hunted in that direction. There was no proof that it had not been the secretary who wrote the anonymous letters. Maigret had not asked her how much she earned with Fumal. She was probably not paid more than the average secretary—perhaps less.

She was Felix's mistress and admitted it quite openly, but made a point of adding:

'We're engaged, as well.'

The chauffeur said the same thing.

'When do you intend to get married?'

'When we've put aside enough money to buy an inn at Giens.'

People don't speak of being engaged when they don't intend to get married for another ten or fifteen years.

As he lay in bed, Maigret did some mental arithmetic. Assuming Louise and Felix spent no more than the strict minimum on their clothes and small expenses—even assuming they saved every penny of their wages—it would be at least ten years before they could buy even the smallest business.

That was not what he'd hit upon just now in his sleep, but all the same it was a point worth bearing in mind.

One or other of them must have some means of getting money more quickly; and since they remained in Fumal's household in spite of their dislike for it, it must be from Fumal they expected to get it.

Fumal had humiliated his secretary, treating her in the most revolting manner.

She had not mentioned this either to Maigret or to the inspectors.

Had she admitted it to Felix? Had the latter kept cool after being told that his mistress had been compelled to strip and, once naked, been told to dress herself again, after a disdainful gesture?

It wasn't that, either. It was something of that kind, but more illuminating.

Maigret felt tempted to go to sleep again and try to recapture his dream, but he couldn't get back to sleep now, his brain was revolving like clockwork.

There was another detail, more recent . . . He almost clenched his teeth in the effort to recall it, to concentrate harder, and suddenly he saw Emile Lentin again in his office, seemed to be hearing his voice. What had Lentin said with reference to Louise Bourges? He had not been speaking directly about her, but about something to do with her. He had admitted . . .

That was it! Maigret was getting somewhere, in spite of everything. Emile Lentin had said that he sometimes went down, in stocking feet, to the office, to take money out of the petty cash—a few hundred-franc pieces each time, he had specified.

Now that money was kept in Louise's desk drawer. She was responsible for it. No doubt she entered her expenditure in a note book, as is done almost everywhere.

According to Lentin this pilfering had been repeated frequently.

Yet she had never mentioned it. Was it credible that she had been unaware of it, had never noticed that her accounts didn't balance?

So there were two points on which, if she had not actually lied, she had kept silent.

Why hadn't it worried her to find that money was disappearing from her drawer?

Was it because she was taking some herself and her accounts were all eyewash in any case?

Or because she knew *who* was committing the thefts and had her own reasons for saying nothing?

He felt the need of a pipe and got up noiselessly, taking nearly two minutes to slip out of bed and creep over to the chest of drawers. Madame Maigret sighed and stirred but did not wake, and he only allowed the match to flare up for a second, shielding it with his hand.

Seated in the arm-chair, he went on with his search.

Though he had still not recaptured the solution he'd dreamt about, he had made some progress. Where had he got to? The thefts from the drawer. If Louise Bourges knew who was coming to her office at night . . .

He thought himself back into that office, where he had spent part of the previous day. Two large windows overlooked the courtyard. Across the yard were the former stables and above them were, not the two or three servants' rooms found in some places of the kind, but two proper storeys, making an independent house.

He had been through those rooms. The secretary's bedroom, where Felix used to join her, was on the right hand side of the second floor, just opposite the office and at a slightly higher level.

He tried to remember the wording of the earliest reports, especially that of Lapointe, who had been first on the scene. Had anything been said about curtains?

The Superintendent could see the windows clearly in his mind's eye; thin muslin curtains were drawn across them, veiling the strong daylight, but they would not be enough, at night, to conceal what went on in the lighted room.

There were other curtains, Empire red in colour. Had they been drawn or pulled back when Lapointe arrived?

Maigret almost rang up Lapointe at home, to ask him this question, which all at once seemed to him supremely important. If those curtains were not habitually drawn, Louise and Felix knew everything that went on in that office.

Did that lead anywhere?

Was he to conclude that they had watched the previous night's drama from their room and knew who was the murderer?

In one corner stood a safe, over three feet high, which was not to be opened until tomorrow, because it could only be done in the presence of the examining magistrate and of Fumal's lawyer.

What did Fumal keep in that safe? No will had been found among his papers. They had telephoned to the lawyer, Maître Audoin, but he did not know of any will.

Maigret, sitting motionless in the dark, went on racking his brains in this direction, with the impression that it was still not the right one. The revelation that had come to him just now, in his dream, had been more complete—a dazzling flash.

Lentin had often gone down to the office, sometimes when Fumal was asleep in his bedroom . . .

That, too, might open fresh prospects. True, there was one room between the office and the bedroom, to act as a buffer. But Fumal was a man who distrusted everybody and had good reason for doing so.

Lentin's thefts had gone on for years. Wasn't it plausible that on one or more occasions the ex-butcher had heard sounds?

He was physically a coward, Maigret knew that. He'd already been one at school; he used to play mean tricks on the other boys, and when they rounded on him he'd wail:

'Don't hit me!'

Or, more often still, he would run to the schoolmistress for protection.

Suppose Lentin had gone down on one of his pilfering expeditions, ten days or so ago . . .

Suppose Fumal had heard sounds . . .

Maigret could imagine the king of the meat market clutching his revolver and not daring to go and see what was happening.

If, as was possible, he didn't know that his brother-in-law was in the house, he must have suspected everybody, including Monsieur Joseph, his secretary and perhaps his wife.

Had he thought of the petty cash? That would almost have amounted to second sight.

Why should some unknown person have come into his office? And wasn't that person going to open the bedroom door? . . .

It all held together. It wasn't the dream, as yet, but it was another step forward. For it might explain why Fumal had begun to write anonymous letters, as an excuse for applying to the police.

He could have done it without that. But then he would have been confessing to the state of terror in which he was living.

Madame Maigret stirred, pushed off the bedclothes and suddenly called out:

'Where are you?'

From the depths of his arm-chair he answered:

'Here.'

'What are you doing?'

'Smoking a pipe. I couldn't sleep.'

'Haven't you been to sleep yet? What time is it?'

He switched on the light. The alarm clock said ten minutes past three. He knocked out his pipe and got back into bed, unsatisfied, still hoping, with no great confidence, that he would recover the thread of his dream; and he did not wake up again until he smelt freshly-made coffee. What surprised him at once was to see the sun, a real slice of sunshine, coming into the room for the first time for at least a fortnight.

'You weren't walking in your sleep last night?'

'No.'

'You remember you were sitting in the dark and smoking your pipe?'

'Yes.'

He remembered everything, all the argument he had held with himself—but not his dream, alas! He dressed, breakfasted, and walked to the Place de la République to catch his bus, buying the morning papers at a stand on the way.

The faces around him were cheerful, because of the sunshine. The air had already lost its damp, dusty tang. The sky was pale blue. The pavements and roofs were dry, only the trunks of the trees were still wet.

Fumal, king of the meat market.

The morning papers recapitulated what the evening ones had said, with further details and fresh photographs, including one of Maigret leaving the house in the Boulevard de Courcelles with his hat pulled down over his eyes and a surly expression on his face.

He was struck by one of the sub-headings:

Fumal said to have asked for police protection on the day he died.

There had been a leakage somewhere. Did it come from the Ministry, where several people must have known about the butcher's telephone call? Did it come from Louise Bourges, who had been questioned by the reporters?

The indiscretion could equally well have been committed, even unintentionally, by one of his inspectors.

A few hours previous to his tragic death, Ferdinand Fumal visited the Quai des Orfèvres, where, it is believed, he informed Superintendent Maigret of the serious threats he is understood to have re-

*ceived. We have reason to suppose that at the very hour when he was
shot down in his office, an inspector from the Judicial Police was on
guard in the Boulevard de Courcelles.*

The Minister was not mentioned, but it was hinted that Fumal had
acquired tremendous political influence.

Maigret went slowly up the wide staircase and raised a hand in
greeting to Joseph; he expected the latter to announce that the Chief
wanted to see him, but Joseph made no sign.

On his desk several reports lay waiting, but he only glanced at them.

The pathologist's report confirmed what he knew already. Fumal had
definitely been killed at point-blank range. The gun had been less than
eight inches from his body when the shot was fired. The bullet had
been found in his chest.

The ballistics expert who had examined the bullet was equally
specific. It had been fired from a Luger automatic such as German
officers carried during the last war.

A telegram from Monte Carlo was about Mrs. Britt: it was not she
who had been seen at the tables, but a Dutchwoman who looked rather
like her.

The bell for the conference rang down the corridor and Maigret set
out, with a sigh, for the Chief's office, where he shook hands absent-
mindedly with those of his colleagues who were assembled there.

As he had expected, he was the centre of attention. The others knew
better than anyone else what an awkward position he was in, and had
a tactful way of showing that they sympathized with him.

The Director, for his part, pretended to treat the matter lightly, with
optimism.

'Nothing new, Maigret?'

'The investigation is going ahead.'

'You've seen the papers?'

'I've just been glancing over them. They won't be satisfied till I make
an arrest.'

The Press would be hard at his heels. This case, added to the mystery
of the Englishwoman's disappearance in the heart of Paris, was not cal-
culated to enhance the prestige of the Judicial Police.

'I'm doing my best,' he added with a sigh.

'Any clues?'

He shrugged his shoulders. Could one call them clues? Each of the
other men spoke of the case he had in hand, and when the meeting
broke up they glanced at him with what looked like commiseration.

The expert from the Finance Department was waiting for him in his office. Maigret listened to him with only half an ear, for he was still trying to recapture his dream.

Fumal's business had been even more extensive than the newspapers imagined. In the course of a few years he had built up what was almost a monopoly in the meat-market.

'Behind these transactions there's somebody who's diabolically clever,' declared the expert, 'and who has considerable knowledge of the law. It'll take months to unravel the tangled skein of companies and subsidiaries that leads up to Fumal. The Internal Revenue will certainly be looking into the matter as well . . .'

The clever brain was probably Monsieur Joseph's, for although Fumal had amassed an impressive fortune before making his acquaintance, he had never done business on such a scale.

Let the Finance Department of the Public Prosecutor's Office deal with all that, and the Internal Revenue too, if they wanted to.

What concerned him was to discover who had killed Fumal, at pointblank range, in his office, while Vacher was walking up and down outside the house.

He was wanted on the telephone. Someone was insisting on speaking to him personally. It was Madame Gaillardin, the real one, who lived at Neuilly; she was calling from Cannes, where she was still staying with her children. She wanted details. She said one of the Riviera newspapers had announced that Gaillardin, after killing Fumal at his house in the Boulevard de Courcelles, had gone to Puteaux and committed suicide.

'I telephoned my solicitor this morning. I shall return to Paris by the *Mistral* today. I want to make it clear to you at once that the woman in the Rue François Premier has no rights whatsoever, that there was never any question of a divorce between my husband and myself, and that we were married under the system of joint property. Fumal robbed him, there's no doubt about that. My lawyer will prove it and claim from the estate whatever sums . . .'

Maigret sighed, holding the receiver to his ear and murmuring from time to time:

'Yes, Madame . . . Very well, Madame . . .'

Finally he asked her:

'Tell me, did your husband possess a Luger?'

'A what?'

'Nothing. Was he in the last war?'

'He was exempted from service because . . .'

'Never mind why. He was never a prisoner, or deported to Germany?'

'No. Why?'

'No special reason. You've never seen a revolver in your flat at Neuilly?'

'There used to be one, but he took it when he went to that . . . that . . .'

'Thank you.'

That woman wouldn't let herself be pushed around. She'd fight like a she-wolf defending her cubs.

He went into the inspectors' office and looked round for a particular one.

'Lapointe's not here?'

'He must be in the washroom.'

He waited.

'Aillevard still away?'

Lapointe came back after a time and blushed at finding Maigret waiting for him.

'Tell me, my boy . . . Yesterday morning, when you went into that office . . . Think carefully . . . Were the curtains drawn or pulled back?'

'They were just as you found them. I didn't touch them and I didn't see anyone else touch them.'

'That is to say they were pulled back?'

'Yes. I could swear they were. Wait a minute! Yes, definitely, because I noticed the old stables across the yard and . . .'

'Come with me.'

It was his custom, during an investigation, to take someone with him nearly always. On the way, in the little black car, he scarcely opened his mouth. In the Boulevard de Courcelles it was he who pressed the brass bell, and Victor came and opened the door in the big gate.

Maigret noticed that he had not shaved, which made him look much more like a poacher than a valet or a concierge.

'Is the inspector upstairs?'

'Yes. They took him up some coffee and rolls.'

'Who did?'

'Noémi.'

'Has Monsieur Joseph come down?'

'I haven't seen him.'

'And Mademoiselle Louise?'

'She was in the kitchen, having breakfast, half an hour ago. I don't know if she's gone upstairs.'

'Felix?'

'In the garage.'

Taking a few steps forward, Maigret saw the man right enough, polishing one of the cars as though nothing had happened.

'The lawyer's not here?'

'I didn't even know he was supposed to be coming.'

'I'm expecting the examining magistrate, too. Show them up to the office when they come.'

'Very good, Superintendent.'

Maigret had a question at the tip of his tongue, but when he was about to ask it, it eluded him. In any case it couldn't be important.

On the first floor they found Inspector Janin, who had been on guard for the latter part of the night. He, too, was unshaven, and could scarcely keep awake.

'Nothing's happened?'

'Nobody moved. The young lady came in just now to ask if I needed her. I told her I didn't, and after a few minutes she went away, saying she'd be in her room and could always be sent for.'

'Did she go into the office?'

'Yes. She only stayed there for a few seconds.'

'Did she open any drawers?'

'I don't think so. She came out carrying some red knitted garment she had had when she arrived.'

Maigret remembered that on the previous day she had been wearing a red cardigan. She had probably left it in one of the first-floor rooms by mistake.

'Madame Fumal?'

'Her breakfast was taken up on a tray.'

'She's not been down?'

'I haven't seen her.'

'Go and get to bed now. There'll be time enough this evening to write out your report.'

The red curtains in the office were still not drawn. Maigret told Lapointe to go and ask the maids if they usually were. He himself looked out of one of the windows. Just opposite, at a slightly higher level, a window was open and a fair-haired young woman could be seen going to and fro, her lips moving as though she were singing softly while tidying the room. It was Louise Bourges.

Struck by an idea, he turned to the safe that stood against the wall opposite the windows. Could that be seen from across the yard?

If it could . . . The idea excited him and he went downstairs, into the courtyard, and up the narrower stairs that led to the secretary's room. He knocked. She said:

'Come in!'

She did not seem surprised to see him, but only said softly:

'It's you!'

He already knew the room, which was a good size and prettily furnished, with a radio on a small table and a bedside lamp with an orange shade. It was the window that interested him. He leant out, his eyes searching the shadows of the office, opposite. He had not thought to turn on the lights before leaving it.

'Would you go and switch on the lights, over there?'

'Where?'

'In the office.'

She gave no sign of alarm or surprise.

'One moment . . . Do you know what there is in your employer's safe?'

She hesitated, but not for long.

'Yes. I'd rather tell the truth.'

'What?'

'A few important files, for one thing, and then Madame Fumal's jewels, some letters I know nothing about; and money.'

'A lot of money?'

'Yes, a lot. You must realize why he had to keep large sums in banknotes on hand. In his business deals there was nearly always a sum that passed "under the counter", a certain amount he couldn't pay by cheque.'

'How much, in your opinion?'

'I've often seen him pay out two or three million francs from hand to hand. He had notes in his safe deposit at the bank, too.'

'So there may well be several million francs in cash in the safe?'

'Unless he took it out.'

'When?'

'I don't know.'

'Go and turn on the lights.'

'Shall I come back here?'

'Wait for me over there.'

Louise's own room had been searched without result. It contained no Luger, no compromising papers and no money, except for three one-thousand franc notes and a few hundred-franc pieces.

The young woman crossed the courtyard. It seemed to Maigret that she took a long time to reach the office on the first floor, but she might have met someone on the way.

At last the lights were turned on, and immediately, through the muslin-veiled windows, the smallest details of the room became visible, including the left-hand portion of the safe, though not the whole of it.

He tried to fix the spot where Fumal had been standing when he was killed, but it was hard to do so with certainty, because the body might have rolled over.

Had it been possible to witness the scene from Louise Bourges's window? That was not certain. What was definite was that anyone coming into the office or going out would be clearly visible.

He crossed the courtyard in his turn and went upstairs without seeing anybody. Louise was waiting for him on the landing.

'Have you found out what you wanted to know?'

He nodded. She followed him into the room.

'You'll notice that from here nearly the whole of my room can be seen, in the same way.'

He pricked up his ears.

'If Monsieur Fumal didn't always draw the curtains in the office, Felix and I had the best reasons for closing our shutters. Because over there the windows have shutters. We're not exhibitionists, either of us.'

'So he sometimes drew the curtains and sometimes didn't?'

'Precisely. For instance, when he worked late with Monsieur Joseph he always drew them. I sometimes wondered why. I suppose it was because on those evenings he had to open the safe.'

'Do you think Monsieur Joseph knew the combination?'

'I doubt it.'

'And you?'

'I certainly don't.'

'Lapointe! . . . Go upstairs to Monsieur Joseph and ask him whether he knows the combination of the safe.'

The key of the safe had been found in the dead man's pocket. Madame Fumal, questioned the day before, knew nothing about it. The lawyer declared that he did not know the combination either, so that they were waiting, this morning, not only for the examining magistrate but for an expert sent from the firm that made the safe.

'You're not pregnant?' Maigret queried abruptly.

'Why do you ask me that? No, I'm not.'

Steps were heard on the stairs. It was the man from the safe-makers, a tall thin fellow with a moustache, who looked at the safe immediately, like a surgeon looking at the patient he is about to operate on.

'We must wait for the magistrate and the lawyer.'

'I know. I'm used to this.'

When the two arrived, the lawyer asked for Madame Fumal, the presumptive legatee, to be present, and Lapointe, who had come downstairs again, went to fetch her.

She was not as drunk as the day before, only a little dazed, and she must have swallowed a gulp of spirits before coming down, to give herself courage, for her breath reeked of it.

The lawyer's clerk had taken his seat at the desk.

'I don't think there is any reason for you to remain here, Mademoiselle Bourges,' said Maigret, noticing that the secretary was still in the room.

He was to regret those words!

He and Planche, the examining magistrate, began chatting in the window while the expert set to work. Half an hour went by, then there was a click and they saw the heavy door swing open.

The lawyer was the first to approach and look in. The magistrate and Maigret stood behind him.

A few yellow, bulging envelopes contained only receipts and letters, more especially ious bearing different signatures.

On another shelf were stacked files relating to Fumal's various businesses.

There was no money, not a single banknote.

Sensing a presence at his back, Maigret turned round. Monsieur Joseph was standing in the doorway.

'Is it there?' he asked.

'What?'

'The fifteen million. There ought to be fifteen million francs in cash in the safe. It was still there three days ago, and I'm sure Monsieur Fumal didn't take it out.'

'You have a key?'

'I have just told your inspector that I have not.'

'Has nobody a duplicate key to the safe?'

'Not to my knowledge.'

As he strode to and fro, Maigret found himself facing the window; opposite, he caught sight of Louise Bourges, back in her own room and singing to herself, as though indifferent to what was going on in the house.

VIII

THE WINDOW, THE SAFE, THE LOCK AND THE THIEF

IT IS said that even the longest dream lasts, in reality, only a few seconds. At that moment, Maigret had an experience which reminded him, not of his last night's dream, which he had still not recaptured, but of the sense of discovery he had had then, the kind of sudden leap forward to a truth he had long been seeking.

Later—so full-packed were those few seconds of life—he could reconstitute his slightest thoughts, his slightest sensations, and had he been a painter he could have depicted the scene as meticulously as a minor Flemish master.

The light from the lamps combined with the sunlight to give the room an artificial appearance that was reminiscent of a stage scene, and perhaps because of this, the persons present all seemed to be acting a part.

The Superintendent was still standing at one of the two tall windows. Opposite, across the courtyard, Louise Bourges was moving about and singing in her room, her fair hair showing pale against the dim background. Below, in the courtyard, Felix, in blue overalls, was turning the stream of water from a hose-pipe on the limousine he had brought out of the garage.

The lawyer's clerk, sitting at the late Ferdinand Fumal's desk, was waiting, head raised, for something to be dictated to him. The lawyer, Audoin, and the examining magistrate, Planche, stood not far from the safe, looking first at its steel bulk and then at Maigret, and the lawyer was still holding a file.

The safe expert had tactfully withdrawn into a corner, and Monsieur Joseph had advanced only two paces into the room; the door was open and young Lapointe could be seen out on the landing, lighting a cigarette.

It was as though for a few seconds life had come to a standstill, every-one holding a pose as if in front of a camera.

Maigret's eyes travelled from the window opposite to the safe and from the safe to the door, and at last he realized the mistake he had made. The door was an old one, of carved oak, with a big lock, made to take a large key.

'Lapointe!' he called.

'Yes, Chief.'

'Go down and fetch Victor.'

Lapointe didn't understand the warning either, and now it was to the safe expert that the Superintendent turned with a question.

'If somebody, watching through that keyhole, had seen Fumal open his safe a certain number of times, and watched his movements carefully, would it have been possible for him to discover the combination?'

The man looked at the door himself, apparently calculating the angle and estimating the distance.

'For me, it would be child's play,' he said.

'And for a man who's not a professional?'

'With patience . . . Following the movements of the hand, and counting the number of times each dial was turned . . .'

They could hear footsteps going to and fro downstairs, and then, from the courtyard, came Lapointe's voice, asking Felix:

'You haven't seen Victor?'

Maigret was sure he had hit upon the truth just now, but at the same time he felt convinced it was too late. Louise Bourges, across the yard, leant out of her window, and he thought he saw a faint smile on her face.

Lapointe came upstairs again, bewildered.

'I can't find him anywhere, Chief. He's not in the lodge, or anywhere else on the ground floor. He's not gone upstairs, either. Felix says he heard the street door open and close again, a few moments ago.'

'Ring up the Quai. Give them a description of him. Tell them to send out an urgent call to all railway stations and police stations. Telephone the nearest police stations yourself . . .'

The man-hunt was beginning and there was no need of innovations there. The radio cars would cruise round the district in steadily narrowing circles. Uniform police and plain-clothes detectives would search the streets, going into the *bistros* and questioning people.

'Do you know how he's dressed?'

Maigret and his inspectors had only seen the man in a striped waistcoat. It was Monsieur Joseph who came to the rescue, observing with an air of repugnance:

'So far as I know he has only one suit, a navy blue.'

'What sort of hat?'

'He has never worn a hat.'

When Maigret had asked Lapointe to go down and fetch Victor, he had not yet been by any means certain. Was it a case of intuition? Or was it the culmination of a vast number of arguments he had held with himself unawares, innumerable observations which, taken separately, were of no importance?

From the outset he had felt convinced that Fumal had been killed out of hatred, for revenge.

Didn't Victor's flight contradict this, or even the fact that fifteen million francs had vanished from the safe? He felt like retorting to himself:

'On the contrary!'

Perhaps because this was a peasant's hatred, and a peasant rarely forgets his own interests, even if driven by passion.

The Superintendent said nothing. The others were looking at him. He felt humiliated, because for him this was a set-back; he had spent too long in beating about the bush, and now he had little confidence in the hunt that was being organized.

'Gentlemen, I need not keep you any longer. If you would like to dispose of the formalities . . .'

The examining magistrate, who was only a tyro, was afraid to ask questions. He only ventured to murmur:

'You believe it was he?'

'I'm sure it was.'

'And he's gone off with the millions?'

It was more than probable. Either Victor had gone off with the money or he had hidden it somewhere outside the house and would be going to fetch it.

Lapointe's monotonous voice was repeating the description over the telephone and the Superintendent went heavily down to the courtyard, pausing for a moment to watch Felix, who was still cleaning the car.

Passing the man without speaking to him, Maigret went upstairs and opened the door of Louise Bourges's room.

Louise's eyes were still full of mischief, and a deep satisfaction as well.

'You knew?' he asked simply.

She made no attempt to deny it. On the contrary, she retorted with:

'Confess it was I you suspected?'

He made no denial either, but sat down on the edge of the bed and slowly filled his pipe.

'How did you realize?' he resumed. 'You saw him?'

He pointed to the window.

'No. Just now, I told you the truth. I always tell the truth. I'm incapable of lying, not because I hate lies, but because I blush.'

'You really used to close the shutters?'

'Always. But I've sometimes come across Victor in parts of the house where he ought not to have been. He had a way of walking without making a sound, moving without stirring the air. Several times I've jumped when I found he was close to me.'

He walked like a poacher, of course! Maigret had thought of that, too, all of a sudden—but too late, while he was glancing from the safe to the door and back again.

The secretary pointed to a bell in a corner of her room.

'You see that? It was put in so that Monsieur Fumal could call me whenever he wanted. It sometimes happened in the evening, even quite late. I'd be obliged to get dressed and go to him because he had some urgent work to give me, especially after a business dinner. It was on those occasions that I sometimes caught Victor on the stairs.'

'He didn't offer you any explanation of his presence?'

'No. He just looked at me in a particular way.'

'How?'

'You know.'

That was true. Maigret had probably understood everything, but he wanted it put into words.

'There was a sort of tacit complicity in the house. Nobody liked the boss. Each of us had some secret or other.'

'You even had one from Felix.'

He had evidence that she blushed easily, for she reddened to the ears.

'What are you talking about?'

'The evening when Fumal made you undress . . .'

She went over to the window and closed it.

'Have you mentioned that to Felix?'

'No.'

'Will you tell him about it?'

'Why should I? I merely wonder why you put up with it.'

'Because I want us to get married.'

'And to set up at Giens!'

'What's wrong about that?'

What was she keenest about, what did she put first,—marriage to Felix, or the ownership of an inn on the Loire?

'How were you getting the money?'

Emile Lentin took it from the petty cash. She, too, must have her system.

'I may as well tell you, for there's nothing illegal about it.'

'Go ahead.'

'The director of "Northern Butchers" was interested in knowing certain figures that went through my hands, because that way he could make big private profits. It would take too long to explain to you. As soon as I had the figures I'd wire them to him, and every month he gave me quite a substantial sum.'

'And the other managers?'

'I feel sure all of them were feathering their own nests, but they didn't need my co-operation.'

So Fumal, the most suspicious of men and the toughest in business dealings, had been entirely surrounded by people who were tricking him. He spied on them, spent his whole life watching them and threatening them, making them feel the weight of his authority.

Yet in his own house a man used to come and sleep several nights a week without his knowledge, going in and out, eating at his expense, and not even hesitating, on some nights, to come close up to the room where he lay asleep, to take money from the petty cash.

His secretary was hand in glove with one of his managers.

Hadn't Monsieur Joseph, too, made a little nest-egg for himself? Probably that would never be known—even the experts of the Finance Department might be baffled.

To make sure of having a bodyguard, a faithful watchdog, Fumal had saved a poacher in his native village from life imprisonment. Hadn't he sent for him, too, to come to his office sometimes of an evening, and given him confidential tasks?

And yet, of all of them, Victor was the one who hated him most. With a peasant's hatred, patient and tenacious, the same that in his poaching days he had so long nourished for the game-keeper he had finally shot dead when the opportunity presented itself.

In Fumal's case, too, Victor had waited for an opportunity. Not only an opportunity to kill him, for that came every day. Not only an opportunity to kill him without being found out; but an opportunity to relieve himself from want at the same time.

Hadn't it been partly the sight of the empty safe, the absence of the fifteen million francs, that had suddenly put Maigret on the track?

He would analyse all that later. The particulars were still jumbled in his mind.

The Luger had played a role too.

'Was Victor in the war?'

'At a military base near Moulins.'

'Where was he during the occupation?'

'In his village.'

The village had been occupied by the Germans. It would have been just like Victor, too, to have got hold of one of their weapons when they retreated. He might even have several hidden in the woods.

'Why did you warn him?' Maigret inquired reproachfully.

'Warn him of what?'

She blushed again, realized it, and this disarmed her.

'I spoke to him on my way down. He was standing at the foot of the stairs, looking worried.'

'Why?'

'I don't know. Perhaps because the safe was being opened? Perhaps because he'd heard you or one of your men make some remark that suggested you were on his track.'

'What did you say to him, exactly?'

'I said: *"You'd better clear out".*'

'Why?'

'Because he'd done everybody a good turn by killing Fumal.'

She seemed to be defying him to contradict her.

'Besides, I felt you'd be getting at the truth. Afterwards it might perhaps have been too late.'

'Admit you were beginning to feel scared.'

'You were suspecting us, Felix and me. And Felix used to have a Luger too. He was in the occupation forces in Germany. When he showed the thing to me—he'd kept it as a souvenir—I insisted on his getting rid of it.'

'How long ago was this?'

'A year.'

'For what reason?'

'Because he's jealous, he has fits of rage, and I was afraid that in one of them he might shoot me.'

She was not blushing. She was telling the truth.

Every police station in Paris was on the alert. Police cars were combing the district, pedestrians were scrutinized as they went along the pavements, and the proprietors of bars and restaurants were being visited by gentlemen who bent towards them to put questions in an undertone.

'Can Victor drive a car?'

'I don't think so.'

They watched the roads, all the same. For a long way out of Paris the local police set up roadblocks and inspected the occupants of all passing cars.

Maigret felt useless. He had done what it was in his power to do. The rest didn't depend on him.

The rest, in point of fact, depended more on chance than on the ability of the police.

It was a matter of finding one man among several million others, and he a man who was determined not to be caught.

Maigret had bungled it. He had got there too late. As he went towards the door, Louise Bourges asked him:

'Do we still have to remain here?'

'For the time being. There will be some other formalities to attend to, and perhaps some questions to put to each of you.'

In the courtyard Felix stared after him mistrustfully and went upstairs at once to join the girl. Was he going to make a jealous scene because she'd spent some time alone with the Superintendent?

The latter walked out of the house and made for the nearest *bistro*, the first along the Boulevard des Batignolles, where he had taken refuge once already.

'A pint of beer?' inquired the proprietor, who had a good memory.

He shook his head. Today he didn't want beer. The bar smelt of *marc de Bourgogne*, and in spite of the early hour, he ordered:

'A marc.'

Afterwards, he called for another and later, thinking of other things, for a third.

It was curious that this drama should have begun at Saint-Fiacre, the tiny village in the Allier where Ferdinand Fumal and he had both been born.

Maigret had come into the world at the château, or rather in a house on the estate, of which his father was bailiff.

Fumal had been born in a butcher's shop, and his mother had worn no drawers, so as not to keep the men waiting.

As for Victor, he had been born in a wooden hut and his father used to eat crows and carrion.

Was that what gave the Superintendent the impression that he understood them?

Did he really want the man-hunt to succeed and the ex-poacher to go to the scaffold?

His thoughts were formless. They were more like a succession of pictures that followed one another while he stared at the tarnished mirror behind the bottles in the bar.

Fumal had been aggressive with the Superintendent because, in the old days when they were at school, he had looked upon Maigret as the son of the bailiff, an educated gentleman who represented the Count in dealing with the peasants.

Victor, for his part, must have regarded as his enemies all those who did not range the woods as he did—all who lived in proper houses and were not openly at loggerheads with the police and the gamekeepers.

Fumal had made the mistake of bringing him to Paris and shutting him up in that big stone box in the Boulevard de Courcelles.

Hadn't Victor felt like a prisoner there? In his lodge, where he lived alone like beast in its lair, hadn't he dreamt about the morning dew and about snaring game?

Here he had no gun such as he'd carried in his woodlands, but he had brought his Luger with him and he must at times have patted it nostalgically.

'The same again, *patron*.'

But he shook his head directly afterwards.

'No!'

He didn't want to drink any more. He didn't need to. He must finish the job he had begun, even if he didn't believe in it; he must go to his office on the Quai des Orfèvres and direct the search.

Not to mention the fact that there was still an Englishwoman to be found!

IX

THE SEARCH FOR THE VANISHED

THE newspaper headline that best summed up the situation was:
'Double failure for the Judicial Police.'

Which implied:

'*Double failure for Maigret.*'

A tourist had vanished from her hotel in the Saint-Lazare district for no apparent reason, had gone into a bar, come out again, walked past a police sergeant and disappeared into thin air.

A man of whom a detailed description had been given, a man who had murdered not only the king of the meat market but a gamekeeper as well, had left a private house in the Boulevard de Courcelles, in broad daylight, at eleven o'clock in the morning, when the house was occupied by the police and the examining magistrate was there too. Perhaps he was armed. He must be carrying on him a fortune of fifteen million francs.

He was not known to have any friends in Paris, any contacts, whether male or female.

Yet, like Mrs. Britt, he had vanished into the city.

Hundreds and thousands of police and gendarmes, all over the country, spent an incalculable number of hours searching for both these people.

Public excitement died away in due course, but the men responsible for the safety of the population still had two names and descriptions, among others, in their notebooks.

For two years there was no news of either the woman or the man.

It was Mrs. Britt, the Kilburn Lane boarding-house proprietress, who was found first, in perfect health, married, and running a boarding-house in a mining camp in Australia.

Credit for finding her was due neither to the French police nor to the British, but, by the sheerest coincidence, to someone who had been in her party on the Paris visit and who afterwards chanced to visit Australia.

Mrs. Britt offered no explanation. There were no grounds for demanding one from her. How and where had she at last met the man of her life? Why had she left the hotel, and then France itself, without a word to a soul? That was her affair, and when reporters called to question her, she showed them the door.

With Victor, matters were different. His disappearance lasted longer, too, for it continued for five years, though his name still appeared in the notebooks of the police and the gendarmes.

One November morning a passenger-carrying cargo boat arrived at Cherbourg from Panama, and among the passengers who landed from it the harbour police noticed a third-class passenger who looked ill and whose passport was a clumsy fake.

'Will you come this way please?' one of the two detectives asked politely after glancing at his companion.

'Why?'

'Just a formality.'

Instead of following the others, the man went into an office where he was asked to sit down.

'What's your name?'

'You've seen it—Henri Sauer.'

'Born at Strasbourg?'

'It's on my passport.'

'Where did you go to school?'

'At Strasbourg, naturally.'

'To the school on the Quai Saint-Nicolas?'

They went on to name several streets, squares, hotels and restaurants.

'It's so long ago,' the man sighed, his face now bathed in sweat.

He must have caught some fever in the tropics, for his body suddenly began to tremble convulsively.

'Your name?'

'I've told you.'

'Your real name.'

In spite of his condition, he didn't give in, but went on repeating the same story over and over again.

'I know where you went in Panama to buy that passport. Only, you see, you were had. One can see you didn't go to school for very long. It's the clumsiest possible forgery and you're at least the tenth person to get yourself caught.'

The policeman went to a filing-cabinet and brought out several similar passports.

'Look. The name of the bloke who sold it to you at Panama is Schwartz, and he's an ex-convict. He really was born at Strasbourg. Not going to talk? Just as you like! . . . Let's have your thumb . . .'

Placidly, the policeman took the suspect's fingerprints.

'What are you going to do with them?'

'Send 'em to Paris, where they'll know at once who you are.'

'And in the meantime?'

'We shall keep you here, naturally.'

The man looked at the glass-panelled door beyond which other policemen were chatting together.

'In that case . . .' he sighed, defeated.

'Your name?'

'Victor Ricou.'

Even after five years that was enough to make the penny drop. The inspector got up, went over to the filing-cabinets again, and finally picked out a card.

'Victor of the Boulevard de Courcelles?'

Five minutes later Maigret, who had just arrived in his office and was looking through his letters, heard this news by telephone.

Next morning, in the same office, he had before him a kind of wreck, a disheartened creature who had no more thought of defending himself.

'How did you get away from Paris?'

'I didn't. I stayed for three months.'

'Where?'

'In a small hotel in the Place d'Italie.'

What puzzled the Superintendent was how Victor, with only a few minutes' start, had got out of the district, although the police had been warned at once.

'I took an errand-boy's bicycle that was standing at the curb and nobody took any notice of me.'

After three months he had made his way to Le Havre, where he had stowed away, abetted by a member of the crew, aboard a cargo boat bound for Panama.

'He began by telling me it would cost me five hundred thousand francs. On board, he asked me for another five hundred thousand. Then, before going ashore . . .'

'How much did he take off you altogether?'

'Two million. On the other side . . .'

Victor had planned to settle in the country, but there was no real country, the virgin forest began almost as soon as one was out of the town.

Feeling homesick, he had spent his time in shady bars, and been robbed again. His fifteen million hadn't lasted more than two years, and he had been obliged to start working.

'I couldn't stick it any longer. I had to come back. . . .'

The newspapers, which had made such a fuss about him, gave a bare three lines to the news of his arrest, for everyone had forgotten the Fumal case.

Victor never even came up for trial. As the preliminaries were long-drawn-out, because the witnesses had all disappeared, he had time to die in the prison hospital at Fresnes, where Maigret was the only person who went to see him, two or three times.

March 4, 1956

MAIGRET IN SOCIETY

I

I T was one of those exceptional months of May which one experiences only two or three times in one's life and which have the brilliance, the taste and the scent of childhood memories. Maigret called it a choral May, for it reminded him both of his first communion and of his first springtime in Paris, when everything seemed new and wonderful.

In the street, in the bus, in the office, he would suddenly come to a halt, struck by a distant sound, by a gust of warm air, by the bright splash of colour of a blouse which took him back twenty or thirty years.

The day before, just as they were setting out to have dinner with the Pardons, his wife had asked him, almost blushing as she spoke:

'You don't think I look too silly, at my age, in a floral dress?'

That evening their friends the Pardons had staged an innovation. Instead of inviting them to their flat, they had taken the Maigrets to a little restaurant on the Boulevard de Montparnasse where the four of them had dinner on the terrace.

Maigret and his wife, without saying anything, had exchanged conspiratorial glances, for it was on this terrace that, nearly thirty years before, they had had their first meal together.

'Is there stewed mutton?'

The owners of the restaurant had changed, but there were still stewed mutton on the menu, wobbly lamps on the tables, evergreens in tubs, and Chavignol in carafes.

All four of them were in high spirits. Over coffee, Pardon had taken a magazine with a white cover out of his pocket.

'You know, Maigret, there's something about you in the *Lancet*.'

The chief-inspector, who knew the famous and austere English medical journal by name, had frowned.

'I mean there's something about your profession. It's in an article by a certain Dr. Richard Fox and this is the passage that concerns you: '"*A skilled psychiatrist, using his scientific knowledge and the ex-*

perience gained in his consulting-room, is in a fairly good position to understand his fellow human beings. But it is possible, especially if he allows himself to be influenced by theories, that he will understand them less perfectly than a good schoolmaster, a novelist or a detective." '

They had talked about this for some time, now jokingly, now more seriously. Then the Maigrets had walked part of the way home through the silent streets.

The chief-inspector could not know that this remark by the London doctor was going to come back to him several times during the following days, or that the memories awakened to him by this perfect month of May would appear to him almost in the guise of a premonition.

The next day too, in the bus taking him towards the Châtelet, he found himself looking at people's faces with the same curiosity as when he had been a newcomer to the capital.

Climbing the staircase of Police Headquarters as a divisional chief-inspector, and being greeted respectfully on the way, seemed strange to him. Was it so long since the time when, very much over-awed, he had first entered this service whose chiefs still struck him as legendary beings?

He felt at once gay and melancholy. With his window open, he went through his post, and sent for young Lapointe to give him some instructions.

In twenty-five years the Seine had not changed, neither the boats passing by, nor the anglers sitting in the same places as if they had never budged.

Puffing at his pipe, he was doing his housework, as he put it, clearing his desk of the dossiers piling up on it, and dealing with unimportant business, when the telephone rang.

'Can you come and see me for a moment, Maigret?' asked the Director.

The chief-inspector made his way unhurriedly to the Director's office, where he remained standing by the window.

'I've just had a curious phone call from the Quai d'Orsay. Not from the Foreign Minister in person but from his principal private secretary. He asked me to send over there straight away somebody capable of assuming responsibilities. Those are the words he used.

' "An inspector?" ' I asked.

' "Somebody of a higher rank would be preferable. It's probably something to do with a crime." '

The two men looked at one another with a hint of malice in their eyes, for neither of them had a high regard for ministries of any sort, least of all a ministry as starchy as the Foreign Office.

'I thought that you would like to go yourself . . .'

'Perhaps it would be best . . .'

The Director picked up a paper from his desk and held it out to Maigret.

'You have to ask for a certain Monsieur Cromières. He is expecting you.'

'Is he the principal private secretary?'

'No. He is the person who is handling the case.'

'Shall I take an inspector along with me?'

'I don't know anything more about the business than what I have just told you. Those people like being mysterious.'

Maigret finally picked on Janvier to accompany him and the two of them took a taxi. At the Quai d'Orsay they were not directed towards the great staircase but towards a narrow, unprepossessing staircase at the back of the courtyard, as if they were being shown in by the side-door or the tradesmen's entrance. They wandered along the corridors for quite a while before finding a waiting-room where an usher wearing a chain, unimpressed by the name of Maigret, made him fill in a form.

At last they were shown into a room where an official, very young and dapper, was standing silent and motionless opposite an old woman as impassive as himself. One had the impression that they had been waiting like that for a long time, probably since the telephone call from the Quai d'Orsay to Police Headquarters.

'Chief-Inspector Maigret?'

The latter introduced Janvier, to whom the young man granted only a distant glance.

'Not knowing what the trouble was, I took the precaution of bringing along one of my inspectors . . .'

'Take a seat.'

Young Cromières was trying hard to look important and there was something very 'Foreign Office' about his condescending manner of speaking.

'If the Quai got in touch straight away with Police Headquarters . . .'

He pronounced the word 'Quai' as if he were talking about some sacrosanct institution.

'. . . it was because, Chief-Inspector, we are faced with a somewhat exceptional situation. . . .'

While looking at him, Maigret also kept an eye on the old woman, who was apparently deaf in one ear, for she bent forward to hear better, cocking her head to one side and watching the movements of the men's lips.

'Mademoiselle . . .'

Cromières consulted a form on his desk.

'Mademoiselle Larrieu is the maidservant, or the housekeeper, of one of the most distinguished of our former ambassadors, the Comte de Saint-Hilaire, of whom you must have heard . . .'

Maigret remembered having seen the name in the papers, but that struck him as going back a very long time.

'Since he retired about twelve years ago, the Comte de Saint-Hilaire had been living in Paris, in his flat in the Rue Saint-Dominique. This morning Mademoiselle Larrieu came here at half past eight and had to wait some time before being shown into the presence of a responsible official.'

Maigret pictured to himself the deserted offices at half past eight in the morning, and the old woman sitting motionless in the ante-room, her eyes fixed on the door.

'Mademoiselle Larrieu has been in the Comte de Saint-Hilaire's service for over forty years.'

'Forty-two,' she specified.

'Forty-two years. She accompanied him on his various missions and she looked after his house. During the past twelve years, she was the only person living with the ambassador in the Rue Saint-Dominique flat. It was there, this morning, that after finding the bedroom empty when she took in her master's breakfast, she discovered him in his study, dead.'

The old woman looked at each of them in turn, with sharp, searching, suspicious eyes.

'From what she says, Saint-Hilaire would appear to have been hit by one or more bullets.'

'She didn't call the police?'

The fair-haired young man assumed a conceited expression.

'I can understand your surprise. But do not forget that Mademoiselle Larrieu has spent a large part of her life in the diplomatic world. For all that the Comte de Saint-Hilaire was no longer on the active list, she considered that in the Service there are certain rules of discretion . . .'

Maigret winked at Janvier.

'She didn't think of sending for a doctor either?'

'It seems there can be no doubt about the question of death.'

'Who is over there in the Rue Saint-Dominique now?'

'Nobody. Mademoiselle Larrieu came straight here. To avoid any misunderstanding and waste of time, I am authorized to inform you that the Comte de Saint-Hilaire was not in possession of any state secrets and that you must not look for a political reason for his death. However, extreme prudence is none the less indispensable. When a well-known man is involved in something of this sort, especially if he has been in the Service, the newspapers are only too apt to give enormous prominence to the affair and to put forward the most improbable hypotheses. . . .'

The young man stood up.

'If you will be good enough to come with me, we will go over there now.'

'You too?' Maigret asked with an innocent air.

'Oh, have no fear. I have no intention of interfering with your inquiries. If I accompany you, it is simply to make sure that there is nothing there which might cause us any embarrassment.'

The old woman stood up too. All four went downstairs.

'We had better take a taxi. That would be less conspicuous than one of the Quai limousines. . . .'

The journey was ludicrously short. The car drew up in front of an imposing late eighteenth-century building outside which there was no crowd, no inquisitive onlookers. Under the archway, once they had gone through the main entrance, it felt suddenly cool, and in what looked more like a drawing-room than a lodge they could see a uniformed concierge as impressive as the usher at the Ministry.

They went up four steps on the left. The lift was standing motionless in a hall of dark marble. The old woman took a key out of her handbag and opened a walnut door.

'This way . . .'

She led them along a corridor to a room which obviously overlooked the courtyard but where the shutters and the curtains were closed. It was Mademoiselle Larrieu who turned on the electric light, and beside a mahogany desk they saw a body lying on the red carpet.

The three men removed their hats in a single movement, while the old servant looked at them with an almost defiant air.

'What did I tell you?' she seemed to be muttering.

Sure enough, there was no need to bend over the body to see that the Comte de Saint-Hilaire was well and truly dead. One bullet had entered by way of the right eye, blowing open the skull, and judging by the tears in the black velvet dressing-gown and by the bloodstains, other bullets had struck the body in several places.

Monsieur Cromières was the first to go up to the desk.

'You see this? It would appear that he was busy correcting proofs . . .'

'He was writing a book?'

'His memoirs. Two volumes have already appeared. But it would be absurd to look for the reason for his death there, because Saint-Hilaire was the most discreet of men and his memoirs were more literary and picturesque than political in character.'

Cromières was talking in flowery language, listening to himself talk, and Maigret began to feel irritated. There they were, the four of them, in a room with the shutters closed, at ten o'clock in the morning, while the sun was shining outside, looking at an old man's disjointed, blood-spattered body.

'I suppose,' muttered the chief-inspector, not without a certain irony, 'that in spite of everything this is still a matter for the Public Prosecutor?'

There was a telephone on the desk, but he preferred not to touch it.

'Janvier, go and phone from the lodge. Get the Prosecutor and the local police inspector . . .'

The old woman kept looking at them, one after another, as if it were her job to watch them. Her eyes were hard, with no sympathy, no human warmth in them.

'What are you doing?' asked Maigret, seeing the man from the Quai d'Orsay opening the doors of a bookcase.

'I am just having a look . . .'

He added, with a self-assurance that was unpleasant in a young fellow of his age:

'It is my duty to make quite sure that there aren't any papers here the divulgation of which would be inopportune . . .'

Was he as young as he looked? To what service did he belong in fact? Without waiting for the chief-inspector's permission, he examined the contents of the bookcase, opening files and putting them back one after another.

In the meantime, Maigret walked up and down, impatient, out of temper.

Cromières started on the other pieces of furniture, rummaging in the drawers, and the old woman remained standing by the door with her hat on and her bag in her hand.

'Will you take me to his bedroom?'

She went in front of the man from the Quai, while Maigret stayed in the study where Janvier soon joined him.

'Where are they?'

'In the bedroom . . .'

'What are we doing?'

'For the moment, nothing. I'm waiting for the young gentleman to be good enough to leave the place to us.'

It was not just Cromières who irritated the chief-inspector. It was also the way in which the case presented itself, and perhaps, above all else, the unfamiliar atmosphere into which he had suddenly been plunged.

'The local inspector will be here in a minute.'

'You've phoned the Criminal Records Office?'

'Moers is on the way with his men.'

'And the Public Prosecutor?'

'I've phoned them too.'

The study was roomy and comfortable. Though there was nothing solemn about it, the place had an air of distinction which had struck the chief-inspector as soon as he had come in. Every piece of furniture, every object was beautiful in itself. And the old man on the floor, with his head practically blown off, retained, in this setting, a certain grandeur.

Cromières returned, followed by the old housekeeper.

'I don't think there is anything more for me to do here. Once again, I recommend prudence and discretion to you. It cannot be a case of suicide, seeing that there is no weapon in the room. We are agreed on that point, I presume? As to whether a theft has been committed, I leave that to you to discover. In any case, it would be regrettable if the Press were to give undue prominence to this affair . . .'

Maigret looked at him in silence.

'I shall ring you up, if you don't mind, to find out what news you have,' the young man went on. 'It is possible that you may need certain information, in which case you can always apply to me.'

'Thank you.'

'In a chest of drawers in the bedroom, you will find a number of let-ters which will probably surprise you. It is an old story which everybody knows at the Quai d'Orsay and which has nothing to do with this affair.'

He retired regretfully.

'I count on you . . .'

The old woman followed him to shut the door behind him, and returned a little later without either hat or handbag. She had not come back to put herself at the chief-inspector's disposal, but rather to keep an eye on the two men.

'Do you sleep in the flat?'

When Maigret spoke to her, she was not looking at him, and she did not seem to have heard him. He repeated his question in a louder voice. This time she cocked her head, turning her good ear towards him.

'Yes. I have a little room behind the kitchen.'

'There aren't any other servants?'

'Not here, no.'

'You do the housework and the cooking here?'

'Yes.'

'How old are you?'

'Seventy.'

'And the Comte de Saint-Hilaire?'

'Seventy-seven.'

'When did you leave him last night?'

'About ten o'clock.'

'He was in his study?'

'Yes.'

'He wasn't expecting anybody?'

'He didn't say so.'

'Did anybody ever come to see him in the evening?'

'His nephew.'

'Where does his nephew live?'

'In the Rue Jacob. He is an antique-dealer.'

'Is he called Saint-Hilaire too?'

'No, he is the son of Monsieur's sister. His name is Mazeron.'

'You've got that, Janvier? . . . This morning, when you found the body . . . Because it *was* this morning you found it, wasn't it?'

'Yes. At eight o'clock.'

'You didn't think of ringing Monsieur Mazeron?'

'No.'

'Why not?'

She did not answer. She had the fixed stare of certain birds and, like certain birds too, she sometimes remained perched on one leg.

'You don't like him?'

'Who?'

'Monsieur Mazeron.'

'That's none of my business.'

Maigret knew now that with her everything was going to be difficult.

'What is none of your business?'

'Family matters.'

'The nephew didn't get on with his uncle?'

'I didn't say that.'

'What did you do, last night, at ten o'clock?'

'I went to bed.'

'When did you get up?'

'At six o'clock, as usual.'

'And you didn't set foot in this room?'

'There was no reason for me to come in here.'

'Was the door shut?'

'If it had been open, I should have noticed straight away that some-thing had happened.'

'Why?'

'Because the lamps were still alight.'

'As they are now?'

'No. The ceiling light was not on. Just the desk lamp and the standard lamp in that corner.'

'What did you do at six o'clock?'

'First of all I washed.'

'And then?'

'I cleaned my kitchen and I went to buy some croissants.'

'The flat remained empty during that time?'

'Like every morning.'

'And then?'

'I made some coffee, I had my breakfast, and finally I went to the bedroom with the tray.'

'Had the bed been slept in?'

'No.'

'Was the room untidy?'

'No.'

'Last night, when you left him, was the Count wearing this black dressing-gown?'

'Yes, as he always did in the evening when he didn't go out.'

'Did he go out often?'

'He liked the cinema.'

'Did he invite friends here?'

'Scarcely ever. Now and then he used to go out to lunch.'

'Do you know the names of the people he met?'

'That is none of my business.'

There was a ring at the door. It was the local inspector with his secretary. He looked at the study in surprise, then at the old woman, and finally at Maigret, with whom he shook hands.

'How is it that you got here before us? Did she phone you?'

'She didn't even do that. She went to the Quai d'Orsay. Do you know the victim?'

'It's the former ambassador, isn't it? I know him by name and by sight. Every morning he used to go for a stroll round here. Who did that to him?'

'We don't know anything yet. I'm waiting for the Prosecutor.'

'The police doctor should be here any minute now . . .'

Nobody touched the furniture or anything else in the room. There was a strange feeling of uneasiness and it was a relief to see the doctor arrive. He gave a little whistle as he bent over the body.

'I suppose I can't turn him over before the photographers get here?'

'No, don't touch him . . . Have you an approximate idea of the time he died?'

'A good while ago . . . At first sight, I should say ten hours or so . . . It's queer . . .'

'What's queer?'

'He seems to have been hit by at least four bullets . . . One here, another there . . .'

Going down on his knees, he examined the body more closely.

'I don't know what the medical expert will think about it. For my part, I wouldn't be surprised if the first bullet had killed him and in spite of that the murderer had gone on firing. Mind you, that's just a theory . . .'

In less than five minutes the flat filled up with people. First came the Public Prosecutor represented by the deputy prosecutor Pasquier and by an examining magistrate whom Maigret did not know very well and who was called Urbain de Chézaud.

Doctor Paul's successor, Doctor Tudelle, arrived with them. Almost immediately afterwards the flat was invaded by the experts from the Criminal Records Office and their bulky apparatus.

'Who found the body?'

'The housekeeper.'

Maigret pointed to the old woman who, with no visible emotion, was still watching everybody's movements and gestures.

'Have you questioned her?'

'Not yet. I've just exchanged a few words with her.'

'Does she know anything?'

'If she does, it won't be easy to make her talk.'

He recounted the story of the Foreign Office.

'Has anything been stolen?'

'At first sight, it seems not. I'm waiting for the Criminal Records people to finish their work to make sure.'

'Any relatives?'

'A nephew.'

'Has he been informed?'

'Not yet. I intend to go myself, while my men are at work, to tell him what has happened. He lives just a few streets away, in the Rue Jacob.'

Maigret could have telephoned to the antique-dealer to ask him to come round, but he preferred to meet him in his own setting.

'If you don't need me any more, I'll go over there now. Janvier, you stay here . . .'

It was a relief to come out into the daylight, and the patches of sunshine under the trees on the Boulevard Saint-Germain. The air was warm, the women were wearing light-coloured dresses, and a municipal watering-cart was slowly sprinkling one half of the roadway.

He had no difficulty in finding the Rue Jacob antique-shop, one window of which contained nothing but old weapons, mostly swords. He pushed open the door, making a bell ring inside the shop, and three or four minutes went by before a man emerged from the shadows.

Seeing that the uncle was seventy-seven, Maigret could not expect the nephew to be a youngster. He was none the less surprised to find himself face to face with something like an old man.

'What can I do for you?'

He had a long pale face, bushy eyebrows and a practically bald pate, and his baggy clothes made him look thinner than he was.

'You are Monsieur Mazeron?'

'Alain Mazeron, yes.'

There were more weapons littering the shop, muskets, blunderbusses, and, right at the back, two suits of armour.

'Chief-Inspector Maigret, of the Judicial Police.'

The eyebrows came together. Mazeron was trying to understand.

'You are the Comte de Saint-Hilaire's nephew, aren't you?'

'He is my uncle, yes. Why?'

'When did you last see him?'

He answered unhesitatingly:

'The day before yesterday.'

'Have you any other relatives?'

'I am married, with children.'

'When you last saw your uncle, did he seem quite normal?'

'Yes, he was even rather gay. Why do you ask?'

'Because he is dead.'

Maigret saw in Mazeron's eyes the same mistrust that the old housekeeper had shown.

'He has had an accident?'

'In a manner of speaking . . .'

'What do you mean?'

'That he was killed last night in his study by several bullets fired from a revolver or an automatic pistol.'

The antique-dealer's face registered incredulity.

'Did he have any enemies you know of?'

'No . . . Certainly not . . .'

If Mazeron had merely said no, Maigret would have paid no attention. The 'certainly not', which came rather as an afterthought, made him prick up his ears.

'You have no idea who would stand to benefit by your uncle's death?'

'No . . . No idea whatever . . .'

'Was he a rich man?'

'He had a small private fortune . . . He lived mainly on his pension . . .'

'He sometimes came here?'

'Sometimes . . .'

'To have lunch or dinner with you?'

Mazeron seemed absentminded, and replied briefly, as if he were thinking of something else.

'No . . . Usually in the morning, in the course of his walk . . .'

'He dropped in for a chat with you?'

'That's it. He used to come in and sit down for a moment.'

'Did you go to see him at his flat?'

'Now and then . . .'

'With your family?'

'No . . .'

'Did you say you had some children?'

'Two . . . Two girls . . .'

'You live in this building?'

'On the first floor . . . One of my daughters, the elder, is in England . . . The other, Marcelle, lives with her mother . . .'

'You don't live with your wife?'

'Not for some years now . . .'

'You are divorced?'

'No . . . It's rather complicated . . . Don't you think we ought to go over to my uncle's?'

He went to look for his hat in the half-light of the back-shop, hung a notice saying that he was out on the door, locked up, and followed Maigret along the pavement.

'Do you know how it happened?' he asked.

You could tell that he was anxious, worried.

'I know next to nothing.'

'Was anything stolen?'

'I don't think so. There was no sign of disorder in the flat.'

'What does Jaquette say?'

'You are talking about the housekeeper?'

'Yes . . . That's her Christian name . . . I don't know if it's her real name, but she has always been known as Jaquette . . .'

'You don't like her?'

'Why do you ask me that?'

'She doesn't seem to like you.'

'She doesn't like anybody except my uncle. If it had been left to her to decide, nobody would ever have been allowed into that flat.'

'Do you think she would have been capable of killing him?'

Mazeron looked at him in astonishment.

'Killing him—her?'

The idea obviously struck him as utterly ridiculous. And yet, a moment later, he found himself thinking again.

'No! . . . It isn't possible . . .'

'You hesitated.'

'Because of her jealousy . . .'

'You mean to say that she was in love with him?'

'She hasn't always been an old woman . . .'

'You think that they were once . . .'

'It's probable . . . I wouldn't swear to it . . . With a man like my uncle, it's hard to tell . . . You've seen the photographs of Jaquette when she was young?'

'I haven't seen anything yet . . .'

'You'll see . . . It's all very complicated . . . Especially happening just now . . .'

'What do you mean by that?'

Alain Mazeron looked at Maigret with a certain weariness and sighed:

'I see that you don't know anything.'

'What ought I to know?'

'I wonder . . . It's a tiresome story. Have you found the letters?'

'I'm just beginning my inquiries.'

'Today is Wednesday, isn't it?'

Maigret nodded.

'Just the day of the funeral . . .'

'Whose funeral?'

'The Prince de V——'s. You'll understand when you have read the letters . . .'

They reached the Rue Saint-Dominique just as the Criminal Records car was leaving, and Moers gave a wave of the hand to Maigret.

II

'W H A T are you thinking about, Chief?'

Janvier was surprised at the effect produced by this question which he had asked simply to break a rather lengthy silence. It seemed as though the words had not penetrated straight away to Maigret's brain, that they were just so many sounds which he had to put in order before he could make out what they meant.

The chief-inspector looked at his companion with big vague eyes and an air of embarrassment, as if he had just given away a secret of his.

'About these people,' he murmured.

Clearly he was not talking about those who were lunching all around them in this Rue de Bourgogne restaurant, but about the others, those of whom they had never heard the day before and whose secret lives it was their job to discover today.

Every time he bought a suit, an overcoat or a pair of shoes, Maigret wore them first of all in the evening, to go for a stroll with his wife through the streets of the district or else to go to the cinema.

'I need to get used to them,' he would say to Madame Maigret when she teased him affectionately.

It was the same when he was immersing himself in a new case. Other people did not realize this, on account of his massive silhouette and the calm expression on his face which they took for self-assurance. In fact, he was going through a more or less prolonged period of hesitation, uneasiness, even timidity.

He had to get used to an unfamiliar setting, to a house, to a way of life, to people who had their own particular habits, their own way of thinking and expressing themselves.

With certain categories of human beings it was relatively easy, for instance with his more or less regular customers or with people like them.

With others he had to start from scratch every time, especially as he distrusted rules and ready-made ideas.

In this new case, he was labouring under an additional handicap. He had made contact, that morning, with a world which was not only very exclusive but which for him, on account of his childhood, was situated on a very special level.

He realized that all the time he had been in the Rue Saint-Dominique he had failed to show his usual confidence; he had behaved awkwardly; his questions had been guarded and clumsy. Had Janvier noticed?

If so, it had certainly not occurred to him that this was the effect of a distant period in Maigret's past, the years spent in the shadow of a château of which his father had been steward and where, for a long time, the Comte and Comtesse de Saint-Fiacre had been, in his eyes, creatures of another species.

For lunch, the two men had picked this restaurant in the Rue de Bourgogne, on account of its terrace, and they had soon noticed that the place was patronized by officials from the nearby ministries, especially from the Premier's department, so it seemed, with a few officers in mufti who belonged to the War Office.

They were not ordinary pen-pushers. All of them had at least the rank of head clerk, and Maigret was astonished to see how young they were. Their self-assurance surprised him too. From the way they talked and behaved, you could tell that they were sure of themselves. Some of them recognizing him and talking about him in low voices, he felt annoyed at their knowing looks and their irony.

Did the people at the Quai des Orfèvres, who were ministry officials too, give the same impression of knowing all the answers?

This was what he had been thinking about when Janvier had roused him from his reverie. About the morning in the Rue Saint-Dominique. About the dead man, that Comte Armand de Saint-Hilaire, an ambassador for so many years, who had just been murdered at the age of seventy-seven. About the strange Jaquette Larrieu and her little staring eyes which penetrated to the very depths of his being while she listened to him, her head cocked to one side, watching every movement of his lips. And finally about the pale and flabby Alain Mazeron, all alone in his Rue Jacob shop, among his swords and his suits of armour, whom Maigret could not manage to class in any known category.

What were the terms used by the English doctor in the article in the *Lancet?* He could not remember. It was something to the effect that a first-class schoolmaster, a novelist and a detective were in a better position than a doctor or a psychiatrist to understand other people.

Why did the detective come last, after the schoolmaster and particularly after the novelist?

That annoyed him slightly. He was in a hurry to feel at home in this new case, as if to give the lie to the author of the article.

They had begun with asparagus and now they had gone on to ray with browned butter sauce. The sky above the street was still as blue as ever and the women passing by were dressed in bright colours.

Before deciding to go and have lunch, Maigret and Janvier had spent an hour and a half in the dead man's flat, which was already more familiar to them.

The body had been taken off to the Morgue, where Doctor Tudelle was engaged in carrying out the post-mortem. The people from the Public Prosecutor and Criminal Records had gone. With a sigh of relief, Maigret had opened curtains and shutters, letting the sunlight into the rooms, where it had given back to the furniture and other objects their normal appearance.

It did not embarrass the chief-inspector to have Jaquette and the nephew following him around, watching his gestures and facial expressions, and now and then he would turn towards them and ask a question.

No doubt they had been surprised to see him coming and going for such a long time, without looking at anything in particular, as if he were inspecting a flat to let.

The study, which had seemed so stuffy that morning in artificial light, fascinated him, and he kept coming back to it with a secret pleasure, for it was one of the most delightful rooms he had ever seen.

It was a high-ceilinged room, lit by a french window opening on to a flight of three steps, beyond which one discovered with some surprise a well-kept lawn and a huge linden-tree standing in a world of stone.

'Who has the use of this garden?' he had asked, looking up at the windows of the other flats.

The reply came from Mazeron.

'My uncle.'

'None of the other tenants?'

'No. The building belonged to him. He was born here. His father, who was still quite rich, occupied the ground floor and the first floor. When he died, my uncle, who had already lost his mother, kept this small flat and the garden for himself.'

This little detail was significant. It was surely a rare thing, in Paris, for a man of seventy-seven to be living in the house where he was born.

'And what happened when he was serving as an ambassador abroad?'

'He closed the flat and opened it up again when he came home on leave. Contrary to what you might suppose, the building brought him in hardly anything. Most of the tenants have been here so long that they pay derisory rents, so that some years, what with repairs and taxes, my uncle was out of pocket.'

There were not many rooms in the flat. The study did service as a drawing-room. Next to it was a dining-room, opposite the kitchen, and overlooking the street there was a bedroom and a bathroom.

'Where do you sleep?' Maigret had asked Jaquette.

She made him repeat his question and he began to think that this was an idiosyncrasy of hers.

'Behind the kitchen.'

There in fact he found a sort of box-room in which an iron bedstead, a wardrobe and a washbasin had been installed. A big ebony crucifix hung over a holy-water basin adorned with a sprig of box.

'Was the Comte de Saint-Hilaire a religious man?'

'He never missed Mass on Sunday, even in Russia.'

What struck him most of all was a subtle harmony, a distinction which Maigret would have been hard put to it to define. The various pieces of furniture were of different styles and no attempt had been made to form an ensemble. Every room was none the less beautiful in itself; each had acquired the same patina, the same personality.

The study was almost entirely lined with bound volumes, while other books in white or yellow covers were arranged on shelves in the corridor.

'Was the window shut when you found the body?'

'It was you who opened it. I didn't even touch the curtains.'

'And the bedroom window?'

'That was shut too. Monsieur le Comte was sensitive to the cold.'

'Who had the key to the flat?'

'He and I. Nobody else.'

Janvier had questioned the concierge. The little door cut out of the main door stayed open until midnight. The concierge never went to bed before that time; he sometimes went into his bedroom, behind the lodge, from which he did not necessarily see people coming in and going out.

The day before, he had not noticed anything out of the ordinary. It was a respectable house, he kept repeating insistently. He had been there for thirty years and the police had never had occasion to set foot in the place.

It was too soon to reconstruct what had happened the previous evening or during the night. He had to wait for the medical expert's report, then for the report of Moers and his men.

One thing seemed clear: Saint-Hilaire had not gone to bed. He was wearing dark grey, pin-striped trousers, a lightly starched white shirt and a bow-tie with spots, and, as usual when he stayed at home, he had put on his black velvet dressing-gown.

'Did he often stay up late?'

'It depends what you mean by late.'

'What time did he usually go to bed?'

'I was nearly always in bed before he was.'

It was infuriating. The most commonplace questions came up against the mistrust of the old servant, who only rarely gave a direct answer.

'You didn't hear him leave his study?'

'Go into my bedroom and you'll see that you can't hear anything there except the lift, which is on the other side of the partition.'

'How did he spend his evenings?'

'Reading. Writing. Correcting the proofs of his books.'

'Did he go to bed at midnight, say?'

'Perhaps a little earlier, or a little later, depending on the day.'

'And when he went to bed, he never called you, he never had need of your services?'

'What for?'

'He might have felt like a hot drink before going to bed, or perhaps . . .'

'He never had a hot drink at night. And if he wanted something to drink, he had his liqueur cabinet.'

'What did he drink usually?'

'Claret with his meals. And in the evening, a glass of brandy.'

They had found the glass, empty, on the desk, and the experts from the Criminal Records Office had taken it away to see if there were any fingerprints on it.

If the old man had had a visitor, he did not appear to have offered him a drink, for no other glass had been found in the study.

'Did the Comte de Saint-Hilaire possess any firearms?'

'Some fowling-pieces. They are in the cupboard at the end of the corridor.'

'He was a keen shot?'

'He sometimes did a little shooting when he was invited to a château.'

'He didn't own a pistol or a revolver?'

Once again she fell silent, and, as before, her pupils narrowed like those of a cat and her gaze became immobile, expressionless.

'Did you hear my question?'

'What did you ask me?'

Maigret repeated his query.

'I think he had a revolver.'

'With a cylinder?'

'What do you mean by a cylinder?'

He tried to explain. No, it wasn't a gun with a cylinder. It was a flat weapon, bluish in colour with a short barrel.

'Where did he keep this automatic of his?'

'I don't know. I haven't seen it for a long time. The last time, it was in the chest of drawers.'

'In his bedroom?'

She showed him the drawer in question, which contained nothing but handkerchiefs, suspenders and braces in various colours. The other drawers were full of neatly folded linen, shirts, pants, handkerchiefs, and, right at the bottom, dress-shirts.

'When did you last see the automatic?'

'Some years ago.'

'How many years ago, roughly?'

'I don't know. Time goes so quickly . . .'

'You never saw it anywhere except in that chest of drawers?'

'No. Perhaps he had put it in one of the drawers in his desk. I never opened those drawers, and in any case they were always locked.'

'Do you know why?'

'Why do people lock pieces of furniture?'

'He distrusted you?'

'Certainly not.'

'Whom then?'

'Don't you ever lock anything, you?'

There was a key, sure enough, a highly ornamental bronze key which opened the drawers of the Empire desk. The contents revealed nothing, except that Saint-Hilaire, like everybody else, accumulated useless little objects, some old empty wallets for instance, two or three gold-rimmed amber cigar-holders which had not been used for a long time, a cigar-cutter, some drawing-pins and paper-clips, and pencils in every conceivable colour.

Another drawer contained writing-paper stamped with a coronet, envelopes, visiting-cards, bits of string carefully rolled up, a pot of paste and a penknife with a broken blade.

The copper trellis-work doors of one bookcase were lined with green cloth. Inside there were no books but instead, on every shelf, bundles of letters neatly tied with string, with a label bearing a date attached to each bundle.

'This is what you were talking about earlier?' Maigret asked Alain Mazeron.

The nephew nodded.

'You know who wrote these letters?'

He nodded again.

'Was it your uncle who told you about them?'

'I don't know if he ever mentioned them to me, but everybody knows about them.'

'What do you mean by everybody?'

'In diplomatic circles, in society . . .'

'Have you ever had occasion to read any of these letters?'

'Never.'

'You can leave us and go and cook your lunch,' Maigret said to Jaquette.

'If you think I'm going to eat on a day like this!'

'Leave us all the same. You can certainly find something to do.'

She was obviously reluctant to leave him alone with the nephew. Several times, he had intercepted glances of something like hatred which she had surreptitiously shot at him.

'You understand?'

'I know that it is none of my business, but . . .'

'But what?'

'A person's letters are sacred . . .'

'Even if they can help in tracking down a murderer?'

'They won't help you to do anything.'

'I shall probably need you soon. In the meantime . . .'

He glanced at the door and Jaquette reluctantly withdrew. How indignant she would have been if she had been able to see Maigret taking the Comte de Saint-Hilaire's place behind the desk on which Janvier was arranging the bundles of letters!

'Sit down,' Maigret said to Mazeron. 'You know whom this correspondence is from?'

'Yes. You will doubtless find that all the letters are signed Isi.'

'Who is Isi?'

'Isabelle de V——. My uncle always called her Isi . . .'

'She was his mistress?'

Why did Maigret think that Mazeron looked like a sacristan, as if sacristans had a particular type of face? Mazeron too, like Jaquette, allowed a certain time to elapse before answering his questions.

'It seems they were never lovers.'

Maigret untied the string round a bundle of yellowed letters dating from 1914, a few days after the outbreak of war.

'How old is the Princess now?'

'Wait a moment while I work it out . . . She is five or six years younger than my uncle . . . So she is between seventy-one and seventy-two . . .'

'Did she come here often?'

'I have never seen her here. I don't think she has ever set foot in the place, or if she has it was before.'

'Before what?'

'Before her marriage to the Prince de V——.'

'Listen, Monsieur Mazeron. I would like you to tell me this story as clearly as you can . . .'

'Isabelle was the daughter of the Duc de S——.'

It was a curious experience for Maigret, coming across names he had learnt at school in lessons on French history.

'Well?'

'My uncle was twenty-six when he met her, about 1910. To be more precise, he had met her when she was a little girl in the Duke's château, where he sometimes spent his holidays. After that he had seen nothing of her for a long time, and it was when they met again that they fell in love with one another.'

'Your uncle had already lost his father?'

'Two years before.'

'Was there anything left of the family fortune?'

'Just this house and a little landed property in Sologne.'

'Why didn't they get married?'

'I don't know. Possibly because my uncle was just starting his career in the Service and he had been sent to Poland as second or third secretary to the Ambassador.'

'Were they engaged?'

'No.'

Maigret felt a certain embarrassment as he looked through the letters spread out in front of him. Contrary to his expectations, they were not love-letters. The girl who had written them recounted, in quite a lively style, the day-to-day happenings of her own life and the life of Parisian society.

She did not use the familiar *tu* form with her correspondent, whom she called her *great friend*, and she signed the letters: *your faithful Isi.*

'What happened next?'

'Before the war—I'm talking about the war of 1914—in 1912, unless I'm mistaken, Isabelle married the Prince de V——.'

'Was she in love with him?'

'By all accounts, no. People even say that she told him so to his face. All I know about it is from hearing my father and mother talking about it when I was a child.'

'Your mother was the Comte de Saint-Hilaire's sister?'

'Yes.'

'She didn't marry into her own class?'

'She married my father, who was a painter who enjoyed a certain vogue at the time. He is almost completely forgotten now, but there is still a canvas of his in the Luxembourg. Later on, in order to earn a living, he became a picture restorer.'

During this part of the morning, Maigret had had the impression that he was having to drag out every scrap of truth almost by force. He could not manage to obtain a clear picture. These people seemed unreal to him, as if they had come out of a 1900 novel.

'If I understand correctly, Armand de Saint-Hilaire didn't marry Isabelle because he wasn't rich enough?'

'I suppose so. That's what I was always told and it seems the likeliest explanation.'

'So she married the Prince de V——, whom you say she didn't love, and she was honest enough to tell him so.'

'It was an arrangement between two great families, between two great names.'

Hadn't it been the same in the old days with the Saint-Fiacres, and when it had been a question of finding a wife for her son, hadn't the old Countess turned to her Bishop for help?

'Did the couple have any children?'

'One child, a boy, after they had been married several years.'

'What became of him?'

'Prince Philippe must be forty-five now. He married a Mademoiselle de Marchangy and lives nearly all the year round in his château at Genestoux, near Caen, where he owns a stud and several farms. He has five or six children.'

'For something like fifty years, to judge by this correspondence, Isabelle and your uncle went on writing to each other. Practically every day they sent each other letters several pages long. Did the husband know that this was going on?'

'So they say.'

'Did you know him?'

'Only by sight.'

'What sort of man was he?'

'A man of the world and a collector.'

'A collector of what?'

'Medals, snuffboxes . . .'

'Did he mix very much with other people?'

'He entertained once a week in his Rue de Varenne house, and in autumn at his château at Saint-Sauveur-en-Bourbonnais.'

Maigret had pulled a wry face. On the one hand, he knew that all this was probably true, but at the same time the people concerned struck him as having no material existence.

'The Rue de Varenne,' he pointed out, 'is only five minutes' walk from here.'

'All the same, I'd be ready to swear that for fifty years my uncle and the Princess never met.'

'Although they wrote to each other every day?'

'You've got the letters in front of you.'

'And the husband knew all about it?'

'Isabelle would never have agreed to conduct a correspondence behind his back.'

Maigret felt almost tempted to lose his temper, as if somebody had been poking fun at him. And yet there the letters were, before his very eyes, full of revealing passages.

'. . . *this morning, at eleven o'clock, the Abbé Gauge called to see me and we talked a great deal about you. It is a comfort to me to know that the bonds which join us are of a sort that men are powerless to break . . .*'

'Is the Princess very devout?'

'She has had a chapel consecrated in her house in the Rue de Varenne.'

'And her husband?'

'He was a Catholic too.'

'He had mistresses?'

'So they say.'

Another letter, from a more recent bundle:

'. . . *I shall be grateful to Hubert all my life for having understood . . .*'

'I suppose that Hubert is the Prince de V——?'

'Yes. He was once a staff-officer at the cavalry school of Saumur. Every morning he went riding in the Bois de Boulogne until last week, when he was thrown from his horse.'

'How old was he?'

'Eighty.'

In this case there was nobody but old people, with relations between them which did not seem human.

'You are quite sure about all that you have told me, Monsieur Mazeron?'

'If you have any doubts, ask anybody you like.'

Anybody in a world of which Maigret had only a vague and doubt-less inaccurate idea!

'Let's continue,' he sighed wearily. 'This is the Prince who, you told me earlier, has just died?'

'On Sunday morning, yes. It was in all the papers. He died from the effects of his riding accident and the funeral is taking place at this very moment at Sainte-Clotilde.'

'He never had anything to do with your uncle?'

'Not as far as I know.'

'And what happened if they met at some social gathering?'

'I imagine they avoided frequenting the same salons and the same clubs.'

'They hated each other?'

'I don't think so.'

'Did your uncle ever talk to you about the Prince?'

'No. He never mentioned him.'

'And what about Isabelle?'

'He told me, a long time ago, that I was his sole heir and that it was a pity I didn't bear his name. It saddened him too that I had two daughters and no son. If I had had a son, he added, he would have applied for a decree allowing the latter to bear the name Saint-Hilaire.'

'So you are your uncle's sole heir?'

'Yes. But I haven't finished what I was telling you. Indirectly, with-out mentioning any names, he spoke to me that day of the Princess. He said something to this effect:

'"I still hope to marry one day, heaven knows when, but it will be too late to have any children . . ."'

'If I've understood you correctly, this is the situation. About 1910 your uncle met a girl whom he loved and who loved him, but they didn't get married because the Comte de Saint-Hilaire was practically penniless.'

'That's correct.'

'Two years later, when your uncle was in an embassy in Poland or somewhere else, young Isabelle made a marriage of convenience and became the Princesse de V——. She has a son, so it wasn't an uncon-summated marriage. The couple must have lived together as husband and wife, at least at the time.'

'Yes.'

'Unless in the meantime Isabelle and your uncle had seen each other again and given way to their passion.'

'No.'

'How can you be so sure? You think that in that particular world . . .'

'I say no because my uncle spent the whole of the First World War away from France, and when he came back the child, Philippe, was two or three years old.'

'All right. The sweethearts saw each other again . . .'

'No.'

'They never saw each other again?'

'I've already told you so.'

'For fifty years, then, they wrote to each other practically every day, and one day your uncle spoke to you about a marriage which was to take place in a more or less distant future. Which means, I suppose, that he and Isabelle were waiting for the Prince to die in order to get married.'

'I imagine so.'

Maigret mopped his forehead and looked at the linden-tree outside the French window, as if he needed to resume contact with a more humdrum reality.

'Now we come to the epilogue. Ten or twelve days ago—the exact date doesn't matter—the eighty-year-old Prince was thrown from his horse in the Bois de Boulogne. On Sunday morning, he died from his injuries. Yesterday, Tuesday, that is to say two days later, your uncle was killed in his study. The consequence is that the two old people, who for fifty years had been waiting for the time to come when they could finally be joined together, won't be joined together after all. Is that right? Thank you, Monsieur Mazeron. Now will you please give me your wife's address.'

'23, Rue de la Pompe, at Passy.'

'Do you know the name of your uncle's solicitor?'

'His solicitor is Maître Aubonnet, of the Rue de Villersexel.'

Again a few hundred yards away. All these people, with the exception of Madame Mazeron, lived practically next-door to one another, in the district of Paris with which Maigret was least familiar.

'You are free to go now. I suppose I can always find you at your shop?'

'I shan't be there very much this afternoon, because I shall have to make arrangements for the funeral and the announcement of my uncle's death, and first of all I intend to get in touch with Maître Aubonnet.'

Mazeron had left reluctantly and Jaquette, suddenly appearing from her kitchen, had gone to shut the door behind him.

'Do you need me at the moment?'

'Not just now. It's lunchtime. We shall be back this afternoon.'

'Am I obliged to stay here?'

'Where would you go?'

She had looked at him as if she did not understand.

'I asked you where you intended to go.'

'Me? Nowhere. Where would I go, indeed?'

On account of her attitude, Maigret and Janvier had not left straight away. Maigret had telephoned to the Quai des Orfèvres.

'Lucas? Have you got somebody there who could come and spend an hour or two in the Rue Saint-Dominique? Torrence? Fine! Tell him to take a car . . .'

With the result that while the two men were lunching, Torrence, for his part, was dozing in the Comte de Saint-Hilaire's arm-chair.

As far as they could see, nothing had been stolen from the flat. Nobody had broken in. The murderer had come in through the door, and since Jaquette swore that she had let nobody in, they were forced to conclude that the Comte himself had opened the door to his visitor.

Was he expecting him? Or was he not? He hadn't offered him a drink. They had found only one glass on the desk, next to the bottle of brandy.

Would Saint-Hilaire have stayed in his dressing-gown to receive a woman? Probably not, judging by the little they knew about him.

So it was a man who had come to see him. The Count hadn't been suspicious of him, since he had sat down at his desk, in front of the proofs which he had been correcting a few minutes earlier.

'You didn't notice if there were any cigarette-ends in the ash-tray?'

'I don't think so.'

'No cigar-stubs either?'

'No.'

'I bet you that before tonight we'll have a phone call from young Monsieur Cromières.'

He was another one who had the knack of getting Maigret's back up.

'The Prince's funeral must be over by now.'

'Probably.'

'So Isabelle will be at home now in the Rue de Varenne, together with her son, her daughter-in-law and her grandchildren.'

There was a silence. Maigret frowned as if he could not make up his mind about something.

'Are you going to go and see them?' Janvier asked, with a certain anxiety in his voice.

'No . . . Not with people like that . . . Are you having coffee? . . . Waiter! Two black coffees . . .'

One would have sworn that he had a grudge against everybody to-day, even including the more or less high-ranking officials who were lunching at the neighbouring tables and eyeing him ironically.

III

As soon as he turned the corner of the Rue Saint-Dominique, Maigret saw them and let out a groan. There were a good dozen of them, re-porters and photographers, in front of the Comte de Saint-Hilaire's house, and some of them had sat down on the pavement with their backs against the wall, as if in readiness for a long siege.

They for their part had recognized him from a distance, and they rushed up to him.

'This is going to please our dear Monsieur Cromières!' he muttered to Janvier.

It was inevitable. As soon as a case was reported to a local police-station, there was always somebody who told the Press.

The photographers, who had dozens of pictures of him in their files, all took fresh shots of him, as if he looked different from the day before or any other day. The reporters started asking questions. These, fortu-nately, showed that they knew less about the case than might have been feared.

'Is it suicide, Chief-Inspector?'

'Have any documents disappeared?'

'For the moment, gentlemen, I have nothing to say.'

'Can we assume that it's probably a political affair?'

They walked backwards in front of him, with their notebooks in their hands.

'When will you be able to give us a statement?'

'Perhaps tomorrow, perhaps a week from now.'

He made the mistake of adding:

'Perhaps never.'

He tried to correct the slip he had made.

'I'm joking, of course. Now please help us by letting us work in peace.'

'Is it true that he was writing his memoirs?'

'So true that two volumes have already been published.'

A policeman in uniform was standing outside the door. A few moments later, in response to Maigret's ring at the bell, Torrence, in shirt-sleeves, came and opened the door to him.

'I had to send for a policeman, Chief. They had got into the building and were having fun ringing the bell every five minutes.'

'Nothing new? No phone calls?'

'Twenty or thirty. The papers.'

'Where's the old girl?'

'In the kitchen. Every time the phone rings, she rushes to it in the hope of answering before I do. The first time, she tried to snatch the receiver out of my hands.'

'She hasn't made any phone calls herself, has she? You know there's another phone in the bedroom?'

'I left the study door open so that I could hear her coming and going. She hasn't been into the bedroom.'

'She hasn't been out?'

'No. She tried to once, to go and get some new bread, so she told me. As you hadn't left me any instructions on that point, I decided not to let her go. What do I do now?'

'You go back to the Quai.'

For a moment, the chief-inspector had thought of going back there himself, and taking Jaquette, whom he wanted to question at leisure. But he didn't feel prepared for this interrogation. He preferred to stay a little longer in the flat and in the end it would probably be in Saint-Hilaire's study that he would try to get the old servant to talk.

In the meantime, he opened the lofty French window to its full extent and sat down in the chair which the Count had so often occupied. His hand was reaching out towards one of the bundles of letters when the door opened. It was Jaquette Larrieu, more sour-tempered and suspicious than ever.

'You haven't any right to do that.'

'You know who these letters are from?'

'It doesn't matter whether I do or don't. It's a private correspondence.'

'You will do me the favour of going back to the kitchen or your bedroom.'

'Can't I go out?'

'Not yet.'

She hesitated, searching for a cutting reply, which she failed to find,
and finally, pale with anger, left the study.

'Janvier, go and fetch me that photograph in a silver frame that I saw
this morning in the bedroom.'

Maigret had not paid much attention to it in the morning. Too many
things had still been unfamiliar to him. It was a principle with him not
to try to form an opinion too quickly, for he distrusted first impressions.

During lunch at the restaurant, he had suddenly remembered a
lithograph which he had seen for years in his parents' bedroom. It must
have been his mother who had chosen it and hung it up. The frame
was white, in the style fashionable at the beginning of the century. The
picture showed a young woman on the shore of a lake, wearing a
princess dress, with a wide ostrich-feather hat on her head and a sun-
shade in her hand. The expression on her face was melancholy, like
the landscape, and Maigret was sure that his mother considered the
picture to be highly poetic. Wasn't that the poetry of the period?

The story of Isabelle and the Comte de Saint-Hilaire had brought
back the memory of that picture to him so clearly that he could see even
the wallpaper with the pale-blue stripes in his parents' room.

Now inside the silver frame which he had noticed in the morning
in the Count's bedroom and which Janvier brought along to him, he
discovered the same figure, a dress in the same style, an identical
melancholy.

He had no doubt that it was a photograph of Isabelle about 1910,
when she was still a young girl and when the future ambassador had
met her.

She was not very tall, and she seemed to have a slim waist, possibly
because of the corset she was wearing, while her bust, as they used to
call it in those days, was rather large. Her features were finely chiselled,
her lips thin, her eyes a pale blue or grey.

'What do I do now, Chief?'

'Sit down.'

He needed somebody there, as if to check his impressions. In front
of him, the bundles of letters were arranged year by year and he took
them one after another, not reading everything of course, for that
would have taken him several days, but a passage here and there.

My good friend . . . Dearest friend . . . Sweet friend . . .

Later on, perhaps because she felt in closer harmony with her correspondent, she wrote simply: *Friend.*

Saint-Hilaire had kept the envelopes, which bore stamps of various countries. Isabelle had travelled a great deal. For a long time, for instance, her August letters were written from Baden-Baden or Marienbad, the aristocratic spas of the time.

There were also letters from the Tyrol, and a good many from Switzerland and Portugal. She recounted in a self-satisfied, lively manner the little happenings which filled her day and gave quite witty descriptions of the people she met. Often she referred to them just by their surnames, sometimes by a mere initial.

Maigret took some time to find his bearings. With the help of the stamp on the envelope and the context of the reference, he gradually managed to solve these conundrums.

Maria, for instance, was a queen still reigning at that time, the Queen of Rumania. It was from Bucharest, where she was staying at court with her father, that Isabelle was writing, and a year later she was at court in Italy.

'My cousin H——.'

The name—that of the Prince of Hesse—was given in full in another letter, and there were others, all first or second cousins.

During the First World War, she sent her letters by way of the French Embassy in Madrid.

'My father explained to me yesterday that it is necessary for me to marry the Prince de V—— whom you have met several times at home. I asked him for three days in which to consider the matter, and during this time I have wept a great deal . . .'

Maigret puffed at his pipe, shot an occasional glance at the garden, at the leaves of the linden-tree, and passed the letters one by one to Janvier, studying his reactions.

He felt a mild irritation in the face of these evocations which seemed so unreal to him. As a child, hadn't he looked with the same sort of embarrassment at the woman on the shore of the lake, in his parents' bedroom? In his eyes, she had been an unreal, impossible creature, surrounded by a false poetry.

Yet here, in a world which had evolved further, which had grown much harder, he had found, in a living person, a very similar picture.

'This afternoon, I had a long conversation with Hubert and I was absolutely frank. He knows that I love you, that we are separated by

too many obstacles, and that I am yielding to my father's wishes . . .'

Only the week before, Maigret had had to deal with a simple, brutal crime of passion, the case of a lover who had stabbed to death the husband of the woman he loved, had then killed the woman, and had finally tried unsuccessfully to cut open his veins. It is true that this took place in the lower-class district of the Faubourg Saint-Antoine.

'He has agreed that our marriage shall remain unconsummated and I for my part have promised never to see you again. He has a high regard for you and does not question the respect you have always shown me . . .'

There were moments when Maigret felt an almost physical sense of revolt.

'Do you believe it, Janvier?'

The inspector was baffled.

'She sounds as if she meant it . . .'

'Read this one!'

It was three years later.

'I know, friend, that this is going to hurt you, but if it is any consolation to you, it hurts me even more than it does you . . .'

It was in 1915. She announced that Julien, the Prince de V——'s brother, had just been killed in Argonne at the head of his regiment. Once again, she had had a long conversation with her husband, who had come to Paris on leave.

What she told the man she loved was, to put it briefly, that she was going to have to sleep with the Prince. She did not use those terms of course. Not only was there not a single brutal or shocking word in her letter, but the subject itself was treated in an almost immaterial fashion.

'As long as Julien was alive, Hubert did not worry, feeling sure that his brother would have an heir and that the name of V—— . . .'

The brother was no longer there. It was accordingly Hubert's duty to ensure the continuation of the family.

'I spent the night in prayer and in the morning I went to see my confessor . . .'

The priest had shared the Prince's opinion. One could not, for a question of love, allow a name to die out which, for the past five centuries, had been found on every page of the history of France.

'I understood where my duty lay . . .'

The sacrifice had taken place, since a child, Philippe, had been born. She announced the birth too, and on this subject there was a phrase which gave Maigret pause:

'Thank God, it is a boy . . .'

Wasn't that saying, in black and white, that if the child had been a girl, she would have had to start all over again?

And if she had had another girl, and then another . . .

'You've read it?'

'Yes.'

It was as if they had both fallen prey to the same feeling of discomfort. They were both of them accustomed to a somewhat crude reality, and the passions with which they came in contact usually took a dramatic turn seeing that they ended up at the Quai des Orfèvres.

Here, on the other hand, it was as difficult as trying to catch hold of a cloud. And when they attempted to grasp the characters, the latter remained as nebulous and unsubstantial as the lady of the lake.

For two pins Maigret would have stuffed all these letters into the green-curtained bookcase, muttering as he did so:

'A lot of rubbish!'

At the same time, he was filled with a certain respect which bordered on emotion. Not wanting to be taken in, he tried to harden his heart.

'Do you believe it all?'

More dukes, princes and dethroned monarchs met in Portugal. Then a journey to Kenya, in the husband's company. Another journey, to the United States this time, where Isabelle had felt rather at a loss because life there was too coarse for her liking.

'. . . The bigger he grows, the more Philippe resembles you. Isn't it miraculous? Isn't it as if Heaven wanted to reward us for our sacrifice? Hubert has noticed it too, I can see that from the way he looks at the child . . .'

Hubert, in any case, was no longer admitted to the marriage bed and he did not fail to look elsewhere for consolation. In the letters, he was not Hubert any more, but H . . .

'Poor H. has a new folly and I suspect that she is making him suffer. He is growing visibly thinner and becoming more and more irritable . . .'

Follies of this kind recurred every five or six months. For his part, Armand de Saint-Hilaire, in his letters, obviously made no attempt to convince his correspondent that he was leading a life of chastity.

Isabelle wrote to him, for instance:

'I hope that the women of Turkey are not as unapproachable as people say and above all that their husbands are not too ferocious . . .'

She added:

'*Be careful, friend. Every morning, I pray for you . . .*'

When he was French Minister in Cuba, then Ambassador in Buenos Aires, she worried about the women of Spanish blood.

'*They are so beautiful! And I, far away and forgotten, tremble at the idea that one day you may fall in love . . .*'

She showed an interest in his health.

'*Are your boils still giving you trouble? In this heat, they must be . . .*'

She knew Jaquette.

'*I am writing to Jaquette to give her the recipe for the almond tart you like so much . . .*'

'Hadn't she promised her husband never to see Saint-Hilaire again? . . . Listen to this . . . It's from a letter sent to this address:

'"*What an ineffable yet painful joy it was for me yesterday to see you from a distance at the Opera . . . I like your greying temples, and a slight paunch gives you an incomparable air of dignity . . . All evening I was proud of you . . . It was only when I got back to the Rue de Varenne and looked at myself in the mirror that I felt frightened . . . How could I have failed to disappoint you? . . . Women fade quickly and I am now almost an old woman . . .*"'

They had seen each other like that, from a distance, fairly frequently. They even gave each other assignations of a sort.

'*Tomorrow, about three o'clock, I shall go for a walk in the Tuileries Gardens with my son . . .*'

Saint-Hilaire, for his part, passed underneath her windows at times fixed in advance.

When her son was about ten years old, there was a characteristic reference to him which Maigret read out aloud.

'*Philippe, finding me busy writing once more, asked me innocently: "Are you writing to your sweetheart again?"*'

Maigret heaved a sigh, mopped his forehead, and tied the bundles up again one after another.

'Try to get me Doctor Tudelle on the phone.'

He needed to find himself back on solid ground. The letters had been returned to their place in the bookcase and he promised himself not to touch them again.

'He's on the line, Chief . . .'

'Hullo, doctor . . . Yes, Maigret speaking . . . You finished ten minutes ago? . . . No, of course I'm not asking you for all the details . . .'

While he was listening, he scribbled words and meaningless symbols on Saint-Hilaire's pad.

'You're sure of that? . . . You've already sent the bullets to Gastine-Renette? . . . I'll phone him a little later . . . Thank you . . . The best thing to do would be to send your report to the examining magistrate . . . That would please him . . . Thank you again . . .'

He started walking up and down the room with his hands behind his back, stopping now and then to look at the garden where a cheeky blackbird was hopping around in the grass a few feet away from him.

'The first bullet,' he explained to Janvier, 'was fired from the front, practically at point-blank range . . . It's a .301 bullet in a nickel-plated copper envelope . . . Tudelle isn't as experienced as Doctor Paul yet, but he's pretty certain that it was fired from a Browning automatic . . . He's absolutely definite on one point: that first bullet caused almost instantaneous death. The body fell forward and slipped from the arm-chair on to the carpet . . .'

'How does he know?'

'Because the other shots were fired from above.'

'How many others?'

'Three. Two in the stomach and one in the shoulder. Seeing that automatics hold six cartridges, or seven if you slip one into the barrel, I wonder why the murderer suddenly stopped firing after the fourth bullet. Unless of course the gun jammed . . .'

He glanced at the carpet, which had been cleaned after a fashion, but where the outline of the bloodstains was still visible.

'Either the killer wanted to make sure that his victim was dead, or else he was in such a state of excitement that he went on firing automatically. Get me Moers, will you?'

He had been too impressed, that morning, by the unusual aspect of the case to attend to the material clues himself, and he had left all that to the experts from the Criminal Records Office.

'Moers? . . . Yes . . . How are you getting on? . . . Yes, of course . . . First of all, did you find the cartridge-cases in the study? . . . No? . . . Not one? . . .'

That was strange and seemed to suggest that the murderer knew that he was not going to be disturbed. After four loud shots—very loud shots if the gun was a .301 automatic—he had taken the time to search the room for the cartridge-cases which would have been ejected quite a long way.

'The doorhandle?'

'The only prints that are reasonably clear are the servant's.'

'The brandy-glass?'

'The dead man's prints.'

'The desk and the rest of the furniture?'

'Not a thing, Chief. I mean there aren't any foreign prints apart from yours.'

'The lock and the windows?'

'The enlargements of our photos show no signs of a forced entry.'

Isabelle's letters might not resemble those of the lovers Maigret usually had to deal with, but the crime was real enough.

Two details, however, seemed at first sight to contradict one another. The murderer had gone on firing at a dead man, at a man who had stopped moving and who, with his head shattered, presented a horrifying sight. Maigret remembered the white hair, still quite plentiful, sticking to the gaping skull, one eye which had stayed open, and a bone protruding from the torn cheek.

The medical expert stated that after the first shot the corpse was on the floor, in front of the arm-chair, in the place where it had been found.

This meant that the murderer, who had probably been standing on the other side of the desk, had walked round in order to fire again once, twice, three times, from above, at close quarters, less than two feet away according to Tudelle.

At that distance, there was no need to take aim in order to hit a given spot. In other words, it seemed that he had hit the chest and stomach on purpose.

Didn't that suggest an act of vengeance, or an exceptional degree of hatred?

'You're sure there isn't a gun anywhere in the flat? You hunted everywhere?'

'Even up the chimney,' answered Janvier.

Maigret too had looked for the automatic which the old servant had mentioned, admittedly in rather vague terms.

'Go and ask the policeman on duty at the door if it isn't a .301 that he's carrying in his holster.'

A good many uniformed policemen were equipped with a gun of that calibre.

'Get him to lend it to you for a minute.'

He too went out of the study, crossed the corridor, and pushed open the door of the kitchen, where Jaquette Larrieu was sitting on a chair, holding herself very stiffly. Her eyes were shut and she looked as if she were asleep. She started at the noise.

'Will you come with me . . .'

'Where?'

'Into the study. I should like to ask you a few questions.'

'I have already told you that I don't know anything.'

Once in the room, she looked all round her as if to make sure that nothing had been disturbed.

'Sit down.'

She hesitated, unaccustomed, no doubt, to sitting down in this room in her employer's presence.

'In that chair, please . . .'

She obeyed reluctantly, looking at the chief-inspector more suspiciously than ever.

Janvier came back with an automatic in his hand.

'Give it to her.'

She shrank from taking it, opened her mouth to say something, then shut it again. Maigret could have sworn that she had been on the point of asking:

'Where did you find it?'

The weapon fascinated her. She found it difficult to take her eyes off it.

'You recognize this gun?'

'How can you expect me to recognize it? I have never examined it closely and I don't imagine it's the only one of its kind.'

'It *is* the type of weapon the Count possessed, though?'

'I suppose so.'

'The same size?'

'I can't say.'

'Hold it in your hand. Is it roughly the same weight?'

She flatly refused to do what they asked.

'It wouldn't be any use, seeing that I have never touched the one that was in the drawer.'

'You can take it back to the policeman, Janvier.'

'You don't need me any more?'

'Stay where you are, please. I suppose you don't know whether your master ever gave or lent his pistol to anybody, to his nephew for instance, or to somebody else?'

'How should I know? All I know is that I haven't seen it for a long time.'

'Was the Comte de Saint-Hilaire afraid of burglars?'

'Certainly not. Neither burglars nor murderers. The proof of that is that in summer he used to sleep with his window open, even though we are on the ground floor and anybody could have got into his bedroom.'

'He didn't keep any valuables in the flat?'

'You and your men know better than I do what there is there.'

'When did you enter his service?'

'Straight after the 1914 war. He had just come back from abroad. His valet had died.'

'Then you were about twenty years old at the time?'

'Twenty-eight.'

'How long had you been in Paris?'

'A few months. Before that, I had lived with my father in Normandy. When my father died, I had to find a job.'

'Had you had any affairs?'

'What did you say?'

'I asked you whether you had had any sweethearts, or a fiancé.'

She looked at him resentfully.

'Nothing like what you are thinking.'

'So you lived alone in this flat with the Comte de Saint-Hilaire?'

'Is there anything wrong in that?'

Maigret was not asking questions in any logical order, for nothing struck him as logical in this case, and he moved from one subject to another as if he were looking for the tender spot. Janvier, who had come back into the room, had sat down near the door. When he lit a cigarette and dropped the match on the floor, the old woman, who did not miss anything, called him to order.

'You might use an ash-tray.'

'Incidentally, did your master smoke?'

'He did for a long time.'

'Cigarettes?'

'Cigars.'

'And recently he stopped smoking?'

'Yes. On account of his chronic bronchitis.'

'But he seemed to be in excellent health.'

Doctor Tudelle had told Maigret, over the telephone, that Saint-Hilaire had obviously enjoyed exceptionally good health.

'A sound body, the heart in perfect condition, no sign of sclerosis.'

But certain organs had been too badly damaged by the bullets to allow a complete diagnosis.

'When you entered his service, he was almost a young man.'

'He was seven years older than me.'

'You knew that he was in love?'

'I used to post his letters for him.'

'You weren't jealous?'

'Why should I have been jealous?'

'You never happened to see the person he wrote to every day here in this flat?'

'She has never set foot in the flat.'

'But you have seen her?'

She made no reply.

'Answer my question. When the case goes to the Assizes, you will be asked much more embarrassing questions and you won't be allowed to remain silent.'

'I don't know anything.'

'I asked you whether you had seen this person.'

'Yes. She used to go past in the street. Sometimes too I took letters to her and delivered them to her personally.'

'In secret?'

'No. I asked to see her and I was taken along to her rooms.'

'Did she talk to you?'

'Sometimes she asked me questions.'

'You are talking about forty years ago, I suppose?'

'Then and more recently.'

'What sort of questions did she ask?'

'Mostly about Monsieur le Comte's health.'

'Not about the people who came here?'

'No.'

'You accompanied your master abroad?'

'Everywhere!'

'As Minister, and later as Ambassador, he had to keep up a large establishment. What exactly was your function?'

'I looked after him.'

'You mean to say that you were not on the same footing as the other servants, that you didn't have to bother about the cooking, the cleaning, the receptions?'

'I supervised.'

'What was your title? Housekeeper?'

'I didn't have a title.'

'Have you had any lovers?'

She stiffened, her eyes more contemptuous than ever.

'Were you his mistress?'

Maigret was afraid that she was going to hurl herself at him with all her claws bared.

'I know from his correspondence,' he went on, 'that he had several affairs.'

'He had a right to, hadn't he?'

'Were you jealous?'

'I sometimes had to show certain persons the door, because they weren't suitable for him and because they would have made trouble for him.'

'In other words, you looked after his private life.'

'He was too good-natured. He had remained very naïve.'

'Yet he filled the delicate role of ambassador with considerable distinction.'

'That isn't the same thing.'

'You never left him?'

'Do the letters say I did?'

It was Maigret's turn not to reply, to insist:

'How long were you parted from him?'

'Five months.'

'When was that?'

'When he was Minister in Cuba.'

'Why?'

'Because of a woman who insisted on him getting rid of me.'

'What sort of woman?'

Silence.

'Why couldn't she stand you? Did she live with him?'

'She came to see him every day and often spent the night at the Legation.'

'Where did you go?'

'I took a little room near the Prado.'

'Did your master come to see you there?'

'He didn't dare. He just used to ring me up to ask me to be patient. He knew perfectly well that it wouldn't last. All the same, I bought my ticket to go back to Europe.'

'But you didn't go?'

'He came to fetch me the day before I was due to leave.'

'Do you know Prince Philippe?'

'If you've really read the letters, you don't need to ask me all these questions. It shouldn't be allowed, going through somebody's correspondence after he's dead.'

'You haven't answered my question.'

'I used to see him when he was young.'

'Where?'

'In the Rue de Varenne. He was often with his mother.'

'You didn't think of ringing up the Princess this morning, before going to the Quai d'Orsay?'

She looked at him full in the face, without flinching.

'Why didn't you, seeing that by your account, you had served for a long time as a link between them?'

'Because today was the day of the funeral.'

'And later this morning, while we were out of the house, weren't you tempted to tell her what had happened?'

She stared at the telephone.

'There has always been somebody in the study.'

There was a knock at the door. It was the policeman on duty in the street.

'I don't know if this is of any interest to you. I thought you might like to see the paper.'

It was an early edition of an evening paper which must have come out an hour before. A fairly prominent headline across two columns at the bottom of the front page announced:

MYSTERIOUS DEATH OF AMBASSADOR

The text was brief.

This morning, at his home in the Rue Saint-Dominique, the body was discovered of the Comte Armand de Saint-Hilaire, who for many years served as French Ambassador in various capitals, including Rome, London and Washington.

'Since his retirement some years ago, Armand de Saint-Hilaire had published two volumes of memoirs, and he was correcting proofs of a third volume when, so it seems, he was murdered.

'The crime was discovered early this morning by an old servant.

'It is not yet known whether some mysterious motive is to be looked for.'

He handed the paper to Jaquette, and looked hesitantly at the telephone. He wondered whether they had read the paper in the Rue de Varenne, or whether somebody had already told Isabelle the news.

In that case, how was she going to react? Would she dare to come here herself? Would she send her son to make inquiries? Or would she just sit and wait in the silence of her house, where, as a sign of mourning, the shutters had doubtless been closed?

Shouldn't Maigret . . .

He stood up, annoyed with himself, annoyed with everything, and went and planted himself in front of the French window, knocking his pipe out on his heel, to Jaquette's indignation.

IV

THE old woman, a small, erect figure on her chair, listened in amazement to the chief-inspector's voice, which had assumed a tone which she had not heard before. Admittedly it was not to her that Maigret was speaking, but to an invisible person at the other end of the line.

'No, Monsieur Cromières, I haven't issued any statement to the Press, and I haven't invited any reporters or photographers along as Ministers are so fond of doing. As for your second question, I haven't anything new to tell you, nor any ideas, as you put it, and if I discover anything I shall report it immediately to the examining magistrate . . .'

He intercepted a furtive glance from Jaquette in Janvier's direction. She seemed to be calling the latter to witness the chief-inspector's ill-concealed anger, and there was a faint smile on her lips, rather as if she were saying to the inspector:

'Well, well! Just listen to your chief!'

Maigret took his companion out into the corridor.

'I'm going to nip round to the solicitor's. Go on asking her questions, not pressing her too hard, but gently—you know what I mean. You may appeal to her more than I do.'

It was true. If he had realized, before setting out that morning, that he was going to have to deal with a tough old maid, he would have brought along young Lapointe rather than Janvier, because, of all the inspectors at Police Headquarters, it was Lapointe who had the greatest success with middle-aged women. One had actually said to him, shaking her head sadly:

'I wonder how a well-bred young man like you can carry on this profession!'

She had added:

'I'm sure it must go against the grain!'

The chief-inspector found himself in the street again, where the reporters had left one of their number on duty while they went to have a drink in a nearby pub.

'Nothing new, old chap . . . It isn't worth your while to follow me . . .'

He was not going far. There was never any need to go far in this case. It was as if, for all those who were remotely or closely connected with it, Paris were reduced to a few aristocratic streets.

The solicitor's house, in the Rue de Villersexel, was of the same period and the same style as that in the Rue Saint-Dominique, with a carriage entrance too, a wide staircase with a red carpet, and a lift which probably went up smoothly and noiselessly. He did not need to use it, for the office was on the first floor. The brass handles of the double doors were highly polished, as was the plate asking visitors to go in without ringing.

'If I find myself faced with another old man . . .'

He was pleasantly surprised to see, among the clerks, a good-looking woman of about thirty.

'Maître Aubonnet, please!'

True, the office was a little too quiet, a trifle austere, but he was not kept waiting and was shown almost immediately into a huge room where a man aged forty-five at the most stood up to greet him.

'Chief-Inspector Maigret . . . I have come to see you about one of your clients, the Comte de Saint-Hilaire . . .'

The other man replied with a smile:

'In that case, it isn't a matter for me but for my father. I'll go and see if he's available just now.'

The younger Maître Aubonnet went into another room and stayed there for some time.

'Will you come this way, Monsieur Maigret . . .'

This time, of course, the chief-inspector found himself in the presence of a real old man, who was not even in very good condition. The elder Aubonnet was sitting in a high-backed arm-chair, blinking his eyes with the bewildered expression of a man who has just been roused from his afternoon nap.

Maître Aubonnet had obviously been very fat at one time. He had retained a certain corpulence, but his body was flabby, with folds every-where. He was wearing a shoe on one foot and a felt slipper on the other, the ankle of which was swollen.

'I suppose you've come to talk to me about my poor old friend? . . .'

The mouth was slack too, and the syllables which emerged from it formed a sort of paste. On the other hand, there was no need to ask any questions to start him talking.

'Just imagine, Saint-Hilaire and I first met at Stanislas . . . That's how many years ago? . . . Wait a moment . . . I'm seventy-seven . . . So it's sixty years now since we were in the sixth form together . . . He intended to enter the Foreign Service . . . My own dream was to join the Saumur cavalry . . . They still had horses in those days . . . They weren't all motorized . . . You know, I've never had a chance to do any riding in the whole of my life? . . . All because I was an only son and I had to take over my father's office . . .'

Maigret forbore to ask him whether this father of his was already liv-ing in the same house at that time.

'Even in his school-days, Saint-Hilaire was a *bon vivant*, but a *bon vivant* of a rather rare type, a person of tremendous distinction . . .'

'I suppose he has left a will with you?'

'His nephew, young Mazeron, asked me the same question just now. I was able to set his mind at rest . . .'

'Does the nephew inherit everything?'

'Not the whole estate, no. I know the will by heart, since it was I who drew it up.'

'A long time ago?'

'The last will dates back ten years or so.'

'Were the previous wills different?'

'Only in minor particulars. I wasn't able to show the nephew the doc-ument, seeing that all the interested parties have to be present.'

'Who are they?'

'Broadly speaking, Alain Mazeron inherits the block of flats in the Rue Saint-Dominique and the bulk of the fortune, which in any case isn't very great. Jaquette Larrieu, the housekeeper, receives a pension which will enable her to end her days in comfort. As for the furniture, knick-knacks, pictures, and personal belongings, Saint-Hilaire be-queaths them to an old friend . . .'

'Isabelle de V——.'

'I see you know all about it.'

'Do you know her?'

'Fairly well. I knew her husband better, because he was one of my clients.'

Wasn't it rather surprising to see the two men choosing the same solicitor?

'They weren't afraid of running into each other in your office?'

'That never happened. The idea that it might probably never occurred to them, and I don't know that they would have found it terribly embarrassing. You see, they were made, if not to be friends, at least to have a high regard for each other, for they were both of them men of honour and, what is more, men of taste . . .'

Even the words he used seemed to come from the past. It was a long time, in fact, since Maigret had last heard the expression *man of honour*.

The old solicitor, in his arm-chair, shook with silent laughter at a fleeting thought.

'Men of taste, yes,' he repeated maliciously, 'and you could add that in one respect they had identical tastes . . . Now they are dead, I don't think I am betraying a professional secret in telling you this, particularly as you too are obliged to be discreet . . . A solicitor is nearly always a confidant . . . Apart from that, Saint-Hilaire was an old friend who used to come and tell me all about his pranks . . . For about a year, the Prince and he had the same mistress, a lovely girl with an opulent bosom who was appearing in some boulevard revue or other . . . They didn't know . . . Each had his own day . . .'

The old man gave Maigret a meaning look.

'Those people knew how to live . . . For several years now, I have had hardly anything to do with the office, where my eldest son has taken my place . . . All the same, I come downstairs to my office every day and I go on helping my old clients . . .'

'Did Saint-Hilaire have many friends?'

'The same was true of his friends as of the clients I mentioned just now. At our age, you see people dying off one after another. I do believe that in the end I was the last person he used to visit. He had kept the full use of his legs, and he still went for a walk every day. He sometimes came up here to see me, sitting where you are sitting now . . .'

'What did you talk about?'

'About the old days, of course, and especially the boys we knew at Stanislas. I could still give you most of the names. It's astonishing, how many of them have had distinguished careers. One of our schoolmates, who wasn't the most intelligent, was Prime Minister I don't know how many times and died only last year. Another is a military member of the Academy . . .'

'Had Saint-Hilaire made any enemies?'

'How could he have made any? On the professional level, he never jostled anybody out of a position, as is so often the case nowadays. He obtained his posts by patiently waiting his turn. And in his memoirs, he didn't pay off any old scores, which explains why few people have read them . . .'

'And what about the V——'s?'

The solicitor looked at him in surprise.

'I've already spoken to you about the Prince. He knew the whole story, of course, and he knew that Saint-Hilaire would keep his word. If it hadn't been for society, I'm convinced that Armand would have been received at the house in the Rue de Varenne and that he might even have had his place at table there.'

'The son knows all about it too?'

'Certainly.'

'What is he like?'

'I don't think he has anything like his father's intelligence. It's true that I don't know him as well as I knew his father. He seems far less communicative, which is probably due to the difficulty, in our day and age, of bearing a name as heavy as his. Social life doesn't interest him. He is very rarely to be seen in Paris. He spends most of the year in Normandy, with his wife and children, looking after his farms and his horses . . .'

'Have you seen him recently?'

'I shall be seeing him tomorrow, as well as his mother, at the reading of the will, so that I shall probably have to deal with both estates on the same day.'

'The Princess hasn't rung you up this afternoon?'

'Not yet. If she reads the papers, or if somebody tells her the news, she will doubtless get in touch with me. I still can't understand why anybody should murder my old friend. If it had happened anywhere except in his own home, I should have sworn that the murderer had killed the wrong person by mistake.'

'I suppose Jaquette Larrieu was his mistress?'

'That isn't the right word. Mind you, Saint-Hilaire never talked to me about her. But I knew him. I knew Jaquette too, when she was young, and she was a very pretty girl. Now, Armand rarely let a pretty girl come within reach without trying his luck. He did that in an aesthetic spirit, if you see what I mean. And it's more than likely that, if the opportunity occurred . . .'

'Jaquette hasn't any relatives?'

'I don't know of any. If she had any brothers and sisters, the odds are that they died a long time ago.'

'Thank you very much . . .'

'I suppose you are in a hurry? In any case, don't forget that I remain entirely at your service. You look a decent fellow too, and I hope you find the scoundrel who's responsible.'

Always this impression of being immersed in a distant past, in a world which had, so to speak, vanished. It was bewildering to find oneself back in the street, in a living Paris, with women in tight-fitting trousers doing their shopping, bars full of nickel-plated furniture, cars throbbing in front of traffic-lights.

He made for the Rue Jacob, but all in vain, for on the door of the shuttered shop he found a card framed in black which announced: 'Closed on account of death in the family.'

He pressed the bell several times without getting any reply, and crossed over to the other pavement to look at the windows on the first floor. They were open but there was no sound to be heard. A woman with copper-coloured hair and big, slack breasts, emerged from the darkness of a picture-gallery.

'If it's Monsieur Mazeron you want, he isn't at home. I saw him go off about midday after closing his shutters.'

She didn't know where he had gone.

'He doesn't talk much to other people . . .'

Maigret could go and see Isabelle de V—— of course, but the thought of that particular visit daunted him slightly, and he preferred to put it off until later, trying in the meantime to find out a little more.

He had rarely felt so nonplussed by other human beings. Would a psychiatrist, a schoolmaster or a novelist, to quote the list in the *Lancet*, have been in a better position to understand people from another century?

One thing was certain: the Comte Armand de Saint-Hilaire, a gentle, inoffensive old fellow, a man of honour, to use the solicitor's expression, had been murdered, in his own house, by somebody about whom he had no suspicions.

The possibility that this was an unpremeditated, accidental crime, a stupid, anonymous murder, could be ruled out, first of all because nothing had disappeared, and secondly because the former ambassador had been sitting peacefully at his desk when the first bullet, fired at close quarters, had struck him in the face.

Either he had gone to open the door to his visitor himself, or else the latter had a key to the flat, although Jaquette maintained that there were only two keys in existence, hers and the Count's.

Maigret, still turning over these rather confused thoughts in his head, went into a bar, ordered a glass of beer and shut himself up in the call-box.

'Is that you, Moers? . . . Have you got the inventory in front of you? . . . Will you look and see if there's any mention of a key . . . The key to the flat, yes . . . What's that? . . . Yes? . . . Where did they find it? . . . In his trouser-pocket? . . . Thank you . . . Nothing new? . . . No . . . I shall be coming back to the Quai late in the day . . . If you've anything to tell me, ring Janvier, who has stayed behind in the Rue Saint-Dominique . . .'

They had found one of the two keys in the dead man's trouser-pocket, and Jaquette had hers too, since she had used it to open the door that morning, when Maigret and the man from the Foreign Office had followed her into the ground-floor flat.

People didn't commit murder without a motive. What remained, once theft had been ruled out? A crime of passion, between two old men? A matter of money?

Jaquette Larrieu, according to the solicitor, received a more than adequate pension for the rest of her life.

The nephew, for his part, inherited the block of flats and the bulk of the estate.

As for Isabelle, it was hard to imagine that, almost immediately after her husband's death, the idea should have occurred to her . . .

No, there was no satisfactory explanation, and the Quai d'Orsay for its part categorically ruled out any political motive.

'Rue de la Pompe!' he said to the driver of a yellow taxi.

'Right, Chief-Inspector.'

A long time ago now, he had stopped feeling flattered at being recognized like that. The concierge directed him to the fifth floor, where a pretty little brunette began by opening the door an inch or so before showing Maigret into a flat which was ablaze with sunshine.

'Excuse the mess . . . I was busy making a dress for my daughter . . .'

She was wearing tight-fitting trousers in black silk which showed the shape of her plump buttocks.

'I suppose you've come to see me about the murder, though I don't know what you hope to find out from me.'

'Your children aren't here?'

'My elder daughter is in England to learn the language. She's living with a family, *au pair*, and my younger daughter is working. It's for her that I'm . . .'

She pointed to the table, where there was some light, coloured material out of which she was cutting a dress.

'I suppose you've seen my husband?'

'Yes.'

'How is he taking it?'

'Is it a long time since you last saw him?'

'Nearly three years.'

'And the Comte de Saint-Hilaire?'

'The last time he came up here was just before Christmas. He brought some presents for my daughters. He never failed to remember. Even when he was in some post abroad and they were still little, he didn't forget them at Christmas and always sent them some small gift. That's how they come to have dolls from all over the world. You can still see them in their room.'

She was not more than forty years old and she had remained extremely attractive.

'Is it true, what the papers say? He was murdered?'

'Tell me about your husband.'

The life promptly went out of her face.

'What do you want me to say?'

'You married for love, didn't you? Unless I'm mistaken, he is much older than you.'

'Only ten years. He has always looked older than he is.'

'You loved him?'

'I don't know. I was living alone with my father, who was sour and embittered. He regarded himself as a great painter who wasn't appreciated at his true value, and it grieved him to earn his living by restoring pictures. I for my part worked in a shop on the Grands Boulevards. I met Alain. Aren't you thirsty?'

'No thank you. I've just had a glass of beer. Go on . . .'

'Perhaps it was the air of mystery about him that attracted me. He wasn't like other men, he talked very little, and what he said was always interesting. We got married and had a daughter straight away . . .'

'You lived in the Rue Jacob?'

'Yes. I liked that street too, and our little first-floor flat. At that time, the Comte de Saint-Hilaire was still an ambassador, in Washington, unless I'm mistaken. During one of his leaves he came to see us, and later he invited us to the Rue Saint-Dominique. I was very impressed by him.'

'How did he get on with your husband?'

'I can't really say. He was a man who was pleasant with everybody. He seemed surprised that I should be his nephew's wife.'

'Why?'

'It was only much later that I thought I understood, and I'm still not sure. He must have known Alain better than I thought, certainly better than I did at the time . . .'

She broke off, as if she were worried about what she had just said.

'I don't want to give you the impression that I'm talking like this out of spite, because my husband and I are separated. Besides, I'm the one who left.'

'And he didn't try to stop you?'

Here the furniture was modern, the walls light-coloured, and he could see part of a neat white kitchen. Familiar noises rose from the street and nearby was the green expanse of the Bois de Boulogne.

'I trust you don't suspect Alain?'

'To be perfectly frank, I don't suspect anybody yet, but I'm not ruling out any hypothesis *a priori*.'

'You'd be on the wrong track if you did, I'm sure of that. In my opinion, Alain is a poor devil who has never been able to adjust himself to life and never will be able to adjust himself. It's surprising, isn't it, that after leaving my father because he was embittered I should marry a man even more embittered than he was? It was a long time before I really noticed. The fact of the matter is, I've never seen him satisfied with anything, and I wonder now if he has ever smiled in the whole of his life.

'He worries about everything, about his health and his business, about what people think of him, about the way neighbours and customers look at him . . .

'Everybody, he imagines, has a grudge against him.

'It's difficult to explain. You mustn't laugh at what I'm going to say. When I was living with him, I had the impression that I could hear him thinking from morning till night, and it was a sound as nerve-racking as the ticking of an alarm-clock. He used to come and go in silence, looking at me all of a sudden as if his eyes were turned towards the inside where I couldn't tell what was happening. Is he still as pale as ever?'

'He is pale, yes.'

'He was already when I met him, and he stayed that way in the country and at the seaside. It was like an artificial pallor . . .

'And nothing showed outside. It was impossible to make contact with him . . . For years we slept in the same bed and sometimes, when I woke up, I found myself looking at him as if he were a stranger.

'He was cruel . . .'

She tried to take the word back.

'I'm probably exaggerating. He thought that he was fair, and he wanted to be fair at all costs. It was a mania with him. He was scrupulously fair and that's what made me talk about cruelty. I noticed it most of all when we had the children. He regarded them in the same way as he regarded me and other people, with a cold lucidity. If they did something naughty, I tried to defend them.

' "At their age, Alain . . ."

' "*There's no reason why they should get into the habit of cheating.*"

'That was one of his favourite words, Cheating . . . Dirty tricks . . .

'He was just as strict about the little details of everyday life:

' "*Why did you buy fish?*"

'I tried to explain that . . .

' "*I said veal.*"

' "When I went to do my shopping . . ."

'He stubbornly repeated:

' "*I said veal, and you had no business to buy fish.*" '

She broke off again.

'I'm not talking too much, am I? I'm not saying silly things?'

'Go on.'

'I've finished. After a few years, I thought I could understand what the Americans mean by mental cruelty and why it has become grounds for divorce over there. There are schoolteachers, both men and women, who, without raising their voices, can impose a sort of reign of terror on their class.

'With Alain, we felt suffocated, my daughters and I, and we didn't even have the consolation of seeing him go off to the office every morning. He was downstairs, under our feet, from morning till night, coming upstairs ten times a day to watch what we were doing with cold eyes.

'I had to account to him for every franc I spent. When I went out, he insisted on knowing which way I was going to go, and when I got back he questioned me about the people I had spoken to, what I had said to them and what they had replied . . .'

'Were you unfaithful to him?'

She showed no indignation. Indeed, it seemed to Maigret that she was tempted to smile with a certain satisfaction, even a certain pleasure, but that she restrained herself.

'Why do you ask me that? Has somebody told you something about me?'

'No.'

'As long as I was living with him, I didn't do anything he could hold against me.'

'What made you decide to leave him?'

'I was at the end of my tether. I was suffocating, as I told you, and I wanted my daughters to grow up in an atmosphere they could breathe freely.'

'You hadn't a more personal reason for wanting to regain your freedom?'

'Perhaps.'

'Your daughters know about it?'

'I haven't concealed the fact from them that I have a lover, and they back me up.'

'He lives with you?'

'I go and see him in his flat. He's a widower of my age, who hadn't been any happier with his wife than I had with my husband, so that it's rather as if we were sticking the bits together again.'

'Does he live in this district?'

'In this building, two floors down. He's a doctor. You'll see his plate on the door. If, one day, Alain agrees to a divorce, we intend to get married, but I doubt if he will ever do that. He's very Catholic, out of tradition rather than conviction.'

'Does your husband earn a good living?'

'He has his ups and downs. When I left him, it was agreed that he would pay me a modest allowance for the children. He kept his word for a few months. Then there were some delays. And finally he stopped paying completely, on the pretext that they were big enough to earn their living. But that doesn't make him a murderer, does it?'

'Did you know about his uncle's liaison?'

'Are you talking about Isabelle?'

'Had you heard that the Prince de V—— died on Sunday morning and that he was buried today?'

'I read it in the paper.'

'Do you think that if Saint-Hilaire hadn't been killed he would have married the Princess?'

'Probably. All his life he had hoped that they would be united one day. I found it touching to hear him talking about her as if she were a woman in a class apart, an almost supernatural creature, when he was a man who appreciated the realities of life, sometimes even a little too much . . .'

This time she smiled openly.

'One day, a long time ago, when I went to see him about something or other, I forget what, I had a job to escape from his clutches. He was a cool customer, and no mistake. In his eyes, it was perfectly normal . . .'

'Did your husband find out?'

She shrugged her shoulders.

'Of course not.'

'He was jealous?'

'In his fashion. We didn't often have intercourse, and it was always cold, almost mechanical. What he would have condemned wasn't that I should be attracted by another man but that I should be guilty of a misdemeanour, a sin, an act of treachery, something he regarded as unclean. Forgive me if I've talked too much or if I've given the impression of wanting to do him down, because that isn't the case. You've seen that I haven't made myself out to be better than I am. I shan't go on feeling a real woman much longer, and I'm making the most of it while I can . . .'

She had a sensual mouth and sparkling eyes. For several minutes she had kept crossing and uncrossing her legs.

'You are sure you won't have something to drink?'

'No thank you. It's time I was going.'

'I assume all this remains confidential?'

He smiled at her and made for the door, where she gave him a hot, plump hand.

'I must carry on with my daughter's dress,' she said, almost regretfully.

So he had managed, after all, to escape for a moment from the circle of old people. Leaving the flat in the Rue de la Pompe, it was without any feeling of surprise that he found himself back in the street, among all its noises and smells.

He found a taxi straight away and told the driver to take him to the Rue Saint-Dominique. Before going into the block of flats, he decided after all to go and have the glass of beer which he had refused at Madame Mazeron's, and in the bar he rubbed shoulders with chauffeurs from the ministries and great houses.

The reporter was still at his post.

'You can see that I didn't try to follow you. You can't tell me whom you've been to see?'

'The solicitor.'

'Did he tell you anything new?'

'Not a thing.'

'Still no clues?'

'No.'

'And it isn't a political affair?'

'Apparently not.'

The uniformed policeman was there too. Maigret rang the bell, next to the lift-shaft. It was Janvier, in his shirt-sleeves, who opened the door to him, and Jaquette was not in the study.

'What have you done with her? Have you let her go out?'

'No. She tried to, after the phone call, saying that there was nothing left to eat in the house.'

'Where is she?'

'In her room. She's resting.'

'What phone call are you talking about?'

'Half an hour after you had gone, the phone rang, and I answered it. I heard a woman's voice, a rather quiet voice, at the other end of the line.'

'"Who is that?" she asked.

'Instead of answering, I asked in my turn:

'"Who is calling?"

'"I should like to speak to Mademoiselle Larrieu."

'"Who shall I say?"

'There was a silence, then:

'"The Princesse de V——."

'All this time, Jaquette had been looking at me as if she knew what it was all about.

'"Here she is."

'I gave her the receiver and straight away she said:

'"It's me, Madame la Princesse . . . Yes . . . I would have come along, but these gentlemen won't allow me to go out . . . There were lots of them all over the flat, with all sorts of apparatus . . . They spent hours asking me questions and even now there's an inspector listening to me . . ."'

Janvier added:

'She looked as if she were defying me. After that, she listened most of the time.

'"Yes . . . Yes, Madame la Princesse . . . Yes . . . I understand . . . I don't know . . . No . . . Yes . . . I'll try . . . I should like to as well . . . Thank you, Madame la Princesse . . ."'

'What did she say then?'

'Nothing. She went back to her chair. After a quarter of an hour of silence, she muttered sadly:

'"I suppose you aren't going to let me get out? Even if there's nothing left to eat in the house and I have to go without my dinner?"

'"We'll see about that later on."

'"In that case, I don't see what we are doing sitting face to face like this, and I'd rather go and have a rest. Have I got your permission to do that?"

'Since then she has been in her room. She has locked the door.'

'Nobody has been?'

'No. There have been a few phone calls, from an American news agency and some provincial papers . . .'

'You didn't manage to get anything out of Jaquette?'

'I started asking her the most innocent questions imaginable, in the hope of winning her confidence. All that happened was that she said in a sarcastic voice:

'"Young man, you can't teach your grandmother to suck eggs. If your chief thought I was going to tell you some secrets . . ."'

'The Quai didn't ring at all?'

'No. Just the examining magistrate.'

'Does he want to see me?'

'He asked if you would call him if you had any news. Alain Mazeron has been to see him.'

'And you didn't tell me?'

'I was keeping it till the end. Apparently the nephew went to see him to complain that you had read Saint-Hilaire's private correspondence without his permission. As executor, he asked for seals to be affixed to the flat until the will had been read.'

'What did the magistrate say to him?'

'He told him to come and see you.'

'And Mazeron hasn't been back?'

'No. He may be on the way, because it isn't long since I had that phone call. Do you think he'll come?'

Maigret hesitated, and finally pulled a telephone directory towards him. After finding what he was looking for, standing there with a serious, preoccupied expression on his face, he dialled a number.

'Hullo. Is that the V—— residence? I should like to speak to the Princesse de V——. This is Chief-Inspector Maigret of the Judicial Police speaking . . . Yes, I'll hold the line . . .'

There was as it were a different kind of silence in the room, and Janvier held his breath as he looked at his chief. Several minutes went by.

'Yes, I'll wait . . . Thank you . . . Hullo . . . Yes, Madame, this is Chief-Inspector Maigret . . .'

It was not his everyday voice, and he felt a certain emotion as when, in his childhood, he had occasion to speak to the Comtesse de Saint-Fiacre.

'I thought that you might possibly wish me to get in touch with you, if only to give you a few details . . . Yes . . . Yes . . . When you wish . . . I will come to the Rue de Varenne then an hour from now . . .'

The two men looked at each other in silence. Finally Maigret heaved a sigh.

'You had better stay here,' he said in the end. 'Ring up Lucas and ask him to send you somebody, preferably Lapointe. The old girl can go out whenever she likes and one of the two of you will follow her.'

He had an hour to wait. To while away the time, he took a bundle of letters out of the bookcase with the green curtain.

Yesterday, at Longchamp, I caught sight of you in a morning coat, and you know how I like to see you dressed like that. You had a pretty redhead on your arm who . . .

V

MAIGRET did not expect to find a house that still smelt of the funeral, as in lower-class or even middle-class homes, with the scent of tapers and chrysanthemums, a red-eyed widow, and relatives from distant parts, dressed in deep mourning, sitting around eating and drinking. On account of his country childhood, the smell of alcohol, and especially that of marc-brandy, remained associated for him with death and funerals.

'Drink this, Catherine,' they used to say to the widow before setting off for the church and the cemetery. 'You need something to buck you up.'

She would drink up, weeping at the same time. The men used to drink at the local inn, and when they returned home.

If hangings decorated with silver tears had adorned the main entrance in the morning, they had been removed a long time ago and the courtyard had resumed its normal appearance, half in the shade, half in the sun, with a uniformed chauffeur washing a long black limousine, and three cars, including a yellow sports car, waiting at the foot of the steps.

It was as huge as the Elysée and Maigret remembered that the house had often served as the setting for balls and charity bazaars.

At the top of the steps, he pushed open a glass door and found himself all alone in an entrance-hall paved with marble. Double doors standing open on his left and right afforded him a glimpse of the state rooms in which various objects, no doubt the old coins and snuff-boxes which had been mentioned to him, were displayed as in a museum.

Should he make for one of those doors, or go up the double flight of stairs leading to the first floor? He was hesitating when a major-domo, appearing from heaven knows where, came up to him in silence, took his hat out of his hands, and without asking for his name murmured:

'This way.'

Maigret followed his guide up the staircase, across another drawing-room on the first floor, and then through a long room which was obviously a picture-gallery.

He was not kept waiting. The servant opened a door a little way, and announced in a soft voice:

'Chief-Inspector Maigret.'

The boudoir which he entered did not look out on to the courtyard but on to a garden, and the foliage of the trees, full of birds, brushed against the two open windows.

Somebody got up from an arm-chair and for a moment he failed to realize that it was the woman he had come to see, the Princess Isabelle. His surprise must have been obvious for as she came towards him she said:

'You expected me to look rather different, didn't you?'

He did not dare to say yes. He made no reply, taken aback by her appearance. In the first place, for all that she was dressed in black, she did not give the impression of being in deep mourning, though he would have been hard put to it to say why. She did not appear to be greatly distressed.

She was smaller than in the photographs, but, unlike Jaquette for instance, she was not bent under the weight of the years. He had no time to analyse his impressions. He would do that later. For the moment, he registered mechanically.

What surprised him most of all was finding a plump woman, with full, smooth cheeks and a dumpy body. Her hips, scarcely hinted at by the princess dress in the photograph in Saint-Hilaire's room, had become as broad as those of any farmer's wife.

Was the boudoir in which they were standing the room where she spent most of her life? There were old tapestries on the walls. The floor shone brightly and every piece of furniture was in its place, something which, for no particular reason, reminded Maigret of the convent where, in the past, he had sometimes visited an aunt of his who was a nun.

'Please take a seat.'

She pointed to a gilded arm-chair to which he preferred an upright chair, even though he was afraid of breaking its delicate legs.

'My first impulse was to go over there,' she confided to him, sitting down in her turn, 'but then I realized that he wouldn't be there any more. The body has been taken to the Morgue, I suppose?'

She was not afraid of words, nor of the pictures which they evoked. Her face was serene, almost joyful, and that too recalled the convent, the peculiar serenity of the good nuns who never really looked as if they belonged to this world.

'I badly want to see him one last time. I shall come back to that later. What I want to know first of all is whether he died in pain.'

'You can set your mind at rest, Madame. The Comte de Saint-Hilaire was killed instantly.'

'He was in his study?'

'Yes.'

'Sitting?'

'Yes. It seems that he was busy correcting proofs.'

She closed her eyes, as if to give the picture time to take shape in her mind, and Maigret made so bold as to ask a question in his turn.

'Have you ever been to the Rue Saint-Dominique?'

'Only once, a long time ago, with Jaquette's connivance. I had chosen a time when I was sure that he wouldn't be there. I wanted to see the setting of his life, so as to be able to visualize him at home, in the various rooms.'

An idea struck her.

'You mean you haven't read the letters?'

He hesitated, then decided to tell the truth.

'I've looked through them. Not all of them though . . .'

'Are they still in the Empire bookcase with the gilt lattice-work?'

He nodded.

'I thought that you would have read them. I don't hold it against you. I realize that it was your duty.'

'How did you hear about his death?'

'From my daughter-in-law. My son Philippe had come from Normandy with his wife and children to attend the funeral. A little while ago, after we had got back from the cemetery, my daughter-in-law happened to glance at one of the newspapers that the servants usually put out on a table in the hall.'

'Your daughter-in-law knows all about it?'

She looked at him with an astonishment which bordered on innocence. If he had not known who she was, he might well have thought that she was playing a part.

'All about what?'

'About your relationship with the Comte de Saint-Hilaire.'

Her smile too was a nun's smile.

'But of course. How could she have failed to know about it? We never made any attempt at concealment. There was nothing wrong about it. Armand was a very dear friend . . .'

'Did your son know him?'

'My son too knew all about it, and when he was a boy I sometimes pointed out Armand to him from a distance. I think the first time was at Auteuil . . .'

'He never went to see him?'

She replied, not without a certain logic, her own logic if nothing else:

'Whatever for?'

The birds went on twittering in the foliage and a pleasantly cool breeze came in from the garden.

'Won't you have a cup of tea?'

Alain Mazeron's wife, in the Rue de la Pompe, had offered him some beer. Here it was tea.

'No thank you.'

'Tell me all that you have discovered, Monsieur Maigret. You see, for fifty years, I have been accustomed to living in imagination with him. I knew what he was doing at every hour of the day. I visited the cities where he was living, when he was still an ambassador, and I arranged things with Jaquette so as to have a look inside all his successive houses. At what time was he killed?'

'As far as we can tell, between eleven o'clock and midnight.'

'Yet he wasn't ready to go to bed.'

'How do you know?'

'Because before going to his room he always wrote me a few words which finished his daily letter. He began it every morning with a ritual phrase:

' "*Good morning, Isi . . .*"

'Just as he would have greeted me if fate had allowed us to live together. He would add a few lines and then, during the day, he would come back to the letter to tell me what he had been doing. At night, his last words were invariably:

' "*Good night, pretty Isi . . .*" '

She gave an embarrassed smile.

'I must apologize for telling you something that probably makes you laugh. For him, I had remained the Isabelle of twenty.'

'He had seen you since.'

'Yes, from a distance. Consequently he knew that I had become an old woman, but for him the present was not as real as the past. Can you understand that? In the same way, he hadn't changed for me. But now tell me what happened. Tell me everything, without trying to spare my feelings. When a woman gets to my age, you know, it means that she is no weakling. Who was the murderer? How did he get in?'

'Somebody got in all right, seeing that no weapon has been found in the room or in the flat. As Jaquette maintained that she locked the door about nine o'clock as she does every night, bolting it and putting the chain on too, we are forced to conclude that the Comte de Saint-Hilaire let in his visitor himself. Do you know if he often received people in the evening?'

'Never. Since his retirement he had become very much a man of habit and he had adopted a daily routine that was practically invaria-

ble. I could show you the letters he wrote to me in the last few years
. . . You would see that the first sentence is often:

'"*Good morning, Isi . . . I send my usual morning greeting, since a
new day is beginning, while I, for my part, am beginning my monotonous circus routine . . .*"

'That was what he called his carefully planned days, in which there
was no room for the unexpected . . .

'Unless I receive a letter by this evening's post . . . But of course not!
It was Jaquette who posted them, in the morning, on her way to buy
croissants. If she had posted one this morning, she would have told me
on the telephone . . .'

'What do you think of her?'

'She was absolutely devoted to us, to Armand and me. When he
broke his arm, in Switzerland, it was she who wrote to me at his dicta-
tion, and when, later on, he underwent an operation, she sent me a
letter every day giving me the latest news.'

'You don't think she was jealous?'

She smiled again and Maigret found it hard to get used to it. This
calm and serenity surprised him, for he had been expecting a more or
less dramatic interview.

It was as if death, here, did not have the same meaning as it did elsewhere, as if Isabelle were living quite naturally with it, without fear,
regarding it as part of the normal course of life.

'She was jealous, but as a dog is jealous of its master.'

He hesitated to ask certain questions, to broach certain subjects, and
it was she who introduced them with a disarming simplicity.

'If, in the old days, she sometimes happened to be jealous in another
way, as a woman, it was of his mistresses, not of me.'

'Do you think she was his mistress once?'

'There can be no doubt about that.'

'He told you so in a letter?'

'He never concealed anything from me, even the humiliating things
which men hesitate to tell their wives. For instance, he wrote to me,
not so many years ago:

'"*Jaquette is nervy today. I must remember to pleasure her tonight . . .*"'

She seemed to be amused at Maigret's astonishment.

'Does it surprise you? Yet it's so natural.'

'You weren't jealous either?'

'Not of that. My only fear was that he might meet a woman capable of taking my place in his mind. Go on with what you were telling me, Chief-Inspector. You don't know anything about his visitor?'

'Only that he fired a first shot with a heavy-calibre weapon, probably a .301 automatic.'

'Where was Armand hit?'

'In the head. The medical expert says that death was instantaneous. The body slipped down on to the carpet, at the foot of the arm-chair. Then the murderer fired three more shots.'

'Why, since he was dead?'

'We don't know. Did the killer get into a panic? Was he in such a state of fury that he lost his self-control? It's difficult to answer that question as yet. At the Assizes, a murderer who has attacked his victim again and again, stabbing him for instance a good many times, is often accused of cruelty. Well, judging by my experience and that of my colleagues, it is nearly always timid characters—I hesitate to say sensitive types—who behave like that. They are panic-stricken, don't want to see their victims suffer, and lose their heads . . .'

'You think that that is what happened here?'

'Unless it is a case of revenge, of hatred held in check for a long time, something which is much rarer.'

He was beginning to feel at ease with this old woman who could say anything and hear anything.

'What would seem to contradict this theory is that the murderer, afterwards, had the presence of mind to pick up all the cartridge-cases. They must have been scattered all over the room, quite a way from the body. But he didn't miss a single one, nor did he leave any fingerprints. There remains one last question which puzzles me, especially after what you have just told me about your relations with Jaquette. After she had found the body, this morning, she doesn't seem to have thought of ringing you up and instead she went, not to the local police-station, but to the Foreign Office.'

'I think I can give you an explanation of that. Just after my husband's death, the telephone kept ringing nearly all the time. People we hardly knew wanted information about the funeral arrangements, or wanted to express their sympathy to me. My son decided to cut the telephone off.'

'So that Jaquette may have tried to ring you up?'

'Very probably. And if she didn't come herself to give me the news, it must have been because she knew that she would find it difficult to see me on the day of the funeral.'

'You don't know any enemies the Comte de Saint-Hilaire had?'

'Not one.'

'In his letters to you, did he sometimes mention his nephew?'

'Have you seen Alain?'

'This morning.'

'What did he say?'

'Nothing. He has been to see Maître Aubonnet. The will is going to be read tomorrow, and the solicitor will be getting in touch with you as your presence is necessary.'

'I know.'

'You know the terms of the will?'

'Armand insisted on leaving me his furniture, so that, if he happened to die before me, I should still have the impression to some extent of having been his wife.'

'Are you going to accept this bequest?'

'It was his wish, wasn't it? Mine too. If he hadn't died, once I had come out of mourning I should have become the Comtesse de Saint-Hilaire. That had always been agreed between us.'

'Your husband knew about your plans?'

'Of course.'

'Your son and daughter-in-law too?'

'Not only them, but all our friends. We had nothing to hide, as I said before. Now, on account of the name which I still bear, I shall be obliged to go on living in this big house instead of going and settling down, as I had often dreamed of doing, in the Rue Saint-Dominique. Armand's flat will be reconstructed here all the same. No doubt I haven't a very long time to live, but however little time I have left, I shall live in his setting, you understand, as if I were his widow.'

Maigret was experiencing a phenomenon which annoyed him intensely. To begin with he was captivated by this woman who was so different from anything he had known before. Not only by her, but by the legend which she and Saint-Hilaire had created and in which they had lived.

At first sight, it was as absurd as a fairy-story or those edifying tales in religious story-books.

Here, in front of her, he found himself believing in it. He began to adopt their way of seeing and feeling, rather as in his aunt's convent he used to walk on tiptoe and speak in a whisper, full of unctuous piety.

Then, all of a sudden, he looked at the old lady in a different way, with the eyes of a man from the Quai des Orfèvres, and he was filled with revulsion.

Were they making fun of him? Were all these people—Jaquette, Alain Mazeron, his wife in the tight-fitting trousers, Isabelle, and even the solicitor Aubonnet—in a conspiracy to fool him?

There was a dead man, a real corpse, with his skull shattered and his belly gaping open. That implied the existence of a murderer, and it could not have been any common criminal who had been able to gain entrance to the former ambassador's flat and kill him at point-blank range without his becoming suspicious and trying to defend himself.

Maigret had learnt, over the years, that people did not kill without a motive, without a serious motive. And even if, in this case, the killer was a madman or a madwoman, he or she was still a creature of flesh and blood, who lived in the victim's circle.

Was Jaquette, with her aggressive mistrust, mad? Was Mazeron, whom his wife accused of mental cruelty, unbalanced? Or was it Isabelle who was not in her right mind?

Every time he started thinking along these lines, he got ready to change his attitude, to put some cruel questions, if only in order to dispel this infectious blandness.

And every time, a surprised or ingenuous or mischievous glance from the Princess disarmed him, made him feel ashamed of himself.

'In fact, you have no idea who could have benefited by killing Saint-Hilaire?'

'Benefited? Certainly not. You know as well as I do the broad lines of the will.'

'And what if Alain Mazeron needed money badly?'

'His uncle used to give him some whenever that was the case and in any event he would have left him his fortune.'

'Mazeron knew that?'

'I don't doubt it. Once my husband died, Armand and I would have married, it is true, but I would never have allowed my family to inherit his money.'

'And Jaquette?'

'She was aware that provision had been made for her old age.'

'She was also aware that you intended to go and live in the Rue Saint-Dominique?'

'She looked forward to my doing so.'

Something in Maigret protested. This was all false, inhuman.

'And your son?'

Surprised by the question, she waited for him to explain what he meant, and as Maigret remained silent, she asked in her turn:

'What has my son got to do with it?'

'I don't know. I'm just feeling my way. He is the heir to the name.'

'He would have been even if Armand had gone on living.'

Obviously. But might he not have considered it demeaning for his mother to marry Saint-Hilaire?

'Was your son here last night?'

'No. He is staying with his wife and children at a hotel in the Place Vendôme where they are in the habit of residing when they come to Paris.'

Maigret frowned, looking at the walls as if, through them, he were gauging the size of the Rue de Varenne house. Surely it contained a goodly number of empty rooms, of unoccupied suites?

'You mean to say that since his marriage he has never stayed in this house?'

'In the first place, he very rarely comes to Paris, and never for long, because he hates society life.'

'His wife too?'

'Yes. In the first years of their marriage they had a suite of rooms in the house. Then they had a first child, a second, a third . . .'

'How many have they altogether?'

'Six. The eldest is twenty, the youngest seven. What I am going to say may shock you, but I cannot live with children. It's a mistake to think that all women are born to be mothers. I had Philippe because it was my duty to have him. I looked after him as much as I was expected to look after him. But it would have been too much for me to bear, years later, to have children shouting and galloping all over the house. My son knows that. So does his wife.'

'They don't hold it against you?'

'They accept me as I am, with all my faults and vagaries.'

'Were you alone here last night?'

'With the servants and two nuns who were watching in the mortuary chapel. The Abbé Gauge, who is my confessor and also an old friend of mine, stayed until ten o'clock.'

'You said a little while ago that your son and his family were here in the house.'

'They are waiting to say goodbye to me, at least my daughter-in-law and the children are. You must have seen their car in the courtyard.

They are going back to Normandy, except for my son who has to accompany me to the solicitor's tomorrow.'

'Will you allow me to have a few words with your son?'

'Why not? I was expecting you to make that request. I even thought that you would like to see the whole family and that is why I asked my daughter-in-law to postpone her departure.'

Was this naïvety on her part? Or was it defiance? To come back to the English doctor's theory, would a schoolmaster have found it easier to discover the truth than Maigret?

He felt more humble and helpless than ever in front of these human beings on whom he was trying to pass judgment.

'Come this way.'

She led him across the gallery, stopping for a moment with her hand on the handle of a door behind which he could hear the sound of voices.

She opened the door and said simply:

'Chief-Inspector Maigret . . .'

And in a huge room, the chief-inspector noticed first of all a child eating a cake, then a girl of about ten who was asking her mother something in a whisper.

The latter was a tall fair-haired woman of about forty. With her florid pink complexion, she reminded him of one of those stout Dutch-women you see in coloured prints and post-cards.

A boy of thirteen was looking out of the window. The Princess introduced everybody and Maigret registered the pictures one by one, planning to put them together again later like the pieces of a jigsaw puzzle.

'Frederick, the eldest . . .'

A lanky young man, fair-haired like his mother, bowed slightly without holding out his hand.

'He intends to enter the diplomatic service too.'

There was another girl, of fifteen, and a boy of twelve or thirteen.

'Isn't Philippe here?'

'He has gone down to see if the car is ready.'

One had the impression that life had been suspended, as in a station waiting-room.

'Come this way, Monsieur Maigret.'

They went along another corridor at the end of which they met a tall man who watched them coming towards him with a slightly annoyed expression.

'I was looking for you, Philippe. Chief-Inspector Maigret would like to have a few words with you. Where will you see him?'

Philippe held out his hand, looking a little vague perhaps, but fairly curious to see a detective at close quarters.

'Oh, it doesn't matter where. Here will do.'

He pushed open a door leading into a study papered in red with ancestral portraits on the walls.

'I will leave you now, Monsieur Maigret, but please don't leave me without news. As soon as the body is brought back to the Rue Saint-Dominique, be good enough to let me know.'

She disappeared, light and unsubstantial.

'You want to talk to me?'

Whose study was it? Probably nobody's, because there was nothing in it to indicate that anybody had ever worked here. Philippe de V—— pointed to a chair and held out his cigarette-case.

'No thank you.'

'You don't smoke?'

'Just a pipe.'

'So do I, usually. But not in this house. My mother hates it.'

In his voice there was a sort of irritation, perhaps even impatience. 'I suppose you want to talk to me about Saint-Hilaire?'

'You know that he was murdered last night.'

'My mother told me a little while ago. It's a curious coincidence, you must admit.'

'You mean that his death might be connected with your father's death?'

'I don't know. The paper doesn't say anything about the circumstances of the crime. I suppose that suicide is out of the question?'

'Why do you ask? Had the Count any reason to commit suicide?'

'I can't think of any, but then you never know what's going on in people's heads.'

'Did you know him?'

'My mother pointed him out to me when I was a child. Later on I came across him now and then.'

'Did you speak to him?'

'Never.'

'Did you bear him a grudge?'

'Whatever for?'

He too seemed genuinely surprised at the questions he was asked. He too gave the impression of being a decent fellow who had nothing to hide.

'All her life my mother kept up a sort of mystic love for him of

which we had no reason to feel ashamed. Indeed, my father was the
first to smile at it with a certain affectionate amusement.'

'When did you arrive from Normandy?'

'On Sunday afternoon. I had come by myself, last week, after my
father's accident, but then I had gone back home because he didn't
seem to be in danger. I was surprised on Sunday when my mother rang
me up to tell me that he had succumbed to an attack of uraemia.'

'You came along with your family?'

'No. My wife and children didn't arrive until Monday. Except for
my eldest son, of course, who is a boarder at the Ecole Normale.'

'Did your mother speak to you about Saint-Hilaire?'

'What do you mean?'

'Perhaps this is a stupid question. Did she tell you, at a given moment, that now she would be able to marry the Count?'

'She didn't need to speak to me about that. I had known for a long
time that if my father died before her, that marriage would take place.'

'You have never shared in your father's social life?'

Everything seemed to surprise him and he thought carefully before
replying.

'I think I can understand your point of view. You have seen photographs of my father and mother in the illustrated magazines, either
when they visited some foreign court or when they attended a big wedding or a society engagement-party. I myself attended some of those
events, of course, when I was between eighteen and twenty-five. When
I say twenty-five, I'm speaking vaguely. After that, I married and went
to live in the country. Did they tell you that I had been to the agricul-
tural school at Grignon? My father gave me one of his estates in
Normandy and I live with my family. Is that what you wanted to
know?'

'You haven't any suspicions?'

'As to Saint-Hilaire's murderer, you mean?'

It seemed to Maigret that the other man's lower lip had quivered
slightly, but he would not have dared to take his oath on it.

'No. You couldn't call it a suspicion.'

'An idea has occurred to you all the same?'

'It's quite preposterous and I'd rather not talk about it.'

'You've thought of somebody whose life was going to be changed by
your father's death?'

Philippe de V—— raised his eyes which he had lowered for a moment.

'Let us say that something of the sort entered my head but I didn't dwell on it. I've heard so much about Jaquette and her devoted loyalty . . .'

He seemed displeased at the turn the conversation had taken.

'I don't want to hustle you. But I have to say goodbye to my family and I should like them to get home before dark.'

'Are you staying a few days in Paris?'

'Until tomorrow evening.'

'In the Place Vendôme?'

'My mother told you?'

'Yes. As a matter of form, I must ask you one last question, which I hope you won't take amiss. I have had to put it to your mother too.'

'Where I was last night, I suppose. At what time?'

'Let us say between ten o'clock and midnight.'

'That's quite a long stretch. Wait a moment. I dined here with my mother.'

'Alone with her?'

'Yes. I left at about half past nine when the Abbé Gauge arrived, because I have no great liking for the man. I went back to the hotel to say goodnight to my wife and the children.'

There was a silence. Philippe de V—— looked straight in front of him, hesitant and embarrassed.

'Then I went for a stroll along the Champs-Elysées . . .'

'Until midnight?'

'No.'

This time, he looked Maigret in the face, with a rather sheepish smile.

'This may strike you as peculiar, in view of my recent bereavement. It happens to be a sort of tradition with me. At Genestoux, I am too well known to be able to indulge in any sort of affair, and the idea has never entered my head. It may have something to do with my youthful memories. In any case, whenever I come to Paris, I am in the habit of spending an hour or two with a pretty woman. As I don't want to have any consequences or to complicate my life, I content myself with . . .'

He made a vague gesture.

'On the Champs-Elysées?' asked Maigret.

'I wouldn't say this in front of my wife, who wouldn't understand. In her opinion, outside a certain society . . .'

'What is your wife's maiden name?'

'Irène de Marchangy . . . I can give you a few details about my companion yesterday, if they are of any use to you. She's a brunette, not very tall; she was wearing a pale green dress; and she has a beauty-spot under one breast. I think it's the left breast, but I can't be sure.'

'You went to her home?'

'I suppose that she lives in the Rue de Berry hotel where she took me, because there were some clothes in the wardrobe and personal belong-ings in the bathroom.'

Maigret smiled.

'Forgive my insistence and thank you for being so patient.'

'Your mind's easy as far as I'm concerned? This way . . . I'll leave you to go down by yourself, because I'm in a hurry to . . .'

He looked at his watch, held out his hand.

'The best of luck!'

In the courtyard, a chauffeur was waiting beside a limousine whose engine was running with a gentle hum which was scarcely perceptible.

Five minutes later, Maigret literally plunged into the fuggy atmos-phere of a café and ordered a beer.

VI

H E was awakened by the sunshine coming in through the slats of the Venetian shutter, and, with a gesture which, after so many years, had become automatic, he put his hand out towards his wife's place. The sheets were still warm. From the kitchen, at the same time as the smell of freshly ground coffee, there came a gentle whistling sound, that of the water singing in the kettle.

Here too, as in the aristocratic Rue de Varenne, there were birds chirping in the trees, though not so close to the windows, and Maigret had a feeling of physical well-being with which, however, was mingled something unpleasant and still rather vague.

He had had a restless night. He remembered having a number of dreams and even, once at least, waking up with a start.

Hadn't his wife, at one moment, spoken quietly to him and handed him a glass of water?

It was hard to remember. There were several stories tangled up to-gether and he kept losing the thread. They had one thing in common: in all of them he played a humiliating part.

One picture returned to his mind, clearer than the rest, the picture of a place which resembled the V—— house, but which was bigger and less luxurious. It had something about it of a convent or a ministry, with endless corridors and an infinite number of doors.

What he was doing there was not very clear in his mind. He knew only that he had a task to perform and that it was of capital importance. The trouble was that he could find nobody to guide him. Pardon had told him that this would be the case when he had taken leave of him in the street. He could not see Doctor Pardon in his dream, nor the street. He was nonetheless certain that his friend had warned him what to expect.

The fact of the matter was that he was not entitled to ask his way. He had tried, at the beginning, before it had been borne in on him that it was not done. The old people just looked at him, smiling and shaking their heads.

For there were old people everywhere. Perhaps it was an almshouse or a home for the aged, although it did not give him that impression.

He recognized Saint-Hilaire, an erect figure with a pink face beneath his silky white hair. An extremely good-looking man, who obviously knew it and seemed to be laughing at the chief-inspector. Maître Aubonnet was sitting in a bathchair with rubber wheels and was amusing himself by driving very fast up and down a gallery.

There were many others, including the Prince de V—— who, with one hand on Isabelle's shoulder, was indulgently watching Maigret's efforts.

The chief-inspector was in a delicate situation, because he had not been initiated yet and nobody would tell him what tests he still had to undergo.

He was in the position of a raw recruit in the army, of a new boy at school. The others kept playing tricks on him. For instance, every time he pushed open a door, it closed again by itself, or else, instead of opening into a bedroom or a drawing-room, it led into another corridor.

Only the old Comtesse de Saint-Fiacre was prepared to help him. Not having the right to speak, she tried to make him understand by means of gestures what was wrong. For instance she pointed to his knees and, looking down, Maigret saw that he was wearing short trousers.

Madame Maigret, in the kitchen, was at last pouring the water on to the coffee. Maigret opened his eyes, annoyed at the memory of this

stupid dream. The long and short of it was that he had as it were offered himself as a candidate for a club which, in this case, was a club
of old people. And if they had refused to take him seriously, it was because they regarded him as a little boy.

Even sitting on the edge of his bed, he was still annoyed, gazing
vaguely at his wife who, after putting a cup of coffee on the bedside
table, was opening the shutters.

'You shouldn't have eaten those snails last night . . .'

To cheer himself up after a disappointing day, he had taken her out
to dinner and he had eaten some snails.

'How do you feel?'

'All right.'

He was not going to let himself be impressed by a dream. He drank
his coffee and went into the dining-room, where he glanced at the
newspaper while he was having his breakfast.

They gave a few more details than the day before about Armand de
Saint-Hilaire's death, and they had found quite a good photograph of
him. There was one of Jaquette too, surprised just as she was going into
a dairy shop. It had been taken the day before, in the late afternoon,
when she had gone to do her shopping with Lapointe on her heels.

'At the Quai d'Orsay, the theory of a political crime is completely
ruled out. On the other hand, in informed circles, the Count's death is
being linked with another death, of an accidental nature, which occurred three days ago.'

That meant that in the next edition or so, the story of Saint-Hilaire
and Isabelle would be recounted at full length.

Maigret still felt dull and obtuse, and it was at moments such as
this that he wished he had chosen a different profession.

He waited for a bus in the Place Voltaire, and he was lucky enough
to get one with a platform on which he could smoke his pipe while he
watched the streets go by. At the Quai des Orfèvres, he greeted the
policeman on duty outside with a wave of the hand and climbed the
stairs which a charwoman was sweeping after sprinkling them with
water to keep down the dust.

On his desk he found a whole pile of documents, reports and photographs.

The photographs of the dead man were impressive. Some of them
showed the whole body, just as it had been found, with one leg of the
desk in the foreground and the stains on the carpet. There were others

too of the head, the chest and the stomach, taken while the body was still fully clothed.

Other numbered photographs showed the hole made by each bullet on entering the body, and a dark swelling under the skin, on the back, where one of the bullets, after breaking the collar-bone, had come to a stop.

There was a knock at the door and Lucas appeared, looking as fresh as a daisy, close-shaved, with some talcum powder below one ear.

'Dupeu is here, Chief.'

'Send him in.'

Inspector Dupeu, just like Isabelle's son, had a large family, six or seven children, but it was not out of irony that Maigret had given him a certain task to perform the day before. He had simply happened to be available at the time.

'Well?'

'What the Prince told you was true. I went to the Rue de Berry about ten o'clock. As usual, there were four or five of them walking up and down. There was only one little brunette among them, and she told me she hadn't been there the night before because she had been to see her baby in the country. I waited quite a while and then I saw another one come out of a hotel with an American soldier.

' "Why are you asking me that?" she said in a worried way when I put my question to her.

' "Is he wanted by the police?"

' "No. It's just a check-up."

' "A big chap, about fifty years old, and rather stout?" '

Dupeu went on:

'I asked the girl if she had a beauty spot under one breast and she said yes, and that she had another one on the hip. Naturally the man didn't tell her his name, but he was the only one she picked up the night before last, because he paid her three times as much as she usually asks.

' "Yet he didn't even stay half-an-hour . . ."

' "What time did he accost you?"

' "At ten to eleven. I remember that because I was coming out of the bar next door where I'd been for a coffee and I looked at the clock behind the counter." '

Maigret remarked:

'If he spent only half-an-hour with her, he must have left her before half past eleven?'

'That's what she told me.'

Isabelle's son had not been lying. Nobody in this case seemed to be lying. It was true that, leaving the Rue de Berry at half past eleven, he could quite easily have got to the Rue Saint-Dominique before midnight.

Why should he have gone to see his mother's old sweetheart? And above all, why should he have killed him?

The chief-inspector had had no better luck with the nephew, Alain Mazeron. The day before, when Maigret had gone along the Rue Jacob just before dinner-time, he had found nobody there. He had telephoned later at about eight o'clock without getting a reply.

He had then told Lucas to send somebody to the antique-dealer's early in the morning. It was Bonfils who in his turn came into the office with some equally disappointing information.

'He wasn't in the least upset by my questions.'

'His shop was open?'

'No. I had to ring the bell. He looked out of the first-floor window before coming down in his braces, unshaven. I asked him for an account of his movements yesterday afternoon and evening. He told me that to begin with he had gone to see the solicitor.'

'That's true.'

'I don't doubt it. After that he went to the Rue Drouot, where there was an auction-sale of helmets, uniform buttons and weapons of the Napoleonic period. He says that there's tremendous competition for these relics between certain collectors. He bought one lot, and showed me a pink form with a list of the things which he has to go and collect this morning.'

'After that?'

'He went and had dinner in a restaurant in the Rue de Seine where he nearly always has his meals. I checked up on that.'

Another one who had not been lying! It was a queer profession, thought Maigret, in which you felt disappointed that somebody hadn't committed murder! Yet this was the case here, and the chief-inspector, despite himself, felt a grudge against each of these people in turn for being innocent or appearing so.

For the fact remained that there was a corpse.

He picked up his telephone.

'Will you come downstairs, Moers?'

He didn't believe in the perfect crime. In twenty-five years of detective work, he hadn't come across a single one. True, he could think of a few crimes which had gone unpunished. Often the police knew the identity of the criminal, who had had time to escape abroad. Or else they were crimes of violence or poisoning.

This was not the case here. No ordinary criminal would have entered the Rue Saint-Dominique flat and fired four shots at an old man sitting at his desk only to go away without taking anything.

'Come in, Moers. Sit down.'

'You've read my report?'

'Not yet.'

Maigret did not confess that he had not had the courage to read it, any more than the eighteen-page report from the medical expert. The day before, he had left Moers and his men to look for material clues, and he put his trust in them, knowing that nothing would escape their notice.

'Has Gastine-Renette sent in his conclusions?'

'They are in the file. The weapon involved is a .301 automatic, either a Browning or one of the many imitations that are to be found on the market.'

'You are sure that not a single cartridge-case was left in the flat?'

'My men searched every square inch.'

'No weapon either?'

'No weapons or ammunition, except for some fowling-pieces and the cartridges to go with them.'

'Any fingerprints?'

'Those of the old woman, the Count and the concierge's wife. I had taken their fingerprints on the off-chance before leaving the Rue Saint-Dominique. The concierge's wife came twice a week to help Jaquette Larrieu with the heavy work.'

Moers too seemed perplexed and annoyed.

'I've added an inventory of everything we found in the furniture and the cupboards. But I've spent a good part of the night going through it without spotting anything suspicious or unexpected.'

'Any money?'

'A few thousand francs in a wallet, some change in a drawer in the kitchen, and in the desk some Rothschild's Bank cheque-books.'

'Any stubs?'

'Some cheque-stubs too. The poor old chap had so little idea that he was going to die that he ordered a suit ten days ago from a tailor on the Boulevard Haussmann.'

'No marks on the window-sill?'

'None whatever.'

They looked at one another and understood one another. They had worked together for years and they could scarcely remember a single case in which, going over the scene of the crime with a fine-tooth comb, as the papers say, they had not discovered a few more or less suspicious details, at least at first sight.

Here, it was all too perfect. Everything had a logical explanation except, of course, the old man's death.

By wiping the grip of the pistol and putting it in Saint-Hilaire's hand, the murderer could have given the impression of a case of suicide. Provided, of course, that he had stopped after the first bullet. But why had he fired the other three?

And why couldn't they find the former ambassador's automatic? Old Jaquette admitted having seen it, only a few months before, in the chest of drawers in the bedroom.

The gun was no longer in the flat and, according to the servant's description, it had roughly the same size and weight as a .301 automatic.

Supposing the former ambassador had let somebody into the flat . . . Somebody he knew, since he had sat down again at his desk, in his dressing-gown . . .

In front of him, a bottle of brandy and a glass . . . Why hadn't he offered his visitor a drink?

Maigret tried to imagine the scene. This visitor going to the bedroom—along the corridor or by way of the dining-room—taking the pistol, coming back to the study, going up to the Count and firing the first shot at point-blank range . . .

'It doesn't make sense,' he sighed.

What is more, there had to be a motive, a motive strong enough for the person who had done this to run the risk of a death-sentence.

'I suppose you haven't submitted Jaquette to the paraffin test?'

'I wouldn't have dared to without asking you first.'

When a firearm is discharged, especially an automatic, the explosion projects a certain distance characteristic particles which become engrained in the skin of the person who fires the gun, particularly along the edge of the hand, and remain for some time.

Maigret had thought of that, the day before. But had he any right to suspect the old servant more than anybody else?

Admittedly she was the best placed to commit the crime. She knew where to find the gun; she could come and go in the flat while her master was working, without arousing his suspicions, go up to him and fire; and it was quite likely that, with the body lying before her on the carpet, she would have gone on pulling the trigger.

She was sufficiently meticulous to have gone round the room afterwards picking up the cartridge-cases.

But was it likely that she would have gone calmly to bed afterwards, a few yards from her victim? Or that, in the morning, on her way to the Quai d'Orsay, she would have stopped somewhere, on the banks of the Seine, for instance, to get rid of the gun and the cartridge-cases?

She had a motive, or an apparent motive. For nearly fifty years, she had lived with Saint-Hilaire, in his shadow. He concealed nothing from her and, in all probability, they had at one time been on intimate terms.

The ambassador did not seem to have attached very much importance to this, nor did Isabelle, who referred to it with a smile.

But what about Jaquette? Wasn't she, to all intents and purposes, the old man's real companion?

She knew about his platonic love for the Princess, she posted his daily letters, and it was she too who had once admitted Isabelle to the flat in her master's absence.

'I wonder if . . .'

The theory was distasteful to Maigret, who considered it too easy. Although he could conceive it, he couldn't *feel* it.

With the Prince de V—— dead and Isabelle free, the old sweethearts were at last entitled to get married. They had only to wait until the end of the period of mourning to go through the marriage ceremony at town hall and church, and after that they would be able to live together in the Rue Saint-Dominique or the Rue de Varenne.

'Listen, Moers . . . Go over there . . . Be nice to Jaquette . . . Don't frighten her . . . Tell her that it's just a formality . . .'

'You want me to carry out the test?'

'It would relieve me of one worry . . .'

When he was told, a little later, that Monsieur Cromières was on the telephone, he sent word that he was out and that it wasn't known when he would be back.

This morning, the Prince de V——'s will was going to be read. There, facing the old solicitor Aubonnet, there would be Isabelle and her son, and, later in the day, the Princess would return to the same room for the reading of another will.

The two men in her life, the same day . . .

He telephoned to the Rue Saint-Dominique. He had hesitated, the day before, to affix seals on the study door and the bedroom door. He had preferred to wait, so that he could inspect the two rooms again.

Lapointe, whom he had left on duty, had obviously dropped off to sleep in an arm-chair.

'Is that you, Chief?'

'Nothing new?'

'Not a thing.'

'Where's Jaquette?'

'This morning, at six o'clock, when I was on duty in the study, I heard her dragging a vacuum cleaner along the corridor. I dashed out to ask her what she was going to do and she looked at me in astonishment.

' "Clean the rooms, of course!"

' "Clean what rooms?"

' "First the bedroom, then the dining-room, then . . ." '

Maigret grunted:

'Did you let her?'

'No. She didn't seem to understand why.

' "What shall I do, then?" she asked.'

'What did you reply?'

'I asked her to make me some coffee and she went out to buy me some croissants.'

'She didn't stop anywhere on the way to make a phone call or post a letter?'

'No. I told the policeman on duty at the door to follow her at a distance. She really did just go to the baker's and she only stayed there a minute.'

'Is she furious?'

'It's hard to say. She comes and goes, moving her lips as if she were talking to herself. Just now, she's in the kitchen and I don't know what she's doing.'

'There haven't been any phone calls?'

The French window leading into the garden must have been open, for Maigret could hear the blackbirds singing over the telephone.

'Moers will be with you in a few minutes. He's already on the way. You aren't too tired?'

'I must admit that I've been asleep.'

'I'll send somebody to relieve you a little later.'

An idea occurred to him.

'Don't ring off. Go and ask Jaquette to show you her gloves.'

She was a devout person and he would have sworn that, for Sunday Mass, she wore a pair of gloves.

'I'll hold the line.'

He waited with the receiver in his hand. It took quite a long time.

'Are you there, Chief?'

'Well?'

'She has shown me three pairs.'

'She wasn't surprised?'

'She gave me a nasty look before going to open a drawer in her room. I caught sight of a missal, two or three rosaries, some postcards, medallions, handkerchiefs and gloves. Two pairs are in white cotton.'

Maigret could imagine her in summer, with white gloves and, no doubt, a touch of white in her hat.

'And the other pair?'

'In black kid, rather worn.'

'Good. See you later.'

Maigret's question was connected with Moer's errand. Saint-Hilaire's murderer could have learnt from the newspapers and magazines that a person who fires a revolver has his hands encrusted with powder for some time after the shot. If Jaquette had used the automatic, mightn't she have thought of putting on a pair of gloves? In that case, wouldn't she have got rid of them?

To clear this point up, Maigret started searching through the file which was still spread out in front of him. He found the inventory, with the contents of every piece of furniture listed room by room.

Servant's bedroom . . . One iron bedstead . . . One old mahogany table covered with a fringed tablecloth in crimson velvet . . .

His finger followed the lines of typescript:

Eleven handkerchiefs, including six marked with the initial J . . . Three pairs of gloves . . .

She had shown the three pairs to Lapointe.

He went out, without taking his hat, and made for the door connecting Police Headquarters with the Palais de Justice. He had never been to see the examining magistrate, Urbain de Chézaud, who had previously been at Versailles and with whom he had never had occasion to work. He had to go up to the third floor, where the oldest offices were, and he finally found the magistrate's visiting-card on a door.

'Come in, Monsieur Maigret. I'm delighted to see you and I was wondering whether to ring you up.'

He was about forty, with an intelligent air about him. On his desk, Maigret recognized the duplicate of the file which he had received himself and he noticed that certain pages had already been annotated in red pencil.

'We haven't many material clues, have we?' sighed the magistrate as he invited the chief-inspector to sit down. 'I have just had a telephone call from the Quai d'Orsay . . .'

'Young Monsieur Cromières . . .'

'He says that he has tried unsuccessfully to get in touch with you and he wonders where this morning's papers obtained their information.'

The magistrate's clerk, behind Maigret, was busy typing. The windows overlooked the courtyard so that there could never be any sunshine in the room.

'Have you any news?'

Because he liked the magistrate, Maigret made no attempt to conceal his discouragement.

'You've read that,' he sighed, pointing to the file. 'This evening or tomorrow I'll send you a preliminary report. Theft isn't the motive of the crime. It seems to me that it isn't a question of financial interest either, because it would be too obvious. The victim's nephew is the only person who benefits by Saint-Hilaire's death. And then he's gaining only a few months or a few years.'

'Has he any pressing financial obligations?'

'Yes and no. It's difficult to get anything positive out of these people without bluntly accusing them. And I haven't any grounds for an accusation. Mazeron lives apart from his wife and children. He has a secretive, rather unpleasant character, and his wife describes him as a sort of sadist.

'From the look of his antique shop, you would imagine that nobody ever goes into it. Admittedly he specializes in military trophies and there's a small number of enthusiasts who are mad about that sort of thing.

'He has been known to ask his uncle for money. But there is no proof that the latter didn't give it him with good grace.

'Was he afraid that once Saint-Hilaire had married he would lose the inheritance? That's possible. But I don't think so. Families like that have a mentality of their own. Every member regards himself as the trustee of property which it is his duty to hand on, more or less intact, to his direct or indirect descendants.'

He noticed a smile on the magistrate's lips and remembered that the latter was called Urbain de Chézaud, a name with a particle.

'Go on.'

'I have been to see Madame Mazeron, in her flat at Passy, and I can see no earthly reason why she should have gone and killed her husband's uncle. The same goes for their two daughters. One of them, in any case, is in England. The other is working.'

Maigret filled his pipe.

'Do you mind if I smoke?'

'Of course not. I smoke a pipe too.'

It was the first time that he had ever met a pipe-smoking magistrate. It is true that the latter added:

'At home, in the evening, while I'm studying my files.'

'I have been to see the Princesse de V——.'

He glanced at the other man.

'You know about that business, I suppose?'

Maigret could have sworn that Urbain de Chézaud moved in circles where people were interested in Isabelle.

'I have heard about it.'

'Is it true that a lot of people knew about her liaison with the Count, if liaison is the right word?'

'In certain circles, yes. Her friends call her Isi.'

'That's what the Count calls her too in his letters.'

'You have read them?'

'Not all of them. And not from beginning to end. There are enough to fill several volumes. It seemed to me, though it's only an impression, that the Princess wasn't as overwhelmed by the news of Saint-Hilaire's death as one might have expected.'

'In my opinion, nothing in her life has ever succeeded in disturbing her composure. I have met her on occasion. I have heard about her from friends. One gets the impression that she has never passed a certain age and that time, for her, has come to a halt. Some say that she has remained as she was at twenty, others that she hasn't changed since her schooldays in the convent.'

'The newspapers are going to publish her story. They've begun making references to it.'

'I've noticed that. It was bound to happen.'

'In the course of the conversation we had together, she didn't say anything that gave me the slightest hint of a line to follow. This morn-

ing, she's at the solicitor's, for the reading of her husband's will. She'll
be going back there this afternoon for Saint-Hilaire's.'

'He has left her something?'

'Just his furniture and personal belongings.'

'Have you been to see her son?'

'Philippe, his wife, and their children. They were all gathered together in the Rue de Varenne. The son has stayed behind in Paris by
himself.'

'What do you think about them?'

Maigret was obliged to reply:

'I don't know.'

Philippe, too, strictly speaking, had a motive for killing Saint-Hilaire.
He had become the head of the historic V—— family which was related
to all the courts of Europe.

His father had tolerated Isabelle's platonic love for the discreet ambassador whom she saw only from a distance and to whom she wrote
childish letters.

Once he was dead, the situation was bound to change. In spite of her
seventy-two years and her sweetheart's seventy-seven years, the Princess
was going to marry Saint-Hilaire, lose her title, change her name.

Was that a sufficient motive for committing a crime and, as Maigret
kept reminding himself, for risking a death-sentence? For replacing, in
fact, a mild scandal with a scandal of a much more serious nature.

The chief-inspector muttered in embarrassment:

'I've checked his movements on Tuesday evening. He booked in with
his family at a hotel in the Place Vendôme, as he was in the habit of
doing. When the children had gone to bed, he went out by himself
and went up the Champs-Elysées on foot. On the corner of the Rue de
Berry he took his pick of the five or six prostitutes who were available
and accompanied one of them to her room.'

Maigret had often known murderers, *after* their crime to go and look
for a woman, any woman, as if they felt a need for relaxation.

He could not remember a single one acting in this way *before*. Could
it have been to produce an alibi?

In that case, the alibi was incomplete, since Philippe de V—— had
left the prostitute about half past eleven, which had left him enough
time to go to the Rue Saint-Dominique.

'That's how things stand at the moment. I shall go on looking for a
new trail, without much hope of finding one, perhaps another of the
former ambassador's friends nobody has told me about yet. Saint-Hilaire

was very regular in his habits, like most old people. Nearly all his friends are dead . . .'

The telephone rang. The clerk got up to answer it.

'Yes . . . He's here . . . Would you like to speak to him?'

And turning to the chief-inspector:

'It's for you . . . It seems that it's very urgent . . .'

'Do you mind?'

'Go ahead.'

'Hullo . . . Maigret, yes . . . Who's that speaking?'

He did not recognize the voice because Moers, who finally gave his name, was in a state of great excitement.

'I tried to get you at your office. They told me that . . .'

'Yes, yes.'

'I'm coming to the point. It's so extraordinary; I've just finished the test . . .'

'I know. Well?'

'It's positive.'

'You're sure?'

'Absolutely certain. There's no doubt that Jaquette Larrieu fired one or more shots within the last forty-eight hours.'

'She let you carry out the test?'

'She was no trouble at all.'

'How does she explain it?'

'She doesn't. I haven't said anything to her. I had to come back to the laboratory to finish the test.'

'Is Lapointe still with her?'

'He was there when I left the Rue Saint-Dominique.'

'You are certain about what you've just told me?'

'Positive.'

'Thank you.'

He hung up, his face serious, a crease in the middle of his forehead, with the magistrate looking at him inquiringly.

'I was wrong,' Maigret murmured regretfully.

'What do you mean?'

'On the off-chance, without taking it seriously, I must admit, I told the laboratory to try the paraffin test on Jaquette's right hand.'

'And it's positive? That's what I thought they were telling you over the telephone, but I found it hard to believe.'

'So did I.'

He ought to have felt a great load off his mind. After an investigation lasting barely twenty-four hours, the problem which had seemed insoluble a few minutes before had now been solved.

Yet the fact was that he felt no sense of satisfaction.

'While I'm here, will you sign a warrant for me,' he sighed.

'You are going to send your men to arrest her?'

'I shall go myself.'

And, hunching his shoulders, Maigret lit his pipe again, while the magistrate silently filled in the blanks of a printed form.

VII

MAIGRET looked into his office on the way in order to pick up his hat. Just as he was going out again, an idea suddenly struck him and, cursing himself for not having thought of it before, he rushed for the telephone.

To save time, he dialled the Rue Saint-Dominique number himself without going through the switchboard. He was anxious to hear Lapointe's voice, to make sure that nothing had happened over there. Instead of the bell he heard the staccato buzz indicating that the line was engaged.

He did not think, and for a few seconds he panicked.

Whom could Lapointe be ringing up? Moers had left him a little earlier. Lapointe knew that he would be getting in touch with the chief-inspector straight away to give him his report.

If the inspector left behind in Saint-Hilaire's flat was using the telephone, it meant that something unexpected had happened and that he was calling Police Headquarters or a doctor.

Maigret tried again, opened the door of the adjoining office and saw Janvier lighting a cigarette.

'Go down and wait for me in the courtyard at the wheel of a car.'

He had one last try, only to hear the same buzz in reply.

A little later he could be seen running down the stairs jumping into the little black car and banging the door.

'Rue Saint-Dominique. As fast as you can. Sound the siren.'

Janvier, who did not know about the case's latest developments,

glanced at him in surprise, for the chief-inspector loathed the siren and
rarely used it.

The car sped towards the Pont Saint-Michel and turned right along
the embankment, while the other cars drew in to the curb and the
passers-by stopped to follow it with their eyes.

Possibly Maigret's reaction was ridiculous but he could not get rid
of the mental picture of Jaquette dead and Lapointe beside her, hanging on to the telephone. It became so real in his mind that he got to
the point of wondering how she had committed suicide. She could not
have thrown herself out of the window, since the flat was on the
ground floor. There was no weapon available, except for the kitchen
knives . . .

The car stopped. The policeman, at his post by the carriage gateway,
out in the sun, was obviously surprised at the siren. The bedroom window was ajar.

Maigret rushed across to the archway, climbed the stone steps, with
a Lapointe who was at once calm and astonished.

'What's up, Chief?'

'Where is she?'

'In her room.'

'When did you last hear her moving around?'

'Just now.'

'Whom were you phoning?'

'I was trying to get through to you.'

'What for?'

'She's getting dressed to go out and I wanted to ask you for instructions.'

Maigret felt ridiculous in front of Lapointe and Janvier who had
joined them. In contrast with the anxiety of the last few minutes, the
flat was quieter than ever. The study was still full of sunshine, the door
open on to the garden, the linden-tree noisy with birds.

He went into the kitchen, where everything was in order, and heard
some slight noises in the old servant's room.

'Can I see you, Mademoiselle Larrieu?'

He had once called her madame and she had protested:

'Mademoiselle, if you please!'

'Who is it?'

'Chief-Inspector Maigret.'

'Just a minute.'

Lapointe went on in a whisper:

'She has had a bath in her employer's bathroom.'

Maigret had rarely been so displeased with himself and he remembered his dream, the old people who looked at him condescendingly, shaking their heads because he was wearing short trousers and because he was just a little boy in their eyes.

The door of the little room opened, and a whiff of scent reached him, a scent which had been unfashionable for years and which he recognized because his mother had always used it on Sundays to go to High Mass.

It was indeed as if to go to High Mass that old Jaquette was dressed. She was wearing a black silk dress, a black tucker round her neck, a black hat trimmed with white silk, and an immaculate pair of gloves. All that was missing was a missal in one hand.

'I am obliged,' he murmured, 'to take you to the Quai des Orfèvres.'

He was prepared to show her the warrant signed by the magistrate but, contrary to his expectations, she showed neither surprise nor indignation. Without a word, she crossed the kitchen, making sure that the gas was turned off, and went into the study to close the French window.

She asked only one question:

'Is anybody going to stay here?'

And as nobody answered her straight away, she added:

'If not, I had better shut the bedroom window.'

Not only, knowing that she had been found out, had she no intention of committing suicide, but she had never been so dignified, so much in control of her feelings. It was she who went out first. Maigret said to Lapointe:

'You had better stay behind.'

She walked in front, giving a little nod of the head to the concierge looking at her through the glass door.

Wouldn't it have been ridiculous, abominable to put handcuffs on this woman who was seventy years old? Maigret invited her to get into the car and took his place beside her.

'You don't need the siren any more.'

The weather was still magnificent and they passed a big red and white coach full of foreign tourists. Maigret could not think of anything to say, any question to ask.

Hundreds of times, he had returned to the Quai des Orfèvres like this, in the company of a suspect, a man or a woman, whom he was going to have to submit to a merciless examination. This could last for hours, and sometimes the interrogation had ended only at daybreak, when the people of Paris were setting out to go to work.

For Maigret, this phase of an investigation was always unpleasant.

Now, for the first time in his life, he was to carry out the operation on an old woman.

In the courtyard of Police Headquarters, he helped her out of the car, but she pushed his hand away and walked with a dignified bearing towards the staircase as if she were crossing the square in front of a church. He had motioned to Janvier to accompany them. All three went up the main staircase and into the chief-inspector's office where the breeze was puffing out the curtains.

'Sit down, please.'

Although he had pointed to an arm-chair, she chose an upright chair, while Janvier, who was familiar with the routine, settled down at one end of the desk and took a note-book and pencil.

Maigret cleared his throat, filled a pipe, walked over to the window, and came back to plant himself in front of the old woman who was watching him with her bright, motionless little eyes.

'First of all I have to inform you that the examining magistrate has just signed a warrant for your arrest.'

He showed it to her. She granted it only a polite interest.

'You are charged with having committed the wilful murder of your employer, the Comte Armand de Saint-Hilaire, during the night of Tuesday to Wednesday last. A technician from the Criminal Records Office carried out the paraffin test on your right hand a little while ago. This test consists of collecting the particles of powder and chemical substances which are engrained in a person's skin when that person makes use of a firearm, particularly an automatic pistol.'

He watched her, hoping for some reaction, but it was she who seemed to be studying him, it was she who was the calmer and more self-possessed of the two.

'You don't say anything?'

'I have nothing to say.'

'The test was positive, which means that it established, beyond any possible doubt, that you used a firearm recently.'

Impassive as she was, she might just as well have been in church listening to a sermon.

'What have you done with that weapon? I suppose on Wednesday morning, on your way to the Quai d'Orsay, you threw it into the Seine with the cartridge-cases? I warn you that the necessary steps will be taken to recover the pistol, that divers will go down to the river bed.'

She had decided to keep quiet and keep quiet she did. As for her eyes, they remained so serene that one might have thought that she was not involved in what was going on, that she was there by accident, listening to a conversation which had nothing to do with her.

'I don't know what your motive was, although I can guess. You had lived for nearly fifty years with the Comte de Saint-Hilaire. You had been as intimate with him as two human beings can be.'

An ephemeral smile hovered over Jaquette's lips, a smile in which there was mingled both coquetry and a secret satisfaction.

'You knew that after the Prince's death your employer would put the dream of his youth into effect.'

It was annoying to talk to no purpose, and now and then Maigret had to keep a firm grip on himself to refrain from shaking the old woman by the shoulders.

'If he hadn't been killed he would have got married, isn't that so? Would you have kept your position in the household? And if you had, would that position have been quite the same?'

With his pencil poised in mid-air, Janvier was still waiting for a reply for him to record.

'On Tuesday evening, you went into your employer's study. He was correcting the proofs of his book. Did you have a quarrel with him?'

After another ten minutes of questions without a single reply, Maigret, utterly exasperated, felt the need to go and relax for a moment in the inspectors' room. That reminded him that Lapointe had been in the Rue Saint-Dominique since the previous evening.

'Are you busy, Lucas?'

'Nothing urgent.'

'In that case, go and take over from Lapointe.'

Then, as it was after midday, he added:

'Drop into the Brasserie Dauphine on the way. Tell them to send up a plate of sandwiches and some beer and coffee for us.'

And, thinking of the old woman:

'A bottle of mineral water too.'

In his office, he found Jaquette and Janvier sitting motionless on their chairs as if they were in a picture.

For half an hour he walked up and down the room, puffing at his pipe, stopping in front of the window, and planting himself a few feet from the servant to look her in the face.

It was not an interrogation, for she remained stubbornly silent, but a long, more or less disconnected monologue.

'It's possible—I'm telling you this straight away—that the experts will find that this is a case of diminished responsibility. Your lawyer will certainly argue that it was a crime of passion . . .'

It seemed ridiculous, but it was true.

'Remaining silent won't help you at all. Whereas if you plead guilty you have every chance of moving the jury. Why not start now?'

Children play a game of this sort: you must not open your mouth whatever your partner may say or do, and above all you must not laugh.

Jaquette neither spoke nor laughed. She followed Maigret with her eyes as he came and went, behaving all the time as if she were not involved, showing no emotion, no reaction of any sort.

'The Count was the only man in your life.'

What was the use? He searched in vain for her Achilles' heel. There was a knock at the door. It was the waiter from the Brasserie Dauphine, who put the tray down on the chief-inspector's desk.

'You had better eat something. At the rate we are going now, we shall probably be a long time yet.'

He offered her a ham sandwich. The waiter had gone. She picked up a corner of the crumby bread and, for a wonder, opened her mouth.

'I haven't eaten any meat for fifteen years. Old people don't need it.'

'Would you prefer cheese?'

'In any case, I'm not hungry.'

He went into the inspectors' room again.

'Somebody ring up the brasserie and tell them to send over some cheese sandwiches.'

He for his part ate as he walked up and down, as if out of revenge, with his pipe in one hand and the sandwich in the other, and now and then he stopped to have a drink of beer. Janvier had put down his useless pencil to have something to eat too.

'Would you prefer to talk to me alone?'

This evoked nothing but a shrug of her shoulders.

'You are entitled as from now to the services of any lawyer you choose. I'm prepared to send for the one you indicate straight away. Do you know a lawyer?'

'No.'

'Do you want me to give you the list of lawyers?'

'It isn't any use.'

'Would you prefer me to choose one for you?'

'There isn't any point.'

They had made some progress, since she was at least talking.

'You admit that you shot your employer?'

'I have nothing to say.'

'In other words, you've sworn to keep quiet, whatever happens?'

Once again there was the same exasperating silence. Pipe smoke was floating about the office, into which the sunlight was falling at an angle. The atmosphere began to smell of ham, beer, coffee.

'Would you like a cup of coffee?'

'I only drink coffee in the morning, with a lot of milk.'

'What would you like to drink?'

'Nothing.'

'Are you planning to go on a hunger strike?'

It had been a mistake to say that, because she suppressed a smile at the idea, which might possibly appeal to her.

He had seen suspects of all sorts here, in similar circumstances, both tough characters and weak characters, some who cried, others who grew paler and paler, and yet others who defied him and laughed at him.

It was the first time that anybody, sitting on that chair, had shown so much indifference and calm obstinacy.

'You still don't want to say anything?'

'Not now.'

'When are you thinking of talking?'

'I don't know.'

'Are you waiting for something?'

Silence.

'Would you like me to ring up the Princesse de V——?'

She shook her head.

'Is there anybody to whom you want to send a message, or anybody you would like to see?'

The cheese sandwiches were brought in and she looked at them apathetically. She shook her head and said again:

'Not now.'

'So you're determined not to say anything, drink anything or eat anything.'

It was a hard chair, and nearly all those who had sat on it had soon begun to feel uncomfortable. At the end of an hour, she was still holding herself as erect as ever, without moving her feet or her arms, and without having changed her position.

'Listen, Jaquette . . .'

She frowned, shocked at this familiarity, and it was the chief-inspector who showed some embarrassment.

'I warn you that we shall stay in this room as long as is necessary. We have material evidence that you have fired one or more shots. All I am asking you to do is to tell me why and in what circumstances. By your stupid silence . . .'

He had used the word unintentionally and he corrected himself.

'By your silence you are running the risk of putting the police on the wrong track and casting suspicion on other people. If, half an hour from now, you haven't answered my questions, I shall ask the Princess to come here and I shall put her in your presence. I shall summon her son too, Alain Mazeron, and Mazeron's wife, and we shall see whether that general confrontation . . .'

He called out angrily:

'What is it?'

There was a knock at the door. Old Joseph beckoned him into the corridor and, with his head bent forward, whispered:

'There's a young man who insists . . .'

'What young man?'

Joseph held out a visiting-card bearing the name of Julien de V——, Isabelle's grandson.

'Where is he?'

'In the waiting-room. He says that he's in a hurry because there's an important lecture he mustn't miss.'

'Ask him to wait a moment.'

He went back into the office.

'Isabelle's grandson, Julien, is asking to see me. Do you still insist on remaining silent?'

It was admittedly exasperating, but it was pathetic too. Maigret thought that he could see signs of a conflict taking place in the old woman, and he felt unwilling to hustle her. Even Janvier, who was just a spectator, looked a little conscience-stricken.

'You'll have to talk sooner or later. In that case why . . .'

'Am I entitled to see a priest?'

'You want to make a confession?'

'I'm just asking for permission to talk to a priest for a few minutes. The Abbé Barraud?'

'Where can I get hold of the Abbé Barraud?'

'At the Sainte-Clotilde presbytery.'

'He's your confessor, is he?'

He did not want to miss the slightest chance, and he picked up the telephone.

'Get me the Sainte-Clotilde presbytery . . . Yes . . . I'll hold the line . . . The Abbé Barraud . . . It doesn't matter how you spell it . . .'

He moved the pipes about on his desk, arranging them in Indian file like soldiers.

'Hullo . . . The Abbé Barraud? . . . This is Police Headquarters . . . Maigret, divisional chief-inspector . . . I have one of your parishioners in my office who would like to talk to you . . . Yes . . . It's Mademoiselle Larrieu . . . Can you take a taxi and come round to the Quai des Orfèvres? . . . Thank you . . . Yes . . . She'll wait here for you . . .'

And to Janvier:

'When the priest arrives show him in here and leave them together . . . There's somebody I've got to see in the meantime . . .'

He made for the glass-sided waiting-room where the only person was the young man in black whom he had glimpsed the day before in the Rue de Varenne in the company of his parents and his brothers and sisters. When he saw Maigret, he stood up and followed the chief-inspector into a little office which was unoccupied.

'Sit down.'

'I haven't got long. I have to go back to the Rue d'Ulm, where I've got a lecture in half an hour.'

In the tiny office, he seemed taller and lankier than before. The expression on his face was serious and rather sad.

'Yesterday, when you came to see my grandmother, I nearly spoke to you.'

Why did Maigret feel that he would have liked to have a son like this boy? He had a natural ease of manner at the same time as a sort of innate modesty, and if he was a little withdrawn, one could tell that it was out of tact.

'I don't know whether what I'm going to tell you will be of any use to you. I thought about it a lot last night. On Tuesday afternoon, I went to see my uncle.'

'Your uncle?'

The young man blushed, a slight blush which disappeared straight away and which he replaced with a shy smile.

'That's what I called the Comte de Saint-Hilaire.'

'You used to go and see him?'

'Yes. I didn't talk about it to my parents, but I didn't try to conceal it from them either. I first heard about him when I was a boy.'

'From whom?'

'From my governesses, then, later on, from my school-mates. My grandmother's love-story is almost legendary.'

'I know.'

'When I was about ten or eleven, I asked her about him, and the two of us got into the habit of talking about Saint-Hilaire. She used to read me certain letters, those, for instance, in which he described diplomatic receptions or gave an account of his conversations with heads of state. Have you read his letters?'

'No.'

'He wrote very well, in a lively style, rather like Cardinal de Retz. It may have been on account of the Count and his stories that I chose the diplomatic career.'

'When did you get to know him personally?'

'Two years ago. I had a friend at Stanislas whose grandfather had also been in the Service. One day, at his home, I met the Comte de Saint-Hilaire and asked to be introduced to him. I thought I could sense his emotion as he looked me up and down, and I was rather moved too. He asked me some questions about my studies and my plans for the future.'

'You went to see him in the Rue Saint-Dominique?'

'He had invited me there, though he had added: "Provided that your parents have no objection."'

'Did you meet him often?'

'No. About once a month. It all depended. For instance, I asked his advice after my baccalaureate, and he encouraged me in my decision to go through the Ecole Normale. He considered, as I did, that even if it didn't help me in my career, it would still provide me with a solid basis.

'One day, without thinking, I said:

' "I feel rather as if I were talking to an uncle."

' "And I to a nephew," he replied. "Why don't you call me uncle?"

'That's why I used the word just now.'

'You didn't like your grandfather?'

'I didn't know him very well. For all that they belonged to the same generation, he and the Comte de Saint-Hilaire were two very different men. My grandfather, for me, remained somebody impressive and inaccessible.'

'And your grandmother?'

'We were great friends. We still are.'

'She knew about your visits to the Rue Saint-Dominique?'

'Yes. I used to tell her all about our conversations. She would ask me for details, and sometimes it was she who reminded me that I hadn't been to see our friend for a long time.'

Although he was drawn to the young man, Maigret nonetheless studied him with an astonishment bordering on mistrust. They were not accustomed, at the Quai des Orfèvres, to meeting young men of this kind, and once again he had an impression of an unreal world, of people who came, not out of life, but out of a book of moral uplift.

'So on Tuesday afternoon you went to the Rue Saint-Dominique.'

'Yes.'

'Had you any special reason for this call?'

'In a way. My grandfather had died two days before. I thought that my grandmother would like to know how her friend was reacting.'

'You didn't feel the same curiosity?'

'Perhaps I did. I knew that they had sworn to marry one day if it were possible.'

'The idea appealed to you?'

'It did rather.'

'And to your parents?'

'I never talked about it to my father, but I've every reason to think that he didn't mind the idea. As for my mother . . . ?'

Since he did not finish his sentence, Maigret prompted him:

'Your mother . . . ?'

'I'm not being unkind about her if I say that she attaches greater importance to titles and privileges than anybody else in the family.'

Probably because she had not been born a princess but simply Irène de Marchangy.

'What happened in the course of this conversation in the Rue Saint-Dominique?'

'Nothing that I can explain at all clearly. All the same, I thought I ought to tell you about it. Right from the beginning, the Comte de Saint-Hilaire seemed worried and it was suddenly borne in on me that he was very old. Before then, he had never looked his age. You could tell that he was in love with life, that he enjoyed every aspect of it, every moment of it, as a connoisseur. To my mind he was a man of the eighteenth century who had strayed into the twentieth. You understand what I mean?'

Maigret nodded.

'I didn't expect to find him broken up by the death of my grand-father, who was two years older than he was, especially seeing that that death had been accidental and hadn't really been very painful. But on Tuesday afternoon Saint-Hilaire was out of spirits and avoided looking at me as if he had something to hide.

'I said something like this:

'"A year from now, you'll finally be able to marry my grand-mother . . ."

'He turned his head away, so I pressed the point:

'"How do you feel about it?"

'I wish I could remember his exact words. It's strange that I can't remember them, seeing that I was so struck by their meaning and all that they implied.

'What he said, in substance, was:

'"I won't be allowed to."

'And when I looked at his face, I thought I could see fear in it.

'As you can see, it's all pretty vague. At the time I didn't attach much importance to it, imagining that it was the natural reaction of an old man hearing about the death of another old man and telling himself that it would be his turn soon.

'When I heard that he had been murdered, that scene came back to me.'

'Did you mention it to anybody?'

'No.'

'Not even to your grandmother?'

'I didn't want to bother her. I could swear that the Count felt that he was in danger. He wasn't a man to imagine things. In spite of his age, his mind was still exceptionally clear and his philosophy of life kept him proof against baseless fears.'

'If I understood you correctly, you think he foresaw what has happened to him.'

'He foresaw something unpleasant, yes. I decided to tell you about it because, ever since yesterday, it has been worrying me.'

'He never talked to you about his friends?'

'About his dead friends. He hadn't any friends left who were still alive, but that didn't upset him too much.

'"When you come to think of it," he used to say, "it isn't as unpleasant as all that to be the last to go."

'And he added sadly:

' "It means there's still one memory in which the others can go on living." '

'He didn't talk to you about his enemies?'

'I'm convinced that he never had any. A few envious colleagues, perhaps, at the beginning of his career, which was swift and brilliant. They too are dead and buried.'

'Thank you. You did right to come.'

'You still don't know anything?'

Maigret hesitated, and nearly mentioned Jaquette who, at that very moment, would be shut up in his office with the Abbé Barraud.

At Police Headquarters, they sometimes called the chief-inspector's office the confessional, but this was the first time that it had really served as one.

'Nothing certain, no.'

'I must be getting back to the Rue d'Ulm.'

Maigret accompanied him to the head of the stairs.

'Thank you again.'

He walked along the huge corridor for a while, with his hands behind his back, lit his pipe, and went into the inspectors' room.

'Is the Abbé next door?'

'He's been there quite a while.'

'What's he like?'

And Janvier replied with a somewhat bitter irony:

'He's the oldest of the lot.'

VIII

'Get me Lucas on the phone.'

'Rue Saint-Dominique?'

'Yes. I sent him to relieve Lapointe.'

He was beginning to lose patience. The conversation was going on in an undertone in the adjoining office, and when he went up to the door, all he could hear was the sort of whispering one heard outside a real confessional.

'Lucas? . . . All quiet over there? . . . Nothing but phone calls from journalists? . . . Go on telling them there's nothing new . . .

What? . . . No, she hasn't talked yet . . . Yes, she's in my office, but not with me or anybody else from Headquarters . . . She's with a priest . . .'

The next minute, the examining magistrate was on the line, and Maigret repeated roughly the same words.

'No, don't worry, I'm not hustling her. On the contrary . . .'

He could not remember being so gentle and patient in the whole of his life. Once again the English article Pardon had read him came back to him and evoked an ironic smile.

The contributor to the *Lancet* had been wrong. It wasn't a schoolmaster in the end, nor a novelist, nor even a detective, who was going to solve the problem of Jaquette, but an octogenarian priest.

'How long have they been in there?'

'Twenty-five minutes.'

He hadn't even the consolation of having a glass of beer, for the tray had been left next door. By the time he got to it, the beer would be warm. It was warm already. He was tempted to go down to the Brasserie Dauphine, but hesitated to leave just then.

He felt that the solution was within reach, and tried to guess what it was, not so much in his capacity as a chief-inspector of the Judicial Police whose duty it was to identify a criminal and get a confession out of him, as in his capacity as a human being.

For it was as a human being that he had conducted this case, as if it had been a personal matter, so much so that in spite of himself, he had brought childhood memories into it.

Wasn't he involved to some extent? If Saint-Hilaire had been an ambassador for several decades, if his platonic love for Isabelle dated back nearly fifty years, he, Maigret, had twenty-five years' service at Police Headquarters to his credit, and as recently as the previous day he had felt convinced that every conceivable variety of individual had passed before him.

He didn't regard himself as a superman; he didn't consider himself infallible. On the contrary, it was with a certain humility that he began all his investigations, even the simplest.

He distrusted the evidence, suspected hasty judgments. He patiently tried to understand, never forgetting that the most obvious motives are not always the most important.

If he hadn't a very high opinion of men and their capabilities, he went on believing in man himself.

He looked for his weak points. And when, in the end, he put his finger on them, he didn't crow with joy, but on the contrary felt a certain sadness.

Since the previous day, he had felt out of his depth, for he had found himself unexpectedly faced with people whose very existence he had never suspected. All their attitudes, their remarks, their reactions were unfamiliar to him, and he tried in vain to classify them.

He wanted to like them, even Jaquette, for all that she got his back up.

He discovered, in their way of life, a grace, a harmony, a certain innocence too which appealed to him.

Suddenly, he coldly reminded himself:

'Saint-Hilaire has been killed for all that.'

By one of these people, that was practically certain. By Jaquette, if scientific tests still meant anything.

For a few moments, he felt an intense dislike for them all, including the dead man, and including that young man who had just aroused in him more keenly than ever before the longing for fatherhood.

Why shouldn't these people have been like others? Why shouldn't they have known the same sordid interests and the same passions?

This all too innocent love-story suddenly annoyed him. He stopped believing in it, and started looking for something else, a different explanation, more consistent with his experience.

Don't two women who have loved the same man for so many years inevitably end up by hating each other?

Wouldn't a family allied to most of the royal families of Europe react strongly to the threat of a marriage as ridiculous as that envisaged by the two old people?

None of them made any accusations. None of them had any enemies. All of them lived in apparent harmony, except Mazeron and his wife who had finally separated.

Irritated by the whispering which was still going on, Maigret nearly flung the door open, and possibly what restrained him was the reproachful glance which Janvier shot at him.

He too had been won over!

'I hope you've got somebody watching the corridor?'

He had got to the point of envisaging the possibility of the old priest's vanishing with his penitent.

All the same, he felt sure that he was on the verge of discovering the truth which had eluded him so far. It was all very simple, he knew that. Human dramas are always simple when you consider them after-wards.

Several times since the previous day, and especially since that morn-ing, though he couldn't have said exactly when, he had been on the point of understanding.

A discreet knocking on the communicating door made him jump.

'Shall I come with you?' asked Janvier.

'It would be a good idea if you did.'

The Abbé Barraud, who was indeed a very old man, was standing up, a skeletal figure with long, untidy hair forming a halo round his head. His cassock was shiny with wear, and it was badly darned here and there.

Jaquette did not seem to have left her chair, on which she was sitting as erect as ever. Only the expression on her face had changed. She was no longer tense, no longer in a fighting mood. She no longer showed any sign of defiance, of a fierce determination to remain silent.

If she was not smiling, she was none the less full of serenity.

'I must apologize, Chief-Inspector, for keeping you waiting such a long time. You see, the question Mademoiselle Larrieu asked me was rather delicate and I had to consider it carefully before giving her a re-ply. I must admit that I nearly asked you for permission to telephone the Archbishop to ask his opinion.'

Janvier, sitting at the end of the table, was taking down the conversa-tion in shorthand. Maigret, as if he felt the need to keep himself in countenance, had installed himself at his desk.

'Sit down, Monsieur l'Abbé.'

'I may stay?'

'I imagine your penitent still has need of your services.'

The priest sat down on a chair, took a little wooden box out of his cassock, and took a pinch of snuff. This gesture, and the grains of snuff on the greyish cassock, brought back old memories to Maigret.

'Mademoiselle Larrieu, as you are aware, is extremely devout, and it is her piety which has led her to adopt an attitude which I have felt it my duty to persuade her to abandon. What was worrying her was the thought that the Comte de Saint-Hilaire might not be given Christian burial, and that is why she had decided to wait until the funeral had taken place before saying anything.'

For Maigret, it was like a child's balloon suddenly bursting in the sunshine, and he blushed at having been so close to the truth without managing to guess it.

'The Comte de Saint-Hilaire committed suicide?'

'I am afraid that that is the truth of the matter. But as I told Mademoiselle Larrieu, we have no proof that he didn't repent what he had done at the last moment. No death is instantaneous in the eyes of the Church. Infinity exists in time as well as in space, and an infinitely small lapse of time, though it may defy measurement by doctors, is sufficient for contrition.

'I don't believe that the Church will refuse its last blessing to the Comte de Saint-Hilaire.'

For the first time, Jaquette's eyes became misty, and she took a handkerchief out of her bag to wipe them, while her lips formed a girlish pout.

'Speak up, Jaquette,' said the priest encouragingly. 'Repeat what you have just told me.'

She swallowed her saliva.

'I was in bed. I was asleep. I heard an explosion and I rushed into the study.'

'You found your master sprawled on the carpet with half his face shot away.'

'Yes.'

'Where was the pistol?'

'On the desk.'

'What did you do?'

'I went to get a mirror from my room to make sure that he had stopped breathing.'

'You made certain that he was dead. After that?'

'My first impulse was to telephone the Princess.'

'Why didn't you?'

'First of all because it was nearly midnight.'

'You weren't afraid that she would disapprove of your plan?'

'I didn't think of it straight away. I told myself that the police were going to come and suddenly I realized that because it was suicide the Count wouldn't be given Christian burial.'

'How long was it from the moment when you knew your employer was dead to the moment when you in your turn fired the gun?'

'I don't know. Ten minutes perhaps? I knelt down beside him and I said a prayer. Then, standing up, I took hold of the pistol and I fired, without looking, and asking the dead man and Heaven to forgive me.'

'You fired three bullets?'

'I don't know. I pulled the trigger until it didn't work any more. Then

I noticed some bright dots on the carpet. I don't know anything about guns. I realized that they were cartridge-cases and I picked them up. I didn't sleep a wink all night. Early next morning I went and threw the gun and the cartridge-cases into the Seine, from the Pont de la Concorde. I had to wait quite a while, because there was a policeman on duty in front of the Chamber of Deputies who seemed to be looking at me.'

'Do you know why your employer committed suicide?'

She glanced at the priest, who gave her an encouraging nod.

'For some time he had been worried and upset.'

'Why?'

'A few months ago, the doctor advised him to give up drinking wine and spirits. He was a great wine-lover. He gave it up for a few days, then he started drinking it again. That gave him stomach-ache and he had to get up in the night to take some bicarbonate of soda. In the end I was buying him a packet every week.'

'What's the name of his doctor?'

'Doctor Ourgaud.'

Maigret picked up the receiver.

'Get me Doctor Ourgaud please.'

And, to Jaquette:

'He had been his doctor for a long time?'

'You might almost say he had always been his doctor.'

'How old is Doctor Ourgaud?'

'I don't know exactly. About my age.'

'And he is still in practice?'

'He goes on seeing his old patients. His son has set up just across the landing from him, on the Boulevard Saint-Germain.'

Right to the very end, they remained not only in the same district but among people who might be said to belong to the same species.

'Hullo. Doctor Ourgaud? This is Chief-Inspector Maigret.'

The doctor asked him to speak louder and closer to the receiver, apologizing for being rather hard of hearing.

'As you may have guessed, I should like to ask you a few questions about one of your patients. Yes, it's him I'm talking about. Jaquette Larrieu is here in my office and has just told me that the Comte de Saint-Hilaire committed suicide.—What's that? . . . You were expecting me to come and see you? . . . You had guessed it was that? . . . Hullo. I'm speaking as close to the receiver as I can . . . She says that for several months, the Comte de Saint-Hilaire had been suffering from stomach-ache . . . I can hear you perfectly . . . Doctor Tudelle, the medical expert who carried out the post-mortem, says that he was surprised to find an old man's organs in such good condition . . .

'What's that? . . . That's what you kept telling your patient? . . . He didn't believe you? . . .

'Yes . . . Yes . . . I see . . . You couldn't manage to convince him . . . He went to see your colleagues . . .

'Thank you, Doctor . . . I shall probably have to trouble you to take your evidence . . . But no! On the contrary, it's very important . . .'

He hung up. His face was serious and Janvier thought he could distinguish a certain emotion in it.

'The Comte de Saint-Hilaire,' he explained in a rather dull voice, 'had got it into his head that he was suffering from cancer. In spite of his doctor's assurance to the contrary, he started going to different doctors to be examined, deciding every time that the truth was being kept from him.'

Jaquette murmured:

'He had always been so proud of his health! In the old days he often used to say to me that he wasn't afraid of death, that he was prepared for it, but that he would find it hard to put up with being ill. When he had the flu, for instance, he used to hide like a sick animal and tried to keep me out of his bedroom as much as possible. He was very touchy about it. One of his friends, several years ago, died of a cancer which kept him in bed for nearly two years. He was given various complicated treatments and the Count used to say impatiently: "Why don't they let him die? If I were in his place, I should ask them to help me to go on as soon as possible."'

Isabelle's grandson, Julien, could not remember the exact words Saint-Hilaire had used a few hours before he died. Thinking he would find him happy to see his dream close to fulfilment, he had found himself in the presence of an anxious, worried old man, who seemed to be afraid of something.

At least, that was what the young man had thought. Because he was not yet an old man. Jaquette, for her part, had understood straight away. And Maigret, who was more than half-way along the road, closer to the old people than to the students of the Rue d'Ulm, understood too: Saint-Hilaire expected to be bed-ridden before very long.

And that just as an old love, which nothing had dimmed in fifty years, was on the point of entering real life.

Isabelle, who saw him only from a distance and who had kept ever-present the picture of their youth, would become a sick-nurse at the same time as she became his wife, and she would know only the infirmities of a worn-out body.

'Excuse me,' he said suddenly, going towards the door.

He made his way along the corridors of the Palais de Justice, went up to the third floor, and spent half an hour closeted with the examining magistrate.

When he came back to his office, the three people were still in the same place and Janvier was chewing his pencil.

'You are free to go,' he told Jaquette. 'A car will take you home. Or rather, I think I ought to have you taken to Maître Aubonnet's, where you have an appointment. As for you, Monsieur l'Abbé, you will be dropped at the presbytery. In the next few days, there will be some formalities to be completed, some documents to be signed.'

And, turning to Janvier:

'Will you take the wheel?'

He spent an hour with the Director of Police Headquarters, and afterwards he was seen in the Brasserie Dauphine, where he drank two big glasses of beer at the bar.

Madame Maigret was expecting him to ring up to tell her that he would not be coming home for dinner, as often happened in the course of an investigation.

She was surprised, at half past six, to hear him coming up the stairs, and she opened the door at the very moment that he reached the landing.

He was more serious than usual, serious and serene, but she did not dare to ask him any questions when, as he kissed her, he pressed her against him for a long time without saying anything.

She could not know that he had just been immersed in a distant past and a rather less distant future.

'What's for dinner?' he finally asked, looking as if he were pulling himself together.

Noland
June 21, 1960

MAIGRET AND THE LAZY BURGLAR

I

A SHRILL noise broke out close to Maigret's ear, and he stirred crossly, as though startled, flapping one arm outside the bedclothes. He was aware of being in bed, and aware of his wife's presence at his side, wider awake than himself, lying in the dark without venturing to speak.

Where he was mistaken—at least for a few seconds—was about the nature of the insistent, aggressive, imperious sound. And it was always in winter, in very cold weather, that he made this mistake.

He thought his alarm-clock was ringing, although never since his marriage had there been one at his bedside. The idea went back even further than his boyhood—to the time when, as a small choirboy, he used to serve at mass at six o'clock in the morning.

Yet he had served at mass in spring, summer and autumn as well. Why did this one memory persist, returning to him unbidden—a memory of darkness, frost, stiff fingers, and thin ice in the lane, crackling underfoot?

He upset his glass of water, as often happened, and Madame Maigret switched on the bedside lamp just as his fumbling hand reached the telephone.

'Maigret here . . . Yes . . .'

It was ten minutes past four, and the silence outside was the special silence of the coldest winter nights.

'This is Fumel, Superintendent . . .'

'What d'you say?'

He could scarcely hear. It sounded as if the caller had a handkerchief stuffed in his mouth.

'Fumel, of the 16th . . .'

The man spoke softly, as though afraid of being overheard by someone in the next room. When the superintendent made no response, he added:

'Aristide . . .'

Oh—Aristide Fumel! Maigret was wide awake now, and wondering why the devil Inspector Fumel, of the 16th *arrondissement*, had woken him at four in the morning.

And also why he was speaking in that mysterious, almost furtive voice.

'I don't know if I'm right to telephone you . . . I informed my immediate superior, the superintendent at my own station, right away. He told me to ring the Public Prosecutor's office and I spoke to the official on night duty there . . .'

Although Madame Maigret could hear nothing except her husband's replies, she was already out of bed, her toes groping for her bedroom slippers. She wrapped her quilted dressing-gown round her and went off to the kitchen, whence came the hissing sound of gas and then the splash of water as she filled the kettle.

'One never knows what to do nowadays, if you see what I mean. The Public Prosecutor's assistant told me to go back to the spot and wait for him. I didn't find the body myself, it was two of the cycle-patrol chaps . . .'

'Where?'

'Beg pardon?'

'I asked where?'

'In the Bois de Boulogne . . . Route des Poteaux . . . You know it? It's a turning off the Avenue Fortunée, not far from the Porte Dauphine . . . A middle-aged man . . . About my age . . . So far as I could make out, his pockets were empty, no identity papers . . . I didn't move the body, of course . . . I can't say why, but it strikes me there's something queer about it, and I felt I'd like to ring you . . . It would be as well for the Public Prosecutor's people not to know . . .'

'Thanks, Fumel . . .'

'I'll be getting back there at once, in case they turn up quicker than usual.'

'Where are you now?'

'In the station in the Rue de la Faisanderie. Will you be coming along?'

Maigret, snug in his warm bed, hesitated, then said:

'Yes.'

'What'll you say?'

'Don't know yet. I'll think of something.'

He was feeling humiliated, almost angry, not for the first time in the past six months. Fumel was a good chap, it wasn't his fault.

Madame Maigret appeared in the doorway to advise:

'Dress up warmly. It's freezing hard.'

Drawing back the curtain, he saw frost-flowers on the window. The street lamp had the special brightness that only comes with intense cold, and along the Boulevard Richard-Lenoir there was not a soul to be seen or a sound to be heard—just one lighted window, in the house opposite; must be someone ill there.

So now 'they' were forcing the police to play tricks! By 'they' he meant the Public Prosecutor's Department, the crowd at the Ministry of the Interior—the whole bunch of college-educated law-givers who had taken it into their heads to run the world according to their own little ideas.

They looked on the police force as a minor, slightly discreditable cog in the wheel of Justice with a capital J—one to regard with suspicion, to watch out for, to keep in its place.

Like Janvier, Lucas and a score or so of Maigret's men, Fumel was the old-fashioned kind; but the others had adjusted themselves to the new methods and rules—all they thought of was passing exams so as to get quicker promotion.

Poor Fumel had stuck at the bottom of the ladder because he could never learn to spell or to draw up a report!

Nowadays the Public Prosecutor insisted that he or one of his staff should be the first to be informed and the first on the scene, accompanied by a sleepy examining magistrate; and the pair of them would give their views as though they'd spent their entire lives finding corpses and knew more about criminals than anyone else.

As for the police, they were sent on errands . . . 'You're to do such and such . . . You're to arrest so-and-so and bring him to my office . . .

'And mind you don't ask him any questions! We must keep strictly to the regulations.'

There were so many regulations—the *Journal Officiel* published shoals, which sometimes contradicted one another—that even the magistrates lost their way among them and went in terror of being caught out by some protesting Counsel.

Maigret dressed himself, crossly. Why did the coffee always taste different on winter nights when he was woken up like this? The flat had a different smell, too, one that reminded him of his parents' house in the days when he used to get up at half past five every morning.

'Will you telephone to the office for a car?'

No! If he arrived on the scene in an official car, they might ask what he was up to.

'Ring for a taxi from the rank.'

He wouldn't get a refund, unless he caught the murderer very quickly—assuming it was a murder. Taxi fares were only refunded if you were successful, these days. And even then you had to prove that there had been no other way of getting to the spot.

His wife handed him a thick, woolly muffler.

'Have you got your gloves?'

He felt in his overcoat pocket.

'Won't you have something to eat?'

He was not hungry. His manner was glum, and yet at bottom this was the kind of moment he enjoyed—even, perhaps, what he would miss most after he retired.

He went downstairs and found a taxi at the door, white steam puffing out of its exhaust.

'The Bois de Boulogne . . . You know the Route des Poteaux?'

'It'd be a poor show if I didn't, after thirty-five years at this job.'

It was with that kind of talk that the older drivers consoled themselves for the passage of time.

The leather upholstery was ice-cold. They met only a few cars, and an occasional empty bus making for its terminus. Even the earliest bars were still in darkness. Cleaners were at work in the offices along the Champs-Elysées.

'Another tart got herself knocked off?'

'I don't know . . . I don't think so.'

'I was thinking she wouldn't find many clients in the Bois in weather like this.'

Maigret's pipe tasted different, too. He thrust his hands deeper into his pockets, reflecting that it must be at least three months since he last met Fumel and that he had known him since . . . almost ever since he himself had joined the force, when he'd been attached to one of the district police stations.

Fumel had been ugly even in those days, and even then the other men had pitied and laughed at him—partly because his parents had been misguided enough to christen him Aristide and partly because, in spite of his appearance, he was always involved in some love-drama.

He married, and after a year his wife disappeared. He moved heaven and earth to find her. For years, every policeman in France had carried her description in his pocket, and Fumel used to rush to the Morgue whenever a woman's body was fished out of the Seine.

The thing had become a byword.

'I can't get it out of my head that something dreadful has happened to her and that it was me they were aiming at,' he would say.

He had a wall-eye—immobile and paler than the other, almost transparent; it made you feel embarrassed when he looked at you.

'I shall love her all my life . . . And I know I shall find her some day.'

Was he still clinging to that hope, now he'd reached fifty-one? It didn't prevent him from falling in love at intervals; and his bad luck persisted, for his affairs invariably landed him in incredible complications and ended disastrously.

He had even been accused of living on immoral earnings—this on the apparently convincing evidence of a strumpet who was making a fool of him—and had narrowly escaped being dismissed from the force.

How did a man, so ingenuous and awkward in private life, manage to be one of the best police inspectors in Paris?

The taxi entered the Bois by the Porte Dauphine and turned to the right. The glow of a pocket torch could already be seen ahead, and soon they came to where some shadowy figures stood beside a path.

Maigret got out and paid the taxi. One of the figures came up to him. It was Fumel.

'You've got here before them . . .' breathed the inspector, stamping on the frozen ground to warm his feet.

There were two bicycles propped against a tree. The cycle police, in their capes, were stamping about too, while a little man in a light-grey felt hat glanced impatiently at his watch.

'Doctor Boisrond, from the registrar's department . . .'

Maigret shook the doctor's hand absent-mindedly and strolled over to a dark shape lying at the foot of a tree. Fumel turned his torch on it.

'I think you'll see what I mean, Superintendent,' he began. 'It strikes me there's something fishy . . .'

'Who found him?'

'These two cycle-patrol men, going their round . . .'

'What time was it?'

'Twelve minutes past three. At first they thought it was a sack someone had dropped there.'

And indeed, the man lying in the stiff-frozen grass looked like a shapeless bundle. He was not stretched out, but huddled, almost curled up, except that one hand projected, the fingers still clenched as though trying to clutch at something.

'What did he die of?' Maigret asked the doctor.

'I was a bit frightened to touch him before the Public Prosecutor's men arrive, but so far as I can tell his skull was fractured by a blow, or blows, from some very heavy object . . .'

'His skull?' queried the superintendent.

For the light of the pocket torch showed him a bruised and blood-stained mass where the face should have been.

'I can't say for certain before the post-mortem, but I would almost swear those blows were struck afterwards, when the man was already dead, or at least dying . . .'

Whereupon Fumel peered at Maigret through the semi-darkness and said:

'You see what I mean, Chief?'

The clothes on the body were good but not expensive—like those of a civil servant or a retired business executive.

'You say there's nothing in his pockets?'

'I felt them cautiously and there were no bulges . . . Now, take a look round . . .'

Fumel moved the beam of his torch over the ground near the man's head; there was no trace of blood.

'It wasn't here that he was bashed. The doctor agrees, because from the nature of the wounds he must have bled freely. So he was brought to the Bois—by car, no doubt. From the way he's huddled up, one would even say he was simply pushed out of the car—that the chaps who brought him didn't bother to get out themselves.'

The Bois de Boulogne lay silent, lifeless, as an empty stage, its widely spaced lamps casting perfect circles of white light.

'Look out . . . Here they are, I think.'

A car was approaching from the direction of the Porte Dauphine—a long, black car, seeking its way. Fumel hurried to meet it, waving his torch.

Maigret stood back, puffing at his pipe.

'This is the place, sir . . . The Superintendent had to go to the Hôpital Cochin for an identification; he'll be here in a few minutes.'

Maigret recognized the Public Prosecutor's deputy, a tall, thin, elegant man about thirty years old, whose name was Kernavel. He also recognized the examining magistrate, as it happened, though he had seldom worked with him: a certain Cajou, a dark-haired fellow in his early forties, who stood, as it were, midway between the old generation and the new. The clerk who accompanied them kept well away from the corpse, as though afraid the sight would turn his stomach.

'Who . . .' began the Deputy Prosecutor.

He looked at Maigret's shadowy figure and frowned.

'Excuse me. I didn't see you at first. How do you come to be here?'

Maigret replied with a vague gesture and the even vaguer words: 'By accident.'

Kernavel was annoyed; he went on speaking, ostensibly to Fumel: 'What exactly happened?'

'Two cycle-patrol men were on their round when they noticed the body, just over an hour ago. I reported to my local superintendent, but as I explained, he had to go to the Hôpital Cochin for an urgent identification and he instructed me to inform your department. As soon as I had done so, I telephoned to Doctor Boisrond.'

The Deputy Prosecutor looked round for the doctor.

'What did you find, Doctor?'

'A fracture of the skull; probably multiple fractures.'

'An accident? You don't suppose he was knocked down by a car?'

'He was struck several times with a blunt instrument, first on the head and then in the face.'

'So you are certain it was murder?'

Maigret could have held his tongue, left things to them, let them go on talking. But he took a step forward.

'It might save time, perhaps, if the Judicial Identity experts were informed.'

The Prosecutor's man said, still addressing himself to Fumel:

'Send one of the cycle men to telephone.'

He was blue with cold. They were all cold, standing round the motionless body.

'A night prowler?'

'He's not dressed like a vagrant, and in this weather they don't come much to the Bois.'

'Been robbed?'

'For all I know—there's nothing in his pockets.'

'Attacked on his way home?'

'There's no blood on the ground. The doctor thinks—and so do I—that the crime was not committed here.'

'In that case it was most likely a private vendetta.'

The Deputy Prosecutor spoke emphatically, pleased at having found a satisfactory explanation of the problem.

'The crime was probably committed in Montmartre and the gang that did it got rid of the body by dumping it here . . .'

He turned to Maigret:

'I don't think this is a matter for you, Superintendent. You no doubt have some important cases on hand. Oh, yes—where have you got to over the Post Office hold-up in the 13th *arrondissement?*'

'Nowhere, as yet.'

'And the previous hold-ups? How many have we had, in Paris alone, in the last fortnight?'

'Five.'

'That's the figure I seemed to remember. So I'm rather surprised to find you here, concerning yourself with a matter of no importance.'

It was not the first time Maigret had heard this kind of thing. The Public Prosecutor's people were alarmed by the crime wave, as they called it, and particularly by the sensational robberies which had been, for some time past, in one of their recurrent periods of crescendo.

It meant that a new gang had been formed recently.

'You still have no clues?'

'None whatsoever.'

This was not absolutely true. Though he had no actual evidence, Maigret had formed a theory that held together and seemed to be borne out by events. But that did not concern anyone else, least of all the Public Prosecutor's department.

'Listen, Cajou, you can handle this business. If you'll take my advice it will be least said, soonest mended. It's a commonplace incident, a quarrel in the underworld, and if the gangsters take to killing one another, so much the better for the rest of us. You see what I mean?'

He turned to Fumel again.

'You're an inspector in the 16th *arrondissement?*'

Fumel nodded.

'How long have you been in the force?'

'Thirty years . . . Twenty-nine, to be precise.'

'Has he a good record?' Kernavel asked Maigret.

'He's a man who knows his job.'

Kernavel took the examining magistrate aside and talked to him in an undertone. When the two of them came back, Cajou seemed rather embarrassed.

'Well, Superintendent, thank you for coming along. I'll keep in touch with Inspector Fumel and give him my instructions. If a time comes when I think he needs help, I'll send someone to ask for your views, or get you to come to my office. Your own work is so important and so urgent that I must not delay you here any longer.'

It was not only from cold that Maigret's face had turned pale, and he bit so hard on the stem of his pipe that it made a faint cracking sound.

'Gentlemen . . .' he said, as though in farewell.

'Have you a car?' asked the Deputy Prosecutor.

'I shall find a taxi at the Porte Dauphine.'

Kernavel hesitated, on the point of offering to drive him there; but the superintendent was already walking away, after a little wave of the hand to Fumel.

And yet, half an hour later, Maigret would no doubt have been able to tell them a good deal about the dead man. He was not certain as yet, that was why he had said nothing.

The moment he bent to look at the body he felt this was someone he had seen before. Although the face had been battered to pulp, he could have sworn he recognized it.

All he needed was one scrap of evidence, and that would be found when the body was undressed.

If he was right, of course, the fingerprints would point to the same conclusion.

On the rank he found the taxi that had brought him.

'Finished already?'

'Take me home to the Boulevard Richard-Lenoir.'

'Okay. But talk about quick work . . . Who is it?'

A bar was open in the Place de la République, and Maigret was tempted to stop the taxi and go in for a glass of something. He refrained, however, feeling it would not be quite the thing.

His wife had gone back to bed, but she heard him on the stairs, and got up to open the door. She, too, was surprised:

'Back already?' she asked; adding at once, anxiously:

'What's happening?'

'Nothing. Those gentlemen didn't need me.'

He said as little as possible about it to her. He seldom mentioned the Quai des Orfèvres and its affairs in his own home.

'Have you had anything to eat?'

'No.'

'I'll get breakfast ready. You'd better have a bath right away, to warm you up.'

He did not feel cold. His anger had given way to depression.

He wasn't the only member of the Judicial Police who had a sense of discouragement, and the Director had twice threatened to resign. He would not have a third opportunity of doing so, because the question of his successor was already under consideration.

The place was being reorganized, as they called it. Well-educated, gentlemanly young fellows, scions of the best French families, were sitting in quiet offices, studying the whole thing in the interests of efficiency. Their learned cogitations were producing unpractical plans that found expression in a weekly batch of new regulations.

To begin with, the police were now declared to be an instrument at the service of justice. A mere instrument. And an instrument has no brain.

It was now the examining magistrate in his office and the Public Prosecutor in his awe-inspiring headquarters who directed investigations and gave orders.

What was more, the orders were no longer to be carried out by the old-fashioned type of policeman, the traditional 'flatfoot' such as Aristide Fumel, some of whom didn't know how to spell.

Now that it was nearly all paper-work, what was to be done with such men, who had learnt their job in the streets, the department stores and the railway stations, getting to know every drink-shop in their own districts, acquainted with every tough and every tart, and able, if need be, to argue with them in their own language?

Now they had to sit for exams and obtain certificates at every step of their career, and when he needed to organize a raid, Maigret had nobody to rely on except the few survivors of his old team.

'They' were not pushing him out yet. They were biding their time, knowing he was only two years short of retirement age.

But they were beginning to keep a close eye on him.

It was still dark as he ate his breakfast, while the windows across the street lit up, one after another. Because of that telephone call he was earlier than usual, and a bit sluggish, as one is after too little sleep.

'Fumel—isn't that the one who squints?'

'Yes.'

'And whose wife ran away?'

'Yes.'

'Was she ever found?'

'It seems she's in South America, married again and with a swarm of children.'

'Does he know?'

'What would be the point?'

Maigret got to the office early, too, and though it was at last beginning to grow light, he was obliged to turn on his green-shaded lamp.

'Get me the all-night station in the Rue de la Faisanderie, please.'

It was he who was wrong. He didn't want to grow sentimental.

'Hallo? Is Inspector Fumel there? What's that? Writing up his report?'

Always this paper-work, this form-filling, this waste of time.

'That you, Fumel?'

The other man was again speaking below his breath, as though making a surreptitious call.

'Have the Identity people finished their job?'

'Yes. They left an hour ago.'

'Did the official pathologist turn up?'

'Yes. The new one.'

For there was a new official pathologist as well. Old Doctor Paul, who had gone on making post-mortems till he was seventy-six, had died and been succeeded by a man called Lamalle.

'What does he say?'

'The same as the first doctor. The man wasn't killed where we found him. He must have bled a great deal, no doubt about that. The last blows, in the face, were struck after the chap was dead.'

'Did they undress him?'

'Partly.'

'You didn't notice a tattoo mark on the left arm?'

'How did you know?'

'A fish . . . A kind of sea-horse?'

'Yes . . .'

'Did they take his fingerprints?'

'By now they'll be dealing with them in Records.'

'The body's gone to the Medico-Legal Institute?'

'Yes . . . You know, I felt very uncomfortable just now . . . I still do . . . But I didn't like to . . .'

'You can put in your report that in all probability the victim is a certain Honoré Cuendet, a Swiss from Vaud, who at one time spent five years in the Foreign Legion.'

'The name rings a bell . . . Do you know where he lived?'

'No. But I know where his mother lives, if she's still alive. I'd rather be the first to talk to her.'

'*They* will find out.'

'I don't care. Make a note of the address, but don't go there before I give you the word. She lives in the Rue Mouffetard. I don't know the number, but it's just above a bakery, nearly at the corner of the Rue Saint-Médard.'

'Thank you, Chief.'

'That's all right. Are you staying on in the office?'

'It'll take me a good two or three hours to write this blasted report.'

Maigret had been right, and it gave him a certain satisfaction, mingled with a touch of melancholy. Leaving his office, he climbed a flight of stairs to the records department, where men in grey overalls were busily at work.

'Who's dealing with the prints of the man found dead in the Bois de Boulogne?'

'I am, Superintendent.'

'Traced him?'

'Just this moment.'

'Cuendet?'

'Yes.'

'Thanks.'

Feeling almost lively by this time, Maigret went along a succession of corridors till he came to the attics of the Palais de Justice. Here, among the Judicial Identity experts, he found his old friend Moers, who was also poring over some forms. Never had there been such a clutter of papers as in the last six months. It was true that even in the old days the administrative work had been considerable; but Maigret estimated that it had recently begun to take up about eighty per cent of the time of all police personnel.

'Have they brought you the clothes?'

'Of the chap in the Bois de Boulogne?'

'Yes.'

Moers pointed to two of his men, who were shaking big paper bags containing the dead man's clothes. This was routine procedure, the first technical operation. In this way all kinds of dust was collected and subsequently analysed, sometimes yielding valuable clues—for example, as to what had been the occupation of some unidentified man, or where he usually lived, or sometimes as to the place where the crime had actually been committed.

'Pockets?'

'Nothing. No watch, no pocket-book, no keys. Not even a handkerchief. Literally nothing.'

'Any laundry-marks, or tabs on his suit?'

'Yes, those weren't torn out or cut off. I made a note of the tailor's name. Do you want it?'

'Not at present. The man's been identified.'

'Who is he?'

'An old acquaintance of mine, a fellow called Cuendet.'

'A criminal?'

'A quiet man, probably the quietest burglar there ever was.'

'Do you think it was an accomplice who did the job?'

'Cuendet never had an accomplice.'

'Why was he killed?'

'That's just what I'm wondering.'

Here again they were working by artificial lights, as in most Paris offices on that particular day. The sky was a steely grey, and out in the street the pavement looked as black as though it were coated with ice.

People were walking fast, keeping close to the houses, a little cloud of vapour floating in front of each mouth.

Maigret went back to his inspectors. Two or three of them were on the telephone, but the majority, inevitably, were writing.

'Any news, Lucas?'

'We're still hunting for old Fernand. Someone thinks he saw him in Paris three weeks ago, but can't say for certain.'

An old con. Ten years ago this Fernand, whose identity had never been definitely established, was a member of a gang that had brought off an impressive number of hold-ups in the space of a few months.

The whole bunch had been arrested, and the case had dragged on for nearly two years. The leader had died in prison, of TB. A few of his subordinates were still behind bars, but the time had come when they were being released, one by one, as the result of good-conduct remissions.

Maigret had not mentioned this just now to the Deputy Public Prosecutor, when he expressed such alarm about the 'new crime-wave'. He had his own ideas on the subject. Certain points about the recent hold-ups had led him to believe that some of the old crowd were mixed up in the business, had no doubt formed a new gang.

All that was needed was to find one of them. And every man who could be spared had been working patiently to that end for nearly three months.

Their inquiries had finally centered on Fernand. He had been released a year ago, and for the last six months there had been no sign of him.

'His wife?'

'She still swears she hasn't seen him. The neighbours bear her out. No one has seen Fernand in that district.'

'Carry on, boys . . . If anyone asks for me . . . If anyone from the Public Prosecutor's department asks for me . . .'

He paused, then added:

'Say I've gone out for a drink. Say whatever you like.'

All the same, they were not going to stop him dealing with a man he had known for thirty years and who was almost a personal friend.

II

IT WAS rare for Maigret to talk about his work, and even rarer for him to pass judgment on any individual or method. He mistrusted ideas as being always too specific to fit the circumstances—which, he knew by experience, were in a state of perpetual flux.

Only to his friend Doctor Pardon, who lived in the Rue Popincourt, did he occasionally, after dinner, mutter something that might, at a pinch, be regarded as confidential.

It so happened that a few weeks before this he had gone to the point of declaring with some bitterness:

'You know, Pardon, people imagine we're there to track down criminals and get confessions from them. That's just another of the mistaken notions that drift around until everyone is so used to them that nobody thinks of calling them in question. In point of fact our chief job is to protect the State in the first place—whatever government is in power, with its institutions; in the second place the currency, public property and private property; and then, last of all, the lives of the individual private citizens.

'Did you ever take a look into the Penal Code? You have to read as far as page 177 before you come to anything about crimes against human beings. One day later on, when I retire, I'll work it out precisely. But let's say that three-quarters of the Code, if not four-fifths, is concerned with goods and chattels, real estate, forged currency, forgeries of public and private documents, falsification of wills, etc., etc. In short, with money in all its shapes and forms . . . To such an extent that Article 274, on mendicancy, comes before Article 295, on wilful homicide . . .'

This although they had dined well that evening, and drunk an un-forgettable Saint-Emilion.

'The newspapers give the greatest amount of space to my service—the Crime Squad, as it has come to be called—because it's the most sensational. But in actual fact we're less important, in the eyes of the Minister of the Interior, for example, than General Information or the Finance Section.

'We're rather like barristers in court. We make a show, but it's the back-room boys who do the serious work.'

Would he have talked like that twenty years ago? Or even six months ago, before the changes he was watching with so much misgiving?

He muttered to himself as, with his coat collar turned up, he crossed the Pont Saint-Michel, leaning against the north wind at the same an-gle as all the other pedestrians.

He often talked to himself like this, with a surly expression on his face; and one day he had overheard Lucas telling Janvier, then a new-comer to the Préfecture:

'Take no notice. When he's in a brown study it doesn't necessarily mean he's in a bad temper.'

Nor even that he was depressed. Only that something was nagging at him. Today it was the attitude of the Public Prosecutor's men in the Bois de Boulogne, and also the stupid end that Honoré Cuendet had come to, with his face battered to pulp after his skull had been smashed in.

Tell 'em I've gone for a drink.

That's what things had come to. What interested the gentlemen in high places was to put a stop to the series of attacks that were causing losses to banks, insurance companies and the Post Office. They also con-sidered that car-thefts were becoming too frequent.

'What about giving more protection to the cashiers?' he had expos-tulated. 'Why leave one man, or a couple of men, to convey millions of francs by a route that anyone can find out beforehand?'

Too expensive, of course!

As for the private cars, was it reasonable to leave such things—worth a fortune, in some cases the price of an average flat, or of a little house in the suburbs—parked along the curb, sometimes without locking the doors or even removing the ignition key?

You might as well leave a diamond necklace, or a wallet containing two or three million francs, in a place where any Tom, Dick or Harry could pick it up.

And so what? It was none of his business. He, more than ever, was a mere instrument, and such questions didn't come within his range.

All the same, he went to the Rue Mouffetard where, despite the cold, he found the usual bustle going on round the pavement stalls and the hand-barrows. Two doors beyond the Rue Saint-Médard he recognized the narrow, yellow-painted front of the bakery, and above it the low windows of the *entresol*.

The house was an old one, tall and narrow. From the far end of the courtyard came the noise of hammering on iron.

Maigret went up the stairs, where there was a rope by way of banisters, and knocked at a door. Soon he heard soft footsteps.

'Is that you, dear?' a voice inquired, as the handle turned and the door opened.

The old woman had grown even fatter, but only in her lower half, from the waist downwards. She had a thinnish face and narrow shoulders, but her hips had become enormous, so enormous that she could hardly walk.

She stared at Maigret in alarmed astonishment, with the expression to which he was accustomed in such people, who went in dread of some misfortune.

'I know you, don't I? You've been here before . . . Wait a minute . . .'

'Superintendent Maigret . . .' he muttered, stepping into a room that was full of warmth and the smell of stew.

'Yes, that's it . . . I remember . . . What have you got against him this time?'

She gave no impression of hostility, only of a kind of resignation, an acceptance of fate.

She pointed to a chair. There was only one arm-chair in the room, a shabby leather affair, and that was occupied by a small sandy-haired dog who bared his pointed teeth with a low growl, and a cat—white with coffee-coloured spots—who scarcely opened his green eyes.

'Quiet, Toto,' said the woman—adding to Maigret 'He just growls, but he's not dangerous. He's my son's dog. I don't know whether it's from living with me, but he's grown to look like me.'

And indeed, the beast had a tiny head with a pointed nose, and spindly legs, but its body was plump, more like a pig's than a dog's. It seemed very old. It had yellow teeth, with gaps between them.

'Honoré picked him up in the street, at least fifteen years ago; he'd had two legs broken by a car . . . Honoré put them into splints, though the neighbours wanted to have the dog put down; and two months later he was running about with the best of them.'

The room had a low ceiling and was rather dark, but remarkably clean. It served both as kitchen and dining-room; there was a round table in the middle, an old dresser, and a Dutch cooking-stove of a type seldom seen nowadays. Cuendet must have bought it in the flea-market, or from a junk dealer, and refurbished it—he had always been clever with his hands. The iron top was nearly red-hot, the brass bits glittered, and it made a faint roaring sound.

Outside, the street market was in full swing and Maigret remembered that at his last visit he had found the old woman leaning out of the window; in fine weather she spent most of her time like that, watching the crowd below.

'Well, Superintendent?'

She spoke in the slow accents of her native Switzerland, and instead of sitting down opposite him she remained standing, on the defensive.

'When did you last see your son?'

'Tell me first whether you've arrested him yet.'

After only a second's hesitation he was able to answer, truthfully: 'No.'

'In other words, you're looking for him? In that case I can tell you at once that he isn't here. You can search the place, as you've done before. You'll find no changes, although that was over ten years ago.'

She pointed to an open door and he looked through into a dining-room that was never used; it was cluttered with useless ornaments, doilies and framed photographs—typical of humble people who are nevertheless determined to keep one room 'for best'.

The superintendent remembered that there were two bedrooms, over-looking the courtyard—the old woman's, which had an iron bedstead by which she set great store, and the one Honoré sometimes used, which was almost as plain but more comfortable.

The smell of fresh-baked bread rose from the ground floor and mingled with the smell of stew.

Maigret was grave, even a little moved.

'I'm not looking for him, either, Madame Cuendet. I would just like to know . . .'

At once she seemed to understand, to guess, and she stared at him more keenly, a glint of anxiety in her eyes.

'If you're not looking for him and you haven't arrested him, it means that . . .'

She had thinning hair and the top of her head looked absurdly small.

'Something's happened to him, isn't that it?'

He bowed his head.

'I thought I'd rather tell you myself.'

'The police shot him?'

'No . . . I . . .'

'An accident?'

'Your son is dead, Madame Cuendet.'

She gazed at him fixedly, dry-eyed, and the sandy dog, which seemed to understand, jumped down from the arm-chair and came over to rub against her fat legs.

'Who did it?'

The words were forced out between teeth as widely spaced as those of the dog, which began growling again.

'I don't know. He was killed, but we don't yet know where.'

'Then how can you tell . . .'

'His body was found this morning beside one of the paths in the Bois de Boulogne.'

She repeated the words, mistrustfully, as though still scenting a trap.

'In the Bois de Boulogne? What would he be doing in the Bois de Boulogne?'

'That's where he was found. He had been killed somewhere else and brought there by car.'

'Why?'

He was patient, careful not to rush her, taking his time.

'That's what we're wondering ourselves.'

How could he have explained his attitude towards Cuendet to the examining magistrate, for instance? It wasn't only in his office on the Quai des Orfèvres that he had come to know the man. And that first rather slapdash investigation had not been enough. It had taken thirty years of his professional life and several visits to this flat, where he no longer felt like a stranger.

'It's in order to find his murderers that I need to know when you saw him for the last time. He hadn't slept here for some days, had he?'

'At his age a man surely has the right . . .'

She broke off, her eyes suddenly filling with tears, and asked:

'Where is he now?'

'You'll see him presently. An inspector will come to fetch you.'

'He's been taken to the Morgue?'

'To the Medico-Legal Institute—yes.'

'Did he suffer?'

'No.'

'They shot him?'

Tears were running down her cheeks, but she was not sobbing, and there was still a shade of distrust in her expression as she stared at Maigret.

'They bashed him.'

'What with?'

She seemed to be trying to reconstruct her son's death in her own mind.

'We don't know. Something heavy.'

Instinctively she raised a hand to her head, with a grimace of pain.

'Why?'

'We shall find out, I promise you. That is why I've come here and why I need your help. Sit down, Madame Cuendet.'

'I can't.'

But her knees were shaking.

'Haven't you anything to drink?'

'You're thirsty?'

'No. It's for you. I'd like you to take a nip of something.'

He remembered she was fond of her glass, and at this, sure enough, she went to the dining-room sideboard and brought out a bottle of plum brandy.

Even at such a moment she couldn't resist cheating a bit.

'I was keeping it for my son . . . He sometimes took a drop after dinner.'

She filled two thick-bottomed glasses.

'I wonder why they killed him,' she resumed. 'A lad who never harmed a soul—the quietest, gentlest man in the world . . . Wasn't he, Toto? You know that better than anyone . . .'

As she wept she patted the fat dog, who wagged his stump of a tail. The Deputy Prosecutor and Cajou, the examining magistrate, would no doubt have found the scene ludicrous.

After all, the son she was talking about was an ex-convict and would still have been in prison, but for his own cleverness.

He had only gone there twice, and on one occasion merely while awaiting trial. Both times it had been Maigret who had arrested him.

They had spent hours and hours in solitary conversation at the Quai des Orfèvres, fencing with one another as though each appreciated the other at his full value.

'How long is it since . . .'

Maigret returned to the attack, patiently, speaking in level tones against a background of market noises.

'A good month,' she said, giving way at last.

'He didn't tell you anything?'

'He never told me about anything he did outside this house.'

That was true, as Maigret had discovered in the old days.

'He never once came to see you during that time?'

'No. Although it was my birthday last week. He sent me some flowers.'

'Where did he send them from?'

'An errand-boy brought them.'

'Was there no florist's name on them?'

'There may have been. I didn't look.'

'You didn't recognize the errand-boy? He wasn't from hereabouts?'

'I'd never seen him before.'

He did not ask to search Honoré Cuendet's room for clues. He was only there unofficially. He had not been put in charge of the investigation.

Inspector Fumel would no doubt be coming along presently, armed with a proper warrant, signed by the examining magistrate. He would probably find nothing. On previous occasions Maigret himself had found nothing, except a neat row of suits, linen on the wardrobe shelves, a few books, and some tools which were not burglar's implements.

'How long was it since he'd last vanished in that way?'

She searched her memory. Her mind was not entirely on the conversation and she had to make an effort.

'He was here nearly all winter.'

'And in the summer?'

'I don't know where he went then.'

'He didn't suggest taking you away to the country or the seaside?'

'I wouldn't have gone. I've lived too much in the country to want to go back there.'

She must have been about fifty, or a little over, when she first discovered Paris, and the only town she had known before that was Lausanne.

She came from Sénarclens, a tiny hamlet in the Canton of Vaud, near a village called Cossonay, where her husband worked as a farm labourer.

Maigret had passed quickly through that part of the country once, long ago, on holiday with his wife, and the inns were what he remembered best.

And it was precisely those clean, quiet inns that had been the ruin of Gilles Cuendet—a little bandy-legged, taciturn man who would sit for hours in a corner, drinking glass after glass of white wine.

From being a farm labourer he had sunk to the level of mole-catcher, going from farm to farm to set his traps, and people declared he stank as badly as his quarry.

The couple had two children, Honoré and his sister Laurence. The girl had been sent to Geneva to work as a barmaid, had ended by marrying someone from UNESCO—a translator, if Maigret remembered rightly—and had gone to South America with him.

'Have you any news of your daughter?'

'She sent me a Christmas card. She has five children now. I'll show you the card.'

She went to the next room to fetch it, more as an excuse for moving about than to convince Maigret.

The card showed Rio bay in the glow of a red and purple sunset.

'Does she never write you more than that?'

'Why should she? We're on opposite sides of the ocean, we shall never see each other again. She's made her own life, after all.'

So had Honoré, but differently. At the age of fifteen he, too, had been sent away to work, apprenticed to a locksmith at Lausanne.

He was a placid, secretive boy, scarcely more talkative than his father. He had an attic room in an old house near the market-place, and it was there that the police suddenly appeared one morning as the result of an anonymous denunciation. At that time Honoré was not yet seventeen. They had found all sorts of things in his room, a jumble of incongruous objects the origin of which he had not even attempted to explain—alarm clocks, tools, tinned foods, children's clothes with the price-tags still on them, two or three wireless sets that he had not even unpacked.

At first the police thought he was a 'pull-in' thief, stealing from parked lorries.

Investigation revealed, however, that he was nothing of the kind—that he used to break into closed shops, warehouses and empty flats and carry off indiscriminately whatever he could lay hands on.

As he was so young they had sent him to the approved school

at Vennes, above Lausanne, where he had been given his choice of
several trades and had elected to be trained as a boiler-maker.

For a year he had been a model pupil, quiet, good-mannered, hard-
working and always obedient to the rules.

Then he had suddenly vanished without trace; and ten years were to
go by before Maigret ran across him in Paris.

The first thing he had done on leaving Switzerland—where he never
set foot again—was to enlist in the Foreign Legion, and he had spent
five years at Sidi-Bel-Abbès and in Indo-China.

The superintendent had had occasion to study his military record
and to have a chat with one of his superior officers.

There again, Honoré Cuendet had been, by and large, a model soldier. The only complaint was that he was unsociable, had no friends
and never mixed with the others even on festive occasions.

'He was a soldier the way another man might be a fitter or a cob-
bler,' said his lieutenant.

He went through three years without a single punishment. Whereupon, for no known reason, he deserted, and was discovered after a
few days in a workshop in Algiers, where he had found a job.

He offered no explanation of his abrupt departure, which might have
got him into considerable trouble, beyond a muttered:

'I couldn't stand it any longer.'

'Why not?'

'I don't know.'

Thanks to his three years of irreproachable service he was let
off lightly. Six months later he ran away again, and this time was
caught after only twenty-four hours of freedom, in a lorry where he was
hiding among a load of vegetables.

It was in the Legion that, at his own request, a fish had been tattooed on his left arm; Maigret had tried to find out why. Most Legion-
aires prefer more suggestive designs.

It was a man of twenty-six who had confronted Maigret on that first
occasion, a shortish, broad-shouldered man with carroty hair.

'Have you ever seen any sea-horses?'

'Not live ones.'

'Any dead ones?'

'One, once.'

'Where?'

'At Lausanne.'

'Where in Lausanne?'

'In a woman's room.'

The words had to be dragged out of him one by one, as it were.

'Who was the woman?'

'A woman I went to see.'

'Before you were shut up at Vennes?'

'Yes.'

'You followed her?'

'Yes.'

'In the street?'

'Yes, right down the Rue Centrale.'

'And there was a dried sea-horse in her room?'

'That's right. She told me it was her mascot.'

'Have you known a lot of other women?'

'Not a great many.'

Maigret thought he understood.

'What did you do when you were demobbed from the Legion and came to Paris?'

'I worked.'

'Where?'

'At a locksmith's in the Rue de la Roquette.'

The police had checked this statement and found it to be true. He had worked there for two years and given entire satisfaction. True, his mates teased him for being 'standoffish', but he was regarded as a model workman.

'What did you do in the evenings?'

'Nothing.'

'Didn't you go to the cinema?'

'Hardly ever.'

'Had you any men friends?'

'No.'

'Any girl friends?'

'Not likely!'

It looked as though women scared him. And yet it was because of the first woman he had ever met, when he was only sixteen, that he'd had a sea-horse tattooed on his arm.

The inquiry had been very thorough. In those days there was time to be fussy. Maigret was still a mere inspector, and only about three years older than Cuendet.

It had happened in rather the same way as at Lausanne, except that on this occasion there had been no anonymous letter.

Very early one morning—about four o'clock, in fact, like the discovery of the body in the Bois de Boulogne—a constable in uniform had spoken to a man who was carrying a large parcel. It happened quite by accident. But for a second the man had made as if to run away.

The parcel contained fur-skins, and Cuendet had refused to account for his strange burden.

'Where were you going with all that?'

'I don't know.'

'Where have you come from?'

'I have nothing to say.'

In the end they had discovered that the skins belonged to a furrier who worked in his own flat in the Rue des Francs-Bourgeois.

Cuendet was then living in a furnished room in the Rue Saint-Antoine, a hundred yards from the Place de la Bastille; and there, just as in his attic at Lausanne, the police had found a large and varied assortment of goods.

'Who were you selling the stuff to?'

'Nobody.'

That seemed highly unlikely; but it proved impossible to discover any evidence of complicity between the Swiss youth and the known receivers of stolen goods.

He had little money on him. His expenditure tallied with the wages his employer paid him.

Maigret had found the case so intriguing that he had persuaded his superior, Superintendent Guillaume, to ask for a medical report on the prisoner.

'He's certainly what we call an asocial type,' said the doctor, 'but he seems to me to have rather more than average intelligence and quite normal emotional reactions.'

Cuendet had the good luck to be defended by a young barrister who later became one of the stars of the profession—Maître Gambier, thanks to whom he was given the minimum sentence.

After an initial period in the Santé prison, Cuendet had spent a little more than a year at Fresnes, where his behaviour had, as usual, been exemplary, so that several months of his sentence were remitted.

In the meantime his father had been killed—knocked down by a car one evening when he was riding home dead drunk on a bicycle with no lights.

Honoré had induced his mother to leave Sénarclens for Paris, so that after living all her life in the quietest corner of the European countryside, she had suddenly found herself transplanted to the noisy, crowded Rue Mouffetard.

She too was phenomenal in her way. Instead of being terrified and taking a dislike to the great city, she had settled down so completely into her district and her street that she had become one of its most popular characters.

Her name was Justine, and by now everybody from end to end of the Rue Mouffetard knew old Justine, with her slow speech and twinkling eyes.

The fact that her son had done time did not disturb her in the least.

'There's no accounting for tastes or opinions,' she used to say.

Maigret had had dealings with Honoré Cuendet on two subsequent occasions, the second time as the result of a big jewel robbery in the Rue de la Pompe, at Passy.

The burglary had occurred in a luxury flat while the owners and their servants were asleep. The jewels had been left that evening on a dressing-table in the boudoir next to the owners' bedroom, and the door between the two rooms had remained open all night.

Neither Monsieur nor Madame D. had heard a sound to disturb their sleep. The housemaid, who slept on the same floor, was positive that she had bolted the front door and found it bolted the following morning. There were no signs of forced entry and no fingerprints.

It was a third-floor flat, so nobody could have climbed in through a window. And there was no balcony along which a burglar could have made his way from a neighbouring flat.

This was the fifth or sixth such robbery within three years, and the papers were beginning to talk about a 'phantom burglar'.

Maigret remembered that spring and how the Rue de la Pompe had looked at all hours of the day; for he had gone from door to door, tirelessly questioning everybody—not only the concierges and shopkeepers, but the residents and their servants.

It was thus, by accident, or rather by sheer persistence, that he had come across Cuendet. In the house opposite the scene of the robbery there had been a room to let, six weeks before—an attic overlooking the street.

'Such a nice, quiet gentleman has taken it,' said the concierge. 'He goes out very little, never at night, and never has women up to see him. Nor anyone else, for that matter.'

'He looks after the room himself?'

'Indeed he does. And I can assure you he keeps it clean.'

Was Cuendet so sure of himself that he had not bothered to move after the burglary? Or had he been afraid that to give up his room would arouse suspicion?

Maigret had found him at home, reading. Looking out of the window, he discovered that he could watch the occupants of the flats across the road in their comings and goings.

'I must ask you to accompany me to the headquarters of the Judicial Police.'

The Swiss had made no protest. Without a word he had allowed his room to be searched. Nothing had been found—not one piece of jewellery, not one skeleton key, not one cat-burglar's tool.

His interrogation at the Quai des Orfèvres had lasted nearly twenty-four hours, with pauses for beer and sandwiches.

'Why did you rent that room?'

'Because I liked it.'

'Have you quarrelled with your mother?'

'No.'

'But you don't live with her any more?'

'I shall go back one day.'

'You have left nearly all your belongings there.'

'Exactly.'

'Have you been to see her lately?'

'No.'

'Who have you seen?'

'The concierge, the neighbours, people going along the street.'

These replies were given in a tone that was slightly ironical—unintentionally so, perhaps, for Cuendet's face remained placid and grave and he seemed to be doing his very best to satisfy the superintendent.

The interrogation had led to nothing, but inquiries in the Rue Mouffetard had produced some circumstantial evidence, revealing that this was not the first time Honoré had vanished for longish periods—usually from three weeks to two months—after which he would return to his mother's roof.

'What do you live on?'

'I do odd jobs, and I have a little put by.'

'In the bank?'

'No. I don't trust banks.'

'Where is this money?'

He did not reply. Since his first arrest he had studied the Criminal Code and knew it by heart.

'It's not for me to prove that I am innocent. It's for you to show that I'm guilty.'

Only once had Maigret lost his temper, and Cuendet's air of mild reproof had made him regret it immediately.

'You got rid of the jewels somehow or other. Probably you sold them. To whom?'

Naturally the police had gone the rounds of the known receivers, given the alarm in Antwerp, Amsterdam and London. They had tipped the wink to their informers as well.

Nobody knew Cuendet. Nobody had seen him. Nobody had been in touch with him.

'What did I tell you?' his mother exclaimed jubilantly. 'I know you're a clever lot, but my son is an exceptional man!'

In spite of his past record, in spite of the attic room, in spite of the circumstantial evidence, they had been compelled to let him go.

Cuendet had shown no elation. He had taken it all calmly. Maigret could still see him, looking for his hat, pausing at the door, extending a hesitant hand as he said:

'*Au revoir*, Superintendent . . .'

As though he quite expected to come back another time!

III

THE STRAW-BOTTOMED chairs gleamed like copper in the dim light. Though the floor-boards were ordinary pitch-pine, and very old at that, they were so well polished that the rectangle of the window was reflected in them. There was a wall clock with a brass pendulum that swung gently to and fro.

Even the most trivial objects—the poker, the china bowls with their pattern of big pink flowers, even the broom against which the cat was now rubbing his back—seemed to have a life of their own, such as one senses in old Dutch paintings, or in a church vestry.

The old woman opened the stove and threw in two shovelfuls of shiny coal, and for a second the flames leapt out at her face.

'May I take off my overcoat?'

'Does that mean you're going to stay a long time?'

'It's well below freezing-point out of doors, and this room is on the warm side.'

'They say old folks feel the cold,' she muttered, speaking more for herself, to occupy her mind, than for him. 'But my stove keeps me company. My son was the same, even as a boy. I can still see him in our cottage at Sénarclens, sitting right up against the stove while he did his homework.'

She looked at the empty arm-chair with its polished wood and shabby leather upholstery.

'Here, too, he'd draw that chair up to the stove and spend the whole day reading, not hearing anything that went on.'

'What used he to read?'

She raised her arms with a helpless gesture.

'How should I know? He used to get books from the lending library in the Rue Monge. Here's the last he took out. He changed them as he went along. He had some kind of subscription. I expect you've read this one . . .'

The volume, bound in black cloth that had been rubbed shiny like a worn cassock, proved to be a book by Lenôtre on an episode during the French Revolution.

'He knew a great deal, Honoré did. He wasn't a great talker but his brain never stopped working. He used to read newspapers too, four or five a day, and thick, expensive magazines with coloured pictures . . .'

Maigret liked the smell of the flat, a mixture of many different smells. He had always had a weakness for houses with a distinctive smell, and now he was hesitant about lighting his pipe, which he had filled automatically.

'Smoke if you like. He used to smoke a pipe too. In fact he was so fond of some of his old pipes that he used to mend them with wire.'

'There's something I would like to ask you, Madame Cuendet.'

'It makes me feel so strange when you call me that. Everybody's been calling me Justine for such a long time now! I don't really believe anyone has ever called me anything else, except the mayor when he gave me his good wishes after my wedding. But ask your question. I'll answer if I feel inclined.'

'You don't work. Your husband was a poor man . . .'

'Did you ever meet a rich mole-catcher? Especially one who drank from morning to night?'

'So you are living on what your son has been giving you.'

'Anything wrong about that?'

'A workman hands over his weekly wages to his wife or his mother; a clerk gives her his monthly salary. I suppose Honoré used to give you money as and when you needed it?'

She looked searchingly at him, as though she grasped the implications of his question.

'And so . . . ?'

'He may also have given you large sums—after each of his absences, for instance.'

'There has never been a large sum in this place. What would I have done with it?'

'He was sometimes away for quite a time, even for weeks on end, wasn't he? If you ran short of money at such times, what used you to do?'

'I never did run short.'

'He gave you enough before he left?'

'To say nothing of the fact that I have accounts at the butcher's and the baker's and the grocer's and that I can buy on credit from any of the shops round here, or even from the barrow-boys. Everybody in this street knows old Justine.'

'He never sent you a money-order?'

'I shouldn't have known how to cash it.'

'Listen, Madame Cuendet . . .'

'I would really rather you called me Justine . . .'

She was still standing up; she added a little hot water to her stew and replaced the lid, leaving a narrow opening for the steam to escape.

'I can't give him any more trouble now, and I've no intention of giving you any. All I want is to find the man who killed him.'

'When can I see him?'

'This afternoon, I expect. An inspector will call for you.'

'And will they give him back to me?'

'I think they will. In order to catch his murderer, or murderers, I need to know certain things.'

'What do you want to know?'

Even now she was wary, like the peasant she had remained at heart, like any almost illiterate old woman, scenting a trap at every turn. She couldn't help it.

'Your son used to leave you several times a year, sometimes staying away for several weeks . . .'

'Sometimes it was three weeks, sometimes two months.'

'What was he like when he came back?'

'Like a man who's glad to be home by his own fire.'

'Used he to tell you he was going away, or did he simply leave without a word?'

'Who would have packed for him, in that case?'

'Well then, he used to tell you. He took away a change of clothes, of underwear . . .'

'He took all a man needs.'

'He had several suits?'

'Four or five. He liked to be well dressed.'

'Is it your impression that when he got back he used to hide anything in the flat?'

'It wouldn't be easy to find a hiding-place in these four rooms. Besides, you searched them—more than once. I remember your men poking about everywhere; they even took my furniture to pieces. They went down to the cellar, though it's shared by all the tenants, and up to the corner of the loft that we're allowed to use.'

That was true, and they had found nothing.

'Your son had no bank account, we made sure of that, and no savings account. But he must have put his money somewhere. Do you know if he ever went abroad—to Belgium, for instance, or to Switzerland or Spain?'

'In Switzerland he'd have been arrested.'

'Quite true.'

'He never spoke to me about the other countries you mentioned.'

The frontiers had been warned on several occasions. For years a photograph of Honoré Cuendet had been among those of the people to be watched for at frontier railway stations and other points of departure from France.

Maigret continued, thinking aloud:

'Obviously he must have sold some of the jewels and other stuff. He never went to professional receivers. And as he spent very little, he's bound to have had a large sum in one place or another.'

He looked more closely at the old woman.

'If he only gave you housekeeping money when you needed it, what will become of you now?'

This idea struck her, and she jumped slightly. He saw a flicker of anxiety in her eyes. But she answered proudly, 'I'm not frightened. Honoré's a good son.'

This time she did not say 'was'. And she went on, as though he were still alive, 'I'm sure he won't leave me without a penny.'

Maigret pursued his reflections:

'He wasn't killed by a tramp. He wasn't killed by a thief. And he wasn't killed by an accomplice.'

She did not ask him how he knew, and he didn't explain. A prowling tramp would have had no reason for smashing up the dead man's face or for emptying his pockets completely, even down to odd scraps of paper, pipe and matches.

Nor would an accomplice have done that, for he would have known that Cuendet had been in prison and could therefore be identified by his fingerprints.

'The man who killed him didn't know him. And yet he had some important reason for getting rid of him. You understand?'

'What am I supposed to understand?'

'That once we know what job Honoré was planning, what house or flat he had got himself into, we shall be well on the way to finding out who murdered him.'

'That won't bring him back to life.'

'May I take a look at his room?'

'I can't stop you.'

'I would rather you came with me.'

She followed him, shrugging her thin shoulders, rolling her almost deformed hips; and the little sandy dog trotted behind, ready to start growling again.

The dining-room was lifeless, expressionless, there was hardly even a smell about it. In the old woman's room the iron bed was covered with an immaculately white bedspread. Honoré's room, which looked onto the courtyard and was rather dark, already seemed to have a suggestion of death about it.

Opening the wardrobe, Maigret saw three suits hanging there—two grey and one navy blue—with a row of shoes along the bottom and a shelf piled with shirts, on top of which lay a bunch of dried lavender.

There was a bookcase containing a red-bound, battered copy of the Penal Code, which must have been bought from one of the second-hand book dealers along the Seine or up the Boulevard Saint-Michel; a few early twentieth-century novels, a volume of Zola and one of Tolstoy, and a much-thumbed plan of Paris.

In a corner, on a small table with a shelf below it, lay some magazines whose titles made the superintendent raise his eyebrows. They did not square with the rest. They were thick, expensive 'glossies', with colour photographs of some of the finest country houses in France and of certain sumptuous Paris flats.

Maigret leafed through a few of them, hoping to find notes or pencil markings.

In his young days as a locksmith's apprentice at Lausanne, Cuendet had lived in a garret and picked up whatever came to hand, including quite worthless objects.

Later, living in the Rue Saint-Antoine, he had shown rather more discrimination, but he still confined himself to haphazard pilfering from local shops and flats.

Then he moved up a step and set to work on middle-class homes, where he found money and jewellery.

Finally, by dint of patience, he had made his way into the fashionable districts. Just now, the old woman had unintentionally given away something important by mentioning that her son read four or five daily newspapers.

Maigret would have been ready to bet that Cuendet didn't read them for their news items, let alone for their political articles, but for their society columns with announcements of weddings, accounts of receptions and first nights.

For these included descriptions of the jewels worn by smart women.

The magazines at which Maigret was now glancing contained information of equal value to Honoré—meticulous descriptions of private mansions and flats, with photographs of individual rooms.

Cuendet used to sit by the fire, musing, weighing the pros and cons, making his choice.

Then he would prowl round the district and take a room in a hotel —or, if he could find one to let, in a private house, as in the case of the Rue de la Pompe.

At the last inquiry, several years ago, they had picked up his trail in this way, finding that he had become a sudden and temporary habitué of various local cafés.

A quiet man who used to sit for hours in his favourite corner, drinking white wine, reading the papers and watching the scene outside . . .

So that after a time a whole block of flats would have revealed its every secret to him.

'Thank you, Madame Cuendet.'

'Justine!'

'Excuse me—Justine. I used to feel very . . .'

He sought for the right word. 'Friendly' was too strong. 'Drawn to-wards' she wouldn't understand.

'I had a great regard for your son.'

That was not quite what he meant, either; but the Deputy Prosecutor and the examining magistrate were not there to overhear him.

'Inspector Fumel will be coming to see you. If there is anything you need, get in touch with me.'

'I shan't need anything.'

'If you happen to discover whereabouts in Paris Honoré spent these last few weeks . . .'

He put on his heavy overcoat and went cautiously down the worn stairs and out into the cold, noisy street. By this time there was a sug-gestion of white powder floating in the air, but it was not snowing and there were no signs of snow on the ground.

When Maigret entered the inspector's office, Lucas said:

'Moers rang you.'

'He didn't say why?'

'He asked if you would ring him back.'

'Still no news of Fernand?'

He had not forgotten that his main job was to catch the hold-up gang. It might take weeks, even months. Hundreds and thousands of police in Paris and the provinces were carrying the photograph of the newly released prisoner. Inspectors were going from house to house like vacuum-cleaner salesmen, asking: 'Excuse me, madame, but have you seen this man recently?'

The hotel squad was dealing with the lodging-houses. The 'vice' squad was questioning prostitutes. In the railway stations, travellers were being scrutinized, unawares, by watchful eyes.

Maigret was not in charge of the Cuendet inquiry. He had no right to take his men off their other work. But he found a way of reconcil-ing duty with curiosity.

'Go upstairs and ask for a photo of Cuendet, the most recent they've got. Have copies of it given to all the men who are looking for Fernand, particularly those who are making the round of the bistros and lodging-houses.'

'All over Paris?'

He hesitated, on the verge of replying, 'Only in the fashionable dis-tricts.'

But he remembered that private mansions and blocks of luxury flats were to be found in the old districts as well.

Back in his own office, he rang through to Moers.

'Found something?'

'I don't know if it's any use to you. When they went over the clothes with a magnifying-glass, my fellows picked up three or four hairs which they put under the microscope. Delage, who knows his job, assures me they are wild-cat's hairs.'

'Whereabouts on the clothes were they found?'

'On the back, near the left shoulder. There were specks of face-powder as well. We may be able to discover what make it is, but that'll take longer.'

'Thank you. Fumel hasn't rung you up?'

'He looked in just now. I gave him the tip.'

'Where is he?'

'In Records, deep in Cuendet's file.'

Maigret wondered for a moment why his eyes felt sore; then he remembered he had been called out of bed at four o'clock that morning.

He had to sign some papers, fill in several forms, and see two people who had been waiting, to whom he listened rather absentmindedly. As soon as he was alone again he telephoned to a big furriers in the Rue La Boétie, where it needed some persistence to get the proprietor himself at the end of the line.

'I am Superintendent Maigret of the Judicial Police. I apologize for bothering you, but I'd like you to give me a piece of information. Can you tell me approximately how many wild-cat fur coats there are in Paris?'

'Wild-cat?'

The man sounded rather annoyed by the question.

'We have none here. At one time, during the pioneer days of motoring, our firm did make them—some for ladies, but mostly for men.'

Maigret recollected some photographs of early motorists, looking like bears.

'Those were wild-cat?'

'Not all of them, but the finest were. They are still worn by some people in very cold countries—Canada, Sweden, Norway, the north of the United States . . .'

'There are none left in Paris?'

'I believe some firms still sell one occasionally, but very few. It's difficult to give you a definite figure. But I would be willing to bet there are fewer than five hundred such coats in the whole of Paris, and most of those must be fairly old. But . . .'

He had had an idea.

'Is it only coats that interest you?'

'Why do you ask?'

'Because we do, very occasionally, make up wild-cat skins for other purposes. For instance, they are made into rugs to cover a sofa or to take in cars.'

'Are there many of those?'

'If I went through our books I could tell you how many we've turned out in the last few years. At a rough guess, three or four dozen. But they are mass-produced by some furriers—in a cheaper quality, of course. Wait a minute; I've thought of something else. While we were talking I remembered that in the window of a chemist's shop not far from here there is a wild-cat's skin, offered as a cure for rheumatism.'

'Thank you very much.'

'Would you like me to get you a list of the . . .'

'If it's not too much trouble.'

This was rather disheartening. For weeks the police had been hunting for Fernand, though they were not even certain he was implicated in the recent hold-ups. That represented almost as much work as would be needed to prepare a dictionary, for instance, or even an encyclo-paedia.

And yet they knew all about Fernand, his tastes, his habits and his quirks. For instance there was one trivial detail that might help them to catch him—the only thing he ever drank was Mandarin-Curaçao.

But so far, the only clue that might lead to Cuendet's murderers was a few wild-cat hairs.

Moers had said they were found on the back of the jacket, near the left sleeve. If they had come from a coat, wouldn't they have been more likely to be on the front of the suit?

Maigret preferred the theory of the rug, more especially a motor-car rug. In which case the car would not have been a small, ordinary one; fur rugs are seldom found in 4 h.p. Renaults.

And for some years past, Cuendet had confined himself to stealing from wealthy houses.

What was really needed was to go the round of all the garages in Paris, putting the same question to every one of them.

Someone knocked on the door. It was Inspector Fumel, with a puffy face and red eyelids. He had had even less sleep than Maigret. In fact, having been on duty the night before, he had had none at all.

'Am I disturbing you?'

'Come in.'

Fumel was one of the few whom Maigret addressed by the familiar 'tu'. Most of these had been in the force for many years, as long as he himself, and had originally spoken to him with the same familiarity, though now they were shy and called him 'Superintendent' or sometimes 'Chief'. Another was Lucas. Not Janvier, though Maigret couldn't have said why not. And then the very young ones, such as little Lapointe.

'Sit down.'

'I've been through the whole file. And now I don't know how to set about the job. A team of twenty men wouldn't be enough. I see from the minutes of the interrogations that you knew him well.'

'Pretty well. This morning I paid an unofficial call on his mother. I broke the news to her and said you'd go round presently and take her to the Medico-Legal Institute. Have you any information about the results of the post-mortem?'

'None. I rang up Doctor Lamalle. He informed me, through his assistant, that he'd be sending his report to the examining magistrate tonight or tomorrow morning.'

Doctor Paul used not to wait for Maigret to ring him up. And sometimes he would even inquire gruffly:

'What am I to tell the magistrate?'

In those days, of course, investigations were left to the police, and the examining magistrate didn't usually take over until the criminal had confessed.

At that time a case used to be taken in three separate stages: the investigation, which in Paris was the responsibility of the Quai des Orfèvres; the examination of the evidence; and later, when the file had been studied by the Grand Jury, the actual trial.

'Did Moers tell you about the hairs?'

'Yes. Wild-cat's hairs.'

'I've just telephoned to a furrier. You'd better look into the sales of wild-cat fur rugs in Paris. And if you question the garage-keepers . . .'

'I'm alone on this job.'

'I know, old man.'

'I've sent in my preliminary report. Maître Cajou wants to see me at five o'clock this afternoon. There'll be a row about that. As I was on duty last night I should have been free today, and somebody's expecting me. I shall ring up, but I know I shan't be believed, and it'll cause no end of complications . . .'

A woman, of course!

'If I come across anything, I'll give you a ring,' said Maigret. 'But for heaven's sake don't tell the examining magistrate that I'm dealing with the business.'

'Right!'

Maigret went home to lunch. The flat was as clean as old Madame Cuendet's, the floors and furniture as well polished.

It was warm, too, and there was a stove burning, in spite of the central heating. Maigret had always been fond of stoves, and had long ago persuaded the administration to leave him one in his office.

There was a good smell of cooking. And yet he suddenly felt that something was missing, though he couldn't have said what.

The atmosphere of Honoré's mother's flat had been even more soothing, more pervasive, perhaps in contrast to the busy street outside. From the window one could almost touch the pavement stalls, and their owners' cries were clearly audible.

The ceilings in that flat were lower, the place was smaller and more withdrawn. The old woman spent her entire time there. And although Honoré was away, one felt conscious that he belonged there.

Maigret wondered for a moment whether he, too, should not buy a dog and a cat.

What nonsense! He wasn't an old woman, nor a country boy come to Paris to live alone in its most crowded street.

'A penny for your thoughts!'

He smiled. 'I was thinking about a dog.'

'Are you planning to buy one?'

'No. Besides, it wouldn't be the same. This one was picked up in the street with two broken legs . . .'

'Aren't you going to take a nap?'

'No time, unfortunately.'

'You seem to be thinking about something that's partly nice and partly nasty . . .'

He was struck by the discernment of this remark. Cuendet's death had left him depressed and mortified. He felt a personal grudge against the murderers, as though Honoré had been a friend, a colleague, or at any rate an old acquaintance.

And he hated the way they had disfigured the man and thrown him out, like a dead animal, beside a path in the Bois de Boulogne where his body must have bounced on the frozen ground.

Yet at the same time he couldn't help laughing when he thought of the life Cuendet had led, and of the man's whims, which he was now trying to understand. It was a funny thing but, although the two of them were so unlike, he had the impression that he was succeeding.

It was true that, at the beginning of his career, if one could call it that, when he was only a skinny apprentice, Honoré had developed his skill by the most commonplace means, indiscriminately pinching whatever came to hand, like all juvenile delinquents born in poor districts.

He had not even sold his spoils, just stacked them in his attic, the way a puppy hides crusts of bread and old bones under its rug.

Why, when he was regarded as a model soldier, had he twice deserted? Clumsily! Stupidly! On both occasions he had let himself be recaptured, with no attempt to run away or resist.

In Paris, when he lived near the Bastille, he had improved his technique and his individual style had begun to take shape. He did not join a gang. He had no friends. He worked on his own.

Locksmith, coppersmith, handyman, clever with his hands, a careful workman, he was learning how to break into shops, workshops and warehouses.

He was unarmed. He had never possessed a weapon, not even a flick-knife.

Not once had he set off an alarm, or left a trace of his passage. He was an essentially silent man, in his work as well as in private life.

What were his relations with women? There were none in evidence in his life. He had always lived under his mother's roof, and if he had occasional brief affairs he must have conducted them discreetly, in remote districts where no one noticed him.

He was capable of sitting for hours in some café, next to the window, with a small pitcher of white wine in front of him. He was also capable of spending whole days watching from the window of a furnished room, or reading beside the fire in the Rue Mouffetard.

His needs were very few. But the list of jewels he had stolen—to speak only of the thefts that could reasonably be placed at his door—represented a fortune.

Did he pass some of his time away from Paris, living in a different style and spending his money?

'I'm thinking about a funny sort of chap, a burglar . . .' Maigret explained to his wife.

'The one who was murdered last night?'

'How did you know?'

'It's in the midday edition of the paper; somebody brought me one just now.'

'Show me.'

'It's only a few lines. I came across it by accident.'

About three o'clock this morning, two constables of the 16th ar-rondissement cycle patrol found a man's body beside a path in the Bois de Boulogne. The skull had been shattered. The man was identified as Honoré Cuendet, an ex-convict of Swiss nationality. Monsieur Cajou, the examining magistrate, who went to the spot, accompanied by Monsieur Kernavel, of the Public Prosecutor's Department, and by the police doctor, believes the man to have been killed in an underworld vendetta.

'What did you say?'

The stock phrase 'underworld vendetta' infuriated Maigret, for it meant that from the official standpoint the matter was as good as closed. As one of the Public Prosecutor's men used to say:

'Let 'em kill one another, down to the last man. That'll save the hang-man trouble and the taxpayers money.'

'What was I saying? Oh yes! Imagine a burglar who deliberately chose occupied houses and flats . . .'

'To break into?'

'Yes. Every year and at every season, so to speak, there are flats in Paris which are left empty for weeks at a time, while their owners are at the seaside, at winter sports, in their country houses or traveling abroad.'

'And they're burgled, aren't they?'

'Yes, they are. By specialists who will never go near a house where they're liable to run into anybody.'

'What are you getting at?'

'At the fact that my friend Cuendet was only interested in occupied flats. He would often wait to break into a place until the owners were back from the theatre or wherever they'd gone, and the wife had taken off her jewels and put them in the next-door room or even, sometimes, left them lying somewhere in the bedroom itself.'

To which the practical Madame Maigret replied:

'If he'd done his job while she was out he wouldn't have found her jewels, since you say she would be wearing them.'

'He'd probably have found others, and in any case there would be valuables, pictures and money.'

'You mean it was a kind of vice he had?'

'That's too strong a word, perhaps; but I suspect it was a mania, that he got some kind of pleasure out of worming his way into the warmth of other people's lives. Once he took a man's watch off his bedside table, while the fellow slept on and didn't hear a sound.'

She, too, laughed at this.

'How often did you catch him?'

'He was only sent to prison once, and in those days he hadn't adopted this system, he worked just like any other burglar. All the same, at the office we have a long list of burglaries which were almost certainly done by him. In some cases he'd rented a room opposite the burgled house for several weeks, and couldn't give any plausible explanation.'

'Why was he murdered?'

'That's what I'm wondering. In order to find out, I need to discover what house he burgled lately—probably last night.'

Maigret had seldom told his wife so much about a case while it was in progress; perhaps because for him this was no ordinary case, and he wasn't even in charge of it.

Cuendet interested him as a person and as an expert—had almost a kind of fascination for him, and so had old Justine.

'*I'm sure he won't leave me without a penny,*' she had declared confidently.

Yet Maigret felt certain she didn't know where her son used to hide the money.

She had confidence, unreasoning trust: Honoré was incapable of leaving her unprovided for.

How would the money get to her? What arrangements had her son made—he who had never in his life worked with an accomplice?

And how could he have foreseen that he would be murdered one day?

The strange thing was that Maigret was beginning to share the old woman's confidence, her conviction that Cuendet would have thought of every eventuality.

He sipped his coffee slowly. In the act of lighting his pipe, he glanced towards the sideboard. Like the one in the Rue Mouffetard, it held a bottle of white spirits—plum brandy in this particular case.

Madame Maigret interpreted the glance and poured him out a small glass.

IV

AT FIVE minutes to four, Maigret, bending over an annotated file that lay in the circle of light thrown by his lamp, was hesitating between two pipes, when the telephone rang. It was the Emergency Calls exchange in the Boulevard du Palais.

'A hold-up in the Rue La Fayette, between the Rue Taitbout and the Chaussée d'Antin. Some shots were fired. Several casualties . . .'

The thing had happened at ten minutes to four, and already the general alarm had been given, the radio cars alerted, and a bus-load of uniformed police was leaving the courtyard of the Municipal Police headquarters, while, in obedience to the Public Prosecutor's orders, the news was being transmitted to him in his tranquil office in the Palais de Justice.

Maigret opened the door, beckoned to Janvier and muttered something indistinct. The two men hurried downstairs, struggling into their overcoats, and jumped into one of the small black-and-white police cars.

A yellowish fog had begun to settle down on the city soon after lunch, so that it was now as dark as at six in the evening, and the cold had become more penetrating instead of diminishing.

'Tomorrow morning it'll be as well to look out for ice on the roads,' the driver observed.

He started his siren and switched on his winking headlight. Taxis and private cars drew in to the curb, and pedestrians stared after the police car. Signs of traffic disturbance were evident by the time they reached the Place de l'Opéra. Bottle-necks had formed. The extra police who had come on point duty were blowing their whistles and gesticulating.

The rush-hour had begun, and in the Rue La Fayette, along the pavement outside the Galeries Lafayette and the Galeries du Printemps, there was a dense crowd, composed chiefly of women: this was also the most brightly lit spot in Paris.

The crowd was being shepherded behind the barricades which had been set up. A length of the street was empty except for the dark figures of a few officials, going to and fro.

The superintendent of police of the 9th *arrondissement* had arrived, with several of his men. Experts were taking measurements and making chalk-marks. A car stood with its front wheels on the pavement; its windscreen was shattered and two or three yards away there was a dark patch with a group of men standing round it, talking in low voices.

A little grey-haired man in black, with a knitted muffler round his neck, stood there, still holding the glass of rum they had brought him from the café across the street. He was the cashier of a big ironmongers in the Rue de Châteaudun.

For the third or fourth time he was retelling his story, his eyes carefully averted from a human form that lay a few yards away, with a piece of some rough material thrown over it.

The crowd was pressing against the barrier of portable wooden railings—of the type used in the city along procession routes—and excited women were talking in shrill voices.

'As usual on the last day of the month . . .'

Maigret had forgotten this was January 31.

'. . . I had been to the bank, behind the Opera, to fetch the money for the staff salaries . . .'

Maigret had often gone past the shop, without realizing how large it was. It had three floors of departments and basements on two levels, and there were three hundred employees.

'I had barely six hundred yards to walk. I was carrying my briefcase in my left hand.'

'It was not chained to your wrist?'

The man was not an official bank messenger, and was not provided with any means of giving an alarm-signal. All he had was a revolver, in the right-hand pocket of his overcoat.

He had crossed the street between the yellow lines, and was walking towards the Rue Taitbout, in a crowd so thick that no attack seemed possible. Suddenly he noticed a man walking close beside him; and glancing back, he saw another at his heels.

After that, everything had happened so fast that he had scarcely followed the course of events. What he remembered best was that a voice had muttered in his ear:

'If you want to keep a whole skin, don't try to show off!'

At the same moment the brief-case was wrenched out of his hand. One of the men rushed towards a car that was crawling towards them, close to the curb. Hearing a shot, the cashier at first thought someone had fired at him. Women were screaming and jostling in the crowd. There was another shot, followed by the tinkle of broken glass.

More shots had followed—some people said three, others four or five.

A red-faced man was standing on one side, with the district superintendent. He looked rather perturbed, not knowing as yet whether he would be treated as a hero or reprimanded.

This was Constable Margeret, of the 1st *arrondissement*. Being off duty this afternoon, he was not in uniform. Then why had he been carrying a revolver? He would have to explain that later.

'I was going to meet my wife, who had been shopping. I saw what happened. When the three men made for the car . . .'

'There were three of them?'

'Yes—one on either side of the cashier and one right behind him . . .'

Constable Margeret had fired. One of the gangsters had fallen on his knees and then sunk slowly to the ground, among the feet of the women who had started to run.

The car drove off at top speed towards Saint-Augustin. The policeman on point duty blew his whistle. Shots were fired from the car, which soon disappeared among the other traffic.

For the next couple of days Maigret had little time to think about his placid Swiss burglar, and on two occasions when Inspector Fumel rang him up he was too busy to take the call.

The police had collected the names and addresses of about fifty eyewitnesses, including a woman who kept a pancake stall near by, a crippled beggar whose pitch was a few yards from the spot, two waiters from the café opposite, and the lady at the pay-desk there—she claimed to have seen all that happened, although the café windows had been steamed up.

There had been a second victim, a man of thirty-five who left a wife and children; he had been killed outright and never realized what was happening.

For the first time since the present series of attacks began, the police had captured a member of the gang—the man shot down by Constable Margeret, who had so miraculously been on the spot.

'My idea was to shoot him in the leg, to stop him from running away.'

In point of fact, however, the man had been hit in the back of the neck, and was now lying in a coma in the Hôpital Beaujon, where he had been taken by ambulance.

Lucas, Janvier and Torrence were taking turns to watch outside his door, waiting till he should be able to make a statement—for the doctors did not despair of saving him.

Next day, as the driver of the police car had predicted, the Paris streets were coated in ice. The light was bad. The traffic crawled along. Municipal lorries scattered sand in the main streets.

The wide corridor of Judicial Police headquarters was full of people waiting in silence. To each of them in turn Maigret patiently put the same questions, while he drew mysterious signs on a plan of the scene which had been drawn up by the appropriate service.

He had gone at once, on the evening of the attack, to Fontenay-aux-Roses, to the address of the wounded gangster, a certain Joseph Raison, described on his identity card as a metal-fitter.

There, in a new building, he had found a bright, trim flat, a fair-haired young woman, and two little girls, aged six and nine, busy with their homework.

Joseph Raison, a man of forty-two, really was a metal-fitter, and worked in a factory on the Quai de Javel. He owned a 2 h.p. Citroën in which he used to take his family for a run in the country every Sunday.

His wife declared that she simply could not understand what had happened, and Maigret believed her.

'I don't see why he should have done such a thing, Superintendent. We were so happy. It's only just two years since we bought this flat. Joseph was earning good wages. He doesn't drink and he hardly ever went out by himself.'

The Superintendent had driven her to the hospital, while a neighbour looked after the children. She had seen her husband for a few minutes and then, on the doctors' orders and despite her protests, had been driven home again.

And now the mass of confused and contradictory evidence must be sorted out. Some people had seen too much, others too little.

'If I say anything, those chaps will hunt me down . . .'

All the same, it added up to a fairly convincing description of the two men on either side of the cashier, and especially of the one who had grabbed the brief-case.

But it was not until late in the afternoon that a witness—one of the café waiters—said he thought he recognized one of the photographs shown to him, which was that of Fernand.

'He came in about ten or fifteen minutes before the attack and ordered a *café crême*. He was sitting at a table near the door, right next to the window.'

Two days after the incident, Maigret secured another scrap of evidence: on the 31st, Fernand had been wearing a heavy brown overcoat.

This was not much, but it showed that the superintendent had not been mistaken in supposing that Fernand, lately released from Saint-Martin-de-Ré, was the leader of the gang.

The wounded man in the Hôpital Beaujon had regained consciousness for a few moments, but only to whisper:

'Monique . . .'

This was the name of his younger daughter.

Maigret was greatly interested by his new discovery—that Fernand no longer recruited his men solely in the underworld.

The Public Prosecutor's Department was ringing him up at hourly intervals and he was writing one report after another. He could not set foot outside his office without being jumped upon by a swarm of journalists.

At eleven o'clock on the Friday night, the corridor was at last empty. Maigret was talking things over with Lucas, who had just arrived from the Hôpital Beaujon and was telling him that a celebrated surgeon proposed to operate on the wounded man. There was a knock on the door.

'Come in!' called Maigret impatiently.

It was Fumel, who, feeling he had chosen an unpropitious moment, shrank back timidly. He had clearly caught a cold, for his nose was red and his eyes watery.

'I can come back another time . . .'

'Come on in!'

'I think I've found the trail. Or rather the hotel police found it for me. I know where Cuendet had been living for the last five weeks.'

For Maigret it was soothing, almost restful, to hear about his placid Swiss burglar.

'Whereabouts was it?'

'In his old district. He'd taken a room in a little hotel in the Rue Neuve Saint-Pierre.'

'Behind the Eglise Saint-Paul?'

This was an ancient, narrow street between the Rue Saint-Antoine

and the river. Cars seldom went along it and there were only a few shops.
'Tell me.'
'It seems to be chiefly a house of call for tarts. But they let a few
rooms by the month. Cuendet was living there quietly, seldom going
out except for meals, which he took at a little restaurant called the Petit
Saint-Paul.'
'What's opposite the hotel?'
'An eighteenth-century house with a fine courtyard and tall windows,
which was completely restored a few years ago.'
'Who lives there?'
'A lady by herself—with servants, of course. A Mrs. Wilton.'
'You've made inquiries about her?'
'I've begun, but the local people know little or nothing.'
In the last ten years or so it had become the fashion for very wealthy
people to buy some old house in the Marais—in the Rue des Francs-
Bourgeois, for example—and restore it to more or less its original state.
This had begun with the Ile Saint-Louis, and now old mansions
were being sought out wherever they still survived, even in the shabbi-
est streets.
'There's even a tree in the courtyard. One doesn't see many trees in
that district.'
'This lady's a widow?'
'Divorced. I went to see a journalist to whom I sometimes give tips,
when it can't do any harm. And this time it was he who gave me one.
Although she's divorced she still sees her ex-husband quite often, and
they go out together now and again.'
'What's his name?'
'Stuart Wilton. Her maiden name, as I found out from the local police files, was Florence Lenoir. Her mother did ironing at a laundry
in the Rue de Rennes, and her father, who died long ago, was in the police. She used to be an actress. According to my journalist she was in
a troupe of dancing girls at the Casino de Paris and Stuart Wilton, who
had a wife already, got a divorce in order to marry her.'
'How long ago?'
Maigret was doodling on his blotter, seeing a vision of Cuendet at
the window of the shady little hotel.
'Ten years, or even less . . . The house used to belong to Wilton. He
has another, at Auteuil, where he's living at present, and he also owns
the Château de Besse, near Maisons-Lafitte.'
'So he keeps racehorses?'

'Not so far as I've heard; he's a keen race-goer, but he doesn't run a stable.'

'Is he American?'

'English. He's been living in France for a very long time.'

'Where does his money come from?'

'I can only pass on what I've been told. He comes of a big manufacturing family and inherited a number of patents that bring him in a lot of money without his raising a finger. He travels for part of the year, rents a villa at Cap d'Antibes or Cap-Ferrat in the summer, and belongs to several clubs. My journalist says he's very well known, but only in a select circle which is hardly ever mentioned in the papers.'

Maigret rose with a sigh, took his coat from its hook, and wound his scarf round his neck.

'Let's get going!' he said; adding, to Lucas:

'If anyone asks for me, I'll be back in an hour.'

Owing to the frost and the icy roads, Paris was almost as deserted as in August, and not a single child was playing in the narrow length of the Rue Neuve Saint-Pierre. The door of the Hôtel Lambert stood ajar; a frosted light-bulb hung above it. In the stuffy office, a man was sitting with his back against the radiator, reading a newspaper.

He recognized Inspector Fumel, and growled as he got to his feet:

'The trouble's beginning, I can see!'

'There'll be no trouble for you if you keep quiet. Is there anyone in Cuendet's room?'

'Not yet. He'd paid the month in advance. I could have let it to someone else on January 31, but as his things were still there I decided to wait.'

'When did he disappear?'

'I don't know. Wait while I calculate. If I'm not mistaken it must have been last Saturday . . . Saturday or Friday . . . We could ask the chambermaid . . .'

'Did he tell you he was going away for a time?'

'He didn't say a word. He was never one for talking, anyhow.'

'Did he go out late on the night of his disappearance?'

'It was my wife who saw him. Customers who bring women here at night don't like to be let in by a man. It embarrasses them. So . . .'

'She hasn't mentioned it to you?'

'Indeed she has. Anyway you can ask her presently. She'll soon be down.'

The air was stagnant, overheated, with a vaguely unpleasant smell that had a suggestion of disinfectant, rather like the Métro.

'According to what she told me, he didn't go out to dinner that evening.'

'Was that unusual?'

'It happened now and then. He used to bring food in with him. We'd see him go upstairs carrying some small parcels and several newspapers. He'd say goodnight and no more would be heard of him till next day.'

'He went out later that evening?'

'He must have, seeing he wasn't in his room the next morning. But so far as that goes, my wife didn't see him. She'd shown a couple upstairs, to a room at the far end of the first-floor corridor. She went to fetch towels for them, and it was then she heard someone going downstairs.'

'What time was that?'

'After midnight. She did mean to look to see who it was, but, by the time she'd shut the linen cupboard and got back to the end of the corridor, the man was already downstairs.'

'When did you discover that he was not in his room?'

'The next morning. It must have been about ten or eleven o'clock when the maid knocked to know if she could do the room. She went in, and saw the bed had not been slept in.'

'You did not inform the police that one of your customers had disappeared?'

'Why should I? He was a free man, wasn't he? He'd paid up. I always make people pay in advance. They're apt to go off like that, without a word . . .'

'Leaving their belongings?'

'He didn't leave much!'

'Take us to his room.'

Dragging his slippered feet, the proprietor shuffled out of the office, behind the two detectives, locked the door and pocketed the key. He was not an old man, but he walked with difficulty and panted as he climbed the stairs.

'It's on the third floor,' he sighed.

There was a pile of sheets on the first-floor landing, and several of the doors along the corridor were open; a servant-girl was bustling about in some room or other.

'It's me, Rose. I'm taking some gentlemen upstairs.'

The atmosphere grew staler as they went up, and the third-floor corridor had no carpet. In one of the rooms somebody was playing the mouth-organ.

'Here we are.'

The figure 33 was roughly painted on the door. The room already smelt stuffy.

'I left everything as it was.'

'Why?'

'I thought he'd be back . . . He looked a decent chap . . . I used to wonder what'd brought him here, seeing he was well dressed and seemed to have plenty of money.'

'How did you know he had money?'

'Both times when he paid, I saw some big notes in his pocket-book.'

'No one ever came to see him?'

'Not to my knowledge, or my wife's. And one or other of us is always in the office.'

'Not at the moment.'

'Well, of course, we do sometimes leave it for a few minutes, but then we listen out, and you'll have noticed I told the chambermaid . . .'

'Did he get any letters?'

'Never.'

'Who's in the next room?'

There was only one, number 33 being at the end of the corridor.

'Olga. A tart.'

The man knew there was no point in trying to hoodwink the police —they were well aware of what went on in his establishment.

'Is she there now?'

'At this time of day she must be asleep.'

'You can go.'

He went off glumly, with his limping gait. Maigret shut the door and proceeded to open a cheap pitch-pine wardrobe with a weak lock.

There was not much inside—a pair of well-polished black shoes, a pair of slippers, nearly new, and a grey suit on a hanger. There was also a dark felt hat of a well-known make.

One drawer held six white shirts, one pale blue one, some underpants, handkerchiefs and wool socks. In another were two pairs of pyjamas and several books—*Impressions of a Traveller in Italy, Every Man his Own Doctor* (published in 1899) and an adventure story.

The room had an iron bedstead, a round table with a dark green velvet cloth, and one arm-chair with half its springs broken. The big curtains were stuck and refused to draw, but the light was softened by half-curtains.

Maigret stood and stared at the house opposite, beginning with the courtyard where a big black car of English make was waiting near the steps that led up to the glass-panelled double doors.

The stone façade of the house had been cleaned; it was now a soft shade of grey; there was graceful moulding round the windows.

A lamp was lit in a ground-floor room, its light falling on a carpet with an involved pattern, a Louis XV arm-chair, and the corner of a small pedestal table.

The first-floor windows were very tall; the floor above was mansard-roofed.

The house was long in proportion to its height, and probably had fewer rooms than one might have supposed at first glance.

Two windows on the first floor stood open, and a manservant in a striped waistcoat was pushing a vacuum cleaner round what looked like a drawing-room.

'Get any sleep last night?' Maigret asked Fumel.

'Yes, Chief. I almost had my eight hours.'

'Are you hungry?'

'Not particularly, yet.'

'I'll send someone along presently to relieve you. All you have to do is to sit down in that chair in front of the window. As long as you don't put the light on the people opposite can't see you.'

Wasn't that what Cuendet had been doing for nearly six weeks?

'Make a note of all comings and goings, and if any cars arrive, try to get their numbers.'

A moment later, Maigret was tapping lightly on the door of the next room. He had to wait some time before he heard a bed creak, and then the sound of footsteps. The door opened, but only a crack.

'What is it?'

'Police.'

'Again?' asked the woman, adding resignedly:

'Come in!'

She was in her nightdress, heavy-eyed with sleep. She had not taken off her make-up before going to bed, and it had smeared so that her face looked all askew.

'Mind if I get back into bed?'

'Why did you say "Again"? Have the police been here lately?'

'Not here, but along the street. They've done nothing but pester us for weeks now, and in the last month I've spent at least six days in the cells. What have I done this time?'

'Nothing, I hope. And please don't tell anybody about my visit.'

'So you're not from the vice squad?'

'No.'

'I seem to have seen your photo somewhere.'

Except for her smears of make-up and her badly dyed hair she would have been quite good-looking; rather plump, but sturdy, and her expression was still alert.

'Superintendent Maigret.'

'What's happened?'

'I don't know yet. Have you been living here long?'

'Ever since I came back from Cannes in October. I always do Cannes in the summer.'

'Do you know your neighbour?'

'Which one?'

'The one in number thirty-three.'

'Oh, the Swiss.'

'How do you know he's Swiss?'

'From his accent. I've worked in Switzerland as well—three years ago. I was a hostess in a German night-club, but they didn't renew my residence permit. I suppose they don't like competition over there.'

'Did he ever speak to you? Did he come to your room?'

'I was the one who went to his. When I got up one afternoon, I found I'd run out of cigarettes. I'd already met him in the passage and he always used to say good-morning, real polite.'

'What happened?'

'Exactly nothing!' she replied, with an expressive grimace. 'I knocked. He took his time opening the door. I wondered what he could be up to. But he was all dressed and there was nobody in his room and it was quite tidy. I saw he was a pipe smoker—he had one in his mouth. I said:

'"I suppose you haven't any cigarettes?"'

'He said he was afraid not; and then, kind of hesitating, he offered to go and buy me some.

'I was the same as when I opened the door to you—with nothing on but my nightdress. There was some chocolate on the table and when he saw me looking at it he offered me a piece.

'I thought we'd go ahead from there. It's only natural, between neighbours. I began to nibble a bit of chocolate and I had a squint at the book he was reading—something about Italy, with old pictures.

' "Don't you get bored, all alone here?" I asked him.

'I'm sure he wanted to. And I don't think I'm all that alarming. For a minute he was hesitating, I realized, and then, all at once, he stammered: "I have to go out. Someone's waiting for me . . ." '

'And that was all?'

'I'll say it was. The walls in this place aren't thick. You can hear every sound from one room to another. And he can't have got much sleep at night, if you see what I mean.

'But he never complained. You may have noticed on your way up that the toilets are at the far end of the corridor, above the stairs. One thing I can say for certain is that he didn't go to bed early, because I met him at least twice in the middle of the night, on his way to the toilet, still fully dressed.'

'Do you ever happen to glance at the house opposite?'

'The madwoman's house?'

'Why do you call her mad?'

'No special reason. I just think she looks mad. You know, one can see quite well from here. In the afternoon I've nothing to do, and sometimes I look out of the window. The people opposite don't often draw their curtains and when it gets dark those chandeliers look gorgeous. Huge glass chandeliers with dozens of lamps . . .

'Her room is right opposite this one. It's almost the only room where they do draw the curtains towards evening; but they pull them back in the morning, and she doesn't seem to realize that she can be seen over here, walking about without a stitch. Or perhaps she does it on purpose. Some women do carry on like that.

'She has two maids to wait on her, but she's just as likely to ring for the manservant when she's got nothing on.

'Some days her hairdresser comes in the middle of the afternoon—or later, on days when she's dolled up to the nines.

'She's not bad for her age, I will say that.'

'What age would you put her at?'

'Oh, forty-five-ish. But with women who take such care of themselves, you can't be sure.'

'Does she do much entertaining?'

'Sometimes there are two or three cars in the courtyard, not often more. It's usually she who goes out. Except for the gigolo of course!'

'What gigolo?'

'I'm not suggesting he's a real gigolo. Though he's a bit on the young side for her, not a day over thirty. He's real handsome—tall, dark, and dressed like a tailor's dummy, and he drives a lovely car.'

'He often comes to see her?'

'I'm not always at the window, you know. I've my own job to do. Some days I begin about five in the afternoon, and that doesn't leave me much time to be staring into people's houses. Let's say he comes once or twice a week. Maybe three times.

'What I do know for sure is that he sometimes stays the night. Mostly I get up late, but on inspection days I have to be out at crack of dawn. One would think your chaps fix their hours on purpose. Well, two or three times the gigolo's car was still in the courtyard at nine in the morning.

'As for the other fellow . . .'

'Is there another?'

'I mean the old one—the one who pays.'

Maigret could not help smiling at Olga's interpretation of the facts.

'What's the matter? Have I said something silly?'

'Go ahead.'

'There's a real swell with grey hair who sometimes comes in a Rolls; he's got the handsomest chauffeur I've ever seen.'

'Does he ever spend the night there, too?'

'I don't think so. He never stays long. If I remember rightly, I've never seen him late in the evening. About five o'clock, that's more his style. For afternoon tea, I expect.'

She seemed delighted to show off her knowledge of the fact that, in a world remote from her own, there were people who took tea at five o'clock.

'I suppose you can't tell me why you're asking me all these questions?'

'No, I can't.'

'And I'm to keep my mouth shut?'

'I am most anxious that you should.'

'I'd better, for my own good—isn't that so? Don't be afraid. I'd heard about you from some of the other girls, but I thought you'd be older.'

She smiled at him, arching her body slightly beneath the bedclothes. After a brief pause, she said softly:

'No?'

And he replied, smiling:

'No.'

At which she burst out laughing.

'Just like my neighbour!'

Then, suddenly serious:

'What's he done?'

Maigret was on the point of telling her the truth. It was a tempta-
tion. He knew he could rely on her. And he knew she would understand things better than Cajou, the examining magistrate, for instance.
Perhaps some clue that hadn't occurred to him would strike her if he
let her in on the story?

Later, if need be.

He turned to the door.

'Will you be coming back?'

'Very likely. What's the food like at the Petit Saint-Paul?'

'The owner does the cooking herself, and if you like chitterlings
they're as good as any you'll find round here. But there are only paper
tablecloths and the waitress is a bitch.'

It was noon when he walked into the Petit Saint-Paul, where he began by telephoning to his wife to say he would not be home for lunch.

He was not forgetting Fernand and his gangsters, but he couldn't
resist this business.

V

IN FACT he was giving himself a change, playing truant as it were,
and he felt slightly guilty about it. But not too much so, because for one
thing what Olga had said about the chitterlings was no exaggeration;
for another thing the Beaujolais, though a little heavy, was very fruity;
and lastly because, seated in a corner, at a table spread with
rough paper instead of a cloth, he could ruminate at his ease.

The *patronne*, a short, stout woman with a bun of grey hair on top
of her head, sometimes opened the kitchen door a crack and threw a
rapid glance round the restaurant. She had a blue apron like the ones
Maigret's mother used to wear long ago; the blue was still dark round
the edges, but had faded in the middle, where it had been rubbed
harder in the wash.

It was also true that the waitress, a tall, dark woman with a pasty
complexion, looked sour and suspicious. From time to time she winced

as though momentarily in pain, and the superintendent would have sworn she had just had a miscarriage.

The other customers included some workmen in their overalls, several Algerians, and a newspaper-woman in a man's jacket and peaked cap.

What would be the use of showing a photo of Cuendet to the waitress or to the heavily moustached *patron* who was attending to the wine? From the table where Maigret was sitting, and which had no doubt been his as well, the Swiss—provided he wiped the steamy window-pane every three minutes—could have kept an eye on the street and on the house that interested him.

He had certainly not confided in anybody. He must have been taken, as he was everywhere, for just a quiet little man; and in a sense this was true.

In his own way, Cuendet was a craftsman; and because Maigret was thinking at the same time about the fellows in the Rue La Fayette —that was what he called ruminating—he found the man slightly old-fashioned—like this restaurant, which would soon make way for a spick-and-span self-service counter.

Maigret had known other solitary workers, such as the famous Commodore, with his monocle and the red carnation in his buttonhole, who used to stay in the most fashionable hotels—a faultlessly attired, dignified, white-haired figure—and was never once caught red-handed.

The Commodore had never seen the inside of a prison, and no one knew how he had met his end. Had he retired to the country with a change of identity, or spent his declining years basking in the sunshine of an island in the South Seas? Had he been murdered by some tough with an eye to his savings?

At that time, too, there had been organized gangs; but their methods of work were not the same as nowadays, and above all they were differently composed.

Twenty years ago, for instance, in a matter like the Rue La Fayette affair, Maigret would have known at once where to look—the exact district and almost the exact tavern frequented by the bad lots. In those days they could scarcely read or write, and their way of life was written all over their faces.

Nowadays they were skilled technicians. This hold-up in the Rue La Fayette, like its forerunners, had been meticulously planned, and the capture of one of the men involved was due to the most improbable accident—the presence in the crowd of a police constable who, in defiance of regulations, was armed although not on duty, and who had lost his head and fired, at the risk of hitting some inoffensive member of the crowd.

Even Cuendet had brought himself up to date, that was true. Maigret called to mind a remark made by the woman in the next room at the hotel. She had referred to people who took afternoon tea at five o'clock. To her, they belonged to a world of their own. To Maigret likewise. But Cuendet had been at pains to make a careful study of such people's habits and customs.

He broke no window-panes, used no jimmy, did no damage.

Out in the street, people were walking quickly, their hands in their pockets, their faces stiff with cold, everyone brooding over his own problems and worries, everyone with his personal drama, everyone compelled to some form of activity.

'My bill, please.'

The waitress wrote down the items in pencil on the paper tablecloth, her lips moving and her eyes turning now and then to the slate on which the prices of the various dishes were marked.

Maigret went back to the office on foot. No sooner was he seated at his desk, with his files and his pipes arrayed in front of him, than the door opened and Lucas appeared. They both opened their mouths at the same time. The superintendent was the first to speak.

'Someone should be sent to take over from Fumel, at the Hôtel Lambert in the Rue Neuve Saint-Pierre.'

Not a member of what might be called his personal team, but a man like Lourtie, for instance, or Lesueur. Neither of these was free, and it was Baron who left the Quai des Orfèvres a little later, suitably briefed.

'And you? What did you want to tell me?'

'There's been a new development. Inspector Nicolas may have put his finger on something.'

'Is he here?'

'Yes—waiting to see you.'

'Send him in.'

Nicolas was an inconspicuous kind of man, and because of that fact he had been sent to prowl round Fontenay-aux-Roses. His job was to get into casual conversation with the Raisons' neighbours, the shopkeepers they dealt with, and the mechanics at the garage where the wounded gangster kept his car.

'I can't say yet if this will lead us anywhere, Chief, but I rather think

we may have got hold of something. Yesterday evening I discovered that
Raison and his wife were on visiting terms with another couple in the
same block of flats. In fact they were great friends. They sometimes
watched television together in the evening. When they went to the
cinema, one of the wives would stay behind to look after the other
family's children as well as her own.

'The name of this couple is Lussac. They're younger than the Raisons.
René Lussac is only thirty-one and his wife is two or three years less
than that. She's very pretty and they have a little boy of two and a half.

'Acting on instructions, I therefore began to watch René Lussac, who
travels for a firm of musical instrument makers. Like Raison, he has a
car—a Floride.

'Yesterday evening I followed him when he left home after dinner.
I had the use of an old car. He had no idea I was trailing him, or he
could easily have shaken me off.

'He went to a café at the Porte de Versailles, the Café des Amis—a
quiet place, popular with the local tradesmen, who come there for a
game of cards.

'Two men were waiting for him, and they began to play *belote*, like
people who are in the habit of meeting round the same table.

'It struck me as a bit peculiar. Lussac has never lived anywhere near
the Porte de Versailles. I wondered why he came such a long way to
play cards in such an unattractive joint.'

'You were inside the café?'

'Yes. I felt certain he hadn't spotted me at Fontenay-aux-Roses, so I
was running no risk by showing myself. He took no notice of me. The
three of them were playing in quite a natural way, but they looked at
the time rather often.

'At precisely half past nine Lussac went to the cash-desk and bought
a counter for the automatic telephone. He shut himself up in the
'phone-box, where he remained for about ten minutes. I could see him
through the glass. It wasn't a Paris call, because after lifting off the receiver he only said a few words and then hung up. He waited in the
booth, and after a few minutes the telephone rang. In other words the
call had been put through by tolls or long-distance.

'When he came back to his table he was looking worried. He said
something to the others and then glanced round suspiciously and signed
to them to go on with the game.'

'What did the other two look like?'

'I went out before they left, and waited in my car. I thought there was no point in following Lussac, who would no doubt be going back to Fontenay-aux-Roses. So I chose one of the others, at random. They both had cars. The one who looked to be the older of the two was the first to drive off, and I followed him to a garage in the Rue La Boétie. He left his car there and walked to a house in the Rue de Ponthieu, parallel with the Champs-Elysées, where he had a one-room furnished flat.

'His name is Georges Macagne. I got the hotel squad to look into that this morning. Then I went up and found his file. He's had two sentences for car thefts and one for assault.'

This was perhaps the long-awaited gleam of light.

'I thought it would be better not to question the café-proprietors.'

'Quite right. I'll ask the examining magistrate for a warrant, and you must take it to the telephone exchange and get them to find out who René Lussac rang up last night. They won't do anything without a written order.'

The inspector was scarcely out of his office before Maigret had rung up the Hôpital Beaujon. He had some difficulty in getting hold of the man who was on duty outside Raison's door.

'How is he now?'

'I was just waiting a few minutes before ringing you. Someone went to fetch his wife. She's just arrived. I can hear her crying in his room. Half a minute. The matron has just come out. Will you hold on?'

Maigret could still hear the muffled sounds typical of a hospital corridor.

'Hello? It's what I thought. He's dead.'

'He didn't say anything?'

'He never even recovered consciousness. His wife is lying on her face on the floor, sobbing.'

'Did she notice you?'

'I'm sure she didn't, not in the state she's in.'

'She came by taxi?'

'I don't know.'

'Go down to the main entrance and wait. Follow her when she leaves, on the off-chance that she may feel like getting in touch with somebody, or making a telephone call.'

'Okay, Chief.'

Perhaps the case might be practically over, and a telephone call would at last lead them to Fernand. It would be quite consistent for him to be lying low somewhere in the country, near Paris, probably in some inn kept by a retired prostitute or an ex-gangster.

If the telephone gave no results they could always make the round of such places, but that might take a long time, and Fernand, the brains of the gang, might very well be in the habit of changing his hide-out every day.

Maigret rang up the examining magistrate in charge of the investigation, told him what had happened, promised him a report, and then settled down to write it at once, for the magistrate wanted to speak to the Public Prosecutor that night.

Maigret mentioned, among other things, that the car used for the hold-up had been found near the Porte d'Italie. As was to be expected, it was a stolen car, and naturally it had yielded no clues whatsoever, let alone any interesting fingerprints.

He was hard at work when old Joseph, the office messenger, came in to say that the Director of Judicial Police would like to see him in his office. For a moment Maigret thought it was about the Cuendet business—that in some mysterious way his chief had got wind of his activities—and he expected a rap over the knuckles.

In point of fact it was about a new case altogether—the disappearance, three days previously, of the daughter of a prominent man. She was a girl of seventeen, and it had been discovered that she was surreptitiously attending a drama school and had done crowd work in several films that were not yet released.

'Her parents want to keep it out of the papers. There's every likelihood that she went off of her own accord . . .'

He put Lapointe on this affair and returned to his report, while the sky outside the windows grew darker and darker.

At five o'clock he knocked on the door of the office belonging to his colleague, the head of General Information, a man with the bearing of a cavalry officer. Here there was no rush, no bustling to and fro, as there was with the crime squad. The walls were lined with green files and the lock on the door was as complicated as that of a strong-room.

'Tell me, Danet, do you happen to know a man called Wilton?'

'Why do you ask?'

'It's still rather vague. Someone's been talking to me about him and I'd like to have a few more particulars.'

'Is he mixed up in some trouble?'

'I don't think so.'

'It's Stuart Wilton you mean?'

'Yes.'

So Danet did know the man, as he knew every foreigner of any standing who lived in Paris or came there for long visits. Among the green files there might even be one bearing Wilton's name; but the head of General Information made no move to produce it.

'He's a very important man.'

'I know. And very wealthy, so I'm told.'

'Very wealthy, yes, and a good friend of France. In fact he chooses to live in this country for the greater part of the year.'

'Why?'

'For one thing because he likes the life.'

'And then?'

'Perhaps because he feels freer here than across the Channel. What puzzles me is your coming to ask me questions, because I don't see any possible connection between Stuart Wilton and your department.'

'There isn't any as yet.'

'Is it because of a woman that you're on to him?'

'One can't even say I am on to him. There is certainly a woman who . . .'

'Which one?'

'He's been married several times, hasn't he?'

'Three times. And no doubt he will marry again one of these days, although he's getting on for seventy.'

'He takes a great interest in women?'

'He does.'

Danet's replies came reluctantly, as though Maigret were trespassing on his own private preserves.

'In others besides those he marries, I take it?'

'Naturally.'

'How do things stand between him and his last wife?'

'You mean the French one?'

'Yes, Florence; the one who—so I'm told—used to belong to a troupe of dancers.'

'He has remained on excellent terms with her—and with his two previous wives, for that matter. The first was the daughter of a rich English brewer, and she gave him a son. She married again and now she lives in the Bahamas.

'The second was a young actress. He had no children by her and left her after only two or three years; he has lent her a villa on the Riviera and she lives quietly down there.'

'And to Florence he's given a house in Paris,' Maigret muttered.

Danet frowned uneasily.

'She's the one you're interested in?'

'I don't know yet.'

'It's not as though she goes in for publicity. But of course I've never had occasion to study Wilton from that angle. I only know what is common knowledge in a certain circle in Paris.

'Yes, Florence lives in a house that used to belong to her ex-husband . . .'

'In the Rue Neuve Saint-Pierre . . .'

'Correct. But I'm not sure the house is hers. As I said, each time Wilton has been divorced he has remained on excellent terms with his last wife. He allows them to keep their jewellery and furs; but I doubt if he would make one of them a present of a house such as that.'

'What about his son?'

'He spends part of his time in Paris, too, but not so much as his father. He does a lot of skiing in Switzerland and Austria, goes in for motor racing and yacht racing on the Riviera, in England and in Italy, plays polo . . .'

'In other words, no professional activity?'

'Definitely none.'

'Married?'

'He was, for a year, to a model; then he divorced her. Listen, Maigret, I don't want to have a battle of wits with you. I don't know what you're after, or what's at the back of your mind. All I ask is that you'll do nothing without telling me. I meant what I said about Stuart Wilton being a good friend of France, and it's not for nothing that he's a Commander of the Legion of Honour.

'He has enormous interests in this country and he's a man to be treated with tact.

'His private life is none of our business, unless he has committed some serious breach of the law, and that would surprise me.

'He's a man for the women. To be quite frank, I shouldn't be surprised to learn that he has some kind of hidden kink. But I'd just as soon not know what it is.

'As for the son and his divorce, I may as well tell you what was rumoured at the time, because you'll find out in any case.

'Lida, the model young Wilton married, was an exceptionally beautiful girl—of Hungarian origin, if I'm not mistaken . . . Stuart Wilton was against the marriage. His son ignored his objections, and they say he discovered, one fine day, that his wife was his father's mistress.

'There was no scandal. In those circles there seldom is; people settle things quietly, like men of the world.

'So young Wilton got a divorce.'

'And Lida?'

'All this happened about three years ago. Since then her photo has often appeared in the papers, because she has had affairs with several internationally celebrated men, and if I'm not mistaken she's now living in Rome with an Italian prince. Is that what you wanted to hear about?'

'I don't know.'

This was true. Maigret felt tempted to lay his cards on the table and tell his colleague the whole story. But their points of view were too far apart.

To put it in terms of what Olga had said that morning, Superintendent Danet probably took afternoon tea now and then; whereas Maigret had lunched at a *bistro* with paper tablecloths, in the company of workmen and Algerians.

'I'll come and see you again when I have some idea. By the way, is Stuart Wilton in Paris at the moment?'

'Unless he's on the Riviera. I can find out. It would be better for me to do it myself.'

'And his son?'

'He lives in the residential part of the Hôtel George V; rents a flat there by the year.'

'Thank you, Danet.'

'Be careful, Maigret!'

'I promise!'

The superintendent had no intention of ringing Stuart Wilton's door-bell and beginning to ask him questions. And at the George V he would get no more than politely evasive answers.

Cajou, the examining magistrate, had known what he was about when he made that statement to the Press, saying that the Bois de Boulogne business was connected with some vendetta in the underworld. It implied that there was no need to get excited, or try to find out too much.

There are some crimes that cause a public sensation. It may be for some quite adventitious reason—the identity of the victim, the manner of the crime, or the place where it was committed.

For instance, if Cuendet had been murdered in a Champs-Elysées night-club he would have hit the front-page headlines.

As it was, his death had passed almost unnoticed, with nothing to capture the attention of people reading their morning paper in the Métro. An ex-convict who had never committed any sensational crime and who could just as easily have been fished up somewhere along the Seine.

Yet Cuendet interested Maigret more than Fernand and his gang, although he had no right to take an official hand in the case.

For the gangsters of the Rue La Fayette, the whole police force was to stand by for action. Whereas Fumel, with no car at his disposal and no assurance that if he ventured to take a taxi the fare would be refunded to him, had sole responsibility for the Cuendet investigation.

He must have gone to the Rue Mouffetard, searched Justine's flat and asked her questions to which she would have replied precisely as she chose.

All the same, Maigret telephoned from his office to the Medico-Legal Institute. Instead of asking for Doctor Lamalle or one of his assistants, he decided to speak to a laboratory attendant he had known for a long time and for whom he had once done a good turn.

'Tell me, François, were you at the post-mortem on Honoré Cuendet, the Bois de Boulogne chap?'

'Yes, I was. Haven't you had the report?'

'I'm not in charge of the case; but I'd like to know, all the same.'

'I understand. Well, Doctor Lamalle thinks this customer had been hit about ten times. To begin with he was struck from behind, so violently that his skull was smashed in and death must have been instantaneous. Doctor Lamalle's a very nice man, you know. We still miss dear old Doctor Paul, of course; but everyone likes Lamalle already.'

'What about the other blows?'

'They were delivered on the man's face when he was lying on his back.'

'What type of weapon do they think was used?'

'They discussed that for a long time and even made some experiments. It seems it wasn't a knife, or a monkey-wrench, or any of the usual things. Not a jimmy or a knuckle-duster, either. I overheard them saying that the object used must have had several projections, and was heavy and bulky.'

'A statue?'

'That's the suggestion they made in their report.'

'Were they able to fix the approximate time of death?'

'According to them it was about two in the morning. Between half past one and three, but nearer two o'clock.'

'Did he bleed a lot?'

'Not only that, but some of his brains came out. There were still traces in his hair.'

'The contents of the stomach were analysed?'

'Guess what it contained! Chocolate, not yet digested. There was some alcohol too; not much, and it was only just beginning to enter the blood-stream.'

'Thank you, François. Unless you're asked, don't say I rang up.'

'Better not for my own sake, too.'

Fumel telephoned the superintendent a little later.

'I called to see the old woman, Chief, and she went with me to the Medico-Legal Institute. It's him, right enough.'

'How did it go?'

'She was less upset than I'd feared. When I offered to take her home she refused, and went off all alone to the Métro station.'

'You searched the flat?'

'I found nothing except books and magazines.'

'No photographs?'

'Only a bad photo of the father in Swiss uniform, and a cabinet photograph of Honoré as a baby.'

'No notes? You went through the books?'

'Nothing. The man didn't write, and received no letters. Nor did his mother, needless to say.'

'There's one trail you might follow up, provided you're very cautious. A certain Stuart Wilton lives in the Rue de Longchamp, where he owns a big house—I don't know the number. He has a Rolls-Royce and a chauffeur. They must occasionally leave the car out in the street or put it into a garage. Try to see if there isn't a wild-cat rug inside.'

'Wilton's son lives at the George V and has a car too.'

'I understand, Chief.'

'That's not all. It would be interesting to get hold of photos of them both.'

'I know a photographer who works in the Champs-Elysées.'

'Good luck to you!'

Maigret spent half an hour signing forms, and when he left the office he set out on foot for the Saint-Paul district, instead of making for his usual bus.

It was as cold as ever and as dark; the city lights seemed unusually bright, and the passers-by were seen in blacker silhouette, as though all half-tones had been eliminated.

As he turned the corner of the Rue Saint-Paul, a voice out of the darkness said:

'Well, Superintendent?'

It was Olga, in a rabbit-fur coat, standing in a doorway. This gave him the idea of asking her for some information he had been meaning to seek elsewhere—particularly as she was the person most likely to be able to supply it.

'Tell me, when you need a drink or want to warm yourself after midnight, what's open round here?'

'Chez Léon.'

'That's a bar?'

'Yes. In the Rue Saint-Antoine, just opposite the Métro.'

'Did you ever meet your neighbour there?'

'The Swiss? No, not at night. Once or twice in the afternoon.'

'Drinking?'

'White wine.'

'Thank you.'

This time it was she who, as she tramped off, called out:

'Good luck to you!'

He had a photo of Cuendet in his pocket, and going into the steamy bar he ordered a glass of brandy—regretting it when he saw there were six or seven stars on the bottle.

'Do you know this man?'

The *patron* wiped his hands on his apron before taking hold of the photograph, which he then studied thoughtfully.

'What's he done?' he inquired cautiously.

'He's dead.'

'How? Suicide?'

'What makes you suppose that?'

'I don't know . . . I didn't see him often . . . Three or four times . . . He never talked to anyone . . . The last evening . . .'

'When was that?'

'I couldn't tell you for certain . . . Thursday or Friday of last week . . . Maybe Saturday . . . The other times he'd come for a quick one at the bar in the afternoon, like a man who's thirsty . . .'

'Only one glass?'

'Two, perhaps . . . Not more . . . He wasn't what you'd call a drinker . . . I can recognize them at the first glance.'

'What time was it, the last evening?'

'After midnight . . . Wait a minute . . . My wife had gone upstairs . . . So it must have been between half-past twelve and one o'clock . . .'

'How do you happen to remember?'

'Well, for one thing, at night we get hardly anybody except the regulars; sometimes a taxi-driver on the crawl, or a couple of police having a glass on the sly . . . I remember there was one couple at the corner table, talking in whispers . . . Otherwise the place was empty. I was busy with the coffee percolator. I didn't hear any footsteps. And when I turned round, there he was, leaning on the bar. It gave me quite a turn.'

'That's why you remember it?'

'And for another reason, because he asked me if I had any real kirsch, not the fancy stuff . . . We don't get many orders for that. I took a bottle from the back row—that one there, with the German words on the label—and he seemed pleased. He said:

' "That's the real thing."

'He took the time to warm the glass in his hand, and drank slowly, looking at the clock. I realized he was wondering whether to ask for another, and when I held out the bottle he didn't say no.

'He wasn't drinking for the sake of drinking, but because he liked kirsch.'

'He didn't speak to anybody?'

'Only to me.'

'The people in the corner took no notice of him?'

'They were a pair of lovers. I know them. They come here twice a week and sit whispering for hours, gazing into each other's eyes.'

'They left soon after he did?'

'Indeed they did not.'

'You didn't notice anyone who might have been watching him from outside?'

The man shrugged his shoulders as though he felt insulted.

'I've been in this place for fifteen years . . .' he sighed.

The implication being that nothing unusual could escape his notice.

A little later on, Maigret walked into the Hôtel Lambert, and this time it was the proprietress who was in the office. She was younger and more attractive than the superintendent would have expected after seeing her husband.

'You've come about number 33, haven't you? The gentleman's up there now.'

On the way up he had to flatten himself against the wall to make way for a couple coming down. The woman was drenched in scent and the man turned his head aside, looking sheepish.

The room was in darkness. Baron was sitting in the arm-chair, which he had drawn up to the window. He must have got through a whole packet of cigarettes, for the atmosphere was suffocating.

'Anything happened?'

'She went out half an hour ago. Before that a woman came to see her, carrying a big cardboard box—a seamstress or a dressmaker, I suppose. They went into the bedroom together and all I could see was their shadows going to and fro and then keeping quite still, with one of them kneeling down, as though a dress was being tried on.'

There were no lights on the ground floor except in the hall. The stairs were lit as far as the second floor, and two lamps were still burning in the drawing-room, on the left; but not the big chandelier.

To the right was the boudoir, where a lace-capped maid in a black dress and white apron was tidying up.

'The kitchen and dining-room must be at the back. The way these people go on, one wonders what they do all day. I counted at least three servants going to and fro with no sign of what they were up to. There've been no visitors except the dressmaker. She came by taxi and left on foot, without her cardboard box. An errand-boy arrived on a box-tricycle and delivered some parcels. The manservant came out and took them from him. Do I carry on?'

'Are you hungry?'

'Beginning to be, but I can wait.'

'Get along now.'

'Shouldn't I stay till someone else takes over?'

Maigret shrugged. What was the use?

He locked the door and put the key in his pocket. Downstairs, he said to the proprietress:

'Don't let number thirty-three till you hear from me. Nobody is to go in there; you understand?'

In the street he caught sight of Olga approaching from a distance, arm in arm with a man, and he felt glad for her.

H E S A T down to dinner with no suspicion that a telephone call was soon to summon him from the rather cloying tranquillity of his flat, that a considerable number of people who were at present making plans for the evening were destined to spend the night otherwise than they had intended, or that every window in the building in the Quai des Orfèvres would be lit up until morning, as only happened on nights when there was a great to-do.

It was a very pleasant dinner, with a cosy sense of tacit understanding between Maigret and his wife. He told her about having chitterlings for lunch at the *bistro* in the Saint-Antoine district. They had often gone together to such places, which were more numerous in the old days, typical of Paris. There used to be one in nearly every street and they were known as lorry-drivers' restaurants.

'You know, the real reason one ate so well there was that they were all owned by people who'd come straight from their native provinces —Auvergne, Brittany, Normandy, Burgundy—and who not only kept up the traditions they'd brought with them, but were in constant touch with home and sent to the country for hams and *terrines* and sausages, sometimes even for bread . . .'

This reminded him of Cuendet and his mother, who had brought with them to the Rue Mouffetard the slow speech of the Vaudois Swiss, with a kind of static placidity that had a suggestion of laziness about it.

'Any news of the old woman?'

Madame Maigret had read his thoughts in his face.

'You forget that officially, for the moment, I'm only dealing with the hold-ups. They're more serious, they are—because they're a threat to the banks and insurance companies, to big business. The gangsters have modernized their methods quicker than we have.'

He said this with a shade of fleeting melancholy. Or rather, of regret for the past. His wife recognized it as such, and knew it never lasted long.

At such moments, incidentally, he was less alarmed by the thought of his retirement, only two years ahead. The world was changing, Paris was changing, everything was changing—men and methods alike.

If it weren't for retirement, though at times it seemed such a bogey, wouldn't he begin to feel lost in a world he no longer understood?

And all the same he was eating with relish, leisurely.

'He was a funny fellow! He had no reason to anticipate what's happened to him, and yet when I hinted to his mother that I was anxious about her future, she only said calmly:

' "*I'm sure he won't leave me without a penny . . .*" '

If that were so, how had Cuendet managed it? What scheme had he finally worked out in his big bullet-head?

And then, just as Maigret was beginning his dessert, the telephone rang.

'Would you like me to answer?'

But he was already on his feet, napkin in hand.

It was Janvier, calling from the Quai des Orfèvres.

'There's some news that may be important, Chief. Inspector Nicolas has just rung me. They've traced the call René Lussac made from the café at the Porte de Versailles.

'It was to a number just outside Corbeil, a villa on the Seine, which belongs to somebody you know—Rosalie Bourdon.'

'*La belle Rosalie?*'

'Yes. I rang the police patrol at Corbeil. They say she's at home.'

This, too, was someone who had frequently spent hours on end in Maigret's office. She was getting on for fifty now, but she was still an appetising creature—plump, florid, and with a flow of vivid, spicy language.

She had begun her career very young, on a stretch of pavement near the Place des Ternes, and at the age of twenty-five she was running an establishment whose clients included some of the most distinguished men in Paris.

Later she had moved to the Rue Notre-Dame de Lorette and opened a night-club of a specialized character, which went by the name of La Cravache.

Her last lover, the great love of her life, had been a certain Pierre Sabatini, a member of the Corsican gang, who had been sentenced to twenty years' hard labour for shooting down two members of the Marseilles gang in a bar in the Rue de Douai.

Sabatini would be at Saint-Martin-de-Ré for quite a few years yet. Rosalie had taken a deeply emotional line at the trial, and after her lover was sentenced she had moved heaven and earth for permission to marry him.

The papers had been full of it at the time. She had declared that she was expecting a child. Some people suspected that she had got herself pregnant by the first comer, in the hope of bringing off the marriage.

In any case, once the Ministry had refused to issue a permit there had been no further suggestion of maternity, and Rosalie had withdrawn from the public eye to her villa near Corbeil, whence she wrote and sent parcels to the prisoner at frequent intervals. She made a trip to the Ile de Ré every month, and the authorities down there kept a close eye on her, fearing that she was plotting her lover's escape.

And Fernand had been Sabatini's cell-mate at Saint-Martin.

Janvier went on:

'I've asked the people at Corbeil to set a watch on the villa. Several men are stationed round it now.'

'And Nicolas?'

'He asked me to tell you he was going back to the Porte de Versailles. What he saw yesterday gave him the impression that Lussac and his two friends are meeting there every evening. He wanted to be settled in the café before them, so as to reduce the risk of attracting their attention.'

'Is Lucas still in the office?'

'He's just back.'

'Tell him to keep a few men in reserve tonight. I'll ring you again in a few minutes.'

He rang up the Public Prosecutor's office, but there was only a subordinate on duty.

'I'd like to speak to Monsieur Dupont d'Hastier himself.'

'He's not here.'

'I know. But I need to speak to him urgently. It's about the latest hold-up, and probably about Fernand.'

'I'll try to get in touch with him. Are you at the Quai?'

'No, at home.'

He gave his telephone number, and then things began to happen in rapid succession. He had scarcely finished his dessert when the telephone rang again. It was the Public Prosecutor.

'They tell me you've arrested Fernand?'

'Not yet, sir, but we may have a chance of arresting him tonight.'

He explained the situation in a few rapid sentences.

'Meet me in my office in a quarter of an hour. I'm dining with friends, but I shall be leaving at once. You've got in touch with Corbeil?'

Madame Maigret made him some strong coffee and brought out the bottle of framboise from the sideboard cupboard.

'Take care not to catch cold. Do you suppose you'll be going to Corbeil?'

'I shall be surprised if they give me the chance.'

He was not mistaken. At the Palais de Justice, in one of the big offices in the Public Prosecutor's department, he found the Prosecutor himself, Monsieur Dupont d'Hastier, in a dinner-jacket, and with him Monsieur Legaille, the examining magistrate in charge of the inquiry into the hold-ups, and Superintendent Buffet, an old colleague of his own from the 'other branch', the Sûreté Nationale.

Buffet was taller, broader and more thick-set than Maigret, with a red face and sleepy-looking eyes—despite which he was one of the most efficient men in the force.

'Sit down, Maigret, and tell us exactly where you've got to.'

Before leaving home he had made another call to Janvier.

'I'm expecting news to come through here, any minute now. One thing I can tell you already—Rosalie Bourdon's had a man in her house at Corbeil for the last few days.'

'Have our men seen him?' asked Buffet; for all his massive body he had a tiny voice, almost like a girl's.

'Not yet, but some of the neighbours have told them about him, and what they said tallies pretty well with the description of Fernand.'

'Are they surrounding the house?'

'Yes—at some distance, so as not to give the alarm.'

'There's more than one way out?'

'Yes, of course. But there are other developments as well. As I told the Prosecutor just now on the telephone, Lussac was friendly with Joseph Raison, the gangster who was killed in the Rue La Fayette, they both lived in the same block of flats at Fontenay-aux-Roses. And Lussac, with at least two friends, is going regularly to a café at the Porte de Versailles, the Café des Amis.

'They were there yesterday evening, playing cards, and at half past nine Lussac went into the telephone-box and rang up Corbeil.

'So that seems to be how the three men keep in touch with their leader. I'm expecting a call from one minute to the next.

'Now if—as we shall soon know—they are meeting at the same place this evening, we shall have a decision to make.'

In the old days he would have made the decision himself, and this kind of council of war in the Public Prosecutor's office would never have been held. In fact it would have been unthinkable, except in a case with political implications.

'A witness has declared that at the time of the hold-up Fernand was sitting in a café exactly opposite the spot where the cashier was attacked and where his accomplices—all but one—jumped into their car.

'Those men went off with the brief-case containing the money.

'It's not likely that Fernand has been able to meet them since then, particularly in view of the accident that took place.

'If it is he who is hiding in Rosalie's house, he must have gone there that same evening, and every evening he issues his instructions by telephone to the Café des Amis . . .'

Buffet was listening sleepily. Maigret knew that his colleague was considering the matter from the same angle as himself, anticipating the same possibilities and dangers. It was only for the gentlemen of the Public Prosecutor's department that he was going into all these details.

'Sooner or later, one of the accomplices will be told to bring all or part of the loot to Fernand. If that happens, of course, we shall have conclusive evidence. But there may be several days to wait. Meanwhile, it's on the cards that Fernand will look for another hide-out, and even with a watch on the villa he might easily give us the slip.

'On the other hand, if there is a meeting at the Café des Amis this evening, as there was yesterday, we shall have a chance to arrest all three men and to get our hands on Fernand at Corbeil at the same time.'

The telephone rang. The clerk handed the receiver to Maigret.

'It's for you.'

It was Janvier, acting as a kind of go-between.

'They are there, Chief. What have you decided?'

'I'll tell you in a few minutes. Send one of our men, and a woman welfare officer, to Fontenay-aux-Roses. Tell him to ring you up as soon as he gets there.'

'Right.'

Maigret rang off.

'What is your decision, gentlemen?'

'To run no risk,' replied the Public Prosecutor. 'We shall get our evidence in the end, shall we not?'

'They will engage the best solicitors and refuse to give anything away, and they've no doubt provided themselves with first-class alibis.'

'Still, if we don't arrest them tonight we may never get another chance.'

'I'll take care of Corbeil,' Buffet announced.

It was not for Maigret to protest. That end was outside his sector.

'Do you think they'll shoot?' asked the examining magistrate.

'Almost certainly, if they have the opportunity; but we'll try not to leave the decision to them.'

A few minutes later, Maigret and his stout colleague moved from one world to another by going through the inconspicuous door that divided the Palais de Justice from the offices of the Judicial Police.

Here the atmosphere was already tense with anticipation.

'We'd better wait before attacking the villa, in case they make a telephone call at half past nine.'

'Right you are. But I'd rather get there ahead of time, so as to have everything ready. I'll ring up to find out how you stand.'

In the dark, cold courtyard a radio car was already waiting, with its engine warming up, and a van loaded with police stood beside it. The superintendent of police for the 16th *arrondissement* must by now be somewhere close to the Café des Amis, with all the men he could muster.

Peaceful shopkeepers were sitting in the café, discussing business or playing cards, with no suspicion of what was going on; and nobody noticed Inspector Nicolas, who was deep in a newspaper.

He had just telephoned his laconic report:

'It's done.'

This meant that the three men were there, as they had been the previous day—René Lussac glancing at the clock now and then, no doubt to make sure he would not be late for his call to Corbeil at nine-thirty.

Spread out round the house at Corbeil, where two ground-floor windows were lit up, men were standing motionless in the darkness, among the ice-coated puddles.

The telephone exchange had been warned and was waiting. At nine thirty-five it reported:

'We have just been asked to ring Corbeil.'

And an inspector at the listening-post recorded the ensuing conversation.

'Everything okay?' asked Lussac.

It was not a man who answered, it was Rosalie.

'Okay. Nothing new.'

'Jules is getting impatient.'

'Why?'

'He wants to go off on a trip.'

'Hold on a minute.'

She must have gone to consult somebody. Soon she was back:

'He says you must wait a bit longer.'

'Why?'

'Just because!'

'They're beginning to look at us suspiciously in this place.'

'Wait a minute.'

Another silence, and then:

'There'll be some news tomorrow, for sure.'

Buffet rang up from Corbeil.

'Okay?'

'Yes. Lussac made his call. It was the woman who answered, but there's someone there with her. It seems that one of the gang, a fellow called Jules, is getting impatient.'

'So we can go ahead?'

'At ten-fifteen.'

The two operations must be synchronized, so that if by some miracle one of the men escaped the raid on the café, he would not be able to raise the alarm at Corbeil.

'At ten-fifteen.'

Maigret gave Janvier his final instructions.

'When you get the call from Fontenay-aux-Roses, tell 'em to arrest Madame Lussac, with or without a warrant, and bring her here, leaving the welfare officer to look after the child.'

'And Madame Raison?'

'No, not her. Not at present.'

Maigret climbed into the radio car. The police van had already left. At the Porte de Versailles a few pedestrians raised their eyebrows as they noticed the air of unusual activity, with men keeping close to the houses and talking in low voices, and others disappearing into dark corners as though by magic.

Maigret got hold of the local superintendent and settled with him how things should be done.

Here again, they had the choice between two alternatives. They could wait for the three card-players—whom they could see from a distance, through the café windows—to emerge and go to their respective cars, which were parked near by, as on the previous evening.

This seemed to be the easiest course. But it was the most risky, for once outside, the men would have complete freedom of movement, and perhaps time to use their guns. And might not one of them manage, during the scuffle, to jump into his car and escape?

'Is there another way out of the place?'

'There's a door into the yard, but the walls are high and the only way to the street is the corridor through the house.'

It took them less than a quarter of an hour to place their men, without attracting any attention in the Café des Amis.

Several men who might pass for tenants of the upstairs flats went into the house, and some of them stood about the yard.

Three others—hearty types and slightly tipsy—pushed into the café and sat down at the table next to the card-players.

Maigret glanced at his watch now and then, like a military commander waiting for zero hour, and at fourteen minutes past ten he went into the café, alone.

His neck was swathed in his knitted muffler and he kept his right hand in his overcoat pocket.

He had only two yards to go, and the gangsters had not even time to jump to their feet. Standing close beside them, he said in an undertone: 'Don't move. You are surrounded. Keep your hands on the table.'

Inspector Nicolas had joined him by now.

'Put the handcuffs on them. You others, too.'

One of the men managed to upset the table with a sudden jerk, and they heard the crash of broken glass; but two inspectors already had him by the wrists.

'Outside . . .'

Maigret looked round at the customers.

'Don't be alarmed, ladies and gentlemen; that was just a police operation.'

Fifteen minutes later the police van deposited the three men at the Quai des Orfèvres, where they were taken to separate offices.

A call came through from Corbeil: it was the burly Buffet, inquiring in his piping voice:

'Maigret? We're through.'

'No hitch?'

'He managed to shoot, all the same, and one of my fellows has a bullet in the shoulder.'

'What about the woman?'

'My face is covered with scratches. I'll bring you the pair of 'em as soon as I've seen to the formalities.'

The telephone never stopped ringing. This time it was the Public Prosecutor.

'Yes, sir. We've got them all. No, I've not asked them a single question. I've put them into separate offices and now I'm waiting for the man and woman Buffet is bringing me from Corbeil.'

'Be careful. Don't forget they'll make out that the police have third-degreed them.'

'I know.'

'And that they have a perfect right to refuse to say a word unless there is a solicitor present.'

'Yes, sir . . .'

In any case Maigret did not intend to question them right away, thinking it better to leave them to stew in their juice, separately. He was waiting for Madame Lussac.

She did not arrive until eleven o'clock, for she was in bed when the inspector got to the flat, and it had taken her some time to get dressed and explain to the woman welfare officer what might need to be done for her little boy.

She was a thin, dark-haired, rather pretty woman of not more than twenty-five or so. Her face was pale and pinched. She said nothing, not bothering to feign indignation.

Maigret asked her to sit down facing him, while Janvier installed himself at the end of the desk with paper and pencil.

'Your husband's name is René Lussac and he is a commercial traveller by profession?'

'Yes, monsieur.'

'He is thirty-one years of age. How long have you been married?'

'Four years.'

'What was your maiden name?'

'Jacqueline Beaudet.'

'Born in Paris?'

'No, Orleans. I came to live in Paris with an aunt, when I was sixteen.'

'What does your aunt do?'

'She's a midwife. She lives in the Rue Notre-Dame-de Lorette.'

'Where did you meet René Lussac?'

'In a record and music instrument shop where I was working as an assistant. Where is he, Superintendent? Tell me what's happened to him. Ever since Joseph . . .'

'You mean Joseph Raison?'

'Yes. Joseph and his wife were friends of ours. We live in the same block of flats.'

'Did the two men often go out together?'

'Sometimes. Not often. Ever since Joseph died . . .'

'You have been afraid the same kind of accident might happen to your husband—isn't that so?'

'Where is he? Has he disappeared?'

'No. He's here.'

'Alive?'

'Yes.'

'Wounded?'

'He might well have been, but he isn't.'

'Can I see him?'

'Not just yet.'

'Why not?'

She added with a bitter smile:

'Silly of me to ask you that! I can guess what you want, why you're questioning me. You're thinking it will be easier to make a woman talk than a man, isn't that it?'

'Fernand has been arrested.'

'Who's he?'

'Do you really not know?'

She looked him straight in the eyes.

'No. My husband has never mentioned him to me. All I know is that someone gives orders.'

She had produced a handkerchief from her handbag, as a concession to propriety, but she was not crying.

'You see it's easier than you were expecting. For quite a time I've been afraid, and I was always imploring René to give those people up. He has a good job. We were quite happy. We were not rich, but we weren't doing badly. I don't know who he met . . .'

'How long ago?'

'About six months . . . It was last winter . . . Or rather, autumn . . . I'm just as glad it's over, because now I needn't be so scared . . . You're sure that woman knows how to look after my little boy?'

'You needn't feel uneasy about that.'

'He's highly strung, like his father. He gets restless during the night . . .'

One could sense that she was tired, rather lost, trying to straighten out her thoughts.

'One thing I can tell you for certain is that René didn't shoot.'

'How do you know?'

'In the first place because he's incapable of it. He let himself be led astray by those people, never imagining things would get so serious.'

'Did he talk to you about it?'

'I'd noticed for some time that he was bringing home more money than he should. And he was going out more often, nearly always with Joseph Raison. Then, one day, I found his gun.'

'What did he say?'

'That I needn't worry, and that in a few months we should be able to go and live quietly in the South. He wanted to have a shop of his own, at Cannes or Nice . . .'

She was crying at last—softly, in little jerks.

'It's the car that's to blame, really . . . He'd set his heart on a Floride . . . He signed some bills . . . And the time came when he had to meet them . . . When he finds out I've told you, he'll be angry with me . . . Perhaps he won't want to have anything more to do with me . . .'

Sounds were heard from the corridor, and Maigret signed to Janvier to take the girl into the next room. He had recognized Buffet's voice.

There were three detectives, pushing in front of them a handcuffed man who threw Maigret a sharp, defiant glance.

'And the woman?' queried the superintendent.

'At the other end of the corridor. She's more dangerous than he is— she claws and bites.'

And indeed Buffet's face was scratched and there was blood on his nose.

'Come in, Fernand.'

Buffet came in as well, while his two officers remained outside. The ex-convict inspected his surroundings and remarked:

'I rather think I've been here before.'

He was recovering his mocking, self-assured manner.

'I suppose you're going to plague the life out of me with questions, like last time. I may as well warn you at once that I shan't answer them.'

'Who is your solicitor?'

'Still the same one. Maître Gambier.'

'Do you want us to send for him?'

'Personally, I've nothing to say to him. But if it amuses you to get the man out of bed . . .'

All through the night people were bustling to and fro in the corridors of the Quai des Orfèvres and going from office to office. Typewriters clicked like falling hailstones. The telephone rang uninterruptedly, for the Public Prosecutor's department was anxious to keep in touch and the examining magistrate had not gone to bed.

One of the inspectors spent most of his time making coffee. Now and then Maigret, as he went about the building, ran into one of his staff.

'Nothing yet?'

'He's not said a word.'

None of the three men from the Café des Amis would admit to recognizing Fernand. They were all playing the same game.

'Fernand—who's that?'

When the tape-recording of the call to Corbeil was played back to them, they replied:

'That's René's business. His love-affairs don't concern us.'

René himself retorted:

'I suppose I can have a mistress, can't I?'

Madame Lussac was confronted with Fernand.

'Do you recognize him?'

'No.'

'What did I tell you?' the ex-convict crowed jubilantly. 'None of these people have ever seen me before. When I left Saint-Martin-de-Ré I was flat broke, and a pal gave me his girl's address, saying she would see I didn't starve. I was in her house, lying low.'

Maître Gambier arrived at one o'clock in the morning and at once began to raise points of law.

According to the new Code of Criminal Procedure, the police could only hold these men for twenty-four hours, after which the case would pass to the Public Prosecutor and the examining magistrate, who would have to take full responsibility for it.

Doubts could already be sensed among the Palais de Justice people.

A confrontation between Madame Lussac and her husband gave no results.

'Tell them the truth.'

'What do you mean, the truth? That I've got a mistress?'

'The revolver . . .'

'One of my buddies slipped me a gun. And so what? I do a lot of travelling, alone in my car . . .'

First thing in the morning they would round up the witnesses, all those who had already filed through the Quai des Orfèvres—the waiters from the café in the Rue La Fayette, the woman at the cash-desk, the beggar, the passers-by, and the police constable in mufti who had shot Raison.

Also first thing in the morning, they would search the flats of the three men arrested at the Porte de Versailles, and perhaps find the brief-case in one of them.

It had all boiled down to a matter of routine—rather sickening and burdensome routine.

'You can go back to Fontenay-aux-Roses now, but the welfare officer will stay with you for the time being . . .'

He told someone to drive her home. She was dropping with fatigue and stared round wide-eyed, as though wondering where she had got to.

While his man continued to press the prisoner with questions, Maigret went out for a breath of air and found that his hat and shoulders were white with the first snowflakes. A bar in the Boulevard du Palais was just opening; he went in and propped his elbows on the counter, eating hot croissants and drinking two or three cups of coffee.

He went back to the office at seven o'clock, trudging along and blinking his eyes, and was surprised to find Fumel there.

'Have you got hold of something, too?'

The inspector seemed highly excited, and began a voluble explanation.

'I was on duty last night. They told me what you were doing in the Avenue de Versailles, but it wasn't my show; so I took the chance to ring up friends in other parts of Paris. They all have Cuendet's photo.

'I said to myself that sooner or later it might lead to something . . .'

'So I was chatting with Duffieux of the 18th *arrondissement*, and I mentioned my chap. And Duffieux said he'd been meaning to ring me on that subject.

'He works with your friend Inspector Lognon. When Lognon saw the photo, yesterday morning, he jumped, and put it in his pocket without a word.

'Cuendet's face reminded him of something. It seems he began asking questions in the bars and little restaurants in the Rue Caulaincourt and the Place Constantin-Pecqueur.

'As you know, when Lognon gets an idea into his head, he sticks to it. In the end he found what he was after—a place called the Régence, right at the top of the Rue de Caulaincourt.

'They recognized Cuendet at once there, and told Lognon he used to come quite often, with a woman.'

'Had he been coming for long?' asked Maigret.

'Yes, that's what's so interesting. For years, according to them.'

'Do they know the woman?'

'The waiter doesn't know her by name, but he's positive she lives close by, because he sees her going past every morning, on her way to the shops.'

The entire staff of the Judicial Police was busy with Fernand and his gang. In another two hours the corridors would again be packed with witnesses, to each of whom the four men would be shown separately. It would take all day, and every typewriter in the building would be needed for copying statements.

Alone and unconcerned amid this bustle, Inspector Fumel, his fingers stained with nicotine from the cigarettes he always smoked to the very end—so that there was even an indelible mark on his lower lip—had come to talk to Maigret about the placid Swiss from Vaud, whom everyone else seemed to have forgotten.

The whole subject had apparently been dismissed. Cajou, the examining magistrate, felt sure he need give no more thought to it.

He had settled the question in his own mind the very first day:

Vendetta in the underworld . . .

Cajou didn't know old Justine, or the little flat in the Rue Mouffetard—let alone the Hôtel Lambert and the mansion it overlooked.

'Are you tired?'

'Not really.'

'Suppose we go up there together?'

Maigret spoke almost furtively, as though suggesting to Fumel that they should play truant from school.

'By the time we get there it will be daylight . . .'

He left instructions for his men, stopped to buy some tobacco at the corner shop by the river, and went off with Fumel—who was shivering with cold—to the Montmartre bus-stop.

VII

DID LOGNON suspect that Maigret was more interested in the man killed in the Bois de Boulogne—and almost universally ignored—than in the Rue La Fayette hold-up and the gang that all the papers would be full of tomorrow morning?

If he did, wouldn't he have followed up the clue he had discovered? In that case one couldn't say how far he might not have gone towards finding out the truth—for he was perhaps the most intuitive member of the Paris police force—the most persistent, too, and the most desperately anxious for success.

Had he been dogged by bad luck, or did the fault lie in his conviction that fate was against him—that he was marked down in advance for victimization?

In any case he would end his career as an inspector at the police station in the 18th *arrondissement,* just like Aristide Fumel in the 16th. Fumel's wife had gone away and left him; Lognon's was an invalid who had not stopped complaining for the last fifteen years.

The Cuendet business had probably been sheer accident. Lognon, busy with some other matter, had mentioned his discovery to a colleague —who had seen no great importance in it, for he had spoken of it quite casually when Fumel rang him up.

The snow was falling fairly hard now, and beginning to settle on the roofs; not in the street, unfortunately. Maigret always felt disappointed to see it melting on the pavement.

The bus was stifling hot. Most of the passengers sat silently, looking straight ahead of them, their heads lolling from side to side, their faces blank.

'No news of the rug?'

Fumel jumped. His thoughts had been far away.

'The rug?' he repeated, as though he had not understood.

'The wild-cat fur rug.'

'I looked into Stuart Wilton's car, but I didn't see any rug. The car not only has a heater, it's air-conditioned as well. It even has a little bar—so I was told by one of the garage men.'

'What about the son's car?'

'He usually parks it outside the George V. I took a quick glance at it, but I saw no rug there, either.'

'D'you know where he gets his gas?'

'Usually from a pump in the Rue Marbeuf.'

'Been round there?'

'I've not had time yet.'

The bus stopped at the corner of the Place Constantin-Pecqueur. There was hardly anyone about. It was not yet eight o'clock.

'This must be the place.'

The lights were on, and a waiter was sweeping up the sawdust on the floor. It was one of the old-fashioned *brasseries* that are becoming very rare in Paris, with metal globes to hold dusters, a marble-topped bar where a woman would arrive later to sit behind the till, and mirrors all round the walls. Notices hung here and there, recommending the *choucroute garnie* and *cassoulet*.

The two men went in.

'Had any breakfast?'

'Not yet.'

Fumel ordered coffee and brioches, while Maigret—who had drunk too much coffee during the night and whose mouth felt clammy with it—asked for a small brandy.

Outside, it seemed difficult for life to start up again. It was neither night nor day. Children were going past on their way to school, trying to catch the falling snowflakes in their mouths, though the snow must have a dusty taste.

'Tell me, waiter . . .'

'Yes, sir?'

'Do you recognize this man?'

The waiter looked knowingly at the superintendent.

'You're Monsieur Maigret, aren't you? I recognize you. You came here a couple of years ago with Inspector Lognon.'

He gave a benevolent glance at the photograph.

'Yes, he's a regular customer. He always comes with the little lady with the hats.'

'Why do you call her the little lady with the hats?'

'Because she has a different hat nearly every time—smart, amusing ones. They usually come for dinner and sit at the back, in that corner. They're a nice couple. She has a passion for *choucroute*. They take their time, and end up with coffee and liqueurs, sitting hand in hand.'

'Have they been coming here for long?'

'For years. I don't know how many.'

'It seems she lives in this district?'

'I've been asked that before. She must have a flat somewhere round here, because I see her going past every morning with her shopping-bag.'

Maigret was delighted, without knowing why, to discover that there had been a woman in Honoré Cuendet's life.

A little later he and Fumel walked into the concierge's lodge of the first house they came to; the morning's letters were being sorted.

'Do you know this man?'

The concierge looked closely at the photograph and shook his head.

'I think I've seen him before, but I can't say I know him. In any case he's never been to this house.'

'You don't happen to have among your tenants a woman who often changes her hats?'

She stared at Maigret in bewilderment and shrugged her shoulders, muttering something he couldn't catch.

They had no better luck with the second and third houses. At the fourth, they found the concierge bandaging her husband's hand; he had cut himself while putting out the dustbins.

'Do you know him?'

'And what if I do?'

'Does he live here?'

'He does and he doesn't. He's the gentleman friend of the little lady on the fifth floor.'

'What little lady?'

'Mademoiselle Eveline, who makes hats.'

'Has she been long in the house?'

'At least twelve years. She was here before I came.'

'Was he with her already?'

'Maybe he was. I don't remember.'

'Have you seen them lately?'

'I see her every day, of course.'

'And him?'

'D'you remember when he was here last, Désiré?' she asked her husband.

'No, but it's quite a time.'

'Did he ever stay the night?'

She seemed to find the superintendent childish.

'What if he did? They're of age, aren't they?'

'He used to stay here for several days?'

'Even for weeks.'

'Is Mademoiselle Eveline at home? What is her surname?'

'Schneider.'

'Does she get many letters?'

The bundle of unsorted letters still lay on the ledge in front of the pigeon-holes.

'Practically none.'

'The fifth floor—on the left?'

'No—the right.'

Maigret went out into the street to see if there was any light showing from the flat. There was, so he began to climb the stairs with Fumel. The house had no lift. The staircase was tidy, the house clean and quiet, with mats outside the doors and here and there a brass or enamel plate.

They noticed a dentist on the second floor, a midwife on the third. Maigret halted now and then to recover his breath, and heard sounds of a wireless.

Reaching the fifth floor, he felt almost reluctant to ring the bell. Here, too, the radio had been playing; but now it was switched off and steps were heard approaching. The door opened, and a small, slim, fair-haired woman, garbed not in a dressing-gown but in a kind of overall, and holding a dish-cloth, stood looking at them with wide blue eyes.

Maigret and Fumel felt no less embarrassed than she, as they watched her expression of astonishment give way to one of alarm. Her lips quivered as she murmured at last:

'Are you bringing me bad news?'

She beckoned them into the living-room she had just been tidying, and pushed aside the vacuum cleaner that stood in the way.

'Why do you ask me that?'

'I don't know . . . Visitors, at this hour of the morning, and when Honoré's been away so long . . .'

She must be about forty-five, but she still looked very youthful. Her skin was clear and her figure firm and rounded.

'Are you from the police?'

'I am Superintendent Maigret. And this is Inspector Fumel.'

'Has Honoré had an accident?'

'You were right in guessing I had bad news for you.'

She was not crying yet, and they felt she was clinging for support to commonplace phrases.

'Please sit down. Do take off your overcoat, it's very hot in here. Honoré likes warmth. You mustn't mind the untidiness . . .'

'You're very fond of him?'

She bit her lip, trying to guess how serious the news might be.

'He's had an accident?'

Then, almost at once:

'He's dead?'

Now she began to cry—like a child, with her mouth open, not caring whether she looked ugly. She grasped her hair with both hands and stared round as though looking for a corner where she could hide.

'I always had a foreboding . . .'

'Why?'

'I don't know . . . We were too happy . . .'

The room was comfortable, cosy, the furniture heavy but good, and the few ornaments not in the worst of taste. An open door led into a cheerful kitchen, with a place still laid for breakfast.

'Please don't take any notice . . .' she kept saying. 'Excuse me . . .'

She opened another door, into the bedroom which was still in darkness; went in, and threw herself face downwards across the bed, crying her heart out.

Maigret and Fumel exchanged glances in silence, and the inspector was the more moved of the two; he always had a soft spot for women, in spite of all the trouble they had brought him.

It didn't last as long as one might have feared; then she went into the bathroom, splashed her face with cold water, and came back looking almost composed.

'I must apologize,' she said quietly. 'How did it happen?'

'He was found dead in the Bois de Boulogne. Haven't you seen the newspapers these last few days?'

'I never read newspapers. But why the Bois de Boulogne? What can he have been doing there?'

'He had been murdered in some other place.'

'Murdered? But why?'

She was trying hard not to burst into tears again.

'You had been friends for a long time?'

'More than ten years.'

'Where did you first meet him?'

'In a restaurant just near here.'

'The Régence?'

'Yes. I used to go there now and then for a meal. I noticed him, alone in his corner.'

Did this mean that about that time Cuendet had been planning a burglary in the district? Very likely. A scrutiny of the list of unsolved burglaries would no doubt reveal one committed in the Rue Caulaincourt.

'I don't remember how we first got into conversation. But one evening we had dinner at the same table. He asked if I were German and I told him Alsatian. I was born at Strasbourg.'

She smiled wanly.

'We used to make fun of each other's accents—he still had his Swiss one and I'd never lost my Alsatian one.'

Hers was a pleasant, sing-song accent. Madame Maigret, too, was from Alsace, and of much the same height and figure.

'He became your lover?'

She blew her nose; it was red, but she didn't care.

'He wasn't always here. He hardly ever spent more than two or three weeks with me, then he'd go off on a trip. At first I used to wonder if he hadn't got a wife and family in the provinces. Some men keep quiet about that when they come up to Paris . . .'

This suggested that there had been other men in her life before Cuendet.

'How did you find out he wasn't like that?'

'He wasn't married, was he?'

'No.'

'I felt sure he wasn't. For one thing, I guessed he had no children of his own, from the way he looked at other people's in the street. One felt he was resigned to not being a father, but that he regretted it all the same. And when he came here he didn't behave like a married man. It's hard to explain. He had a kind of bashfulness that a married man would have lost. The first time, for instance, I realized he felt shy about being in my bed, and when he woke up next morning he was even more embarrassed . . .'

'He never talked to you about his occupation?'

'No.'

'And you never asked him?'

'I tried to find out without seeming to pry . . .'

'He told you he travelled a lot?'

'He said he had to go away. He never explained where, or why. One day I asked him if his mother was still living, and he blushed. That

gave me the idea that perhaps he lived with her. Anyway he had someone to mend his clothes and darn his socks—someone who didn't do it
very well. Buttons were always coming loose, for instance; I used
to tease him about it.'

'When did he leave you for the last time?'

'Six weeks ago. I can look up the exact date . . .'

It was her turn to ask a question.

'And when . . . when did it happen?'

'On Friday.'

'And yet he never had much money on him.'

'When he came to stay with you, did he bring a suitcase?'

'No. If you look in the wardrobe you'll find his dressing-gown and
slippers, and there are shirts, socks and pyjamas in a drawer.'

She pointed to the mantelpiece and Maigret saw three pipes there,
one of them a meerschaum. Here too, just as in the Rue Mouffetard,
there was a coal stove with an arm-chair beside it—Honoré Cuendet's
arm-chair.

'I am sorry to be indiscreet, but there is a question I must ask you.'

'I can guess what it is. You mean, about money?'

'Yes. Used he to give you any?'

'He suggested it, but I refused, because I make quite a good living.
I did allow him to pay half the rent—he insisted, and it made him uncomfortable to live here without paying his share.

'He used to give me presents. He bought the furniture of this room,
and had my trying-on room done up. I'll show it to you . . .'

It was a very small room, furnished in the Louis XVI style, with a
profusion of mirrors.

'He painted all the walls too, including the kitchen, and papered the
living-room. He loved doing odd jobs.'

'How did he spend his days?'

'He went out for walks—not long ones, just round here, always the
same way, like somebody taking out a dog. And he sat in his chair,
reading. You'll find heaps of books in the cupboard, nearly all of them
travel books.'

'You never went away with him?'

'We had a few days at Dieppe, the second year. Another time we
went on holiday to Savoy and he showed me the Swiss mountains in
the distance and told me that was his country. And another time we
took a coach trip to Nice and along the Riviera.'

'He spent money lavishly?'

'It depends what you mean by lavish. He wasn't stingy, but he didn't like to be cheated, and he always looked over our hotel and restaurant bills.'

'I take it your age is about forty?'

'Forty-four.'

'So you have some experience of the world. Did you never wonder why he was leading this double life? Or why he didn't marry you?'

'I've known other men who didn't propose marriage.'

'But were they his type?'

'No, of course they weren't.'

She pondered for a moment.

'I did wonder about things, naturally. At first, as I told you, I thought he must have a wife in the provinces and a job that brought him to Paris several times a year. I shouldn't have blamed him. It would be tempting to have a woman to welcome him here, and a home to go to. He loathed hotels, I noticed that the first time we went away together. He felt uncomfortable in a hotel. As though he were afraid of something all the time.'

(Only natural!)

'Later, from the way he behaved and the way his socks were darned, I decided he must live with his mother and that he didn't like to tell me about it. There are more men than you'd suppose who don't marry because of their mothers, and are as much in awe of them at fifty years old as when they were little boys. It might have been that way with him.'

'All the same, he had to earn his living.'

'He might have had a small business somewhere.'

'You never suspected another kind of activity?'

'What kind?'

She was perfectly sincere; there was no question of her acting the innocent.

'What do you mean? I'm ready for anything now. What did he do?'

'He was a thief, Mademoiselle Schneider.'

'He—Honoré?'

She gave a nervous giggle.

'You don't really mean that, do you?'

'Wait a moment! He had been a thief all his life, from the age of sixteen, when he was apprenticed to a locksmith at Lausanne. He ran away from an approved school in Switzerland and joined the Foreign Legion.'

'He said something about the Legion when I noticed his tattoo marks.'

'He didn't mention that he'd spent two years in prison?'

Her knees gave way and she sat down abruptly, and listened as though the Cuendet she was hearing about were a different man from her Honoré.

Now and then she shook her head, still incredulous.

'I arrested him myself on that first occasion, mademoiselle, and since then he had been brought to my office several times. He was no ordinary thief. He had no accomplices, never associated with criminals, and led a very regular life. From time to time he would get an idea for a burglary by reading the newspapers and magazines, and for weeks he would watch a particular house, with all its comings and goings . . .

'Until the moment when he felt confident enough to go in and pick up the jewels and money he found there.'

'I simply can't believe it! It's too incredible!'

'I can quite understand you. But you were right about his mother. For part of the time he didn't spend here he used to be with her, in a flat in the Rue Mouffetard where he also kept belongings.'

'Does she know?'

'Yes.'

'She's known all along?'

'Yes.'

'And she didn't try to stop him?'

She was not indignant, only astonished.

'Is that why he was killed?'

'More than likely.'

'The police?'

She stiffened, her expression became less friendly, less trustful.

'No.'

'Was it the people where . . . whose house he had burgled, who killed him?'

'I imagine so. Now listen to me. I am not in charge of the investigation; it is in the hands of Monsieur Cajou, the examining magistrate. He has given certain tasks to Inspector Fumel.'

Fumel bowed.

'This morning the inspector is here unofficially, without instructions. You would have been entitled to refuse to answer our questions. You could have refused to let us in. And if we were to search your flat, we should be exceeding our authority. You understand?'

No. Maigret perceived that she did not grasp the implications of what he had been saying.

'I think . . .'

'To put it more precisely, nothing you have told us about Cuendet will appear in the inspector's report. It is to be expected that when he finds out about your existence and your relations with Honoré, the examining magistrate will send Fumel or another inspector to call on you, with a proper warrant.'

'What should I do then?'

'When that happens, you will be entitled to ask for your lawyer to be present.'

'Why?'

'I said you would be entitled to. The law does not insist on your doing so. Perhaps Cuendet may have left something in your flat, in addition to his clothes, his books and his pipes . . .'

At last he saw understanding dawn in Mademoiselle Schneider's blue eyes. Too late, for already she was murmuring, as if to herself:

'The suitcase . . .'

'It would be only natural for Honoré, since he spent part of the year under your roof, to have left in your care a suitcase containing personal effects. It would also be only natural for him to have given you the key, telling you—for instance—to open it if anything should happen to him . . .'

Maigret rather wished Fumel were not present; and as though aware of this, the inspector had put on a glum, absent-minded expression.

As for Eveline, she shook her head.

'I haven't got the key . . . But . . .'

'That doesn't matter, either. It is quite on the cards that a man like Cuendet would have taken the precaution of making a will, instructing you to see to various things in the event of his death—if only to take care of his mother . . .'

'Is she very old?'

'You will be seeing her yourself, since it appears that you two were the only women in his life.'

'You believe so?'

She could not help being pleased, and showing it by her smile. When she smiled she had dimples, like quite a young girl.

'I don't know what to think, myself.'

'When we've gone you will have time to think things over at leisure.'

'Tell me, Superintendent . . .'

She paused, suddenly blushing to the roots of her hair.

'He never . . . he never killed anyone?'

'Never—I can assure you.'

'You know, if you'd told me he had, I shouldn't have believed you.'

'I'll tell you something else, more difficult to explain. Cuendet lived on part of what he got by theft, that's certain . . .'

'He spent so little!'

'Precisely. It is possible, even probable that he felt a need for security, a need to know that he had a nest-egg to fall back on. But I wouldn't be surprised if in his particular case there was another essential factor.

'As I told you, he used to study the life of a house for weeks on end . . .'

'How did he set about it?'

'By choosing a convenient *bistro* where he would sit for hours in the window; or, when he had the opportunity, by renting a room in the house opposite.'

Eveline was struck by the same idea that had occurred to Maigret.

'Do you suppose that when I first met him, at the Régence . . . ?'

'Very likely. He didn't wait for a flat to be empty, for the owners to go out. On the contrary, he used to wait till they got home . . .'

'Why?'

'A psychologist or a psychiatrist could answer that question better than I can. Was the sense of danger necessary to him? I'm not so sure. You see, he didn't only break into a strange flat, but into the lives of the people who lived there, so to speak. They'd be asleep in their beds, and he brushed past them. It was rather as though, as well as their jewellery, he carried off a little of their private lives . . .'

'You don't seem to have any feeling against him . . .'

It was Maigret's turn to smile at this, but he only growled:

'I have no feeling against anybody. Goodbye, mademoiselle. Don't forget what I said to you, not a single word of it. Think it over quietly.'

He shook hands with her, to her great surprise, and Fumel did the same, more awkwardly, as though in the grip of emotion.

They were no sooner on the stairs than Fumel exclaimed:

'That's a wonderful woman!'

He would be back again, hanging round the neighbourhood, even after everyone had forgotten Honoré Cuendet. He couldn't help himself. He was already saddled with a mistress who gave him endless trouble, and he would now be doing his best to complicate his life still further.

Outside, the snow was beginning to settle on the pavements.

'What do I do now, Chief?'

'You must be sleepy—no? Anyhow, let's have a drink.'

By this time there were a few customers at the Régence; one of them, a commercial traveller, was copying addresses from the trade directory.

'Did you find her?' asked the waiter.

'Yes.'

'Nice, isn't she? What will you have?'

'A hot grog for me.'

'The same for me.'

'Two grogs, two!'

'This afternoon, when you've had some sleep, you'll be writing your report.'

'I'm to put in about the Rue Neuve Saint-Pierre?'

'Yes, of course, and about the Wilton woman who lives opposite the Hôtel Lambert. Cajou will send for you to ask for details.'

'He'll tell me to go and search Mademoiselle Schneider's flat.'

'Where, I hope, you will find nothing except a suitcase full of clothes.'

In spite of his admiration for the superintendent, Fumel felt uneasy, and puffed nervously at his cigarette.

'I understood what you were saying to her.'

'Honoré's mother told me. "I'm sure my son won't leave me without a penny."'

'She said the same to me.'

'You'll see, Cajou won't be at all keen for this case to go any further. As soon as he hears the name of Wilton . . .'

Maigret sipped his grog slowly, paid for the drinks, and decided to take a taxi back to the office.

'Can I drop you anywhere?'

'No, I have a direct bus.'

Perhaps, fearing that Eveline had not quite understood, Fumel intended to go back for a word with her.

'By the way, I'm bothered about that matter of the rug. So keep on looking into that . . .'

And thrusting his hands into his pockets, Maigret walked off to the taxi rank in the Place Constantin-Pecqueur, from where he could see the windows of Inspector Lognon's flat.

VIII

AT THE Quai des Orfèvres everyone was worn out—the inspectors, as well as the men who had been arrested during the night. The witnesses had been fetched from their homes and they were all over the place, some of them half-asleep and very peevish, plaguing Joseph, the office messenger, with questions:

'How much longer will they keep us hanging about?'

What could the old man tell them? He knew no more about it than they did.

The waiter from the Brasserie Dauphine was arriving with yet another tray of rolls and coffee.

The first thing Maigret did on getting back to his office was to ring through to Moers, who was equally busy upstairs, in the Judicial Identity service.

The 'paraffin test' had been applied to the four men's hands, so that if any of them had used a firearm of any kind within the past three or four days, gunpowder would be found in the pores of his skin, even if he had taken the precaution of wearing gloves.

'Have you got the results?'

'They've just come from the laboratory.'

'Which of the four?'

'Number three.'

Maigret glanced down the list, which bore a number against each name. Number 3 was Roger Stieb, a Czechoslovak refugee who had worked for a long time in the same factory as Joseph Raison, on the Quai de Javel.

'The expert is quite positive?'

'Absolutely.'

'Nothing from the other three?'

'Nothing.'

Stieb was a tall, fair-haired youth who had been the most docile of the lot during the night's questioning. Torrence was still pressing him hard, but he merely gazed at the inspector with bovine placidity, as though he did not understand a word of French.

All the same, he was the gang's killer, responsible for covering their escape after an attack.

The other man, Loubières, was a burly, hirsute fellow, born at Fécamp, who now kept a garage at Puteaux. He was married, with two children. A team of experts was searching his premises at the moment.

Nothing had been found at René Lussac's flat, or in Rosalie's villa.

Rosalie herself had been the noisiest of the lot, and Maigret could hear her yapping although the office where she was having her *tête-à-tête* with Lucas was two doors farther down the passage.

Some of the witnesses were now being confronted with the prisoners. The two waiters were too scared to speak positively, but said they thought they recognized Fernand as the customer who had been in the café at the time of the hold-up.

'You're sure you've caught the whole bunch?' they had asked before the identification began.

They were told that was so, although it was not strictly true. One member of the gang—the driver of the car—was still at large and the police had no clues to his identity.

He must be a crack driver, as always in such cases, but probably he played no part in the actual operations.

Maigret had to take a call from the Public Prosecutor.

'Yes, sir . . . We're getting on . . . We know who did the shooting—it was Stieb . . . Yes, he denies it . . . He'll deny it to the bitter end . . . They all will.'

Except poor Madame Lussac, who was in a state of collapse at home, where the woman welfare officer was helping her to look after her baby.

Maigret could hardly keep his eyes open, and the hot grog he had drunk at the Régence was no help. He was reduced to fetching the bottle of brandy he kept in his cupboard for special occasions, and taking a reluctant nip from that.

'Hello? Not yet, sir.' This time it was the examining magistrate.

Maigret kept getting calls on two telephones simultaneously, and not till twenty past ten did the one he wanted come through—from Puteaux.

'We've found it, Chief.'

'The lot?'

'Down to the last note.'

The newspapers had been allowed to announce that the bank had the numbers of the stolen notes. This was not true, but it had prevented the thieves from trying to get rid of them. They had been waiting for a chance to unload them in the provinces or abroad. Fernand was cunning enough to bide his time and to stop his men from leaving Paris while the search was in full cry.

'Where?'

'In the coachwork of an old car. That Loubières woman is the bossy type, she stuck to us like a leech . . .'

'You think she was in the know?'

'I do. We searched the cars one by one. More or less took 'em to pieces, in fact. Anyhow—we've got the stuff!'

'Don't forget to make Madame Loubières sign the statement.'

'She won't. I've tried.'

'Then get some witnesses.'

'That's what I've done.'

For Maigret this practically settled the matter. He would not be needed while the witnesses were being questioned, separately and in pairs. That would take hours.

Afterwards, the inspectors would make their individual reports to him, and he would have to draw up a general report.

'Would you get me Monsieur Dupont d'Hastier, the Public Prosecutor?'

A moment later he announced:

'The notes have been found.'

'And the brief-case?'

The man expected too much. Why not ask for nice, clear fingerprints?

'The brief-case is floating down the Seine by now, unless it was burnt in someone's stove.'

'Where was the money found?'

'At the garage.'

'What does the garage-owner say?'

'Nothing, so far. He hasn't been told about it.'

'Take care to have his solicitor there. I don't want any complaints, or any trouble in court when the case comes up for hearing.'

Once the corridors were cleared the two men would be taken to the Central Police Station, and the woman Rosalie, too—she would be put in a room by herself—and there they would be made to strip to the skin and go through the anthropometrical inspection. At least two of them had had that experience before.

They would probably spend the night in a ground-floor cell, because the examining magistrate would want to see them in the morning before committing them to the Santé prison.

It would be several months before the case came up for trial, and other gangs would have had time to form by then, in the same way, for reasons with which the superintendent was not concerned.

He opened one door, then another, and found Lucas sitting in front of a typewriter, typing with two fingers, while Rosalie paced to and fro with her hands on her hips.

'So there you are! Pleased with yourself, I suppose? The idea of Fernand being out of clink was keeping you awake at night, till you found an excuse for getting your paws on him again. You're not even ashamed to torment a woman; you forget that in the old days you sometimes came to my bar for a drink, and you weren't above picking up the bits of information I could give you . . .'

She was the only one who was not sleepy, whose energy showed no sign of flagging.

'And on purpose to humiliate me, you turn me over to the smallest of all inspectors. A fellow I could swallow at one gulp!'

Maigret made no reply, merely saying to Lucas, with a wink:

'I'm going home for a couple of hours' sleep. The money's been found.'

'What's that?' screeched the woman.

'Don't leave her alone. Send for whoever you like to keep her company—a tall chap if she'd rather—and go and sit in my office.'

'Right, Chief.'

He had himself driven home in a police car. The courtyard was full of them, for all resources had been mobilized since the previous evening.

'I hope you're going to bed?' said his wife as she turned down the sheet. 'What time shall I call you?'

'At half past twelve.'

'As early as that?'

He hadn't the energy to take a bath at once. He would have one when he woke up. He was just dozing off, warm to the ears, when the telephone rang.

He reached out for it and growled:

'Maigret speaking—yes?'

'Fumel here, Superintendent . . .'

'I'm sorry. I was half-asleep. Where are you?'

'Rue Marbeuf.'

'Go ahead.'

'I have some news. About the rug.'

'You've found it?'

'No. I doubt if it will ever be found. But it did exist. The man at the gas pump in the Rue Marbeuf is positive. He noticed it again about a week ago.'

'Why did he notice it?'

'Because it's unusual to see a rug in a smart sports car—especially a fur rug.'

'When did he see it last?'

'He's not certain, but he says it was quite recently. But two or three days ago, when young Wilton called in for gas, it had gone.'

'Put that in your report.'

'What will happen, in your opinion?'

Maigret, eager to bring the conversation to an end, replied laconically:

'Nothing!' and hung up. He needed sleep. And he felt almost certain he was right.

Nothing would happen!

He could imagine how supercilious the examining magistrate would look if he, Maigret, went and told him:

'On the night of Friday to Saturday, about one o'clock, Honoré Cuendet broke into the private house belonging to Florence Wilton, née Lenoir, in the Rue Neuve Saint-Pierre.'

'How do you know?'

'Because for the last five weeks he had been studying the house, from a room in the Hôtel Lambert.'

'So, just because a man takes a room in a shady hotel, you jump to the conclusion . . .'

'This was no ordinary man, it was Honoré Cuendet, who for nearly thirty years . . .'

He would describe Cuendet's ways.

'Have you ever caught him red-handed?'

Maigret would be compelled to admit that he hadn't.

'He had no keys to the house?'

'No.'

'Accomplices inside it?'

'And Mrs. Wilton and the servants were there at the time?'

'Cuendet never broke into unoccupied houses.'

'You are suggesting that this woman . . .'

'Not she. Her lover.'

'How do you know she has a lover?'

'I was told by a prostitute named Olga, who also lives opposite.'

'Has she seen them in bed together?'

'She's seen the man's car.'

'And who is this lover?'

'Young Wilton.'

Here the picture became a little blurred, because Maigret saw the examining magistrate laugh derisively, which was out of character.

'You are insinuating that this woman and her stepson . . .'

'Well, the father and his daughter-in-law didn't hesitate . . .'

'What's that?'

Maigret would relate the story of Lida, who had been the father's mistress after marrying the son.

Come, come! As though such things were possible! How could a conscientious magistrate, belonging to one of the best professional families in Paris, contemplate for a single moment . . .

'I hope you have further evidence?'

'Yes, sir . . .'

He must be asleep, for he saw himself bringing out of his pocket a twist of tissue-paper containing two almost invisible threads.

'What is this?'

'These are hairs, sir.'

Another proof that this was a dream, that it could only be a dream: now the magistrate was saying:

'Whose hairs?'

'They come from a wild-cat.'

'Why wild?'

'Because the rug in the car was made of wild-cat fur. For once in his long career, Cuendet must have made a noise, knocked something over, given the alarm, and they bashed him over the head.

'The lovers couldn't call the police without . . .'

Without what? His ideas were growing slightly confused. Without Stuart Wilton finding out what was going on, of course. And Stuart Wilton held the purse-strings . . .

Neither Florence nor her lover knew the unknown man who had suddenly appeared in their room. Wasn't it a wise precaution to make his face unrecognizable?

He had bled profusely, so they had been obliged to clean up . . .

And then the car . . .

And there, he had messed up the rug . . .

'You understand, sir . . .'

There he would be, apologetically, with his two hairs.

'In the first place, who told you these were wild-cat hairs?'

'An expert.'

'And another expert will come into the witness-box to jeer at him and declare they are hairs of some completely different animal . . .'

The magistrate was right. That was how it would happen. There would be a burst of laughter in court, and Counsel for the Defence would raise his hands dramatically and protest:

'Now, gentlemen, please let us be serious . . . What is the evidence against my client? Two hairs . . .'

Things might, of course, be done differently. For instance, Maigret might pay a call on Florence Wilton, put questions to her, poke about the house, question the servants.

And in the quiet of his own office, he might have a long talk with young Wilton.

But that sort of thing was against regulations.

'That will be enough, Maigret. Forget all this far-fetched stuff and take away those hairs . . .'

In any case he didn't give a damn. That was why he had winked at Fumel this morning.

Would the inspector, so unhappy in love, be more successful with Eveline than he'd been with other women?

At all events, the old lady in the Rue Mouffetard had been right. *I know my son . . . I'm sure he won't leave me without a penny . . .'*

How much money was there in the . . . ?

Maigret was sound asleep.

No one would ever know.

Noland
January 23, 1961